THE ART OF LOVE (& LOATHING)

A NOVEL

by

STEPHEN DANIEL RUIZ

VERB'D MEDIA

Copyright © 2019 by Stephen Daniel Ruiz

All rights reserved, including the right to reproduce this book or portions thereof in any form whatsoever.

This book is a work of fiction. Names, characters, businesses, organizations, places, events and incidents either are the product of the author's imagination or are used fictitiously. Any resemblance to actual persons, living or dead, events, or locales is entirely coincidental.

Published by Verb'd Media
contact@verbdmedia.com

ISBN: 978-1-7322212-2-2

1 2 3 4 5 6 7 8 9   23 22 21 20 19

To my children.

For myself.

PART ONE

CHAPTER ONE

Every year, thirteen people are crushed to death by vending machines.

It's not the most romantic way to go, and it doesn't leave much contribution to a memorable epitaph. In fact, it's a bit sad in a pathetically human way. The most likely cause of this accident—if we are to call it that—is from said victim trying to retrieve the nondispensing item they had paid good money for. Sometimes all it takes is a solid whack on the side of the machine. Other times, however, it takes everything you've got to get what you want, the thing that is rightfully yours, and it ends up killing you.

Within a single year, the odds of being killed by a dog are one in 11,273,142. The odds of being murdered with a gun are one in 24,974—depending on your demographic of course. Falling down a flight of stairs, 157,300. Asteroid collision, one out of 74,817,414, and the chances of winning the lottery, one in 175,000,000.

Now, I'm not a mathematician. I got all those statistics from the internet, so there's a vulnerable certainty I feel in those numbers. Yet, as I stood in the convenience store watching the old man in the yellowed t-shirt and faded jeans recycle his money for more scratch-offs, I wondered what he thought his chances of winning actually were. Not just winning but transforming his life. Something in my gut told me that even if he did win, he'd end up right back at that convenience store counter gnawing at his toothless gums, smelling like piss and PBR. I considered telling him that he had a better chance of getting killed by an asteroid than winning, but I couldn't recall the last time I'd even heard about someone being killed by an asteroid. It made me curious as to who this mysterious 74,817,415th person was each year—the lucky bastards.

Incidentally, the safest age is ten years old.

Moments later, I was staring through the fogged glass door at the shelves of cool, refreshing beer just on the other side. I could almost feel the bottle perspiring in my hand, hear the crisp exchange of carbon dioxide and oxygen as the cap twists off. My body ached as the tingling heat once again surged the entire system of my veins. I turned away feeling parched, and after purchasing a bottle of water, smoked a cigarette while waiting outside for my cab. When it arrived, I loaded my suitcase into the trunk and settled into the back seat. The air lent me the thick scent of the chewing tobacco that the driver had plugged into his bulging cheek. It was a silent ride, thankfully, and in forty-seven minutes I was freely breathing the filtered oxygen of the city airport, listening to the echoing instructions of a pre-recorded voice, the little plastic tires on luggage pecking along the faux granite floors. The smell of coffee and kitchen bleach. Cha-ching. Va-room. Clickity-clack. Thump-thump. All those wondrous signs of that which we call life.

I stood waiting with my boarding pass, staring out the window at the stallion of the skies. It was much smaller than I'd imagined it should be, then I cursed for not checking what the odds were of dying in a plane crash.

"Sir, we'll need to verify your carry-on with the certificate of cremation." The woman clad head to toe in navy blue smiled apologetically.

"Sure," I said, already prepared. She took the document from my hand and studied it diligently.

"Your name?"

"Arthur Kimble." She typed into her computer.

"And the death certificate?"

"What about it?" I asked after a pause.

"Just to verify that they're really dead."

"I'm pretty sure they're dead," I said, indicating the urn under my arm.

"I just need the certificate, sir. I apologize."

"Well, I don't have the certificate on me."

"I'm sorry, but airline policy requires that we verify the death with the certificate."

"They're a pile of ashes in a wooden box. How much more dead can a person get?"

"Policy states we have to verify both the certificate of cremation and the death certificate before we can permit it as a carry-on."

"It's interesting that neither the ticket counter nor the TSA agents said anything to me about it."

"I apologize that they failed to mention this to you when you checked in, but it's not a federal regulation. It's the policy of our particular airline."

"I checked your website, and all it said was certificate of cremation, so all I have with me is the certificate of cremation."

"Again, airline policy requires we verify that they're legally dead. I apologize."

"As opposed to being illegally dead?" The woman's eyes fluttered closed then open again.

"This is standard procedure, sir. If you want it as a carry-on, we need the proper paperwork. If you don't have the proper paperwork, you can register it as checked baggage."

"Checked baggage..." So, this is what happens after you die.

"Yes, sir."

"Do I have any other choice?"

"You can always take the train."

The jet engine rumbled as we picked up speed on the runway. They had us packed in like pickles in a jar, fermenting at 30,000 feet, and I wondered if the process worked faster or slower at higher altitudes.

"Human flight is a truly remarkable thing," Huxley marveled. "I wonder if we birds would have the ingenuity to create it ourselves were we not natural creatures of the sky."

"Ingenuity is meaningless without the opposable thumb," I said.

"Who's to say that the ingenuity of your species hasn't been diminished by this natural asset?"

"You never know," I said, growing bored of his conjecture. "I honestly haven't spent much time contemplating thumbs."

"That's because you take them for granted."

"Like you and flight?"

"Not at all," said Huxley. "Birds don't take everything for granted the way your kind does. Particularly English birds. We're a humble flock."

"You and I both know you're not humble," I laughed. "A showman if ever I saw one."

"What is life without a bit of dramatic flair?" he asked, waving a wing. "Even in the worst of times, we keep a stiff upper beak and press on. Which, by the way, may I extend to you my deepest condolences, Arthur. I understand how difficult it must be."

"I'm fine," I said.

"Yes, of course you are." I watched Huxley reflected in the window, his eyes solemn beneath the brim of his bowler hat. A high, crisp collar framed his face, and a satin Windsor knot tied his three-piece suit together in pure gentle-birdly fashion. Never had there been more stately a pigeon.

"Excuse me," said a voice to my right which I assumed was not addressing me. "Excuse me, sir. What is that you're drawing?"

I stopped the movement of my pen on paper to look at the passenger beside me. A woman looked back through remarkably tired eyes, her lipstick needing either removed or reapplied.

"It's just a doodle," I said.

"I like it," she smiled. "I feel like I've seen it somewhere before."

"It's possible. Do you read *Verb'd Magazine?*" I asked. She shook her head.

"You're an artist for a magazine?"

"A writer, mostly."

"Oh," she smiled. "That sounds exciting."

"Yeah," I shrugged, fooling myself into assuming the exchange was over. A few moments later she cleared her throat.

"How long?" she asked.

"How long?" I repeated.

"I know it's not my business, but…"

"I'm not sure I follow." She extended her arm, pulling up the sleeve to reveal a long thin scar down the center of her wrist. I looked down at my own, a similar, pinker scar visible where my sleeve had risen. I pulled it back down.

"Do you always ask people that?"

"Only the ones that survived," she said.

"Survival is a relative term." I sighed, attempting to relax. "If it's all the same to you, I'd rather keep my scars to myself."

"But isn't that how it got there in the first place?" I studied her for a long moment, tapping the end of my pen against the small drawing pad.

"I was raised to believe that failures are beneficial, so long as we learn from them. It avoids repetition."

"Why do you think you're a failure?"

"I never said that, but I'm still alive, aren't I?"

"Fair enough," she said after a pause. "I tried twice in '96 and again in '97."

"Well, don't let it get you down," I smiled. "Thomas Edison failed a hundred times before he finally got the light bulb right."

"Failure is a relative term, too." Her eyes stole a long glance out the window. "You know what they say: death is just a part of life. If that's true—and I believe it is—then the only way to fail at dying is to fail at living."

We said nothing to each other again until we landed, and she stopped me momentarily in the boarding bridge. "Here's my card," she said, holding one out to me, "in case you ever want to talk."

I looked down and read the dark letters raised on a white background. I should've guessed she was a shrink.

A vertically challenged man named Gregery sat across from me, peering through a pair of 30-year-old glasses at a 20-year-old computer. The clicking of the keys echoed hollow in his office, backed by the almost imperceptibly shrill hum of the incandescent light. The pair of sounds were as vexing as a mosquito tapdancing in your ear.

"Oh…" he said for the tenth time before mumbling, squinting with his efforts.

"What?" I asked for the seventh time. His clicking stopped, and he turned to me, calmly folding his hands on the desk.

"We don't have it, sir."

"Yes," I nodded. "I know that. If you did, I wouldn't be sitting here."

"Correct, sir." Gregery cleared his throat, "but I mean that we literally don't have it. It's currently in the possession of another airline."

"How the hell is that even possible?" I asked after a long inhale.

"It was loaded on the wrong plane."

"You're shitting me."

"No, I'm not," he said with a stupidly regretful smile.

"I could see that happening with luggage, but cremated remains?" My fingers dug into the seat of my chair, and I exhaled. "So, where is the plane that it's on?"

"Where is it?" he asked. I nodded. "Let me check that…" More clicking. "Oh…oh…okay…It's currently en route to Washington."

"As in Seattle or as in D.C.?"

"Let me check that…" He studied the screen. "As in Seattle." He smiled again apologetically.

"Well…" I shook my head toward the floor. "What do I need to do at this point?"

"Let me check that…"

Lonnie Lemmon stood a short way off from the entrance of the airport waving at me with his smartphone. He was taller than me by a couple inches, athletically thin but without exercise. His signature black tee and jeans gave him a stagehand appearance, though he was so accustomed to hijacking the center of attention, he seemed to have developed a spotlight expectation.

"How was the flight?" Lonnie didn't wait for an answer. He rarely ever did. "You should've taken the train."

"Tell me about it." I said, following him towards the parking lot.

"Well, taking a train is one of the most classic modes of transportation," he said, perceiving my words to be literal. "I kind of wish we still used those steam engine trains though. There's something so innovative about that puff of rising smoke."

"Steam."

"Say again?"

"It's steam that rises out of a steam engine. Not smoke." Lonnie laughed and said that was what he meant before leading me to an unfamiliar vehicle that was angularly double-parked. "I see you've got yourself a new ride. Again."

"The new Tesla. It's fantastic. Quiet as heck. Zero to sixty in less than five seconds. I'm going to have to give you the full experience, man. It's pretty Zen." Lonnie said that about almost anything he liked, though it seemed to have a way of ruining things for him over time.

"No, you really don't," I said. He laughed again as we climbed in, and I was accosted by a large rectangular display. "Christ, Lonnie. That's kind of excessive, isn't it?"

"It's like I always say: excess is simply wealth with a purpose."

"I've never heard you say that. I'm not even sure that means anything."

"Of course, it does. It's part of my new book *Survival of the Prosperous*," he said matter-of-factly. "Don't you remember? I sent you a copy with the pills."

"Oh. Yeah, of course," I lied.

"It's in chapter three, 'Beyond Our Means'." The parking lot behind us appeared on the screen as he put the car into reverse. "It's such an antiquated idea, living within guidelines that we place upon ourselves as if it's the Great Depression." We began moving slowly until we reached the main road, and he floored it, the acceleration forcing my body into the seat. "Oh, yeah!" he cheered before slowing down just enough to still push past other vehicles on the road. He continued his thought. "You were raised like that. I was raised like that. We were trained to settle for what we have already instead of what we could have. That's why the majority of people will live their entire lives scraping away for a living that gives them just enough to survive while their inner selves are suffocating. We were meant for more, every one of us. In different ways, obviously, but you know. I'm not discounting the people who reach their potential working in fast food or as a cashier or custodian. Not everyone is equally yoked, you know. Not mentally or intellectually. Not physically, for sure. But all people are capable of more than that menial slog of monotony. I was thirteen when I got my first job scraping algae and shit off the hulls of luxury yachts in Florida. Made three bucks an hour busting my ass for these millionaires who were spending half the year on vacation."

"I thought you made three-fifty," I interjected, recalling the last time he told this story which was fifty cents fewer than the time before that.

"The point is," Lonnie rolled his eyes, "all I wanted was to have my own boat, my own place on the water. So, I saved, and I worked, and I saved some more. After a few years, I had just about enough, but then when my dad split, I had to use what I made to support my mother and my two younger brothers all while still going to school. She preached over and over to me about how we had to 'live within our means'." He chicken-scratched the air. "And I get why she thought that. Her parents were poor farmers whose parents were also poor farmers and so on. They only had what they could grow and sell. My mom though," Lonnie chuckled, "it's like she just couldn't understand that times were different. So, she cleaned houses and ran a register at an old gas station down the road. You know what I did though?"

"No, what?" I lied again.

"I said, to hell with that. Too many people live within their means like it's some kind of tried and true course of action. You know what it is though? Really?" He looked sideways at me, and I said nothing to avoid lying again. "Fear. Fear is the reason why people define their means as this minimalist expense and reward system, but they don't ever get anywhere. You know the majority of people in this country die where they're born, and less than half of those people don't ever travel outside a hundred-mile radius of that place? All because of fear."

"That's all, huh?"

"That's fucking all, man," he said enthusiastically. "And it's because they've already decided what their limits are. So, they grind through that daily motion from birth to death, thinking that what they've got is all they need, and everything else, all their dreams and desires, their wants, they think *that's* excess. Until a person raises the limits of their means to the same level as their wants, they'll never break through their personal glass ceiling. Just like my mother."

I thought of that wooden box flying high above the earth. Elegantly scrolled text embossed on a brass nameplate put a face to the ashes inside. It gave the contents an identity, motivations, weaknesses and strengths, knowledge and wondering, failures and successes, hopes—and yes, fears. It gave them a history. Perhaps, even love. But they were only ashes, and the nameplate was but an ode to one who no longer existed, if they ever truly had at all.

"My mother was a nurse at a mental institution," I said, looking out the window.

Lonnie drove silently for several moments. "You hungry?"

"I think I'll just find something at home," I said, though it occurred to me that what little food had been there would likely be spoiled after having been away for three months.

Several minutes later, we arrived outside my apartment building, its tall gray face as inviting as dinner with the Dahmers.

"Hey," Lonnie began as I exited the car. "I got you a little something-something." He shook a medicine bottle containing several pills. "Happy birthday."

"It's not my birthday." He stared at me. "Look, I'm just not really trying to get into that anymore. Thanks anyway."

"If it's money, man, don't worry. It's on the house."

"No, thanks."

"Come on."

"I'm good, Lonnie."

"Okay, suit yourself," he shrugged. Once I'd unloaded my luggage, he shifted into gear. "Hey, Art." I looked up just in time to see an orange blur flying at me. It hit my chest and fell to the ground. "You'll thank me later!" The bottle looked up at me from the sidewalk as he sped away.

The door of my fourth-floor apartment closed behind me, the metallic click of the latch striking with a sense of familiarity and calm. It was like entering someone else's home though, recognizing that scent associated with a particular place or person. Everyone everywhere has one, for better or worse, though most people are so assimilated to themselves that they'll never know. Talk about your grade-A metaphor. It's a remnant of our ancient survival instinct that tells us when something is different or abnormal. Of course, to determine this, there must be some kind of baseline. From birth, that baseline is being established, and every minute of every day until death, that instinct remains in action. It's a funny thing though, that no matter how complex and capable the human brain proves to be, it never seems to be naturally self-aware. It takes a conscious effort and years of shitty experiences and mistakes to identify the self, to establish that baseline. In a world that's constantly changing, it's no wonder that we're all at least a little insane and have absolutely no idea.

Seated on my couch, I dialed the number I'd been given from Gregery and waited. I pressed one, then five, then five, then five again as directed by the prompt, until I was serenaded by synthesized jazz and a midi-generated flute. After seven minutes, I turned on the speakerphone and opened up my text messages to type.

Back in town. Can I see the kids?

Waiting for a reply, I held up the bottle of pills to the light, clattering them around inside. I didn't want them, but I didn't *not* want them. Without a clear choice of what to do, I decided to stash them away in my usual spot which, perhaps, was a choice in itself. I reasoned that, in knowing they were there, it might serve as a way of strengthening my resistance. The more times you say no, the easier it had to get, right?

The dots of a pending reply appeared on my phone as I moved to the kitchen.

...Didn't know you were back already
Yeah, just got in today. Can I see the kids?
...They're busy
Doing what?
...At school
What about after school?

As the hold music continued to play, I stood on my toes to reach the small porcelain Buddha I'd kept pushed to the very back of a high kitchen cabinet, that perfect smile of nirvana waiting to greet me as in days long past. His head came off as the top of a jar, and I looked down into the pit of his bulging gut. The pills clinked and jingled merrily as I poured them inside, ten in all, and I felt oddly relieved to see them. My phone buzzed.

...They have rehearsal for the school musical
Okay. I could get them dinner
...They have school in the morning. They can't be out till all hours of the night
Why would they be out that late? I wouldn't do that
...K
Then let me just pick them up and bring them home
...Fine. Pick them up at 6 but don't be late
Why would I be late?
...
...
...

Goddamn text bubbles. I hated them almost as much as that shitty hold music. Sick of waiting, I ended the call and returned to the couch. My eyes closed immediately as I commenced the painstaking avoidance of thought.

"-down to the upper twenties in the region...Tomorrow, partly cloudy, slight chance of flurries in the evening, highs in the mid to upper forties...And now the news at six..."

I listened to the radio broadcaster's voice, his inflections assuring factuality as he informed me of all the goings-on I should know, the relevant happenings in the world and what it all meant—but mostly didn't mean—for me. The light was disappearing quickly behind the horizon, and the temperatures were taking their plunge. I felt compressed by the invading cold that I'd become unaccustomed to and blasphemed the effects of earth's orbit around its star. The radio began to wane out in static spurts, the syllables and annunciations indiscernible at each stoplight. Then it would come back. Then it would fade. Then return, and so on.

I'd woken with a start on my couch, cursing under my breath for falling asleep, for not waking up on time, and most of all, for not having eaten. A fifteen-minute drive brought me to a faded, brick building just off the main road. They called it Queen City High School, and a crumbling sidewalk led up to and beneath a banner hanging over its crypt-like entrance. "Keep Dreaming," it read, and I felt like a slug trapped in the growing shadow of a descending shoe. I parked, rushed from my car to the indoors, and began making my way to the auditorium, rubbing my hands vigorously for warmth.

Walking through the halls unearthed long-repressed memories of my own high school, due, perhaps, to its uncanny resemblance of a graveyard. They'd made a half-assed attempt at hiding it with a fresh coat of paint here and there and computers and projectors and televisions. The school board said it was all to keep up with the times, to prepare our children for the future, because there was surely nothing new to learn, only new ways to learn it. But the lockers still appeared as headstones, the teachers as morticians, the principals as groundskeepers, and I extrapolated that each parent must, therefore, be a gravedigger.

Clusters of students were scattered in the seats as I entered the auditorium, most of them falling into their smartphones, their faces illuminated like hypnotized ghosts in the dark. The stage was lit, and a chorus line of teens were stepping out a high school teacher's best crack at choreography. They sang along to an instrumental track of Leonard Bernstein's "America", butchering Hispanic accents, their voices diminishing and rising again as they performed flamboyant movements with unsteady footing. Mid-verse, the music stopped abruptly, sending a thrash of silence across the auditorium and causing all the distracted teens to look up in bewilderment. From the front and center seat, a heavy-set woman with teased orange hair let loose an alarming frenzy of criticisms. The students looked down at her from the stage but likewise appeared to be cowering beneath her.

Once I'd established that there was no recognizable face in the lineup, I diverted my attention to the darkened rows, looking for a recognizable back-of-the-head, disregarding the couple swapping spit in the seats several feet off in the same way they had disregarded me. Within a few moments, I saw a familiar mess of hair and recognized the sneakers propped on the back of the seat in front of it. As I drew closer, I watched my son sketching away in a college-ruled notebook, headphones on, apparently disconnected from his surroundings. He didn't notice me until I shuffled through the row and plopped into the seat beside him.

"Hey, Ryan," I smiled. He stared at me for a long moment.

"What are you doing here?"

"I came to pick you guys up. Is Abi around?"

"I thought you were on your trip until next month," he said looking down at his notebook.

"I got back early. I missed you." I wrapped an arm around him and squeezed gently while he remained motionless. It was like hugging a tree, only chillier. "Do you know where Abi is?"

"Nope," Ryan said before putting his notebook into his backpack and rising to his feet.

"Excuse me, Dad." He slid past me to make his way up the aisle and out the double doors. I watched him silently, feeling something like regret or guilt, though I couldn't discern which or why, then reined in my mind with deliberate sharpness.

I resumed my search among the adolescents, all appearing as obnoxious as ever and poised with indifference to anything but others' perceptions of themselves. To fit in was the purpose of all things while simultaneously claiming self-expression and individuality. I knew this because it was a common disposition of all teenagers, and while I recognized it as a byproduct of coming into one's self, it stirred within me a dormant hate for those pimple-faced pubescents all with sneers embedded under the skin and eyes loosened just enough to roll freely but not fall out. "Not my baby though," I thought with a sudden relief. "She's not one of them."

"Dad?" I turned to the whisper and was halted momentarily when I saw that Abi's golden hair was down around her shoulders, bangs swept over her forehead. Small hoops decorated her ears, and her clothes bore no more pink. I realized I'd been foolishly looking for a girl much younger than the one seated before me, and I forced a smile through my embarrassment. I slid into the seat next to the young lady and put my arm around her.

"You're back!" Abi sighed wrapping her arms around my neck.

"Hey, Sprout. I missed you so much!"

"I missed you too, Daddy."

"How are you? How's it going?"

"I'm okay, I guess. You saw that right?" Abi's voice was strained with anxiety.

"Yeah. That was a bit overboard, wasn't it? She's probably just as nervous as the rest of you though." Abi looked up at me disagreeably.

"We're not nervous—at least we wouldn't be if she didn't flip out about everything. I don't know…" She shrugged and looked back at the stage where the dancers had continued their rehearsal.

"What part are you playing?" I asked.

"Anybodys." Abi was dismal with her reply which had thoroughly confused me.

"Anybody's? You mean you're an understudy or something?"

"No. Anybodys is a tomboy that wants to be in the Jets. It's a stupid part. I don't even get to sing or anything." Abi tucked her knees up under her chin and hugged them listlessly.

"If you're playing the part, there's no way it could be stupid. At least you got a part. Right?"

"Yeah, because that's what matters, Dad. Thanks." Abi's sarcasm put my admittedly pathetic consolation to shame, and as we sat there watching, I searched my inner author and all my writer's avenues and alleyways for something I could say that wouldn't sound so unforgivably generic. But as the moment passed and my brain turned up nothing, it became pointless.

"It'll be all right, Sprout." I put my arm around her, and as she tucked her head against my shoulder, the feeling of failure dissipated.

A short while later, Ryan, Abi, and I rode with the heat blasting, the engine softly growling, burning away my money. Abi had moved on from the stress of the theatre, her tone cheerful as she told me about a writing assignment in her English class that she was weighing ideas for. She asked my advice, and I gave it sparingly, my personal rule being to leave Abi to her own devices concerning creativity as much as possible. Ryan stared out at the passing city from the backseat, and I tried to pull him into the conversation, but his mind remained dormant between his headphones.

"So, Dad, how did your trip go?" Abi asked.

"It was good. I got a lot accomplished, a lot of research. A lot of traveling, too."

"Really? Like where?"

"You know, all around. Some western states, up north, some south."

"Did you go to California?"

"I did, actually. Why?"

"I was just wondering if you heard about Fletcher Price. About the accident." Abi leaned in.

"Yeah, I did." I looked inquisitively at her. "How did you hear about that?"

"We're reading one of his books in my English class, and our teacher Ms. Graves told us about it. It must really suck being in a coma. I wonder if he'll still be able to write when he wakes up."

"*If* he wakes up," I said before I could avoid my own morbidity. "What I mean is, he hasn't written anything in a long time. I'm just not sure he would want to if he does."

"No, I mean if he'll be able to. I did some research online, and there are some pretty crazy things that can happen from going into a coma. One time, there was a woman in England who had a coma for six weeks and when she woke up, she thought it was the 1990s again. There was this other guy in England, too. He thought he was a famous actor, and he spoke French fluently when he'd never spoken it before. And did you know that there are over sixty recorded cases of people speaking with different accents after coming out of comas?"

"Not that I doubt the possibility of coma-induced personality changes, but don't you think it's slightly possible that they were faking it? At least with the accents? Besides, how does someone who doesn't speak French suddenly wake up and speak it fluently? The knowledge couldn't be there from nowhere, could it?"

"I guess that's true. I don't know why someone would wake up from a coma and not want everything to go back to normal though. Talk about unnecessary drama."

"I suppose," I chuckled.

"Can you imagine waking up one day and finding that nothing in the world is at all what you thought?" Abi looked out the window, folding up an old gum wrapper into tiny squares. "That must be scary."

"Yeah," I said, the humor evaporated. "It must be."

"There are a lot of people saying some mean things about him, too. I don't know why people have to be so nasty all the time. Especially to an old man. The only thing he ever did was write books and stuff."

"Well, even people who write books and stuff aren't exempt from public persecution." The brakes squeaked softly at an intersection. The stoplight reflected red against Abi's face as she began rolling the wrapper up into a tiny ball, rotating it over and under between her thumb and forefinger.

"Do you think he's going to die?" she asked.

"Everyone dies."

"I know that," she said with mild sarcasm. "I mean right now."

"I don't know, Sprout. I guess he might."

"I hope he doesn't. We're all hoping he gets better." She said this casually, but the information struck me unexpectedly.

"Who's we?" I asked.

"Just a bunch of us at school. One kid in my class even started this online movement last week called Faith For Fletcher, and it's already gotten over eight hundred followers from all different parts of the country. I even joined it."

"You joined it?"

"Yeah. On Facebook."

"Since when did you have a Facebook account?" I frowned.

"That's not the point," she deflected. "The idea is for people to rally behind him. That's how I look at it anyway."

"I think it's retarded," Ryan interjected suddenly, and I seized the moment.

"You shouldn't say that word, Ryan," Abi scolded, facing him. "It's insensitive."

"It's accurate," he countered.

"Why do you think it's stupid?" I asked earnestly, looking at him in my rearview.

"Because he's old. He's going to die soon anyway. And how is some stupid internet group going to help him? It's not like they can change anything."

"That's not the point," Abi objected. "We're all supporting him."

"Life support is supporting him," Ryan countered. "In a couple weeks, no one's going to give a crap about Fletcher Price because no one actually cared to begin with. There'll be something new for them to rally behind, or protest, or whatever. They just want to feel like they're doing something because their own lives suck."

"Well, I joined it, and my life doesn't suck," said Abi, proudly defending her position. "What about you, Dad?"

"Does my life suck?"

"Do you want to join Faith For Fletcher?"

"I don't really know about that stuff." Abi looked back out, thinking deeply, the ends of her mouth drawn back and the gum wrapper now a flat, aluminum disc. "But I could take a look into it." Her eyes lit up with her smile. Ryan's eyes almost fell out again. I accelerated.

A few minutes later, I steered into the driveway of a nice house at the end of a nice cul-de-sac. It had a nice picket fence out front that matched all the other nice picket fences. In fact, between all the lights and décor, the entire neighborhood was about as coordinated as my gay uncle. He was nice, too, but as nice as it all was, driving through that Stepford wonderland gave me the urge to take a nice, giant dump on someone's lawn.

Ryan spared no time for goodbyes when I parked as he all but tucked and rolled out of the car, leaving Abi and me behind to watch him disappear through the front door. With a half-hearted smile, I left the car running as we moved quickly through the chill.

"I missed you, Abi."

"I missed you, too." She paused. "Is everything okay, Dad?" Abi must have heard the tightness in my throat, the heaviness in my voice. I held the screen door open for her and looked beyond the threshold into the warm, inviting living room.

Ryan was already seated on a corduroy couch, his shoes kicked off, the remote in his hand. His lips parted in the faintest smile as he talked to his mother seated beside him. She was manicured, pedicured, eyeshadowed and lipstuck. It was all for herself, but necessary because, as she always said, it made her feel good. Her voice wasn't strange or spectacular, but I could discern it in a crowd, the same as her laugh, the same as her scolding.

Talking with them from the kitchen doorway was a tall figure, a man a few years my senior wearing his usual argyle sleeveless sweater, the cuffs of his button-up rolled just past his wrists as if trying to assert a working-man image, though the overpriced watch, slacks and loafers gave away his pencil-pushing status. The three of them laughed about something that had nothing to do with me, and Abi watched as I shrank away from the entrance into the cold.

"Everything's fine. I'm fine," I said. "Tired. That's all." Abi looked into my face as I stared past her into the house.

"You're still not coming in," she neither asked nor stated. I said nothing, and as the talking and laughter continued beyond us, she nodded in understanding. Abi was like that, and the love I felt for that trait of hers was accompanied by a stab of shame that it should ever exist in the first place. "I love you, Daddy."

I love you, she said.

"I love you too, Sprout." I smiled, hugged her, breathed in the scent of her hair, kissed her cheek, and walked back to my car, that unsettled rush returning to my sternum, boiling ever restlessly like a cauldron. I looked to the sound of a squeaking screen door and my name being called.

"Leaving so soon, Arthur?" The sweatered man stood smirking, his hands behind his back. "I thought maybe you'd enjoy a family meal."

"Tell me, does the food taste bitter when it's stolen?"

"I wouldn't know. It was given to me quite freely," he said. "You know, Julia and I have actually started going to a Kamasutra class to awaken us from our sexual slumber."

"Sex and slumber are two words that have no relation in my vocabulary," I replied before lighting a cigarette.

"The Kamasutra is about more than just sex, Art. It's about intimacy. It's about connection and fulfillment on multiple levels. But that's clearly not in your vocabulary either, is it?" His hands remained uncomfortably behind his back as he took a few steps closer. "Care to take a guess what I'm holding?" he asked with a grin.

"The record for most paper clips held between two ass cheeks?" I responded, blowing smoke towards him.

"It's a for-sale sign," he said without hesitation, though the expression on my face gave him pause. "That's right. Julia and I have decided to sell the old homestead."

"She didn't mention anything to me about that."

"How could she? You've been off finding yourself or whatever." I watched him stride past me to the end of the drive and stick the sign into the ground, just off target from a pair of existing holes. "Speaking of which, did you find him?"

"Who? Jesus?" I replied, getting back into the heat of my car.

"Funny," he smiled, walking back up. "I was referring more to the father, not the son."

"Nothing but ghosts," I replied.

"So I heard."

As he returned to the house, I stared momentarily at the for-sale sign in the front yard, the yard Julia, Ryan, and I had stood in while gazing fondly at our new home. The yard I'd push-mowed with Ryan asleep on my shoulders. The yard he and Abi had dashed back and forth through the sprinkler in. Taking a long drag from my cigarette, I searched myself for something astute and likewise cutting to respond with.

"Hey, Argyle," I said, and he turned back to me. "Go fuck yourself."

Cutting the wheel, I punched the gas and backed over the sign, flipping him off as he reminded me of his real name, as if I'd forgotten. Grinning with sadistic satisfaction, my attention turned back to the road. Yet, as I drove onward, the feeling of pleasure disintegrated as the hint of a tremor revived itself in my hands.

Sometimes you win. Sometimes you lose. But there's no more of a confounding feeling than when you do both at the exact same time.

CHAPTER TWO

In my bedroom, the sun was beginning to invade the shadows through pale curtains, fingers of light caressing the room, the chair, the clothes on the floor, a row of small toes poking out from under the sheets of the bed. Vivian Ward lay asleep, her dark hair draped across her bare shoulders and neck. One arm wrapped itself lovingly around my middle. She wasn't beautiful in the traditional sense, but she wasn't by any means unattractive. Popular beauty relies heavily on symmetry which for her was broken simply by the slight offset of her nose. When awake, one eye remained ever so slightly wider than the other, and her crooked smile had permanently left its evidence in the crease by her mouth. Vivian was fit, clear-skinned with freckles that only fully revealed themselves in the sun. Her eyes were both bright and stormy, seeing what others could not, things as they are and things as they could be, but always finding beauty. At times it felt as if sleeping with her was an act of desecration. She was not holy; neither saint, nor angel. Vivian was a woman, lovely, and I the unrighteous defiler.

  I glanced about the room before sliding stealthily out from under the blankets until my feet touched the floor. Vivian remained asleep as I crept around, throwing on a t-shirt and sweatpants before entering the kitchen. The coffee pot was already sputtering as it brewed to the timer. I stood there staring at it with my mug in hand, looking like some unemployed man in a bread line during the Great Depression. The faint green light of my laptop indicating a full charge caught my attention. I opened the screen and looked again over the property listing.

121 WINNOW LANE

$217,500

Make this tastefully renovated and beautifully preserved 3-bedroom, 1½-bath home yours for Christmas! All 1,854 square feet are move in ready! Recent upgrades include a stunning new kitchen with stainless appliances, a beautifully appointed master suite, large walk in closets, his and her sinks, refinished original hardwood floors, washer and dryer hookups, tons of space, all conveniently located within walking distance of Queen City's historic district.

Contact Agent: Sherrie Mardeleaux

Sherrie's 4.8 out of 5-star rating didn't make me feel any better.

"Beautifully preserved, indeed," said Huxley, perched on the counter beside me. "I am a bit confused as to why you'd want to buy it, however."

"Who said I wanted to buy it?" I asked.

"It doesn't take a master of deduction like myself to recognize that twinkle of desire in your eye," he said. "I know it when I see it. Even Farnaby could see it."

"Farnaby's perceptive enough," I said. "How is your nephew, anyway?"

"Oh, I'm sure he's off chasing some tailfeather 'round the city. He's at that age, I suppose. It's quite irritating to have him so distracted all the bloody time though."

"You mean to tell me that you weren't like that?"

"I never had to chase anyone. They flocked to me," Huxley laughed. "Still, I was always a very focused lad. I only wish he were as well."

"Why not let him have a little fun?" I asked. "You're only young once."

"It's not the fun that worries me. It's all the risk that comes with it. Tarnish is a difficult thing to polish out of a reputation." Huxley looked at the computer screen and sighed.

"You have to allow some room for mistakes."

"Mistakes are understandable. It's the repetition of mistakes that is worrisome. One can find good in any rotten situation if a lesson is learned. If not, then what the hell was all the struggle worth?"

"God has given you one face, and you make yourself another," Vivian uttered softly from behind her camera. She'd snuck up on me from the bedroom, but despite my immediate annoyance, I forced a smile.

"Not another," I replied, shutting the laptop, "just uncaffeinated. You should try photographing someone when they're ready some time."

"That would be boring," she said, pressing the shutter button again.

"I'm sure there'd be something stimulating if you looked hard enough," I said, casually closing the laptop. Vivian approached me, lowering the camera and sliding an arm around my waist.

"I think I found some stimulation right here." She kissed me.

"I haven't brushed my teeth yet."

"Neither have I." Vivian kissed me again.

"Yes, I know." We both smiled and laughed, encouraging curious hands and inciting goosebumps. "You should take the day off."

"I wish I could," said Vivian before pulling away. "I can't though. I've got final edits to submit before tomorrow which, honestly, means working late since I was so distracted from my work last night." She winked at me.

"Procrastination has its perks." I moved in again.

"You don't have to convince me," Vivian smiled, "but I do need to get dressed. I'll be right back."

The coffee pot beeped, and I turned to pour us each a cup, adding only two or three scoops of sugar to both. I carried them to the bedroom and stood at the door. Vivian was straightening a muslin shirt over her torso, and I momentarily lost myself in the loosely hanging material that drifted down over her unconfined breasts.

"Hey," Vivian said softly as she picked up a pair of glasses from the table beside her. She blinked a few times and refocused on me with a smile. "What are you thinking?"

"Where thou art, there is the world itself, and where thou art not, desolation," I smiled, offering her coffee.

"Shakespeare is contagious, isn't he?" I saw her lips begin to form a sentence, then halt themselves. "Thank you."

The glow of the morning shone softly through, and I studied the shadowlight of her movements. The light shifted, however, casting a shadow over me once more as I remembered the truth of it all, who she was, and who I was. I'd heard once that forbidden love was the greatest of all stories, yet it seemed ever increasingly trite to me. In the twenty-first century, the only people forbidding love were antiquated and—with any luck—close to extinction. This wasn't some forbidden love scenario like Romeo and Juliet, or Tristan and Isolde, and not even Dagny and Hank. In truth, there was nothing forbidden at all about Vivian and me, and I wasn't sure why it put me so on edge.

Sipping my coffee as I sat on the bed, contemplating the day ahead without much enthusiasm, my eye caught a folded magazine sticking out of Vivian's purse on the chair in the corner. This would have meant nothing, even with the name Fletcher Price printed in large font on the front amid several other high-profile names. Still, it was the name of the magazine that made this impossible to ignore.

"*Slander Magazine* did an article about Fletcher Price?" I asked, bringing the issue to the bathroom and holding it up in the mirror for her to see.

"Going through my things now, are you?" Vivian raised an eyebrow.

"It was begging to be found," I said. "Dare I even ask what it says?"

"Nothing you'd want to read, I assure you." She laughed carelessly.

"You're probably right." I stepped back out and sat down again, eyeballing the magazine in my hands.

"You going to read it or not?" she asked, squeezing a liberal amount of toothpaste onto her toothbrush in a line fit for advertising. "I know you want to know what it says," she said, half-ignoring the look of revulsion on my face. "Jesus, it's not like it's going to give you leprosy. It's just a magazine."

But *Slander Magazine* wasn't just a magazine. It was a publication founded for the sole purpose of feeding frenzied and wrung-out minds filler substance like fried spam. They served up nothing but fragmented rumors and shoddy photographs developed into unbelievable stories to smear the names of all and anyone they could, no holds barred. They did it all in the name of the people's right to be informed about the private lives of the rich and the famous, whether the information was anyone's business or not, whether there was any truth to it or not. And, I had considered, perhaps it was *Slander*'s ever-increasing popularity, its exploitation of the public's institutionalized ignorance, that evoked my deepest disdain for it.

Regardless of my personal feelings, Vivian's statement had been a challenge that I reluctantly accepted. Taking the glossed pages in hand, I followed the contents guide to a large, poor quality image of an old man whom I immediately recognized. He was bleary-eyed and smiling drunkenly, well-dressed but simultaneously haggard compared to his formerly polished appearance. On the opposing page, a large headline in bold print interjected their assertion. I read aloud:

FLETCHER PRICE IS DEAD

For three of the past four decades, Fletcher Price has shone brightly among the stars as one of the most talented and successful playwrights and authors of the 20th (and into the 21st) century and was—at one time—even hailed a modern Shakespeare. He is a multigenerational household name whose culmination of works have turned him into one of the most successful and richest celebrities of all time. But since the unprecedented flop of his book *Happy* nearly a decade ago, Fletcher Price's career began a plummet from bad to worse to let's-not-talk-about-it. While there were still many fans who blamed his failures on the unexpected mental breakdown and death of his wife Miriam Price, those fans have been long lost as he is now better known for his drinking binges and sex parties than for his work. Over the past ten years, he's been twice rumored to have filed bankruptcy and seven times to have died, three of those times by suicide.

Needless to say, it is with much surprise that Fletcher Price's publicist announced a new novel after a three-year hiatus, even more surprising since the author is still hospitalized in a coma. However, the lack of a title or even a plot leaves an overwhelming skepticism of this claim being true. If and when he wakes up, Fletcher Price is still to show his face to the public in any respectable way, and recent photos of him boozing it up with scantily clad models [*opposite page*] time and again makes it doubtful that he's been doing any writing at all. His reputation has accurately morphed from prolific genius to drunken playboy to disheveled failure. For those with any doubt, *Slander* is here to assure you that, whether breathing or not, in a coma or not, Fletcher Price is indeed dead, and that any indication of his resurrection should be disregarded as a desperate publicity stunt from an old, washed up has-been.

"Well," I stopped reading and looked at Vivian, "I see that *Slander Magazine* is still living up to its name."

"I warned you," she said, taking the magazine back and folding it into her purse.

"You know, his wife's mental breakdown thing was just a rumor. No one has ever proven it," I said. Vivian shrugged.

It was in those moments that I wondered how—or even why—Vivian was a photographer for *Slander Magazine*. It was difficult for me to imagine her as being naive to the fact that she was better than that. Of course, everyone needs to make a living, but she had the capability of being a self-sustaining, independent photographer, a fact which I'd made clear to her many times before. Vivian would of course turn the tables on me and ask me what I'm doing as an under-achieving writer at *Verb'd Magazine*, but I would tell her it's not the same. It was different, because the magazine I worked for exalted artistry and was built on principles that upheld the enrichment of people's lives and the broadening of their understanding of art. It didn't sling mud at hard-earned reputations with lies and rumors, and certainly never kicked the dog when it was down. She didn't feel it was any different, however. "The issue," she'd argued, "isn't the work we do. It's the contrast of our work against our potential, which is why you're right, and I'm right." It was a rebuttal I conceded to, but only with the proverbial agreement to disagree. Then she would smile, knowing as I knew that we truly were the same.

The tone of Vivian's voice rose in a question, though I had become oblivious to her words. She sat on the edge of the bed with her phone in hand.

"What?" I asked blankly.

"I said, speaking of him, did you see this?" She raised her phone for me to see what she'd been looking at. "Apparently there's a group of people reading his books and putting on his plays. They're lighting candles and praying outside his hospital at night."

"Interesting," I said. Vivian looked up at me.

"It's interesting how as untouchable some people might seem, celebrities are just as subject to bad things happening to them as anyone else. Though, I guess it shouldn't come as a surprise for him particularly, considering his lifestyle. And his age. It's kind of a miracle that he's still alive."

"True."

"It's pretty sad, honestly."

"Yeah."

"What's wrong?" she asked. I shook my head and shrugged. "Come on. What is it? I know there's something wrong when you give one-word responses like that." I laughed at this, realizing that she was too observant for my own good.

"I promise, nothing's wrong at all. I feel kind of like you do, that it's a miracle he's gone this long without dying."

"It's okay to be upset," Vivian said.

"I'm not upset," I laughed again.

"You have practically every book he's written."

"As I do of John Steinbeck and Aldous Huxley and Ernest Hemingway."

"Yes, but Fletcher Price is the one still alive." I opened the top drawer of my dresser and began absentmindedly tidying the folded clothes.

"I appreciate his work as I do many other people's, but he's not special to me," I said, chuckling with a streak of condescension. "That's just ridiculous."

"I just thought…Okay." She tucked her phone into her purse and began slipping her feet into the shafts of a pair of high-heeled boots. An instant wave of regret hit me as I realized that, in response to her only taking an interest in what she'd thought was important to me, I'd been rude. I closed the drawer and turned back around.

"Fletcher Price is someone I would consider influential for me, and I enjoy reading what he's done. So, you're right, I guess. I just try not to be surprised when things like that happen to people. That's life."

There. Just as good as an apology.

Vivian looked at me closely before smiling. "It's okay." She stood up, approached me, held me as in countless times before, her head on my chest, one hand gently resting on my shoulder. "I missed you so much, Arthur. You have no idea. I'm proud of your decision to go to rehab, but I'm glad you're home."

"Thanks. Me too."

The benefit of speaking while hugging is that no one can see your facial expression when you do it. I felt slightly annoyed for a reason I wouldn't take the time to regard. Six minutes later, I closed the door behind her, watching through the peephole as she stepped onto the elevator down the hall.

"Yeah, my name is Arthur Kimble," I said into my phone, back in the kitchen. "I'm calling about an item, cremated remains. They were loaded onto the wrong plane a few days ago…My flight number was ZE1173…Yes…Well, it wasn't lost. It was loaded on the wrong plane…That flight number? It's—let me look. It's R448. It was headed to Washington…As in Seattle…I don't know if it was going to Seattle specifically. I…I don't know. Can't you see based on that flight number?…How do you not have access?…You're the billing department…Okay…No, I don't need a refund. I need to talk with someone about an item being loaded onto the wrong—yes…Okay, I'll hold…"

After twenty minutes of some musical pop-reggae-salsa concoction, I opted to receive a call back.

Winter was toying with the idea of arriving early in Queen City, and it seemed the warmth of the sun only increased the chill of the air around, just as its increased brightness appeared to cast darker shadows. What I thought was dressing warmly was still inadequate, and even my own exhalation was bitter at me for having released it into the cold. Queen City possessed its share of pomp and glamour and the occasional scar of graffiti. A bus stop served as a refuge from the cold for the poor and huddled masses yearning to breathe free, but only breathing in what another had exhaled just moments before. Second-hand air was stale and as cancerous as July, even in late October. The scene was repulsively mesmerizing. The driver behind me laid on his horn as I'd missed the changing of the traffic light.

Calvin "Cal" Little was born on July 4th, 1876, in Goings, Alabama, a small town about thirty miles south of Montgomery. His mother, Naomi, worked in the Clayton house, the home of a wealthy white family that, despite the havoc wrought by the Civil War, managed to maintain the majority of their wealth. Calvin's father, John Little, had become a sharecropper on the plantation where he was previously a slave. They lived in a shack, working just as hard as before, and treated with as much disdain. John and Naomi loved their son, and despite the hardships endured simply for the color of their skin, it did not diminish this fact. They insisted he spend more time learning letters and numbers than working in the field.

At the age of seventeen, Calvin attended the Tuskegee Institute and became overcome with visions of life up north, away from Jim Crow and oppression. In 1902, he moved to Queen City. There he found work playing piano and fiddle for vaudeville shows. He fell in love with a white woman name Katharine. They started Cal's Diner together and, despite living well above the Mason-Dixon line, experienced more hate and resentment than either had ever known. It was three days after their twin son and daughter were born that Calvin was lynched in the middle of the night. In his memory, Katharine remained steadfast and oversaw the diner on her own, passing the business onto their children, who in turn passed it onto theirs, and so on. It became famous for its brisket and had become mine and Samwell Epstein's favorite place to eat.

Apparently, in the few months that I'd been gone, it had been turned into a Starbucks.

I stood staring in disbelief up at the green queen herself, though for some reason I was hardly surprised. Through the glass windows, I watched several patrons scattered from table to table diligently focused on papers, laptops, and tablets. Some wore headphones. Others were talking into Bluetooth earpieces. All of them couldn't care less what this place used to be and why. I didn't dare ponder the question whether it had all been worth it.

"Yeah, I couldn't believe it either," Samwell remarked as we sat facing each other with our coffees. "But hey, easy come, easy go." He blew the steam gently away from his mug. "It's great to see you, Art. I'm sorry I keep saying it, but I missed you around the office."

"I missed you too, man. It's good to be back."

"And a little early, I might add. Everything went well, huh? You're looking good; healthy. Did you drop a few pounds?"

"Thanks. Yeah, it's amazing how much weight you lose when you stop drinking."

"I can imagine," he said with a smile. "I'm proud of you, man. Seriously."

"Thanks. I'm proud of myself," I said, looking down at my sandwich. Sam nodded, staring out the large window overlooking the sidewalk.

"Have you seen the kids yet?"

"Yeah, I took them home from school on Wednesday. They're doing pretty well. About the same."

"How are things between you and Julia?"

"About the same there, too. You know, she's got the house up for sale and didn't even bother telling me."

"It's hers isn't it? Didn't she get it in the divorce settlement?"

"It hasn't been finalized yet," I said after a pause.

"You two were dealing with that shit months ago. What the hell is taking so long?" he asked.

"I was gone for three months."

"Well, now that you're back, you need to deal with it."

"Okay, Sam," I said, trying to end the conversation. I smiled, "Hey, you want to buy a house?"

"What the hell would I do with some rickety, old house that's probably got crayon all over the walls?" Sam chewed a mouthful of his sandwich. "Besides, I just got the place back to myself."

"What do you mean? Jason moved out?"

"The way of the universe, right?" he commented.

"Man, I'm sorry. It really seemed like things were going well. How long had it been, two years?"

"Yeah, but it's fine. It's not so fresh now. This happened just over a month ago. I know it's not sixteen years of marriage or anything, but I can understand a little more now why it was so difficult for you when Julia left." Sam wiped his hands. "What about Vivian? How's that whole situation?"

"You know. Keeping it simple," I said.

"Open?"

"No. Just...you know, simple. Easy."

"Oh, I see. Still haven't said the 'L' word, huh?"

"You mean labia?" I watched Sam gag as he always did with any reference to female genitalia.

"Well, you might not want to say it, and she might not have said it, but saying it or not doesn't matter when love is something you do."

"I think she would have said it if she does."

"And if she did, what would you do?" I looked at him without an answer. "Exactly. You know, nothing says 'I love you' more than sticking around through a mental breakdown."

Samwell Epstein was a good-looking man, tall and broad-shouldered. Some could have even considered him the poster boy of the corporate sector despite the fact that he had a subversive streak to him. In many ways, he was very much a lion. An exceptionally well-groomed lion. He began his career with *Verb'd Magazine* as a young man fresh out of Yale, much to his parents' chagrin. They had paid for him to become a journalist at what they considered a "real magazine", like *TIME* or *The New Yorker*. The problem with Sam wasn't that he was ungrateful, or even that he had a desire to do something else with his life as many college graduates discover once it's too late. He simply had no interest in politics, which he believed was the crux, underlying or not, of every mainstream publication. Politics, he thought, were simply for people who wanted to argue. Sam had no desire to argue with anyone. That's not to say he only wanted to get along with people. He couldn't care less about that and would confirm this fact himself. If he agreed with you, he'd say so, and that would be the end of it. Sam wouldn't waste his time exchanging unpleasantries, unless of course, you were dishonest. This he could and would never tolerate.

Jack Dorset, the editor-in-chief of *Verb'd Magazine*, had hired him because of all this and for the fact that, during his interview, Sam told Mr. Dorset that he wasn't especially fond of certain columns in most recent issues and informed him how they should be fixed. Jack Dorset did fix them. Within a year, Sam had been promoted to head writer, and within two, to writing director.

"Let's talk about something else," I evaded, putting a melted string of cheese from my sandwich into my mouth.

"Okay," Sam nodded. "Let's talk about Huxley. The December issue is the last remaining installment you have sitting in the queue, and I need to get January's submitted to the visual editor by December twelfth."

"Don't worry," I said. "I actually have a whole new concept for Huxley."

"Yeah, like what? A new villain or something?"

"Nothing like that. More of a fresh perspective, a new feel altogether. Something more thought provoking and cerebral that examines who Huxley is as a character. There would also be only one graphic."

"Only one?" Samwell sipped his coffee. "You think it's a good idea to change things up like that?"

"I don't think it's a bad idea."

"I don't either necessarily. I can't help but wonder what's prompted the idea. You don't feel like it's already good the way it is? It's like my mama always said, 'if it ain't broke, don't fix it'."

"I'm pretty sure everyone's mother said that," I said with a laugh before sipping my coffee. "No, I feel like it's been great, but I just think Huxley is ready for something different." In my peripheral vision, I watched a well-dressed pigeon smile at me.

"Hopefully, your readers feel the same way," said Samwell before stuffing the last bite of his sandwich into his mouth. "You going to eat your pickle?"

We walked along between the chains of painted brick buildings rising up on either side of the main strip like the parting of the Red Sea. I'd recalled seeing old photographs of that area of town, the black and white frames capturing a bygone era of antiquated capitalism when horses were in direct competition with combustion engines.

The offices of *Verb'd Magazine* were on the third and fourth floors of an old building in Queen City's historic district. I wanted to ride the newly installed elevator, but Samwell insisted on taking the stairs. By the time we reached the top and entered the lobby to our offices, I was out of breath, clearly having been away for too long. He laughed at me as he turned down the hall toward his office. I continued on my own way in the direction of a young woman's familiar face just visible over the high counter of the receptionist's desk. Upon looking towards me, she squinted for a moment.

"Mr. Kimble?" she smiled. "I thought you were gone for a couple more weeks. What are you doing here?"

"Yeah, I was supposed to be, but I'm back early. How have you been, Stacy? You look well." Stacy Whittaker stepped out to me, visibly excited at my arrival with her hands clasped together. Her hair fell freely to her shoulders, a barrette keeping her bangs out of her eyes. The bell sleeves of her blouse swayed with each gesture she made.

"Oh, you know me. Always keeping busy. Notice anything different?" Smiling, she ran her hands down her front, revealing a small, abdominal bump.

"Oh, shit," I said somberly. "You have a tumor."

"No!" Stacy frowned. "I'm pregnant! I'll be eighteen weeks tomorrow."

"Wow." I looked at her closely for a confused moment. "Please, don't take this the wrong way, but I thought you were a lesbian."

"Invitro fertilization. It's where they take the egg of the mother and the sperm—"

"You don't have to go into detail. I've got the gist of it," I said awkwardly. "Well, congratulations."

"Thank you. Bailey and I are so happy. We'll be finding out what it is in a couple of weeks."

"But, if you're both lesbians, won't it be a lesbian, too?" I asked after a pause.

"I meant, to find out if it's a boy or a girl," said Stacy, hardly amused.

"Yeah. Of course."

Stacy followed me to the door of my office. "Anything you need? Do you want me to let Mr. Epstein know you're here?"

"No, I already saw him. Thanks though."

"I'll have the cleaning guys hit your office today. I don't think anyone's been in there since you left."

"Sounds good," I said flipping the light switch on. "It'll probably need it."

My office was no more special than any other cramped office with its small, south-facing window. I remembered twelve years earlier when I first entered it and saw a cozy little sanctuary of creative possibilities. Somewhere along the line, it had mutated into a crypt, and I suspected the dust and cobwebs may not have had everything to do with that. Against the wall to my left, several books—mostly the ones abandoned by my predecessor—lined a small shelf. I had determined to read them, imagining something sacred in studying old books that someone else had read when the pages were crisper and the binding pristine. Second and third editions of novels like *Atlas Shrugged* and *To Kill a Mockingbird* remained untouched except during the occasional high that would lift my fingertips to brush over their spines in something like stupefied awe. My own additions to the collection seemed amateur with their flimsy, vibrantly colored bodies, and despite them including titles like *Invisible Man*, *A Raisin in the Sun*, and *The Winter of Our Discontent*, it made me feel foolish. Perhaps, in a past life, I would never have judged a book by its cover; only for its content. But words were not what they once were. Not anymore.

"Don't judge yourself so harshly, Arthur," said Huxley. "You don't truly believe that only the proles are inclined to superficiality, do you?"

"But it's true, Hux."

"Words are what you make them," he said, fluttering to my desk, a feather drifting to the floor. "As are most things in life."

"Some things are made by others," I said. "Some things make themselves."

"And yet, we concede to our perceptions the basis of all reality." Huxley sighed. "Disappointment has many names, but only what we give it."

"I've got a list of names."

"People?"

"Sure."

"Is your name on that list, I wonder." he said.

I reached out and took the one book that was not as dusty as the rest, a copy of *Brave New World* which Julia had given me as a present when I'd first landed the job. It opened naturally to pages 76 and 77, the tiny dimples in the paper evidence of where I used to stash my emergency pills and powder. Fanning to the front, I read the inscription in the cover written in scarlet cursive:

To Arthur,

May you find this book an inspiration as you enter your own brave new world.

Love Always,

Julia.

Love always, she said.

I guessed she didn't realize it was a dystopian novel.

Becca Monahan fluently spoke French, Italian, Spanish, and some Pashto. That was her pastime, learning languages. She was a software developer for a private contracting company called Hexicom. From what I understood, she liked the job because, ironically, she didn't have to talk to anyone. She couldn't stand most people, and I was fairly certain that I was one of them, especially after the seventh or eighth time I'd passed out drunk on hers and Lonnie's living room floor. I think it was fair to say that we'd only found each other annoying when we were together. How she came to date someone like Lonnie I had no idea, but as much as he liked to talk and as much as she didn't, I figured it was simply a matter of convenient compatibility.

Becca sat opposite me in the booth, Lonnie to her right. He had done what he usually did and set up plans to meet at the last second, then laid on the guilt trip when I declined his offer.

"But we haven't seen each other in ages. You can bring Vivian along," he'd said.

"I saw you a few days ago, and Vivian has to work late tonight."

"We hardly saw each other, and it was forever before that."

"It was three months, Lonnie."

"I can't believe you, man. Here I went and got us reservations because I wanted to spend time with my two favorite people."

"I thought you said Vivian was invited?"

"My three favorite people."

"Did you really get us reservations?"

"Not yet. I was going to, but now that I realize you don't want to go, I won't."

"Okay."

"Don't you know how short life is? You never know when your ticket's going to get punched. Now I'll just have to go about my days wondering if it was the last time. And what if it was? You'd feel terrible. I couldn't bear doing that to you."

"If I died or something?"

"No, if I died, and we didn't get to say goodbye. How do you think I'd be able to live with that?"

"You'd be dead, Lonnie."

"But not to you, Art. To you, I would always remain here in this conversation. The conversation when you said no. The conversation—"

"Damn it, Lonnie. Okay!"

The restaurant he picked boasted "Best Authentic Mexican", the letters probably stenciled onto the window by someone's cousin. Despite the impression of the exterior, however, they weren't exaggerating. They also weren't taking reservations.

"What do you think is in this?" Lonnie picked at the ravioli on his plate revealing a pale gray filling. "Some milk-based substance, obviously, but what else?"

"It's ricotta cheese," I informed him. "Like always."

"It seems different."

"How does it taste?"

"I don't know. I haven't tried it yet."

"Maybe you should taste it," I suggested.

Lonnie placed his fork down on the plate and stared at me incredulously. "Do you just eat whatever is put in front of you? Are you that much of a socially conformed non-individual?"

"It's ravioli. Mexican ravioli, but ravioli."

"I know that," he huffed. "It's the principle of it. Our society has been engineered to accept whatever is given to them without questioning what it is or where it came from. That's the problem with people. Nobody asks questions because they're too afraid of the answers they might get. So, they go through life just assuming that what they've been told is fact even though they've never actually verified it for themselves. It leads to generation after generation of ignorant, unaspiring people. Followers. Conformists."

Lonnie had a piggy face. Not to say he was overweight, but he had unusually pinkish skin, an uplifted nose and an oddly round structure to his overall visage. It made me wonder why Becca was even with Lonnie, a woman in her early twenties who would be socially rated an easy seven if you're shallow like that…which I am.

"It's just ravioli in some tomato-based sauce, and it came from a restaurant kitchen," I said finally. Becca sipped her water.

"Use the straw." Lonnie glared at her.

"What?"

"The straw! Use the straw! You think those glasses are clean?

Don't even try to kiss me until you've brushed all that bacteria out of your mouth."

"Lonnie, I'm sure it's clean," I said.

"You know what? It's fine. Don't worry about the bacteria," said Lonnie. "I'm not going to let anyone get under my skin tonight. I've got some pretty amazing news."

"About what?"

"I—am—" Lonnie rubbed his hands together, "the new morning host of WRPS 103.3!" He released a triumphant laugh. "Or at least between the hours of 7am and 10am EST."

"Really?" My surprise was genuine. "How the hell did that happen? I didn't know you were trying to get into broadcasting."

"The station manager over there has been wanting to have a motivational morning host where someone talks to callers and gives uplifting life advice as they get started with their day. Well, I gave my book to Zach Hatchett, you know the evening host, who then passed it along to the station manager. Once he read my book, he knew he had to have me. Crazy, huh?"

"It sure is."

"Well, it's not completely crazy," Lonnie backtracked. "This is my rise to the top. My ascension."

"You're not exactly Jesus Christ, but I guess you have to start somewhere."

"I've already talked to my publicist about this, and she says this is a slamshot for my new book. We're even considering a tour to promote both it and the show."

"A slamshot?" I asked.

"That's what she said."

"What about the class you teach over at the college?" asked Becca.

"I'm leaving after this semester."

"Don't you have a contract?" she pressed.

"What did you think I meant when I said I was leaving after this semester?"

"You're teaching at the college?" I asked, surprised again.

"What's the class?"

"It's a creative writing course, something right up your alley, actually." Lonnie chuckled. "Right up your alley...*right* up—creative *writing*. See what I did there?"

"You seriously teach a creative writing class?"

"Yeah. What? I'm a great writer. I've published more books than you," he said, and the truth of it stung a little. "Actually, now that we're discussing it, I have an offer to do a series of lectures next month that'll require travel for about three weeks. Obviously, I can't be there and here at the same time. You want to cover my classes for me while I'm gone? I could make it worth your while. There's good money in education."

"There is?" I asked dubiously.

"For you, sure."

"Thanks, but I'm good," I said, not completely sure what he meant. "I probably wouldn't have much time for it anyway. I'm back at work, and we've got a lot going on."

"I'll be gone the sixteenth of November to the seventh of December. That's only two classes."

"But that's over Thanksgiving," said Becca.

"Yeah, it's over Thanksgiving," Lonnie repeated, either missing or disregarding Becca's inference. "That's why it's only two classes."

"I'll pass."

"Damn. All right. Let me know if you change your mind." Lonnie resumed picking at his ravioli. "What's this green stuff?" He held up a small sample of his food with the end of his fork and stuck it in Becca's face. "Is that mold?"

"Yes," said Becca flatly.

"It is?" He studied it closely, then frowned. "No, it's not. That's parsley or something. You shouldn't say something is something if you don't know, Becca."

"Sorry."

"Don't say sorry if you don't mean it. I just don't understand why you would want me to think it was mold."

"I didn't."

"You wanted me to think something."

"You're right. I shouldn't say things I don't know about." He looked at her for a long moment, then smiled with a shake of his head.

"I don't know where you'd be without me. You're lucky I've taken the time to teach you what I know." Lonnie smiled and gave her a peck on the side of her head. I watched Becca shrink down and continue eating. "Anyway, Art, I meant to ask you. How was the funeral last month?"

"It was a funeral," I shrugged.

"Come on. I know it must have been difficult for you. Tell me about it. You know I'm always here to listen."

"The flowers were nice."

"How was your dad taking it?"

I looked blankly at him. "He was pretty quiet."

Lonnie took a bite of his ravioli and closed his eyes indulgently. "Damn, this is so Zen! Becca, you've got to try this."

Lonnie held his fork laden with food in front of her face, and she silently accepted. Her jaw tensed and relaxed with the motion of her chewing. When prompted, Becca made a noise of agreement that satisfied him, but her eyes made me question if she had the same bitter taste in her mouth that I did.

I excused myself to use the restroom, hoping that it would somehow speed up time, and I could go home. As I was about to walk back, my phone started ringing, and I realized I'd completely forgotten that the airline was supposed to be contacting me.

"Hello?"

"Thank you. Please hold for the next available representative or press 9 to receive a call back."

The number nine beeped under my thumb. Putting my phone away, I found myself wondering the location of the nearest vending machine.

CHAPTER THREE

Shares. Comments. Likes. Adds. Swipes. Memes. Selfies. Views. Upvotes. Avatars. Forums. Podcasts. Blogging. Vlogging. Microblogging. Tweeting. Retweeting. Tagging. Hashtagging. Geotagging. Following. Trolling. Trending. Friending. Blocking.

The world has never been smaller than in the 21st century. Social media has made it possible for people to remain in constant contact, sharing with each other every aspect of their lives from the absolute mundane to the most intriguing. "Check out these shoes." "Look what I had for dinner." "See this injustice." "Hear me." "See me." "Acknowledge me." But this is personal public relations. The flaw of its design is that, while we might have a hundred, a thousand, or even tens of thousands of friends, we only know what those so-called friends have chosen to reveal through the proverbial filter. "Like me," they beg. "Like me based on the image I've created. Respect me for the opinions I swear I've formulated on my own, because we're the same. Be my friend. Please, be my friend! Because the world has never been smaller, and I've never felt so alone."

As it had been months since I'd logged on, Facebook required me to verify that I was indeed Arthur Kimble, whoever that was. Once I was in, I felt the clutter of almost two hundred notifications, the newest being a friend request from Abi which I accepted before clearing the rest. I immediately began stalking my daughter's profile. She was smiling everywhere, most of her posts regarding one current social topic or another. Welcome immigrants displaced by war. Support your local businesses. Demand climate policy reform. Federalize the pharmaceutical industry. Though I couldn't fault her for promoting a cause (or four), I likewise couldn't establish why it didn't sit well in my stomach.

As an artist of the new millennium, I'd of course learned to monopolize on the many platforms of social media. Years before, I'd started a website, a blog, and an account on pretty much anything that presented the possibility of a good audience. For better or worse, it was the best medium for exposure. However, it required constant attention, and for the past year, I'd given it virtually none. My lack of action apparently lost me over three hundred followers, and my blog site was no different. Although, the readers gave me the courtesy of announcing how much of a disappointing shitbag I apparently was.

greekgod4889: *Real artists don't stop creating!*

arielr08: *Did you die? I hope so*

justinthyme: *Your stuff was kind of declining anyway. Kudos for knowing when to quit.*

xxxmaria69: *Want to chat with REAL naked women? Click* HERE*!*

Apparently, the link was expired.

A comment about my website not even working prompted me to check for myself. It appeared that www.arthurkimble.com was unable to be found, and I realized that I'd forgotten to pay for the hosting. I seemed to be staring at a ball of mud-soaked yarn that I would either have to meticulously unravel or let roll away. There was no one to blame but myself for the current state of things, and I tried to massage away the tension building in my neck.

"Mr. Kimble." Stacy knocked and poked her head into the room. "Mr. Dorset wants to see you."

I walked into a small hallway which opened to a bright anteroom where a secretary sat, the tips of her fingers hopping about from key to key, her eyes glued to the nearly illegible document she was effortlessly transcribing. As I entered, she looked up and smiled, straightening her back to accentuate her endowments.

"Well, look what the cat dragged in," she sighed. "You know, I heard you were back, but I just didn't believe it."

"Really? Why not?" I laughed.

"Because I thought for sure that if you were in the building at least one time, you'd have made certain to come see me. You're a real heartbreaker, you know that, Arthur Kimble?" Helen shook her head with a smile.

A sudden thud and raised voice from inside the office ended the banter, and a moment later, Stanley Dorset burst from the room, lines of anger augmenting his thin face. He tossed a file of paperwork onto Helen's desk, covering the document she'd been typing.

"Make three copies of each. Send two down to my secretary and the other to Mr. Grant." She sat back with a silent expression of disgust. Ignoring her reaction, he began walking past but stopped and looked back over his shoulder upon noticing me. "I thought you died," he commented with a hint of disappointment.

"Call me Lazarus."

Stanley glared then continued down the hall. Jack Dorset appeared a moment later in his doorway with another man whom I did not recognize but surmised to be Mr. Grant. He clutched the handle of a briefcase as it brushed against the trousers of his three-piece suit. Mr. Dorset shook his hand without a word, and the man solemnly followed the path that Stanley had taken.

"It's all right, Helen," said Jack Dorset. "Just see that it gets done. Thank you." Mr. Dorset turned towards me with a smile. "Come on in, Arthur," he said cheerfully, leading the way into his office. The walls were shadowed, the blinds to his panoramic window closed, allowing through only a few streams of light which lined the floor before hitting his executive desk. Finally seated, he leaned back with a sigh, removing his glasses. "So, tell me, Arthur. How are you?"

"I'm well, thanks. How about you?"

"Have you ever checked for your own pulse and felt nothing? In that instant you suddenly are on a mission to find it. Feel one wrist, feel the other," he demonstrated, with a worried look on his face. "Nothing. The carotid—ah. There it is. I knew it was there somewhere." I nodded an expression of consideration, not completely sure if he was going for humor. "But for all that time, the question has burrowed into your consciousness: am I really alive? I'm not as senile as some people think. I am very much alive." Mr. Dorset leaned forward and winked. "But don't tell anyone. It keeps them guessing, and the last thing you want is to be predictable."

"Mum's the word," I said.

"Now then, Arthur," he crossed his hands, "how was your journey?"

"Good. It went very well."

"Did you find what you were looking for?"

"What I was looking for, yes. What I expected, no."

"Expectation is the scourge of happiness." Jack Dorset reached for a walnut from a bowl on the corner of his desk and picked up the metal nutcracker and pick lying beside it. "Remind me again, where was it you were staying?"

"I traveled all around; Carson City, Flagstaff, Santa Fe, Venice, Sacramento—"

"Venice…" He whispered, squeezing the walnut in the nutcracker until it opened with a splintering crack. "No other place quite like it, I think."

"Probably not." I watched as he took up the pick and began prying the flesh from inside the shell.

"You know, I was a bit surprised when I was told you'd returned early."

"I felt like I accomplished what I set out to do."

"I'm very glad to hear that." He chewed the pieces slowly, working the fragments until he swallowed. After a long pause, "Arthur, we haven't had a chance to discuss what happened before. You gave us all quite a scare."

"I know. I apologize."

"Please, you don't owe anyone an apology. I didn't bring the matter up to guilt one out of you. I only mention it because it's very serious and I—we—care about you."

"Yes, I know."

Mr. Dorset nodded thoughtfully, rubbing his thumb across his fingers before casting his gaze out the window and grasping the end of his bristled chin.

His face was stoic and weather-worn, tough even in his old age, long wisps of white hair falling over the permanently tanned leather of his forehead. His hands were as equally rugged, striations lining his fingernails from years of hard labor. Even with the look of a wizened outdoorsman, his presence still invoked an offering of respect. With a sigh, he reached for a silver cigarette case in a drawer then stood and walked around to where I sat. Leaning against the edge of his desk, he offered me one which I accepted, then lit them both. He puffed the smoke out of his nostrils.

"Arthur, I know that the past several months have been difficult for you. Clearly. Now, I'm not fishing for details, but I've heard—and far be it from me to give credence to rumors—but I've heard that some of what happened may have stemmed from troubles at home." I wasn't sure if he was looking for a confirmation or not, so I just looked back at him. "Arthur, we take care of our own. *Verb'd* is a family, or at least I'd like to think I've fostered that kind of environment here." He stood and moved back around his desk. "We want you to be well. It was the primary reason for me approving your trip to sort things out. I was glad to hear from Samwell that you were doing some writing. It can be quite therapeutic as we both know."

"I did, and yes, it is. I truly appreciate your doing that for me."

"But the problems are not gone, Arthur. They didn't evaporate while you were away, and now you're back and will have to face them."

"Jack, I understand the concern, and again, I appreciate you and everyone caring about my well-being, but I've gotten myself to a much better state of mind. I needed to give myself a moment to clear my head, and with your help I've done that."

"All the same, I'd feel better knowing you were still actively taking care of yourself. I know I can't make you, and I would never try, but I feel strongly that utilizing the services of a counselor or a therapist would be of great benefit to you."

"Jack—"

"I know, I know. I might be overreaching, but it's important, Arthur." Mr. Dorset removed his glasses and leaned forward. "It's important."

Why it's difficult to accept the fact that good people might actually care about you, I don't know. Perhaps it's a side effect of self-loathing, or maybe a handicapped ability to trust. Whatever the reason, I didn't have time to figure it out just then, but likewise couldn't leave him hanging with such a genuine concern.

"I'm already seeing a therapist," I lied.

"Really?" Mr. Dorset smiled, mildly surprised as I opened my wallet to retrieve the business card I'd been given. As I handed it to him, I wondered how I'd come to put it there in the first place.

"Dr. Margaret Hollande," he read aloud. "I'm very happy for this. Very happy. If there's anything at all you need, don't hesitate." After handing it back to me, he set his burning cigarette in the holder of an ashtray and took up another walnut. "So, Arthur, I hope that while you've been gone, perhaps you've developed the next installment of your column. Not that I want you to feel under pressure, but as you might be aware, we're in need of another story for Theodore Huxley." He smiled with satisfaction at the sound of a splitting walnut shell.

"Don't worry. I've got the next one coming along nicely," I said, trying to convince myself as much as trying to convince him.

"Well, good." His eyes laughed over his glasses as he picked at the walnut. "You know, in the past forty years that we've been printing, your column has proven to be one of my favorite elements of them all."

"Thank you." I kept smiling. "I'm actually working on a new angle with Huxley. I don't want to give anything away just yet, but you won't be disappointed."

"Oh, come now, Arthur. Can't you humor an old man?" I laughed with him, almost as amused as I was agitated.

"Well, you could say that's kind of counter to the idea. I'm going to leave the humorous elements behind. Make it more cerebral."

"Really?" Mr. Dorset asked, lacking enthusiasm as he chewed.

"I'd like to make it less focused on action and more on characters. Only a single graphic, maybe."

"What would it be about?"

"Well, Huxley still," I said.

"Of course, but what would be happening?"

"The same as always except with a closer examination of the characters and their motivations. Where they come from, where they're going."

"That's quite a leap from the norm, Arthur. I'm not sure how our readers would enjoy it or react."

"I think it's where Huxley is going in his evolution though, which I believe readers would appreciate."

"I don't have any reservations about your expanding the character. A character without growth is no character at all. However, I don't think it's a good idea to change something we have such great traction with. People love action and adventure. They're familiar with this series being in the traditional format with the illustrations. That's what you've always given them." He took up the pick. "And I'm not sure this wouldn't be just a way for you to project yourself into the character, and that could be even more detrimental."

"Detrimental to what?" I asked, and Mr. Dorset shook his head dismissively.

"Why don't you just go ahead and write it, draw it up, and then we'll see. Maybe that will help me understand your perspective." He cleared his throat. "And sooner rather than later, please."

"Okay," I said after a pause.

"Until then, I stand by my conviction. Huxley should remain as he's always been."

"Okay."

"Excellent." He smiled before jabbing the point of the pick into the walnut.

I watched the meticulous work of Jack Dorset freeing the tiny bits from their shell, fumbling to pick them up with the tips of his calloused fingers, then chewing the bites that wouldn't have satisfied a bird. I considered what a laborious toil it must be to reap so small a reward.

"Blood pressure."

"Sorry?"

"My blood pressure," Mr. Dorset explained quietly. "The doctor says these will help." He gnawed the bits of nut. "Tastes like paper." His lips curled with disgust as he picked yet another walnut.

I put out the cigarette in the ashtray where his was still burning down with neglect. As I shut the door to his office, I heard him let out a deep-chested cough followed by a sputtering of muttered curses.

Abi and Ryan were home alone when I arrived at Julia's that afternoon to pick them up for my weekend visitation. Ryan greeted me at the door with an empty expression as Abi was chattering to herself down the hall. When she appeared, she was applying black makeup around her eyes, the contrast against the pale foundation hollowing out her features. She smiled at me with her blackened lips.

"Hi, Dad! I only have a little left to do. What do you think?"

"I think Frankenstein is one lucky monster," I said.

"Frankenstein wasn't the monster. He was the scientist."

"You know you can't go trick-or-treating this year, right?" I said, ignoring her correction. "You're too old."

"I already told her," informed Ryan dryly as he walked past the door.

"There's no rule that says I can't dress up. Someone has to sit with the candy when the kids come by."

"We're not going to do candy."

"What?" Abi's jaw dropped. "Why not? You said trick-or-treating is tonight in your building."

"Yes, but there aren't that many kids in my building."

"Not *many* kids."

"Right."

"There are still kids though. They should be able to get candy."

"Sprout, I love your festive spirit, but it's really not going to matter if we have candy for the handful of kids in the building."

"It matters to them, and if it matters to them, it matters to me."

"I don't have candy."

"We can buy some. I'll pay. I have my allowance money."

"Sprout—"

"Please, Daddy?" She looked at me with eyes tender and pleading.

"Well, I guess I need to get some groceries anyway," I surrendered.

"Thank you, Daddy!" Sprout cheered, opening the screen door to give me a peck on the cheek. She left a set of black lip prints. "You're the best!"

You're the best, she says.

"It takes a quarter."

"What do you mean it takes a quarter?"

"They do it to save money on their end, so you can save money on yours. It's in their advertisements." I looked at the chains linked to the lines of grocery carts, each with a coin slot. "You'll get it back," Abi assured me.

We entered the store and began walking through the aisles. I had never been there before, but Abi had nearly staged a protest that I shouldn't go to any other store except this new one. It was eco-friendly, cheap, and nice to dead animals.

"You have to thump it," she told me, taking the cantaloupe I'd just put in the cart. "Like this." Abi flicked the side of the melon, producing a hollow thumping sound from within. "Now you know it's ripe."

"Well, what do you know?" I remarked, feigning ignorance of the practice but pleased at my daughter's satisfaction with teaching me something. She hurried to the kiwis a few feet away and picked a pair for me to see.

"You want to hold them in your hands like this and gently squeeze. If they—"

"Yeah, I know about that one," I interrupted, taking the pair of fuzzy fruit that she was innocently fondling. "Let's just put these back," Abi shrugged, and we mulled along past the produce toward the frozen aisles.

"Where did Ryan go?"

"I'm sure he'll turn up when we get to the chips," I said before spotting him poking at the cow tongues and livers. He was nodding along to the music playing in his headphones. A couple minutes later, Ryan approached us and dropped a handful of frozen chimichangas into the cart.

"Those are so unhealthy," said Abi. "There's loads of sodium."

"So? They're not for you," Ryan said before wandering off again.

Ryan had grown almost as tall as me, his shoulders just as broad and the shadow above his lip already shaved away. He fit the mold of a brooding adolescent; except he was my brooding adolescent which occasionally made it an adolescent pain in the ass.

After debating with herself over which bag of candy would be best, Abi finally tossed one into the cart so we could leave. Ryan remained sullen as we walked back to the car, the beat thumping audibly even outside the confines of his headphones. After loading the few bags of groceries into the trunk, Abi elected to return the cart. When she reached the corral, an older woman was fumbling with putting her quarter into the slot. I watched as Abi said something to her before letting her take the cart we'd been using and hurried back.

"That sweet old lady!" said Abi as she hopped into the passenger seat. "She couldn't figure out how to get the cart free. I had to give her ours."

"Yeah, I saw," I said, starting up the engine. "That was very kind of you, Sprout,"

"I just felt so bad for her, all hunched over and old. Why aren't her kids helping her?"

"Maybe she doesn't have kids."

"That's even more sad, going through your whole life and ending up alone." She looked out the window as we pulled out of the parking lot, narrowing her eyes wistfully. "I hope that doesn't happen to me."

"Why do you think that would happen to you?"

"I don't know. I mean, look at most of the people out there today. It seems like almost everyone is alone. Over half of all marriages end in divorce. Did you know that?"

"Being divorced doesn't mean you're alone. I'm not alone." Abi shot me a dubious glance. "What? I'm not. What was that look for? I have you and Ryan. I'm not alone at all."

"What about all the days that we're not with you? You're not alone then?"

"I'm too busy thinking about the next time we're together to be lonely," I smiled.

"Okay, okay. Regardless," she continued, "it sucks to be alone. I still feel bad for that lady."

"Well, I'm sure she's very thankful for what you did. I'm proud of you. It's always good to think of others." I drove along silently for a moment. "Hey, let me get my quarter back. I'll save it for next time."

"Oh, that old lady has it," Abi said casually.

"But she gave you her quarter, right?" I asked. "She exchanged the quarter in her hand for the quarter in the cart."

"She wanted to, but I told her to keep it."

"But that was my quarter."

"I'm not taking money from a little old lady," she said, repulsed at such an idea.

"You wouldn't be taking her money. You would be exchanging it. Now you gave her my quarter for nothing."

"So, it's just a quarter. Besides, she's not even going to keep it."

"How do you know?"

"She couldn't get it in. She's not going to be able to get it out."

"That's what she said," Ryan suddenly voiced up. I gave him the look in the rearview, though he wasn't paying attention.

"So," I said to Abi, "now some random person's going to walk off with my quarter."

"You shouldn't think of it like that," Abi said candidly. "Think of it as a random act of kindness. Maybe the next person who gets that cart will do something nice for someone else just because you did something nice for them. Maybe it'll become this chain of good deeds. Maybe by giving that quarter, you were directly involved in making the world a better place."

"Maybe they keep the quarter," I said. "Then there's *no* chain of good deeds." Abi pondered something for a long moment.

"Maybe. But at least now there's a fifty percent higher chance that there will be a chain of good deeds than if I just gave it back to you. It seems worth a quarter to take that chance. Don't you think so?" Sprout smiled at me. "A quarter's-worth of change. Change for a quarter." She laughed, sufficiently pleased.

I found myself marveling at Abi, wondering at the evolution she'd undergone. Not long ago, she was just a young girl with little opinion about anything outside of her personal existence. Suddenly, she was a thoughtful and observant individual who no longer viewed the world as hers, but everyone's. She was a better person than me, and I was okay with that.

After dinner, Abi stationed herself at the door in her full Bride of Frankenstein costume with the bag of candy in a large mixing bowl. I spent the next twenty minutes cleaning up the kitchen and the dishes while Ryan remained on the couch scrolling through the channels. Once I was certain he'd scanned through the loop at least twice, I took a seat beside him.

"What are you watching?"

"I don't know," he frowned.

"A hundred channels and nothing on. You know, when I was a kid we only picked up one channel in our town. Everyone knew when the soaps were on, the local and national news, *Wheel Of Fortune* and *Jeopardy!* Late night sitcoms. The world was a simpler place."

Ryan ignored my nostalgia by flipping faster through the channels, but I pressed on. "You know what we should watch? It's a perfect Halloween movie." He raised his eyebrows in irritation. "*Young Frankenstein.*" Only his eyes creaked toward my direction. "You know who Mel Brooks is, right?" His eyes creaked back.

"Yes, I know who Mel Brooks is," he said in a gasp. "I don't care."

"Perfect." I stood and approached my shelf of DVDs and VHS tapes. Once located, I put the cassette into the VCR. The screen shifted over and a few white lines danced across the black screen for a second or two. "Good old VHS. They don't make them like they used to." As if on cue, the screen turned blue, and 'REW' flashed at the top.

"For obvious reasons," Ryan grumbled. "I'm going to sit with Abi." Ryan tossed the remote down and headed to the front door.

I sat, listening to the whir of the tape rewinding, thinking about all the times I'd tried to tell myself that he couldn't hate me forever, then began to wonder how long ago that had been. There are a lot of things that change on their own. People's minds aren't one of them, at least not the people whose minds are worth changing. You have to convince them. Evidence. Facts. Arguments. Closing statements. The burden of proof ever remains in the hands of those who can't seem to wield it, despite knowing and understanding all the ways in the world one could make their case. Yet, the words simply don't flow.

To tell the truth is one thing. To convince someone of the truth, that requires imagination, and despite my profession, it was clear that I had little.

The VCR clicked, its gears adjusting to play the video.

"Dad!" Ryan rushed back into the room. "Abi's not here."

"What do you mean she's not here? Did you check the bathroom?"

"She's not here!" he repeated more insistently.

I rose quickly from the couch and, after a swift walkthrough of my apartment, stepped out into the hall and around the corner. Her name reverberated back to me, empty.

"She's got to be around here somewhere," I said to Ryan.

"Why would she just walk off?" Ryan asked. "There's no reason for her to go anywhere."

"It's okay, Ryan. We'll just check the other floors. She couldn't be far." I had to consciously relax my stride as I walked towards the elevator. I stood after pressing the button, but Ryan walked past toward the stairs, commenting on how that would take too long. "Ryan, hold on," I said, knowing he'd ignore me. "You should stay at the apartment in case she comes back."

"Whatever." Ryan kept moving.

"Someone needs to be there if she comes back."

"Then you stay!" he shouted.

"What the hell's wrong with you, lately?" I asked, forcing him to face me. "You've had a chip on your shoulder for a long time, but ever since I've been back it's like it festered."

"So?"

"So, I want to know why."

"It's none of your business."

"You're my son," I said. "That makes it my business."

"Well, you never bothered asking before, so either it isn't your business, or you just never gave a shit."

"Don't talk to me like that, Ryan," I warned.

"Just following your example, Dad." Ryan pushed past, and I listened to him return to the stairs as I remained inhaling the scent of carpet cleaner. There it was, the sensation enveloping me like a powerful storm surge, and I couldn't swim.

"Fuck it."

I took out a cigarette and lit it as I headed back. Once in my apartment, I made a beeline for the kitchen where, far back in a cupboard, a long-neglected bottle of scotch had been waiting for me. Beside it was a single lowball glass, the shapes of diamonds ornamentally cut into the side in alternating rows. The bottle was smooth and cool in my grasp, the familiar texture of the label increasing the intense pounding of my heart. A remarkable sensation of fire and ice radiated from my sternum and into my limbs, down the muscles and ligaments, then into my fingers and toes. Such sensations multiplied with each movement I made; the twist of the top, the sound of the plastic cap clattering on the counter; the weight shifting in my hand with the decline of the bottleneck; the contents disturbed, lapping back and forth before being released and hitting the bottom of the glass with the swirl of a breaking wave.

The drink hit my lips, wet my tongue, warmed my chest, released the energy. I closed my eyes, relishing the internal electric burst. When I opened them, my children were standing there, watching. Abi looked at me, either puzzled or concerned. I couldn't tell. Ryan shook his head in disgust.

"Found her." Ryan walked quickly to his room and slammed the door.

"Hey, Sprout," I said to her quietly. "Where were you?"

"Ms. Foster needed help looking for Mr. Skiddles, so I went around with her to look."

"Who is Mr. Skiddles?"

"Her cat," said Abi. "We didn't find him."

"Oh," I said. After a moment, "I didn't know she has a cat."

"She doesn't. Not anymore, at least." She looked at the bottle on the counter, then back at me. "I'm sorry, Daddy," she said softly.

I'm sorry, she says.

A minute later, I remained at the counter, at the bottle.

"Perhaps," said Huxley from the dining table, "you should have waited until they were asleep to do that."

"I didn't feel like waiting that long."

"Didn't feel like or couldn't?"

"How was I supposed to know they'd be walking in right at that moment?" I asked.

"As a writer, you of all people should know that anything is possible, and the more possible, the more probable."

"Don't give me that shit, Huxley."

"I'm merely making an observation, Arthur. Don't get uptight because you see the validity of my point."

"I'm not being uptight."

"Did you want them to see you drink?" Huxley asked. I stared at him.

"Did I want them to see? Why would I want them to see? You of all people should know that I would never do that on purpose. Not after what they've been through."

"All this as you hold your second shot."

I'd apparently filled the glass absentmindedly. Without a word, I dumped it down the drain, though Huxley knew that it wasn't without a bold streak of anxiety.

On Ryan's tenth birthday, Julia and I gave him a blue bicycle. It was for big kids, a step up from his tricycle minus the training wheels. This new bike had handlebar brakes, deep treaded tires, and even a place for a water bottle to attach to the down tube. Ryan didn't know how to ride a bike though, not without the training wheels at least. It had been an arduous task to battle through, and I spent countless spring and summer days trying to help him find his balance and stride. Regardless of this, I could hardly get him a few feet forward before he would panic, turning the handlebars side to side and sticking his feet out towards the ground.

"Whoa! Dad, don't let go!" Ryan would cry. I assured him repeatedly that I had him. That he was safe. That I wouldn't let anything happen to him.

But Ryan continued to falter in his movements, and eventually he didn't even want to try. He assumed that he could not do it. I tried to boost his confidence. "You can do anything you put your mind to, buddy." Julia made attempts, pointing out the fact that all the other kids were riding bicycles, and wouldn't it be fun to ride with them. He didn't seem to care about that though, stubbornly convinced that he couldn't do it.

Ryan's inability to ride the bicycle stirred an anger inside me, a frustration, not because he wasn't capable yet, but because he'd assumed he was incapable. He was afraid, a trait in anyone that I didn't understand or have patience for. Ryan was afraid to fall, though he knew I held him. He knew he was safe, yet he doubted the facts, dreading the worst. I never expected for him to be especially courageous or daring, but a lack of courage didn't, in my mind, constitute the presence of fear, just as a lack of fear didn't constitute the presence of courage. For him to simply try, to put forth effort, to take a risk on what others all around had proven possible was all I expected from him.

As the summer was drawing nearer to its end, Ryan was yet to ride that damn bicycle more than a yard, and as the morning on one late summer day ticked by, I was resolute that the time had come for him to get it done. I had decided. It was then or never, and I wasn't going to put another minute of work into teaching him what he had decided he couldn't learn.

"Ryan," I'd said, "get your helmet, pads, and gloves on. Meet me outside with your bicycle in ten minutes. Today's the day."

I left not even the hint of room for protest or discussion. When we got to the street, I told him to mount his bike, holding the handles for him as he lifted one foot over the frame, cautiously resting it on the pedal.

"Okay," I said. "Both hands on the handlebars…one foot on the ground, one on the pedal…just like that…now push off the ground with one foot and push the pedal with the other…no, at the same time…you have to push harder than that…no, I'm not going to let go…good. Now pedal. Push on the pedals…keep the handlebars straight…yes…all right, keep going…keep going…"

I decided in that moment, as the wheels began to spin faster and his control of the bars steadied, to do what I had never done before. I removed one hand from the handle, gripping the back of his seat with a push. Ryan continued to pedal, the tires spinning faster, the spokes shimmering like water under the sun.

I released the faux leather from my grasp, watching his focus, the deep concentration of his squinted eyes and the tip of his tongue poking through the corner of his mouth. He was doing it. Ryan was sailing off, finally feeling the wind on his face, the first sensation of freedom and control a person has in life. Perhaps, I thought, all it took the whole time was for me to let go. He was riding his bike. It was happening.

Until he realized it was happening.

Ryan looked back at me, terror striking his once determined eyes as he understood that he was on his own. It was only a half moment, then the handlebars began to shake again. He forgot which foot was pushing down and which was rising up. With a howl and the cry of my name, he toppled over, rolling less than a foot on the asphalt. I jogged the fifty to sixty feet he'd ridden to reach him, cheering that he'd done it, that he'd conquered it, hoping it would outweigh the fall. But when he looked at me, his cheeks slick with salty tears, he accused me of betrayal with a dirty finger. Ryan yelled, not because he was hurt, but because I'd let him go. He blamed me for the fall, telling me if only I'd held on to him, stayed with him the whole way, he wouldn't have hit the ground at all. I tried to point out the significant success he'd just had, but it made no difference to him. He had fallen.

Finally, I snapped. "You can't just quit! You can't just give up because it didn't work right the first time! Things don't always happen the way we want, but that doesn't mean we sit around and cry about it! You can't just stop trying! You can't sit there and feel sorry for yourself, and I'm not going to feel sorry for you either! Now get up and try it again, or I'm giving the bike away!"

Ryan stopped crying, surprised by the emotion in my outburst. He looked at me, wiping his face and dusting off his clothes as he sat, and then he thought. He watched the other boys down the street riding around as if it was a biological attachment they'd been born with. He looked at our house and down at the bicycle, its bright blue body once full of possibility and adventure now scratched and dirty like the cover of a used textbook. Ryan stood without a word and walked into the house. Later the same evening, I took a sledgehammer to that fucking bike.

CHAPTER FOUR

I replaced the coffee pot on the burner and flicked a pair of sugar packets before tearing them open and dumping the contents into a Styrofoam cup. Gripping one of the tiny black straws between my fingers, I made a lame attempt at stirring the contents together. Without the resistance of the liquid as with a spoon, however, there was zero satisfaction in the act, and I began to seriously question the agenda of coffee companies and their related manufacturers. It was a conspiracy among the lot of them. The stirrers would poorly mix the sugar and creamer, causing the drinker to add more for a better taste. This would either mean that the drinker would pour less coffee into the cup and be back for seconds sooner, or a larger coffee cup would be required, meaning that more coffee would be poured. More sugar and creamer mixed in. More coffee cups used. It was actually quite genius in a corporately evil way. They were raking in the profits all thanks to those shitty coffee stirrer straws.

"And why the hell are they straws?" I asked. "Nobody drinks through them."

"Probably to cut manufacturing costs," Linus Federley reasoned. "I seriously doubt it's some giant plot to rip off coffee drinkers though."

"Why should we be forced to accept poorly stirred coffee so that some company no one's ever heard of can save a few bucks?" I asked.

"Think of it as an eco-friendly way to stir your coffee."

"But no one recycles these things. They all end up stuck to the inside of a garbage bag."

"Well, I don't know," he sighed in exasperation. "Why does it matter?"

"You're the marketing director. You of all people should understand the importance of questioning convention."

"Sure, when it matters."

"But how do you know it doesn't matter?" I asked, following him to sit at the conference table. "How do you know until you question it?"

"Okay, so it doesn't matter to me. What matters is that I have stirred coffee." He sipped and squinted at his cup. "What the hell?"

"See? It doesn't stir well enough."

"No, I think this is decaf. What's the point of decaf coffee? Now there's something that matters."

As he and I sat, I noticed the room slightly emptier than I had recalled. There was Jan from design but not Frank; Regina in accounting without Willy Baker. Dan and Lisa who ran the creative department were both present; Veronica and Pam from sales. Crystal Sheridan from publicity was missing, and she never missed anything.

Before I could mention it to him, Samwell, Stanley, and Jack walked in together with a quick suction of air as the glass door opened. Jack moved with a startling briskness for an older man whom I'd witnessed hacking up a lung only days before. Linus tapped my shoulder and nodded.

"Who's that?"

Until then, I hadn't noticed the apparent visitor to our staff meeting. The same gentleman from the other day who'd exited Jack Dorset's office behind Stanley was preparing himself a cup of the same coffee.

"I don't know. I think his name is Grant." We watched him

trace circles in his coffee with one of the idiotic stirrer-straws. Then he capped the straw with a finger and brought the other end to his lips to taste the coffee. Satisfied, he nodded and put the straw down on a napkin.

"Okay, so maybe it's not a conspiracy," I admitted.

"Whoever he is, I don't trust him," said Linus. Before we could speculate further, Jack cleared his throat at the head of the table.

"Let's get started, shall we?" he began, quieting the room. "I just received the print for November's issue, and I first want to say that everything looks excellent."

He held up the magazine, the cover an abstract painting of a tiger collared to a sparkling leash, the end of which was in the hand of a long-legged woman with caramel skin and a single piece of cloth wrapped around her body. I had no idea what it symbolized.

"You all are doing a splendid job with keeping us on schedule," Jack continued, "even with some of the cost cutting we've had to implement over the past few weeks." I shot an inconspicuous glance at Sam. Mr. Dorset scanned the loose pages in his open folder, his thumb pressed against the varicose vein at his temple. "As a reward for your efforts and as an early Christmas present, I'm happy to be getting that vending machine you've been asking for. It should be installed within the next few weeks"

Linus let out a hissing, "Yessss."

"It probably won't have any baked apple pies," I whispered.

"Now, on a more important note, I'd like to welcome back Arthur Kimble from his much-deserved trip." Mr. Dorset gestured towards me, smiling. "Arthur, I'm glad you've returned to us. Now, get your ass back to work." Everyone chuckled as I smiled and nodded politely, wishing he'd move on with more important matters.

"Let's get into the business of the week." Jack Dorset cleared his throat again while flipping a page. "Our HR representative will be here Wednesday with updated insurance information as we've just switched companies. Please see to it that all of you and your departments have gone online to fill out your coverage electives before then, and that all required paperwork has been signed. Everyone should be getting an email to remind you. Also, on a more important note…" Jack Dorset removed his glasses and wiped the bridge of his nose. "There's a new face in the room, and I'm sure you're wondering who he is. This is Mr. Jerry Grant from the Operations Solutions Group in Minneapolis. You'll be seeing him around for the next few weeks observing how we work, understanding the way our magazine functions, and looking for ways to improve our day-to-day activities by weeding out unnecessary and excessive processes. Would you say that's accurate Mr. Grant?"

"Yes, sir. Simply put, I'll be looking for ways to increase productivity," Mr. Grant smiled. "Usually when I do this, people can be nervous by seeing me around. Please know that I am not here to be a spy or a rat or a big brother looking over your shoulder. I'm here to help, and I look forward to getting to know you folks over the next couple of weeks."

"Thank you, Jerry. We're glad to have you with us. As he said, there's no need to be nervous. And speaking of nervousness, there's a matter I need to address with you all." Jack Dorset cleared his throat. "I want to remind everyone that we are having an auditor come through the third week of November to see where we can trim the fat financially, so I expect the departmental expense reports to be completed by this coming Monday. I believe all the questions I received about it have been answered, and I appreciate your cooperation with getting those in punctually. It seems that there have been concerns regarding these reports and the auditor, and I'd like to address you all together and hopefully quell those concerns, however justified.

"First, there have been rumors throughout the workplace that *Verb'd Magazine* is going bankrupt, that we are losing our readership, and that we are even to become solely internet-based. I want to assure you that these rumors are completely false. For the past thirty-eight years, this publication has been in a constant state of growth and maturation, and the recent months are no exception. However, for us to stay viable in these days of new technology and business methods, it is imperative that we keep up with the times. This means some restructuring, some reorganizing. Let's call it a renovation. And, yes, I realize that change is uncomfortable. But change for the greater good is never undergone without some growing pains. Take comfort in knowing that these renovations will in no way impact the foundation of who we are and what we do. *Verb'd Magazine* has built a solid reputation of presenting the finest of artistry to its readers by remaining thorough, unbiased, and explorative. It is my intention for that to continue in the decades to come." He looked at each of us and nodded. "With the group sitting around this table today, I'm confident that we can."

"I guess that explains the shitty coffee," Linus whispered.

"I understand the reason behind going paperless, but there's something to be said about turning physical pages and reading printed words. Of all the ways to cut costs, I wish that wasn't one of them." Samwell frowned out the window of Starbucks holding his sandwich with both hands.

"It's better than firing people," I said.

"Yeah." He spoke the word quickly in a tone that made me pause.

"What's the matter?" I asked. Samwell huffed and looked at his plate.

"I already filled out the expense reports for the writing department."

"And?"

"There's always somewhere and some way to cut costs, but the quickest and most effective is to cut people. There's always someone expendable. Even if we don't want them to be. It's just the way it is."

"You don't think Jack will actually let that happen, do you?"

"The man isn't God."

"Why would he need to be God to avoid firing his own employees?" I asked.

"Like I said, I filled out the expense reports for us, and if the other departments look anything similar, something more effective is going to happen. I'm not saying it's that, but something. You don't need to worry though."

"I'm under contract. Why would I worry?"

"I know, I'm just saying. Contracts can be bought out," he said.

"Is there something I should know?" I asked warily.

"I was just speaking hypothetically, but that's not even a possible scenario." He smiled and shook his head, an action I found somehow calming, yet it did not clear the questions that were clouding my mind. Sam took a bite of his food and changed the subject. "Did you get my email about P.J. Goring?"

"Yeah, I—" The ringer on my phone began sounding off, and when I saw that it was the airline, my blood pressure spiked. Excusing myself, I went to stand by the pastry display.

"Hello?"

"Hello, I'm calling for Mr. Arthur Kimble," a woman said.

"Speaking."

"Mr. Kimble, my name is Sri. I'm calling in regard to the remains that were misdirected from your flight last week. I'm so sorry that this happened to you. I can't imagine how horrible it must feel being separated this way from a loved one."

"I'm used to it, but thanks."

"I'd also like to apologize that you've had such a rough go of getting through to anyone. I see you've talked to a couple different people without much resolution."

"Without any resolution," I corrected her. "The last person I spoke with was Gregery something at Columba Regional Airport."

"Gregery Samsan, yes. I spoke with him just a short time ago while we've been tracking down the remains. It was—"

"Tracking down?"

"Yes, sir."

"As in, you don't know where they are?"

"We know where they've been which gives us a good idea as to where they're going to be."

"So, they're completely lost?!" I shouted, attracting the eyes of everyone in the cafe, Samwell's particularly curious.

"Mr. Kimble, please understand that we don't take this lightly, and anything and everything I can do to recover the remains I will do."

"How the hell could this even happen?"

"That is something I will be investigating as well. It is our responsibility to ensure that all passengers and cargo arrive at the correct destination, and we take that responsibility very seriously. That's why I have been assigned to your claim."

"What's your name again?" I asked.

"My name is Sri. I am an internal recovery specialist."

"You mean this kind of thing happens so frequently there's a position dedicated to it?"

"A department, actually," she clarified. "Again, Mr. Kimble, I can understand how upset you must be. If it might ease your mind, I do want to let you know that I have a 97.3% recovery rating."

"There's a rating system?"

"Yes, sir."

"Wow."

"The reason I am calling is to let you know that we've tracked the remains to an airport in Toledo. It was processed for a transfer last night, but to which flight is still unknown. Out of the over four hundred flights going out daily from there, I've been running searches through each of the manifests. I feel confident I'll have an answer soon."

"Okay. What do I do now?"

"Where are you?"

"Where am I?" I asked, a bit confused. "In a Starbucks."

"Well, I suggest you get yourself a cup of coffee." Once she disconnected the call, I returned to the table where Sam was puzzling at me.

"What was that all about?" he asked. "What's lost?"

"All hope," I said. "What were we talking about?"

"I don't remember…Goring. I asked if you'd gotten my email."

"Oh, right. I haven't started reading his novel yet, but I did leave a message with his publicist's firm. You'd think there'd be an easier way to reach him, like a manager or an agent or something. How the hell is anyone supposed to get in contact with you when you live off the grid?"

"That's probably the point. The man is known to like his privacy. I can't say I blame him. I feel like that's a growing trend with authors."

My phone rang once more, and I looked down at a number that

I was sure I'd seen somewhere yet couldn't place. Samwell watched me stare at it momentarily before asking if I was going to answer.

"Hello?" I said, once again at the pastries.

"Hello, Mr. Kimble. This is Dr. Hollande. Is this a bad time?"

"Maybe," I said hesitantly.

"Do you remember me?" she asked.

"Yes. Why are you calling me? How did you even get my number?"

"Your secretary. She's very sweet."

"Are you stalking me now?"

"No, nothing like that," she chuckled. "I'm calling you because Jack Dorset reached out to me." Upon hearing her words, the blood rushed to my head, and my ears started to burn.

"Reached out?"

"Yes, Mr. Kimble. It seems that he is under the impression you're seeing me for therapy. I'm not sure why or how he thought this, but he called me to ask if there was a way he could cover the copayments of your sessions."

"What did you say?"

"Don't worry. He has no idea that you aren't seeing me; doctor-patient confidentiality and all that. I told him I couldn't tell him whether you were or weren't."

"Okay. Good," I sighed. "Thanks. So, is that why you called?"

"I'm calling to find out why you told someone you're seeing me for therapy when you aren't."

"Why is that any of your business?"

"When someone calls to pay for someone else's therapy, that means they must truly care about that person's mental health, and mental health is my business."

"Not my mental health. I don't need therapy, lady."

"If you really believed that, why would you lie about going to a therapist? Wouldn't the lie itself be an admittance that you need it?" Dr. Hollande asked. I found myself without a reply to her logic which in and of itself was a reply. "I'd very much like for you to come in for a session, Mr. Kimble. Free of charge. I think you'd find it beneficial."

"That's a pretty bold statement considering you know absolutely nothing about me."

"On the contrary. Within the past few months at most, you attempted suicide. You survived which means either you called 911 yourself, implying your lack of desire to die, or someone else did for you, which means you weren't alone and that someone cares enough to do it. Now you have someone calling to make it easier for you to receive treatment. People love you, yet you can't seem to accept it."

"Takes one to know one, doesn't it?"

"I'll leave a slot open for you on Thursday at four o'clock. If you do decide to come in, I suggest arriving early to fill out your paperwork."

"Is this a joke?"

"Not at all, Mr. Kimble. I hope to see you Thursday." Dr. Hollande hung up, and I must've stood for nearly a minute with the phone to my ear. Samwell suddenly appeared beside me, apparently done with his food.

"No, I'm really not interested in—" I began, speaking into the phone until it rang. Sam frowned at me, and I shrugged. "I guess it got disconnected."

"You're popular today," he said as I answered the phone once more.

Queen City High School was just as dismal and depressing in the early afternoon as it had been when I'd arrived at night the week prior.

The third phone call I'd received was from the principal's office requesting my presence in regard to an undisclosed incident involving Ryan. The mixture of emotion I felt was odd in that, while I was anxious to discover what had happened that I should be needed, I was pleased to be needed at all. There was no mixed emotion when I found Julia already seated in the lobby of the school. Pure nausea.

"They called you?" she asked, clearly surprised at my arrival.

"Why wouldn't they?" Julia didn't answer, turning her head away with a roll of her eyes. "Do you have any idea what this is about?"

"They wouldn't tell me over the phone."

"My guess is a fight," I remarked sitting down on the same bench though with at least a foot of space between us.

"Why the hell would Ryan get into a fight?" Julia snapped back.

"I don't know. It's just a guess. He's a boy. Boys get into fights."

"He's not a boy anymore. He's almost an adult, and unlike some people, he can control himself." Julia was an expert at passive aggression.

"Look, as much as I know you hate my guts right now, can we at least try to pretend that we're two united parents? For our children's sakes?"

"Sorry it took me so long, Julia. I got over here as fast as I could." I turned, disbelieving the sight of Argyle hurrying towards us from the entrance. He slowed his pace upon recognizing me. "What are you doing here?"

"I could ask you the same question," I returned, standing to look at him directly. "What are *you* doing here?"

"I called him," said Julia rising from her seat.

"You called him?" I repeated. "And you weren't going to call me?"

"Ted is just as much an influential part of Ryan's life as you are, Arthur. He's the man of the house."

"You mean the one that's up for sale?"

Julia had opened her mouth to respond when Ryan suddenly appeared around the corner alongside the school security officer who was separating him from another boy of roughly the same age. Both were bruised and bloodied, their shirts stretched out of place, but the other boy had one eye swollen almost completely shut. Julia covered her mouth in a gasp, then held out her hands to delicately touch the wounds on Ryan's face.

"Ryan! What happened?"

"You okay?" Argyle asked in a stern voice much deeper than natural.

"I'm fine," Ryan flinched before pulling away from his mother in irritation.

"What happened, Ryan?" I asked, trying to establish my superiority by stepping in front of Argyle. Ryan ignored me, however, and the security officer interjected a request to wait until the other boy's parents had arrived and were all in Principal Sorkin's office together. Julia took a closer look at Ryan's opponent then widened her eyes in recognition.

"Charlie. You too?" she stammered, then looked as the voices of his parents broke in from behind us.

"Charlie!" A woman ran past us to her son, fawning over his injuries. "Phil, just look at his face!" A suited man sauntered up behind her with an expression of pure boredom.

"Yup," he replied dryly. The woman turned and opened her mouth in surprise equal to Julia's at the sight of whom her son had been fighting.

"You and Ryan? I don't believe this! Julia," she said tragically, "I don't understand how this could have happened."

"I have no idea, Cathy. We're just as shocked as you are. Why did you two get into a fight?" Ryan and Charlie glared at each other then looked away in silence.

"Wait," I interjected. "How do you all know each other?"

"Who are you?" Cathy asked.

Before offering an answer, the group of us looked over as the door of the principal's office opened and a tall, stout woman stepped out in a long, floral-print dress. "Hello, Mrs. Kimble, Mr. Bowman, Mr. and Mrs. Hollister...and Mr. Kimble. Please come in. Burt, stay with the boys out here." The security officer nodded and had the boys take seats on either end of the bench.

The principal's office was bright, filled with books and several filing cabinets, the walls decorated with inspirational quotes and pictures of rock climbers and cats dangling from unlikely places. Four chairs had been arranged at her desk. Charlie's parents and Julia sat, but before I could take my place beside her, Argyle plopped down in the seat.

"What are you doing?" I whispered angrily. Argyle glanced at me, indifferently crossing his legs.

"If you wouldn't mind standing, this shouldn't take too long," said the principal. I folded my arms and chose not to press the issue. Principal Sorkin interlocked her fingers on the desk. "I never enjoy having these discussions. However, in a high school, these conversations are inevitable."

"Can you just tell us what happened?" Cathy asked.

"While we're not completely certain of the details that initiated the confrontation, it seems that the boys got into a fight over a certain female student."

"This was all over some girl?" asked Argyle.

"Not just some girl," she answered. "Your daughter, Abigail."

"Why would they get into a fight over Abi?" I asked.

"You are aware," Principal Sorkin began in slight surprise, "that Charlie and Abigail are a couple, aren't you?" My eyes fell on Julia who remained motionless.

"We were aware," said Argyle taking Julia's hand. I looked down at him, envisioning my knuckles making impact with the back of his head before slamming his nose into the desk. My arms remained folded.

"But what does this have to do with Abi?" Cathy asked.

"Well, this isn't an easy subject, but it seems that a rumor has been circulating about Abi and Charlie."

"What kind of rumor?" I asked.

"Now, keep in mind that this is only a rumor. What's being said is that Abi and Charlie have been—experimenting—with certain physical acts of intimacy."

"What acts of intimacy, specifically?" asked Julia.

"Specifically…oral sex."

The room fell silent, though I noticed the evidence of a hidden chuckle on Mr. Hollister's face. Principal Sorkin shifted uncomfortably.

"That's obviously not true," I said, trying to avoid making my anger at such an outrageous statement too apparent. "Abi would never do something like that."

"And that's Ryan's position on the subject, but he also seems to think that Charlie is the one who started the rumor."

"That's ridiculous! Charlie wouldn't ever start a rumor like that," said Cathy. "Especially about Abi. He's crazy about her."

"I realize that this may be shocking to hear, but that is the current situation, and I would like to know if any of you believe that there might be any validity to the rumor?" Principal Sorkin looked at each of us, receiving a series of shaking heads. "Well, despite this being my first year as principal at this school, I have been educating children for over thirty years and have learned that rumors of this nature, true or not, are generally based on some kind of factuality."

"Are you serious?" I asked. "We're talking about a bunch of high school kids."

"They're not really kids though," said Argyle. "They're prone to do things like that at this age."

"Not Abi," I replied with a resolute shake of my head. "She's not that kind of girl."

"No one is suggesting that she is, Mr. Kimble, and no one is suggesting that Charlie is that kind of boy. I didn't call any of you to determine whether or not they are, but as their parents, I'm sure you care about their reputations, and I believe it would behoove you to have a serious discussion with them about these things. We all must accept, to a degree, that Mr. Bowman has a valid point. They aren't children anymore. This is the time in their lives that they will begin to experiment and act upon these developing, natural urges."

"Our daughter doesn't get urges like that," I argued.

"And you would know that how, Arthur?" Julia asked with a disgusted expression.

"Please," said Principal Sorkin. "Let's try to stay on topic here. I feel you should be aware of what's going on with them at their school so that you can take the helm of this issue as parents should. Whatever the reason for Ryan's and Charlie's disagreement, I can't justify their threatening not only each other's welfare but the welfare of the students around them. We are adamant on solving our problems through nonviolent means, so it should be no surprise to any of you when I say that, in accordance with our zero-tolerance policy for violence, both boys will have to be suspended for two weeks."

"But shouldn't the person who started the fight be the one who gets suspended?" Cathy chimed in. "I'm sure Charlie was just defending himself."

"What makes you think it wasn't Charlie who started it?" Julia asked.

"I think it's pretty obvious that your son started the fight with his accusations."

"There wouldn't have been a fight in the first place if your son wasn't spreading rumors about Abi." The two began arguing over each other, Argyle reaching unsuccessfully for Julia's hand to calm her, and Phil sitting back silently watching the two with the same look of boredom as before.

"Ladies! Control yourselves!" Principal Sorkin stood, her fingertips pressed against the top of her desk. "Hostility cannot be resolved with more hostility. Now, as the head of this high school, I have over six hundred other students that require my supervision and have no time to waste trying to figure out who said what and why and who threw the first punch. They will both receive a two-week suspension, and that's final." She took her seat again. "Now, what I would appreciate for you all to do as their parents is talk to them about the unacceptability of fighting, talk to them about appropriate behavior while dating, listen to what they say and feel, and help them with resolving this issue in a peaceful and wholesome manner. And one of the best ways to do that is by simply setting the example. Can you agree to that?" Julia and Cathy nodded reluctantly, resembling students themselves. "Good. Now, unless there are any more questions…I consider this meeting concluded. Again, thank you all for coming."

The three of us walked a short distance behind Ryan through the parking lot. Overhead, the clear November sky had been blanketed by a thick sheet of darkening gray, concealing any sunlight that might have elevated the mood from completely miserable to mildly depressing. Ryan didn't respond to any line of questions or comments and slammed the passenger door after climbing into Julia's car.

"How could you not tell me that Abi was dating someone?" I asked Julia, catching up with her steps. "I thought we'd agreed that sixteen was the dating age. She's not old enough to be dating. She doesn't know what she wants."

"She's fourteen. She's plenty old enough to know what she does and doesn't want."

"But you can't make that choice without me. You can't just keep me in the dark."

"That's what you're so concerned about, Arthur?" She asked wheeling around. "That you didn't know something?"

"I would've appreciated it considering you made me look like an idiot in that meeting," I said as she shook her head with an incredulous smile. "What kind of father doesn't know who his own daughter is dating, much less that she is dating at all?"

"That's a great question, Arthur, but I don't really feel like I need to answer that."

"You need to answer why you didn't bother telling me. I'm her father."

"And as her father, maybe you should be more concerned about her reputation with her peers and what's being thought and said about her instead of yourself. All you've ever been concerned about is you and how you feel and how things will affect you."

"That's not true."

"This is all about our kids and their lives and wellbeing, so if you can't get on board with that, then maybe you have no business getting involved in the first place."

"I love Ryan and Abi," I said evenly after a moment. "You know I do, Julia."

"Yeah, well," she said in bursts of visible breath, "it takes more than a little love to raise a kid, Arthur, and if you can't manage to figure that out, then you will always do more harm than good. Instead of getting all pissed off at me for not telling you, maybe you should spend your energy trying to figure out why it is that Abi didn't tell you herself." She took a few steps then looked back. "Oh, and by the way, I heard about the other day. About the drinking."

"So, that's why you're pissed? Because of one fucking drink?" I asked.

"I'm pissed because instead of thinking how that might make them feel given everything that happened, you did it anyway, because you couldn't be bothered to consider how your actions might affect them. As usual."

Julia turned away into the quickening wind of an impending storm, a single drop of rain falling into her tousled hair. My steps had ceased as I watched her walk away from me to join Argyle where he'd been waiting. She slipped her arm under his, and a second drop of rain hit me right in the goddamn eye.

"Bloody women. Damn, bloody women."

"What if she's right, Hux?"

"Do you truly believe that she is?" asked Huxley before taking flight.

I wasted another couple of hours at work doodling on sticky notes before heading through the downtown strip. It was as moderately quiet as any other Monday night. With Vivian still indisposed at work, I soon found my hands on the ten and two of my steering wheel, guiding the vehicle involuntarily to park on a side street illuminated red by a neon sign reading "Baron's". I sat listening to the buzz of the glowing letters, unsure of what invisible force had guided me there. Even though it was the only bar I could truly tolerate since it wasn't completely overrun by college kids and hipsters, I hadn't planned to enter its doors again, at least not quite so soon. Whatever it was, I felt the need to be there, and not simply because of what I knew was available.

After hurrying through the unrelenting rain to the entrance, I stepped into a volley of memories hitting me with a familiar scent and comforting ambiance. A slight smoky musk; leather and whiskey; red, green, and vanilla. An older man sat upon a stool wearing a Hawaiian shirt under a brown leather jacket and relaxed, navy blue jeans, a straw fedora pushed back to reveal a far receded hairline. The gold chain and watch completed the picture of a man caught in the wrong hemisphere in the wrong decade.

"Hey there, Ricky," I greeted, taking the stool beside him. Ricky González turned his head slowly towards me.

"Arthur fucking Kimble," he smiled broadly, addressing me with his brusque hint of a Cuban accent. "Of all the faces I didn't expect to see today! What the hell brings you in here? It's been ages!" Ricky turned to the bartender. "A double scotch, neat, for my good friend here. And...another for me."

"Thanks, but I'll just take some water."

"Feeling dehydrated?" Ricky chuckled. "Okay. A water for Arthur Kimble." He patted my shoulder. "Where have you been hiding out? You take a vacation or something?"

"Or something," I smiled, watching as his drink was poured. "It's a little quieter than I remember," I remarked looking around the nearly empty bar. "Why aren't you throwing a costume party? It's Halloween."

"We did that last night thinking we'd get more people on a Sunday night than a Monday night. Still wasn't a huge success," he sighed. "It's been getting worse over the past few months. But hopefully that'll change once the renovation is completed."

"The renovation?"

"Oh, that's right. I forgot you haven't been here since it started. In the back. Come on, I'll show you." Ricky led me past the tables occupied by a handful of people toward a set of double doors. Behind them were two large plastic curtains hanging as a divider. He held it aside for me to walk through and into a spacious, empty room.

"What's this? What happened to all the tables?"

"This, Arthur, is the new dance floor." He stretched out his hands. "This is the new Baron's."

"The new Baron's?"

"Yes, sir. Up on that platform we'll have a house DJ during the week and special guest DJ's through the weekend. The sound system is state of the art, and the lighting system is synced to it so the strobes and lasers keep time to the beat." Ricky moved around the room as he spoke. "And a second bar. A shot bar."

"A shot bar?"

"Strictly for shots."

"I understand the concept, Ricky, but what pushed you to do all this exactly? Has business been that bad?" Ricky lowered his head, abandoning the demeanor of the grand showman.

"It hasn't been very good. No."

"But you always said how you'd never own a club. You hate clubs."

"It's these millennials. They love clubs. Local rock bands and karaoke nights just don't seem to cut it anymore."

"And this was your solution to the problem?"

"Well, it's not going to be my problem. Not for long anyway," said Ricky, taking a sip of his drink.

"What do you mean?"

"My son's taking it over. This was actually all his idea." He sighed and looked around the construction. "Between you and me, I fucking hate it. But since I won't have to be here to deal with it, I figured what the hell."

"But I thought Baron's was like your baby."

"Yeah, well, you've got to let them go eventually." He looked around the room, nodding to himself. "Christ, this is depressing. Let's head to the back." We walked together in silence towards the bar then down a small hallway. We entered his office at its end, and he locked the door behind us.

"Ricardo González, retired. I never thought I'd see the day." Ricky opened a drawer and moved a small square mirror to the top of his desk upon which a small mound of blow had already been chopped up into fine bits of powder.

"Neither did I. Like you said, this has been my baby, but while I was busy taking care of this baby my three real babies have grown up and moved out. I missed it all." Ricky paused, the tone in his voice changing from his usual nonchalant evenness to something I'd never heard before. It was calm, yet serious, as if stating the fact that the world was doomed and simultaneously coming to terms with one's inability to do anything about it. "I've missed too much, Arthur. I may not be able to get those years back, but I'm not going to let whatever time I've got left go to waste. You know I've got three grandchildren now?" He leaned over after producing a shortened straw from the same drawer and inhaled a small section of the cocaine, then sat back with a sigh, his eyes wide. "Jesucristo! Besides," he continued after sniffling, "I've been thinking about retiring for a few years. This just takes away any excuse for me not to, and it stays in the family." He partook again and pinched his nose. "Goddamn! Here, have some."

"Thanks, but I shouldn't."

"What?" Ricky chuckled, waving the straw at me. "You're a funny man."

"For real," I smiled. "I'm good."

"Seriously?" he squinted.

"Yes," I said with some hesitation.

"You're really getting clean?"

"I'm cleaning up."

"Well, you could get away with just this, couldn't you?" Ricky produced a cigarette and tapped the open end of it into the powder. "Yeah?" I felt my heart begin to rattle, a tightening in my diaphragm of familiar longing.

"Thanks, Ricky, but no."

"I know they tell you that once you're an addict, you're always an addict. But I think that's bullshit. You've got the power to say no if you want. Why not say yes once in a while?"

"Because even though it takes saying yes many times to label something an addiction, it only takes saying yes one time to get it started." He held the flame to the whitened tip of the cigarette, and it crackled faintly under the heat.

"Self-discipline. I can respect that."

"You made a very compelling argument though," I said, producing my own cigarette. "You should've been a lawyer."

"Any bar you have to go to college for isn't my kind of bar." We both gave in to a brief laugh, then he took a drag from the cigarette before speaking again. "Seriously though, I'm kind of looking forward to retirement. I've got enough money to buy a place down in the Keys. Besides, my wife's getting bored with me, and I can't have that. I think she fucked the pool boy this past summer."

"Didn't you fuck your masseuse last year?"

"They're called happy endings, Art. Whose side are you on, anyway? The point is, I opened this place twenty-seven years ago. Twenty-seven!" He pointed his cigarette at me. "I wanted this place classy. I didn't want some Patrick-fucking-Swayze roadhouse bullshit. I wanted something like…*Cheers* meets the roaring twenties. You know?"

"Like Norm Peterson doing the Charleston?"

"I was thinking more like Ted Danson, but anyway, it's just not what it used to be. I thought I had the place I wanted. Then over the past few years, people have changed too much. Times are changing too much. It's like the '80s all over again. Nobody gives a shit about where they are anymore. They just want to get fucked up to a good beat."

"That sounds like pretty much any decade."

"Yeah, well," he smiled. "Honestly, it really comes down to my family. Fuck those millennials. Fuck this bar. Fuck the patrons and the money. What the hell does it matter without family, Arthur? What the hell does it really matter?"

I stared at the edge of his desk, contemplating his words. I had a million things to say, a thousand that wouldn't do, a hundred that were appropriate, but only one forefront that I wouldn't allow myself to speak because of the fraud I was afraid it would make me in uttering it. But Ricky said it for me.

"Family first. Right?"

"That's right."

Ricky took a sip of his drink then raised his eyebrows. "Speaking of which, how's your family doing? How old are Ryan and Abi now?"

"Abi's fourteen now, and Ryan will be seventeen next April."

"Well, goddamn," marveled Ricky with the wipe of his forehead. "They grow up too fast. Things better with you and Julia now? I mean, I know you two got divorced, but maybe you're cordial now?"

Why Ricky cared at all, I didn't understand. He hadn't cared before when I was buying cocaine from him three to four times a week. It was as if in the last twenty minutes he'd had a costume change from a drug dealing bar owner to a warm, philanthropic family man. I wanted to slap him out of it, to shake him back into that man who was supposed to be my tempter, who was the enemy I'd developed an understanding with. It was in the same thought that I realized he had always been this man, successful at it or not, and I couldn't fault him for it.

"Things are a lot better," I said. "We don't really ever fight anymore." Ricky's eyes glistened with satisfaction.

"You know I never got to say—I should have said I'm—you know."

"I know, Ricky."

"I've always wanted you to have things good at home, but here I was selling you—well, I wasn't helping like a friend should."

"It's the past. Everything is better now."

He held up his scotch. "A la familia."

I held up my water. "A la familia."

Ricky stared at my glass of water for a long moment, then blinked away his thoughts before we drank.

I left Baron's a half hour later, unable to decipher why exactly I felt so unsettled. The only thing that entered my mind after that was how much better I would be feeling with a shot of whiskey and a line of cocaine.

For some inexplicable reason I was surprised that my key worked when I pushed it into the lock. The tumblers were depressed correctly, and the door opened with a slight squeak on the hinge. A lamp had been left on for me, illuminating the way to the living room where I found Vivian asleep, her glasses on, photographs in hand. As I reached to touch her, I was forced to pause. Her face was so relaxed, at peace, but still this quality of—something difficult to describe. There was so much potential at rest, I could see it on her skin, hear it in her breathing. On the coffee table beside her were a dozen photographs spread out. They weren't of the usual celebrities in their various states of 'oh shit'. These were simple, black and white photos of the city, or rather, little pieces of it. The metalwork in an old iron fence; the etching in a cornerstone; the imprint atop a railroad spike that protruded from the tie. I'd never consciously seen these things, but instantly recognized them. I realized how blind I was, or perhaps, just too visionary to notice.

"You're here," Vivian said sweetly, waking. "I got pizza if you want some."

"Thanks. I'm not really hungry though." I sat beside her on the couch. "I see you've been burning the midnight oil."

"Yeah, I was doing some work, but I got sidetracked with some personal stuff." She smiled, wrinkling her nose.

"What are you working on?"

"Just looking through the pictures from the past several months. I got a little bit infatuated with hidden designs. There are some beautiful little things out there that we miss so easily." Vivian shrugged up her shoulders in a stretch and sighed. "Those other ones are of you and me." She reached for a few photos peeking out from beneath the others. "Remember this one? This is the night we met in Chicago, and we bonded over trashing the ballet we just saw."

"You're lucky I had to stick around to watch the whole thing. If it wasn't for *Verb'd*..."

"Well, I'm glad you had to suffer through it. You'll have to thank *Slander* for the same thing." I made a gagging gesture, and she giggled before looking at another picture. "I feel like this was in March or April. I can't remember."

The photo was of me smiling at the camera through the reflection of a bathroom mirror, clean paths running through shaving cream. She stood behind the camera in a long t-shirt, hair in a messy bun. I was a different man altogether it seemed, and as I studied my own face, I couldn't help but wonder if I'd been high at the time.

"And this one," she continued. "This one is my favorite I think."

The image was a selfie of her and me in bed. I'd always felt that the selfie was a pretty ridiculous concept, but the selfie of someone pretending to sleep was pretentiously stupid to me. She and I lay together, I asleep, she with her eyes closed, pillows crunched up underneath her. My mouth was slightly open as I rested on her chest, my countenance uncharacteristically tranquil. She wore a Deadpool t-shirt. The fingers of her left hand had found a place in my hair. A small collection of hair bands and a leather bracelet decorated her wrist. The monochrome of the picture enhanced the freckles across her nose and that smile she wrestled to hide. Then it occurred to me that she wasn't pretending to sleep at all. Vivian's eyes had been closed in contented felicity. It wasn't stupid. It wasn't pretentious. It was humble, unabashed love.

Like a phantom, a detail at the bottom corner of the picture made me forget.

"You know when I took this?" she asked

"Yeah. I do." We looked at it for a long time in silence.

"I wasn't afraid then, you know," said Vivian quietly, "and I'm not afraid now."

There's no telling how it happens or when. Perhaps it exists in there all along. There's a theory I heard somewhere that we live our lives over and over until we get it right, and that through it all, you remain connected to one other person, even as different people. I'm the last person to know what happens in the ever after, but I felt in that moment, for the first time, a certainty, albeit fleeting, about the here and now.

"Neither am I," I lied.

"I love you, Art."

I love you, she says.

CHAPTER FIVE

For centuries, men and women alike, adventurers, pilgrims, priests and pagans, emperors and slaves, dictators, saints, even fictional characters have all searched for the Holy Grail. Whether you believe in all of that doesn't really matter. More often, it's the lack of belief that compels the quest for such things. It's the sinners who go to church in search of a savior. People go to haunted houses to be convinced that ghosts do exist, and anyone who attends a magic show is there to be pulled away from their disbelief. Every one of those things is a personal holy grail, you might say. There's no evidence that it exists, yet there's no evidence that it doesn't.

I came one step away from ruining my personal holy grail when I discovered that the fast speed on my windshield wipers kept time to "Ob-La-Di, Ob-La-Da" by The Beatles, and the mid speed kept time to "Red House" by Jimi Hendrix. I hadn't discovered what song the slow speed matched rhythm to, and I decided I never would. I got the strange feeling that if I did, the sun would explode, or I'd become immortal. Either way it would be a shit deal, and for this reason, I never under any circumstances used the slow speed.

"Dad! How can you stand that dry squeaking noise?" Abi complained with her hands over her ears. "It sounds like a dying cat. It's not raining hard enough for the wipers to go that fast."

"I'd explain it to you, but you'd just think I'm crazy," I answered, never taking my eyes off the road, a light misting of rain wetting the street ahead. "I bet you'll never miss the bus again."

"Haha, very funny." Sprout concealed the corner of a smile. The squeaking continued, and I finally had to admit that it was indeed annoying as hell.

"All right, I'll cut it off for now." The sudden silence was almost as disturbing as the squeaking had been. "How have rehearsals been going?"

"Pretty good."

"Pretty well," I corrected.

"Pretty well," she sighed.

"Good, I'm glad." The car rumbled. "Anything special going on?"

"Not really."

"Did you finish that book you were telling me about?"

"Yeah." I started to panic at her uncharacteristic deficiency of words.

"You want to get some ice cream?"

"Are you kidding? It's, like, ten degrees outside. Besides, I have to go to school."

"We can throw it into the microwave and have ice cream soup. You remember doing that when you were little? Me and you and your brother?" She nodded, looking firmly out the passenger window. "Abi."

"Hmm?"

"What's wrong, honey?"

"Nothing."

"You're pushing your cuticles back with your fingernails."

"So?"

"That's your tell." Abi rolled her gaze to look at me.

"Okay." After a long moment, "I don't want to move." I kept my eyes on the road and nodded. "I don't want to have to get used to a new house and a new room. There's nothing exciting about it. I don't care what Mom says."

"I can understand that feeling," I said.

"Why can't I just stay with you?"

"With me?" I repeated, scouring my brain for any reason but the truth.

"Yeah, why not?"

"Well…you'd still be moving, and if it's the change in location that's really bothering you, that won't help."

"But at least I'd be with you," she whimpered. "I don't want to live with Ted."

"You guys are moving in with Arg—with Ted?" I could feel my neck and face going flush with anger.

"Yeah, in December. You didn't know that?"

"Yeah, I knew," I lied. "It just slipped my mind."

"Why can't I pick where I go?"

"It's just not as simple as that, Sprout. There's a lot of things involved."

"Like what?"

"It's complicated."

"That's not an answer."

"It's the best one I've got for now, Abi. Sometimes we don't get to decide what happens, and we just have to accept it." I'd inadvertently raised my voice slightly and caught myself. She sat back in her seat and looked out the window. "I mean, this is just part of living, Sprout. There are things you love that go away. There are good things that hopefully replace them. You can't control that, good or bad. You can control how you react though, and that's what matters. What are you going to do when life sucks?"

"What do you do?"

"Me? I write," I said, a dated answer.

"Besides that?"

"I don't know," I shrugged. "I guess I just wait it out."

"You just wait?"

"For things to get better, yeah."

Sprout looked at me, completely deflated after receiving the worst advice a parent ever gave their kid. Or maybe she was disappointed in me because she recognized it. I couldn't decide which was worse. It's true that you can't impress your kids forever. They get older, they have experiences, they get smarter (hopefully), and then they start to see you for the human being you've been hiding all along, no better, no stronger, and no more put together than them. And once that picture is sullied, the only thing you can do is hope they'll love you anyway.

"I just wish things could go…" Sprout's words trailed off, though I knew how her wish ended. It had been the same as mine.

Stephen King penned the phrase, 'wish in one hand, shit in the other, see which fills up first.' But what do you do when that hand gets full?

You throw it.

"Ah! A man on a mission, I see!" Huxley laughed triumphantly. "How invigorating!"

"It really is, Hux," I said. "I don't know why I ever let myself get into my own head."

"Who can say. We all do it from time to time." He made himself comfortable on the dash. "You, perhaps, more than others."

"Maybe it's just a matter of confidence, locating that reason to go after something and owning it."

"You've located it?"

"Sprout gave it to me. You know I've been thinking about buying that house, but what was the likelihood I'd actually try to get it? There are a few things in my life that need to change, one of them being my lack of assertiveness. If a person wants something, life doesn't just hand it over. You've got to take it."

"Indeed, Arthur," Huxley said with an excited growl. "Indeed."

"I'll show them."

"Show who?" he asked.

"You know. The universal them."

"Does that include you? Because truthfully, I believe that's all that really matters. Everyone else is simply a footnote in your accomplishments."

"What about Abi and Ryan?" I asked, looking over at her lost in thought. "This whole thing is for them. I'd say they're more than just a couple of footnotes."

"Well, if that's the case, then I stand corrected," he sighed. "Though I can't remember the last time that happened."

After dropping off Abi, I drove to Lonnie's house only to be received unenthusiastically by Becca who had no idea where Lonnie was. A minute later I was headed in the direction of Queen City Community College. It was a cluster of old brick buildings on the edge of town in dire need of expanded parking and a new mascot.

The original mascot, selected in 1982, was a golden toad, and it took two decades and the invention of the internet to enlighten everyone that the golden toad had in fact been extinct since 1979. The faculty took the opportunity to vote on a new mascot and it was decided to be the queen chess piece. An official drawing by one of the students was approved and displayed all over the campus. It was an elaborate affair updating all the banners, coffee mugs, sweatshirts, bumper stickers, and the painted entrance hall floor. The school spent tens of thousands of dollars on this mascot before some chess club middle-schooler pointed out that the mascot design was in fact a rook and not a queen. By then it was too late, and no one was willing to take the blame for the obvious mistake which earned them the nickname Queen City Rookies. That story always gave me a good chuckle. There was nothing funny about the parking situation though. That shit was terrible.

Once inside the school, I found Lonnie passed out in his coffin of an office and kicked lightly at the chair he was drooling on.

"Welcome back to the land of the living," I said when he began to stir. Taking a seat behind his desk, I found myself reveling for some unknown reason in his lack of coherence.

"How did you know I was here?" Lonnie asked, sitting up.

"Because you weren't home."

"How did you know I wasn't home?" he asked scrunching his face.

"Because you weren't at home," I said, pausing momentarily from spinning his seat to look at him. "Where else would you be?"

Lonnie's face looked like it had met the underside of the fat lady after she was done singing, his eyes red and puffy, and one side of his hair standing up.

"Fuck man," he said with a deep breath. "I need coffee."

"You need a shower and a toothbrush."

"I need coffee." He stood slowly. "But first, I need amphetamines."

"Amphetamines?"

"Top left drawer." I looked where he directed and found a square aluminum case with four pills, two pale pink uppers like the ones he'd given me, and two unfamiliar white pills.

"What are these?"

"Muscle relaxers. You can have one if you want."

"That's the last thing I need."

"Best way to get to sleep in my opinion."

Upon viewing the pills, Lonnie moved with a greater urgency as he locked the door. He selected an upper and broke it into fourths. After crushing and lining it with his faculty ID that was already lightly dusted with powder, he bent over, the straw to his nose, and vanquished them. At the third line, he stood straight and offered me the straw.

"I'm good," I lied. He shrugged and cleaned the plate.

"Now coffee," he smiled.

Ten minutes later, we sat on a bench overlooking the quad under the risen sun, watching the dew evaporate off the grass. A line of women was jogging around the small field, young and spandexed.

"You know, I've never understood how in the movies a woman can wear a pair of glasses and have her hair in a bun, and no one will know how hot she is until they take her glasses off and let her hair down. Then it's this amazing transformation, like no one actually had a fucking clue." Lonnie blew gently over his coffee. "I wonder who came up with that phrase 'beauty is in the eye of the beholder'. As if beauty was truly a subjective thing. Either they're hot or they're not, right?

"There's a reason why all the guys will chase around that one woman with the firm ass and perky tits and not the schlumpy one with bad teeth and back boobs. Of course, the ones that do chase them know exactly what they're getting into. Maybe that's why. There's no uncertainty, no risk factor. I guess that's how even the ugly chicks get laid. And the ugly men, too. Vice versa and whatever." Lonnie sipped his coffee. "It isn't love or even lust that keeps our species from extinction. It's insecurity."

A trickle of iridescent oranges and reds fluttered from the oak trees toward the earth.

"I heard somewhere though," he continued after lighting us each a cigarette, "that the fundamentals of physical attraction are linked back to human survival. You subconsciously look for the strongest, fittest, most likely to effectively carry on the line. But what place does that have in modern society? We don't have to be afraid of predators like lions or any of that shit anymore. There's no need to keep the watch-fires burning at night. It's reasonable to believe that we'll live long healthy lives in most places on earth. If anything, people in this day and age should be chasing down the nerds and computer geeks to reproduce. I don't give a shit how many muscles you have. You need brains to deal with technology and information. Survival of the techiest, you could say. But still we chase the curves and the muscles and the symmetry, as if it really mattered anymore." He chuckled. "I guess I've got best of both worlds with Becca."

"Yeah? And what does she get out of it?" I joked. Lonnie shot me a glance and smirked.

"What doesn't she get out of it? I mean, come on. I'm about to have my own radio show, for Christ's sake."

"When does that start, anyway?" I asked.

"January. It would've been sooner, but I've got those lectures I told you about."

"You've got a lot on your plate."

"Everybody wants a slice of the Lemmon." He chuckled to himself. "Slice of the Lemmon…I kind of like that. What do you think? I should use that as a catchphrase."

"You really should," I lied.

"Truthfully though, I'll be glad to ditch this place. Most of these kids don't even know how to read," he sputtered, "and I know it's not necessarily their fault. Education has gone to hell, but still."

"You know, Lonnie, I was thinking about what you were saying the other night, and I think I'd be willing to take the reins for those couple of weeks." He looked at me over his sunglasses.

"Really? Why?"

"I'm thinking about moving places, and I could use the extra money. You said it would be worth my while."

"You are? Where to?"

"The house on Winnow Lane." Lonnie stared at me for a long moment then exhaled with widened eyes.

"Seriously?" He shook his head. "Well, to be completely honest, Art, the pay is terrible. Like, seriously. There's no money in education."

"Didn't you say you were making good money here?"

"Why the hell would I say that?"

"You literally said that just the other night."

"Oh. Well, you know my memory is shit," he laughed.

"Why did you say there was good money in education?" I asked. Lonnie sat up slowly, looking around carefully.

"There's good money *here*," he said, "but not from the teaching."

"I don't know what you're talking about, Lonnie," I said, getting annoyed.

"This is a college campus, community or not. There's a market here hardly tapped at all."

"What market?"

"The drug market," Lonnie whispered.

"Are you shitting me?" I asked with disgust. "You're a goddamn drug dealer?"

"You've been buying uppers from me for years, Art. Don't get all high and mighty on me." He paused. "Well, you can get high, just not mighty."

I watched him laugh, amused with himself, then he looked at me and frowned. "I'm not dealing, okay? Relax. I'm just a supplier of sorts. That's where the real money is. I'm literally walking away with over twenty grand a week just from this place."

"What kind of pills are you supplying to make twenty thousand dollars in a week?" I questioned, disbelieving.

"It's not pills, man. Get serious," Lonnie said into his coffee cup. He took a long drawn out sip. "It's cocaine. Or, should I say, cocaína. The premium stuff. You want a sample?"

"No, Lonnie." I blinked angrily away from him.

"Why are you getting mad? This shouldn't come as a surprise."

"It's not a surprise," I said.

It really wasn't, and I felt conflicted in my reasoning for even being angry about it. It was one thing to just be some dealer, a low-level guy doing the grunt work, more than likely for the sole purpose of making ends meet. I could almost conjure up in my head something honest and justified about it. They go out and commit their sins in the light of day. Suppliers, on the other hand, despite being only a step above, immediately brought to mind the image of some cheap sleaze ball slithering around in the shadows, and for some unknown reason, wearing crocodile skin loafers.

"So, this is why you wanted someone to sub for you," I put together. "To keep the supply going. Why don't you just ask Becca to do it?"

"Becca doesn't know about this, and she doesn't need to. Look, do you want to do it or not? I'll give you twenty-five percent. For two weeks, that should get you around thirty grand."

"What kind of math is that? Twenty-five percent of forty thousand is only ten thousand."

"Well…" he said, blowing out a cloud, "I have two other connections out in town."

"This is getting ridiculous," I began, but he continued.

"Over two weeks, that's going to bring the total to about a hundred and twenty grand. That's ninety for me, and thirty for you. Why would you not want to do it? Most people don't make that in a year."

"And what is 'doing it', exactly?" I asked.

"All you have to do is drive, pick up, drop off, collect money. You literally interface with no one."

"Drive? So, a delivery boy basically."

"I think they're known as mules," he said. "Doesn't matter. You want to do it or not?"

"I don't know…"

"Look," Lonnie sighed with exasperation, "whether you do or don't makes no difference to me. I'd rather have you do it because we're friends, and I know you'll look out for me the way I always look out for you." He was laying it on thick. "We've been friends almost half a lifetime. That means something to me. Do I think you're insane for your reasons to do it? Hell, yeah. But I'm your friend, and if it means that much to you, I'm willing to help."

"You do remember that you were the one asking me, right?" I reminded him. Lonnie raised his eyebrows expectantly. "Can I think it over?"

"Sure. I just need to know by tomorrow so I can inform the department head. Okay?"

"Jesus! The department head is in on this, too?"

"What? No! I have to tell him if you're going to be teaching the class." Lonnie laughed, shaking his head as he flicked his cigarette into the grass.

"Knock, knock," said Jerry Grant. That was probably the most annoying way possible for anyone to enter a room.

"Yes?" I said, looking up from my reading.

"Arthur, right?"

"Yeah," I said, unenthused by his presence and his presumption to take a seat across from me without invitation. It was the first good look I'd ever had of the man, and it annoyed me that he was one of those people you just liked to look at. He was well-dressed, not ostentatiously so, but smartly in a suit that fit him well. His hair was short, combed to the side, and he was younger looking than I had originally thought.

"What are you reading there?" he asked, putting his briefcase down beside the chair before craning his neck to see. I held up the book. "*Opportunity Cost* by P.J. Goring. Never heard of him."

"No kidding."

Mr. Grant produced a notepad which he opened with the flick of his wrist. A ballpoint pen made its appearance as well, and he crossed his legs before looking at me.

"Don't let me interrupt you."

We looked at each other for a long time.

"What are you doing?" I asked finally.

"Observing. Pretend like I'm not even here," he smiled.

"That's not easy," I said. "Since you're just sitting there."

"Would you prefer me to stand? I recently purchased these fantastic insoles with extra arch support."

"No." As put together as he appeared, it was clear that Jerry was simply an annoyance.

"Just keep doing what you're doing."

"You're going to watch me read this book?"

"That's my job," he smiled again. I nodded dubiously, then returned to the book. I was half a paragraph in when he asked, "Is it good?"

"I don't know yet," I answered without looking at him.

"What's it about?"

"Opportunity cost, I imagine."

"Oh," said Jerry. "Opportunity cost is a real thing, you know. Actually, it's one of the main ways I measure productivity. What is the opportunity cost of one action over another? The bottom line for productivity is choice. Sometimes, it's not how well you know a certain task that ensures productivity. It's knowing how to do it most effectively. You'd think the two would go hand in hand, but you'd be surprised. Not everyone is a natural thinker like that. It takes analysis, weighing the gain against the cost. There's a whole psychology behind it…"

I had been on the fence as to whether or not I'd go to that appointment with Dr. Hollande, still unsure as to whether the truth might make its way back to Jack Dorset. I had no interest in therapy but sitting there listening to Jerry Grant ramble on made it seem like the less objectionable alternative. I looked at the clock. Only 2:45, but who cared?

"Jerry," I suddenly interjected. "I actually need to get going. I have an appointment across town I can't afford to miss."

"Oh, of course," he said, looking almost hurt. It was incredibly satisfying.

A few padded chairs formed a row against one of the walls in Dr. Hollande's empty waiting room, and the trickle of water falling in an electric fountain mingled with the soothing strings of a koto, attempting to lull the anxiety out of me. Between the music and the dimmed lighting, I would have likely dozed off if I hadn't had to fill out a medical information sheet and a supplemental questionnaire wanting to know everything about me, my parents, my kids, marriage, sex life, you name it. Of course, those were the easy questions in comparison to the last section entitled "Stress".

Why did you choose therapy? I didn't. What are your personal goals for therapy? To break through the fourth wall. What are your concerns about therapy? That it just might work. I let out a brief laugh when I read the question asking me to rate my level of happiness on a scale of one to ten, the concept of rating happiness at all striking me as an absurdity.

A few minutes after her secretary took back my paperwork, Dr. Hollande stepped out from her office. She looked significantly more put together than last time with a loose, flowery button up and a long skirt. Her eyes were piercing bright now, the lines at their corners manifesting with her broad smile, and her long black hair was now close-cropped. I almost commented on it but didn't want to give the false impression of enthusiasm.

"Mr. Kimble," greeted Dr. Hollande. "Good to see you again. Please." I followed her into a large office lighted with a pair of floor lamps. The proverbial leather couch awaited me, positioned opposite a single chair and a side table. To the right, a bookshelf covered the entire wall, and to the left was her desk which appeared rarely used. She gestured for me to take a seat, and in a few moments, we were facing each other as she looked over the answers I'd written on the sheet. "So, tell me, how are things? How have you been?" she asked, still looking at the paper.

"I thought that's what the exam was for."

"Yes," she smiled, "but I'd like to hear it from you."

"It's not going to be any different."

"I wouldn't expect it to be," she began, glancing down again. "You rated your level of overall happiness on a scale of one to ten as…pi. I see you've got a good sense of humor," she chuckled.

"I'd say it's more like irony, a circular answer on a linear scale."

"Quite thought provoking."

"It doesn't mean anything," I said. "Just a little word play."

"That's quite a statement coming from a writer. I would've thought you'd say that there is meaning in all words."

"Words only have as much meaning as we give them. On their own, they're just symbols and sounds."

"That's an interesting perspective." Dr. Hollande held her chin on her knuckles. "Do you think that applies only to words or could it possibly carry over into other things?"

"Sure, it could. It does."

"To life itself, maybe?"

"Sure."

"You know, humans have been pondering what the meaning of life is for as far back as back goes. You've perhaps solved that in less than five minutes."

"Hardly," I scoffed.

"You don't think so?"

"If you really believe that, then you and I should be trading seats."

"Indeed," she smiled reflectively. "While it is difficult to discover one's meaning to life, however, it is impossible to do so if one ends it." There it was. I had been expecting this, but not right out the gate. "Why did you try to end your life?"

"Why does anybody?" I sighed. "I guess I just wasn't happy."

"Why not?" she asked. I shrugged and shook my head. "Do you expect to be happy in life?"

"No."

"Why not?"

"Is that a serious question?" I asked. Dr. Hollande lifted her eyebrows. "Happiness isn't exactly a byproduct of living, you know."

"Well then, if you don't expect to be happy, do you expect to be miserable?"

"No. I don't know," I said, fantasizing about burning tobacco.

"Then what exactly do you expect out of life, Mr. Kimble?"

"What do I expect?" I repeated, briefly pondering a question I'd never truly asked myself before. Or hadn't allowed myself to answer. "I don't expect anything."

"Why not?"

"You're the doctor."

Dr. Hollande smiled and blinked at the floor. "I've always found it interesting, people's preconceived ideas about psychologists and psychiatrists and therapy. People come to me every day looking for answers, but what so many fail to realize is that I am the one type of doctor who doesn't have the answers. In fact, probably ninety percent of the people that walk in here already have the answers, but just don't realize it because they're so lost in the fray of their struggles. So, I can't tell you why you expect nothing out of life. What I can tell you, however, is that in all my years of practice, I've never met anyone who has said that and truly, deeply didn't expect anything, even if they honestly believed it. Just because something is convenient doesn't make it true, but again, only you would know the truth. Regardless of what you expect or don't expect, you've nonetheless had a significant breakthrough."

"Really? In under ten minutes? Does that cost extra?"

"The time it takes is of no significance. And as I told you, this session is free."

"So, what exactly is this breakthrough?"

"You admitted that you're not happy."

"Tell me, who is exactly?"

"Many people, Mr. Kimble, believe it or not."

"Well, I don't believe you," I said through a bemused chuckle.

"Why not?" she asked.

"Because it's just not possible to feel happy all the time."

"No, but it is possible to feel happy overall. Just as it is possible to not feel miserable all the time." I breathed in deeply and leaned back on the couch.

"Look, I didn't come here to change my outlook on life or anything, okay?"

"Then why did you?"

"Because you strong-armed me into it. If I didn't then you were going to tell my boss."

"I said no such thing," corrected Dr. Hollande. "You can tell yourself whatever you'd like, but nobody walks through that door because they were forced to, just like no one is forced to stay once they enter."

"So, you're telling me I'm here because I've chosen to be here?" Dr. Hollande extended her hands.

"We always have a choice, Mr. Kimble, and for many that's a far more terrifying prospect than having none at all."

"I'm not afraid of having a choice, Dr. Hollande. That idea in general seems ridiculous to me."

"Why does it seem so ridiculous?"

"Because—look, I understand what you're saying. If people believe they don't have a choice, then it takes away the burden of responsibility when things go south. But that's not me. When anything goes wrong, I prefer to blame myself. I'd rather know that something went wrong because of a mistake *I* made instead of someone else coming along and screwing things up."

"Do you think that you are the sole person responsible for everything that goes on in your life?"

"It's my life, isn't it?"

"Of course, but no one's life is isolated. Don't you believe that there are things that just happen to us? Things out of our control?"

"Are you referring to fate or being a victim?"

"Either."

"I'm not convinced there is such a thing as fate, and I choose not to be a victim."

"Just moments ago, you accused me of strong-arming you into being here, that you didn't have a choice. That sounds very much like being a victim."

"Being a victim is a choice."

"Even when you have no control in a situation?"

"I thought you said that we always have a choice."

"Always having a choice isn't the same as always being in control. Things do occur that are beyond our control, but no matter what happens, in or out of our control, we always have a choice in how we react."

"But that's not the same as choosing to be here."

"Isn't it?"

"It isn't," I insisted. Dr. Hollande held a finger against her lips in thought, then went back to the questionnaire. "Let's talk about your family."

"Let's not." She glanced up at me with a sharp inhale, then shrugged. "Okay, then. Let's talk about work. Do you enjoy being at *Verb'd Magazine*?"

"For the most part."

"And you're a writer, yes?"

"For the most part."

"What kinds of things do you write?"

"I do interviews occasionally, book reviews, other stuff."

"What other stuff?"

"I had a short story column."

"You say you *had* one. You don't anymore?"

"That's yet to be seen. It all depends on whether I can write it and if they like it."

"You sound uncertain of your abilities."

"I wouldn't say uncertain. I just feel tired."

"Are you not enjoying it anymore? It seems to me that the creative aspect of your work would be the most enjoyable."

"Creativity requires inspiration, and that's been in short supply."

"You're referring to writer's block?" she asked.

"I wouldn't say that. More like I just don't have the energy to think about it."

"Do you feel it as a point of stress?" she asked. I shrugged. "What *do* you have energy to think about?"

"I don't know. Not much of anything."

"Why is that?"

"Maybe you missed the memo, but life has a reputation for being kind of shitty," I snapped. "It's not much fun to sit around and ponder."

"How does thinking about your life make you feel?"

"What kind of question is that? How do you feel when you think about your life? How does anybody feel? Lucky? Sad? Nostalgic?"

"It's just a question, Mr. Kimble."

"It's a bullshit question, and you know it. You think you already know the answers, but you don't. You don't know me or anything about me, and all your goddamn diplomas and all your stupid scars don't change that."

"Why are you suddenly so hostile?"

"I'm not being hostile, and I'm not going to sit here and be treated like a goddamn puppet."

"So, you're angry right now because you feel out of control in this situation?"

"You're goddamn right."

"You need to feel in control?"

"I don't *need* to feel in control. I *like* to feel in control, and that's no different than anyone else."

"What if that feeling is false?"

"I'm not going to let you nitpick my words."

"Well, I'll remind you that you are free to leave at any time you choose. I cannot make you stay, nor will I try."

"Good, because I am taking control, and I am leaving," I announced, rising abruptly.

"Mr. Kimble, I—"

"Save it for your patients."

I had already pulled a cigarette from my pack by the time my hand was on the doorknob, and I didn't bother waiting until I was outside to light it.

Two feline eyes watched me coldly from the wall of the elevator in my apartment building. Beneath the furry face was a shaky, handwritten plea for any and all assistance in finding Mr. Skiddles. I thought of telling Ms. Foster that she may find more success by offering some type of reward, but as I looked back at the deadpan stare of the cat, I realized that no amount of money could tug at my heartstrings enough to assist in the search.

"I've never understood your species' obsession with pets."

"Some people are worse than others," I said.

"The whole institution of pet ownership seems wrapped around the idea of being the master of another living being," Huxley observed. "It's barbaric."

"Most people do it for companionship, more like having a friend than a possession."

"Arthur," said Huxley.

"Yes, Hux?"

"I'm not your pet, am I?"

"Well," I paused, "I suppose in that sense of it, you just may be."

"I refuse!" he shouted. "I refuse to be your pet! I will not be the object of such a savage practice!"

"Why not? You might like being a pet."

"Over my plucked and bleeding body, Arthur Kimble! You take that back!"

"What?" I laughed aloud. "You wouldn't want to be my pet?"

"I am a proud English pigeon, and one of the greatest sleuths the world has ever seen! How dare you, sir!"

"Hux," I said facing him, "don't get your feathers all ruffled. You're not my pet. You're my character. You always will be."

"Bloody goddamn right, I am!" he smiled.

I entered my apartment and went straight for the scotch, pouring slowly into a glass until the bottom inch was filled with the liquor, then added a second inch. Placing the bottle back in the cabinet, I kept my eyes averted from the Buddha's disarming smile.

A few minutes later, 121 Winnow Lane was shining from my computer screen with its vanilla cream siding and burgundy shutters. All that was left of the tire swing that had been hung from the oak tree in the front yard was a pathetic stump. It didn't matter though. There was more than all that, more than the picket fence, the cracked concrete driveway, and the painted shutters. There were all the pieces in between, all the possibilities, limited only by imagination and desire. Could it ever be real? Had it ever been? There was no evidence to suggest either way, and though my belief was a matter of personal deliberation, I nonetheless picked up my phone.

So, Viv, how would you feel about going to look at a house with me?
...What kind of house??
The cohabitation kind

I added a winking smiley face for good measure.

CHAPTER SIX

"What do you think?" I asked with a smile. Vivian got out of the car and nodded approvingly.

"It looks nice enough. I like the neighborhood. It's how many square feet?"

"1,854," I said. "Not counting the unfinished office space in the basement."

"It has a basement?" She glanced down at her phone. "Where does it say that?" It didn't.

"You can tell from the way the foundation is laid," I said.

"You really like this place, huh?"

"It's hard to say just yet." Vivian took my arm and we climbed the small flight of stairs to the front door, mahogany brown with a brass knocker. A sign on the knob invited us to enter for the open house.

It was just like in the photographs. To the right of the vestibule was a large living room, furnished to inspire the imagination of potential renters. A couch by the far wall of the living room, a recliner to its side. A coffee table stacked with copies of rough drafts, the wall decorated with books of all sizes and stories. The television across just there, cartoons playing.

To our left was the dining area where a long wooden table was surrounded by a set of matching chairs situated in homely fashion. The centerpiece was a fruit basket, beside it a spread of cheeses, crackers, and small deli meat rounds.

"Well, hello!" A petite woman with a small nest of hair on her head greeted Vivian and me from the top of a flight of stairs, her excessively cheerful voice a perfect match to her cherry lips and bright blue dress. She was, I imagined, the equivalent of June Cleaver on crack. "Hello, hello, hello! Welcome! How are you all today? I was just tidying the upstairs. I hope you haven't been waiting long."

"We're doing well, thanks," Vivian answered for the two of us.

"My name is Sherrie Mardeleaux. I'm hosting the open house today. What are your names?" Sherrie held out a plump, manicured hand.

"I'm Vivian. This is my boyfriend Arthur." I was relieved for her to take the lead on this.

"Oh!" she exclaimed. "Are we moving in together?"

"Just her and I," I said with a smirk that Sherrie didn't notice. Vivian smiled though.

"Yes, we're taking the plunge. Seeing how it goes."

"I wish things were that way back in my day. I remember when I first got married, and I'll tell you. You don't really know somebody until you live together. Biggest mistake of my life."

"Divorced, huh?" asked Vivian.

"Oh, no. We've been married for thirty-one years. Happily, of course." Sherrie cleared her throat, pasting her smile back on. "Would you like me to give you the tour?"

Sherrie led the way through the house, one room at a time. The doorway to the living room had a few dings in it from where a piano had been brought in at one point. They'd been painted over with the same turtle shell brown as the rest of the doorways in the house. The bedrooms had been freshly painted as well, new carpet on the floors. Prints from where glowing stars had decorated the ceiling above a bed were still visible in one of the rooms.

"Are you okay?" Vivian quietly asked me as we looked at each other in the bathroom mirror.

"Yeah, why?" I asked casually.

"You just seem...off."

"I'm very much on," I smiled then turned to look at her directly. "Very, very much on." Vivian's eyes gleamed mischievously before hugging me.

"I like this place. It's warm. You know?"

What should have been a heart-warming moment between us was instantly frozen as, looking over Vivian's shoulder in our embrace, I saw through the window as Julia and Argyle stepped out of his car in the driveway.

"I don't know." I said, doing my best to conceal my inner panic. "I think we should still visit some of the other houses." I took her hand and led her quickly down the stairs. "We didn't get to look out back. Let's go that way." I took her through the kitchen to the back door and out onto the small wooden deck.

"Why are you in such a rush?"

"I'm not in a rush. Don't you want to see the back?"

"Well, yes, but—"

"Let's go around the side," I said, guiding her along.

"But it's kind of overgrown."

Vivian followed me around the house. Ahead was her car which we'd fortunately taken instead of mine, and I whispered a sigh of gratitude to the universe. We were almost to it when Julia and Argyle suddenly appeared in front of us, a look of shock slapping them on their faces.

"Arthur, what are you doing here?" Julia halted, causing Argyle to almost knock her over.

"It's an open house isn't it?" I pointed out as relaxed as I could be. Perhaps too relaxed. Vivian reached me and put her hand around my waste. "Julia, I'd like you to meet my girlfriend, Vivian. Vivian, this is my ex-wife, Julia. And her boyfriend, Argyle."

"My name is Ted, actually, and I'm her fiancé," Argyle corrected.

"You are?" I asked.

"I am."

"Hi," Vivian said without moving, save for the squeeze of my side in her hand.

"We were just leaving," I informed them, sliding past with Vivian's hand in mine. Though I couldn't see it, I could feel Julia stabbing me with her glare. Two minutes later, I watched the house disappear in the side view mirror as we drove away.

"So that's your ex-wife," she commented. "Pretty."

"Pretty horrible," I said. "I didn't know she was going to be there."

"No, but that's why you hurried us out of the house, isn't it?" I said nothing, gnawing lightly at my index finger. "Why didn't you just tell me instead of putting me in an awkward position like that?"

"I didn't know that she'd be there."

"I believe you didn't, but instead of telling me when you realized she was, you made us leave the house as if you didn't want her to know we were there. You practically ran away from her, and I don't understand why."

"I introduced you."

"Only because you had to. If you had your way, I would never have met her, and you would never have told me." I said nothing again. "Isn't that true?"

Sometimes, it's not the truth but the reasons for the truth that are so difficult.

Students and their families packed into the heated lobby of Queen City High School, shivering as they transitioned from the cold night. I had arrived just before the lights dimmed, and the school orchestra struck up with the overture to *West Side Story*. The diminishing chatter of the audience was overwhelmed by the deep brass and piping woodwinds. Once the song ended and the curtain rose, a group of Jets began snapping together in time to the music before cutting loose.

As a teenager, I'd been in only one show at my high school and never was again, my experience playing Jud in *Oklahoma* underwhelming, to say the least. However, there was a certain satisfaction in playing the guy people didn't like, mostly because I didn't really like the people playing the good guys. There were never any genuine people in high school, which as an adult might seem like a ridiculous expectation, but back then it seemed to make sense. I always assumed that people would just be honest, because why not? It's easier. But then I became an adult and realized that the only difference between them and me was that they had already honed and perfected their ability to bullshit. I was the late bloomer.

Abi appeared on stage, her hair styled short for her character, but she was probably the most believable person up there. Although I might've been biased, it didn't seem far-fetched that she could understand Anybodys' mentality: misunderstood, trying to be a part of something, yet still enough of a child to have a conscience.

Ryan was nowhere to be seen, which didn't surprise me, though his name did appear in the playbill as Officer Krupke. I was disappointed that I wouldn't be able to watch him portray the iconic lawman due to his suspension. At intermission, I stepped outside into the cold and was about to light up a cigarette when I saw the no-smoking sign bolted into the brick wall of the building. I searched around for a secluded spot, away from the visibility of any parents or faculty, until I found myself by an industrial dumpster that was pleasantly out of the path of any breeze. After a few puffs, huddled in my jacket, I heard a pair of voices approaching from the opposite side of the dumpster.

"Here?" a girl asked.

"Yeah. It's perfect," said a boy, his voice familiar.

"Are you sure there aren't any cameras back here?"

"I'm sure." The metallic clinking of spray cans echoed slightly as they hit the ground. "What did you bring?" she asked.

"Liquitex," he answered. "I've got all the primary and secondary colors, and some black and gray for shading. And a can of white." A few moments later as I hunkered down by the dumpster taking secret puffs on my cigarette, I listened to the clip-clapping of the spray cans being shaken followed by spurts of shushing.

"Hey, Ryan, look," the girl said, and my jaw tightened with confirmation of my suspicions. "I got this at Roy's Hardware." The shush stopped.

"I didn't know he sold spray paint...Holy shit, Plutonium? How much was that?"

"He let me have it for free."

"No," he said after a pause. "There's no way."

"Well, if you don't pay for something, then it must be free."

"Did you lift it?" Ryan asked. The girl giggled. "Trish, you shouldn't do that. What if you got caught?"

"But I didn't."

"You can't even use that here," said Ryan. "It's acrylic."

"Says who?" she laughed again, and the shushing continued to Ryan's disapproval. "Stop being so uptight! Seriously. It's just a wall."

"Some of us still go to school here though. I don't feel like getting expelled."

"Whatever. High school is all part of the conspiracy," she said.

"The conspiracy of what?"

"Brainwashing. Everyone knows that the whole point of public education is to institutionalize every generation of American citizens for the capitalist agenda."

"What the fuck are you talking about?" Ryan laughed, and in a moment, Trish joined him.

"What are you painting?" she asked, though without receiving a reply. Clip-clap-clip-clap. "Seriously though, you should drop out."

"I don't want to," said Ryan.

"But you hate school."

"I hate *this* school."

"All schools are the same," she said. "You trying to go to college or something?" Shusshh.

"Maybe. I don't know."

"I bet your parents are beating you over the head with applications." Clip-clap.

"Not really," said Ryan. "My mom told me it was my choice, and as long as I'm happy, she's happy."

"That's pretty cool. What about your dad?"

"My dad probably doesn't even know I'm graduating this year," he said, and I frowned, trying to exhale the smoke slowly.

"Sure, he does. It's not like he isn't around like my dad." Shusshhh.

"He's around, but he isn't *around*. It's like his head is always somewhere else, and he has no idea what's going on. I mean, he just came back after being gone for three months. He didn't even know Abi was dating someone."

"Being gone for three months is better than your dad being gone your whole childhood. At least he cares enough to come back."

"I told you he tried to kill himself, didn't I?" Ryan asked, and I shut my eyes. Clip-clap-clip-clap.

"Yeah." A lighter flicked once on the other side of the dumpster. "Take a hit. It'll help." A second flick soon followed.

Ryan began a fit of coughs before regaining his ability to speak. "Why do people like that?"

"It's an acquired taste," she chuckled.

"I don't know," he said, finally catching his breath. "I just don't understand how he can try to kill himself and turn right around and say he loves me and Abi. Suicide is fucking selfish. Sure, life sucks, but that doesn't mean you should just bail on everyone. Not the people who need you the most." Clip-clap. Shusshhh. Clip-clap. "I like that."

"Thanks," she said, and I could hear her smile.

As the orange ember of my cigarette neared the filter, I became lost in its glow, in the rhythm of its breathing, the shine and the dimming. There are times when people hear the truths they have been too afraid to admit to themselves, and it seems as though the past, present, and future become rolled up into one giant rock, and that rock replaces their brain. This is a condition that tokers refer to as being 'stoned'. Without the weed, however, it's simply dissociation.

"Shit!" I yelled as the burning end of my cigarette caught my fingertips.

"The fuck was that?" Trish asked. In a moment, the two of them were on my side of the dumpster, leaving me with no time to hide or run. For some reason, I determined the best option was to stand and take a relaxed leaning pose.

"Hey, guys," I smiled. "What's up?"

"Dad! What are you doing back here?!" Ryan exclaimed in terrified recognition, pulling his bandana down.

"That's your dad?" she asked.

"Yeah, I'm Ryan's dad."

The girl remained silent for a moment, then smiled. "Hi, Mr. Kimble. I'm Trish."

"Nice to meet you, Trish," I said, shaking her hand while trying my best to conceal my own shock.

"I'm gonna go," Trish said to Ryan, breaking the several awkward seconds of silence.

"Okay," he said, staring at the ground between us.

"Nice meeting you," she smiled at me, then disappeared. We stood there stupidly for some excessive amount of time before I summoned up the courage to speak.

"She seems nice."

"Why are you back here? Were you spying on us?"

"I came out for a smoke." Ryan looked to where the girl had walked away, then closed his mouth and looked down without a word. "You know, I've been told a lot lately that times have changed. People have changed. But I see that the best place to sneak some weed at school is still behind the dumpsters. It's nice to know there are some things that stay the same." Ryan nodded and looked up at me, his eyes narrowed in concentration.

"What?" he asked blankly before starting to chuckle.

"Never mind."

"Oh..." It didn't take a genius to realize that Ryan was baked with his bloodshot eyes and sudden onset of uncontrollable giggles. After a few seconds, however, he began to rub his stomach, frowning.

"You okay?" Before he could answer, Ryan doubled over, spraying the asphalt between us with something that could have been chewed up pizza or Chinese food mixed with the odor of a very cheap liquor. "Jesus Christ," I muttered as he spit.

A short time later, Ryan and I sat, our backs against the dumpster on the opposite side from where he'd wretched. The muted sounds of the impending rumble between the Sharks and Jets floated to us from within the auditorium. I'd lit up another cigarette as he sipped on an overpriced bottle of water purchased from the concession. I glanced at him beside me, the fog having lifted from his face. The welts from the fight were nearly gone, and the cut on his lip had dried out, appearing chapped.

"I didn't know you could paint," I said, looking up at the wall they'd graffitied.

"It's stupid." Ryan shrugged before turning the bottle over in his lap, watching the water remain in place within the roll.

"I'm not really an expert in the urban arts, but it doesn't look bad to me. Certainly not stupid. What is that, a phoenix or something?"

"The beginning of a phoenix."

"I like it."

"Thanks," he muttered.

"Why are you smoking weed?" I finally addressed the elephant in the dumpster. He shrugged again.

"I don't know…stress reliever. It feels good."

"Really? It didn't seem like it a few minutes ago."

"I mean…It just relaxes me."

"Why not just talk about whatever you're stressed about?"

"I do, pretty much."

"With your mom?"

"No." I sat back and nodded, breathing down my annoyance.

"With Ted?"

"What do you care? It's not like you'd understand."

"You don't know that."

"Yes, actually. I do know that."

"Try me." I looked him in the face, but he kept his gaze removed before breathing deeply.

"No, thanks."

"Come on. Let's talk about that fight you got into. What was that about?" Ryan finally looked at me with sobered eyes.

"I don't want to talk about it."

"What did Abi have to do with it?"

"I just said…" He shook his head and turned away. "Charlie

wanted Abi to give him a blowjob, but when she wouldn't, he got pissed off and spread a rumor that she did."

"You know it was him for sure?"

"Everyone knows it, and I told him that he better stop with the rumors and tell people the truth."

"And that's why you got into the fight. Because he wouldn't do it."

"People get into fights all the time, and it's so stupid because it's usually over nothing. But this isn't nothing, and I'm not about to let some asshole trash-talk my little sister."

"Why didn't you just bring the issue up with me or your mom?"

"Because it would've only made things worse. Don't you get that?"

"No, it wouldn't have. We would've dealt with it in a way that didn't get you suspended. We would've brought it up to his parents and the principal."

"Seriously?" He exhaled with frustration. "This is why I don't talk to either of you at all. You don't understand. You don't listen. You're both so wrapped up in your own problems that it's almost as if Abi and I don't even exist!"

"That's not true, Ryan."

"It's only not true when it benefits you and Mom. It's like we're bargaining chips or something. Like we're leverage. You only need us when you have something to prove to each other."

"So that's why you talk to Ted? Because you don't feel like he'll use you?"

"Of course not. He uses us all the time to impress Mom. I'm not stupid. But he at least takes the time to listen. He doesn't give a shit about what I say, but he doesn't try to act like he does and that he has all the answers." Ryan's voice began to waiver, but his eyes remained steady.

"I never said I had all the answers, Ryan. Nobody does. I can't help but want to give you advice when you tell me your problems though."

"You don't give me advice. You just tell me I'm wrong, and that

I should do or think something else."

"That's not true."

"See?!" Ryan let out a laugh of indignation. "You just proved my point! Whether you think it's true or not, it is to me, and I'm not the only one who feels that way. I'm just the only one with enough guts to say it."

"You mean Abi? She feels this way, too?" Ryan said nothing. "Okay…" I thought for a long while, trying to think of a way to get him to trust me when I opened my mouth. "So, what do you want us to do? How would you like it to be?"

"Now you're asking me how you should raise me?"

"That's not what I'm asking, Ryan. Just give me something I can work with."

"Fine. You can stop acting like Abi and I are only here to make you feel good about yourself. Stop trying to prove to yourself that you're a good parent and start trying to prove it to us."

"I don't see how I'm like that, but if it helps, I'll think about it and see if I can understand your point of view."

"Okay," Ryan scoffed.

"What?"

"You're doing it right now. You don't care about my point of view. You just want to figure out how you can get me on your side. How you can change my mind because there's no way I'm actually right. I understand how this all works."

"I don't know how else to be, Ryan," I said. "I'm doing my best. So is your mom. What more do you want that we're not giving you?"

"Honesty, Dad! Try starting there!"

"I am honest with you. When have I not been?"

"Okay. Where were you for the past three months?" His focus charged into me, and for a moment I could've believed that he was able to read my mind. It was as though he'd paralyzed my brain, and I could only remain in that moment of thought. Ryan finally shook his head. "It's okay, Dad. It doesn't really matter anyway. People are who they are, and I guess you can't expect any more than that."

I had never expected to be a complete success in life. I had never held myself to unreasonable standards because I knew myself well enough. There was no way to be perfect, or understand all the time, or to always be present for everything. All children, at one point or another, have to face things alone. There will inevitably be moments of disappointment, loneliness, and heartbreak. I never thought I would be the cause of this, however. I hoped, despite my imperfections, that I would always be reliable, the dad that they knew they could depend on no matter how much of a mess life turned into. That would have been success to me. Not only had I fallen short, but they didn't believe that I could be any better.

"Abi prays for you, you know," he said. "Every night."

"She does?" I asked, frantic for some glimmer of hope.

The sound of a squeaking door from around the corner and the mingling of voices and congratulations brought us to our feet. Ryan took up his backpack and began walking toward the growing crowd.

"What about the wall?" I asked Ryan. He looked back at it and shrugged.

"It's water-based. A little rain, and it'll be like it was never there." As I followed him, I wanted to assure Ryan that I wouldn't tell his mother about what happened, that no one needed to know he had been smoking and drinking, to prove that I was trustworthy. But as I was about to speak, I suddenly understood that if I did tell him, it would only be evidence of his point. What was the purpose in telling him, but to receive appreciation and, in return, loyalty? To satisfy my own need to feel like a decent parent? Within a few more moments, the crowd had engulfed us like a giant amoeba. Ryan was suddenly hidden from sight, and I was left apart.

I searched for Abi, scanning the crowd until I'd made it inside, scouring the auditorium until I'd eventually walked backstage where a couple of students were chatting. I returned to the other side of the room, the seats emptied, and only a couple adults remained, conversing cheerily. When I walked back out to the parking lot, most of the cars had disappeared from their spaces. I was a stranger in a small group of stragglers, a few parents smiling and hugging their students still in stage makeup, pouring love and pride over them. But Sprout was gone. I'd missed her, and the fear that had been riding up in my chest suddenly sank to the floor of my heart as I contemplated all the possibilities of her thoughts. That her father didn't show up. That her father didn't care enough to be there for her. That she had wasted her prayers on a lost cause.

In the elevator, the poster that had requested any information about Mr. Skiddles had been amended with a permanent marker, a reward of $100 added to the pot. It was as though the old lady had heard my thoughts. A hundred bucks was little compensation to spend time looking though, especially since, after a couple of weeks in the cold, the cat was likely dead in a ditch somewhere. Still, I had to give her credit for persistence.

When I'd left Vivian to attend Abi's show, she had been fervently looking at color schemes and do-it-yourself decor ideas. I hadn't ever seen her so involved in anything outside of her work and on occasion had felt like a footnote in her mind. For some reason or another it hadn't really bothered me unless she sought my input, which was frequently. Rather than actually get involved in the conversation of swatches and shades, however, I just agreed with her, and she remained placated. Vivian was where I'd left her when I'd gone, and a part of me wondered if she'd even noticed.

"Do you like granite or slate better?" Vivian asked in lieu of a greeting.

"Granite's nice," I said.

"But slate is such a nice color."

"That's what I was just about to say." I stepped into the kitchen, wishing like hell for a shot of whiskey. Just as I had convinced myself that she wouldn't notice a little liquor on the breath, Vivian appeared in the doorway, smiling at me.

"This is so exciting," she said, approaching me for an embrace. "Are you sure this is okay with you?"

"Why wouldn't it be? I initiated the whole thing, didn't I?"

"That's true," she said before kissing me. "It just feels…"

"What?" I asked after several seconds of silence.

"You seem different. I'm not saying that in a bad way," she quickly explained. "Just different."

"I guess I've had a lot to think about," I said.

"Like what?" Sometimes it annoyed me that she cared so much.

"They're doing some downsizing at work. They've got some auditors there and this guy is following people around to make sure they're working."

"Oh, no. Are you worried?"

"Why should I be worried?" I asked. "I've been there a long time. I do great work, and they know it. They would never let me go just like that."

"Why do you seem anxious then?" she asked.

"I guess…I don't know. I just don't want to see other people get hurt, that's all."

"Why are they making all these changes?"

"I don't know…" I couldn't hide my eyes from her.

"You know, it's not the only writing gig out there," she said quietly. "It never hurts to put your feelers out, get the lay of the land."

"I'm not doing that," I insisted. "I couldn't do that to them."

"To them?"

"Samwell. Jack. Stacy. They need me where I am."

"I'm glad you feel that way," she smiled. "It's good to feel needed. It doesn't change the fact that you've been thinking a lot about it."

"It's difficult not to," I lied.

"Well," she smiled, backing away, "why don't you think about joining me in the shower. I bet I know a way to distract you."

"I know you do."

The oversized t-shirt she'd been wearing slipped easily over her head and fell to the floor. Vivian looked back at me over her bare shoulders just before disappearing into the bedroom. Her panties suddenly landed in the doorway, and I smiled.

As soon as the sound of shower water reached me, I reached for the bottle, planted my lips, and drank, savoring the soothing heat nothing else could ever emulate. I half-returned the bottle to the cabinet before stealing a second swallow.

A loud knock at the door nearly caused the liquor to shoot up through my nose, bringing tears to my eyes. I shuttered and coughed before returning the bottle and hurrying to the front door. Another series of knocks erupted before I answered to find Julia with her arms crossed. She pushed past me into my apartment.

"Julia, what are you doing here?" I asked alarmed.

"I should ask you the same question." She swung around to face me with an expectant glare.

"I live here," I said slowly.

"Why weren't you at the show?"

"I was there, Julia. I couldn't find any of you after it was over. It's not my fault."

"Is that so?"

"Yes."

"Which character did Abi play?"

"Anybodys, the girl who wanted to be in the Jets."

"And who else?" I froze, realizing that I'd potentially missed her second role when I was outside with Ryan.

"She didn't play anyone else," I guessed hesitantly, hoping it had been a trick question.

"Jesus, Arthur," Julia muttered. She took a couple steps away, staring towards the sound of the shower. After a quick shake of her head, Julia dropped her arms. "Abi thinks you're mad at her."

"Why would I be mad at her?"

"Because of the rumor and the boys' fight. She feels like it's her fault that everything happened the way it did."

"That's ridiculous. I know that she couldn't control what happened."

"That's what I told her, but I don't think she really hears me. They don't listen, either one of them. Not because they don't care, but because somewhere along the line we all became disconnected, and I just can't figure out why." Watching Julia talk to the floor made me wonder if she was still addressing me or simply thinking aloud. "I often find myself wondering at what point everything shifted, what caused it. But that's when I have to ask myself, was it one thing, or one person?

And does awareness have anything to do with being the culprit?"

"What do you mean?" I asked.

"I just wanted us to be a family, Arthur. So did you. We wanted a family that was always there for each other and supported each other and listened." Her eyes began to moisten.

"We were, Julia," I said, unsure if I was consoling or convincing her. "At least that's what I thought."

"And what, I fucked it up, right?" I shrugged silently, feeling that no answer was necessary. "Sometimes I wonder if you've always had one foot in the dark or if you just turned off the lights one day. Either way, it wasn't my fault. Not solely."

"I'm pretty sure most people would disagree with you."

"I didn't marry most people, Arthur. I married you." Julia caught her tear midfall. "I had children with you. I gave the best of myself and the best of my years to you."

"Yeah, and your youth and your independence and your career. Did you come over simply to beat a dead horse, or was there something else? Because I can have a shitty night without you."

"Yeah," she chuckled. "I'm sure you can."

"Jesus Christ, Julia. Tell me what you want or get the fuck out. I don't have the time or the patience for this." I moved to where my cigarettes and lighter lay on the coffee table.

"Okay, fine," she breathed, collecting herself. "I need the papers."

I paused mid-lift of the flame to my cigarette, then continued silently until a puff of smoke rose up to the ceiling. I turned, going back into the kitchen to open a drawer where, beneath an array of useless items, I'd hidden the divorce papers from myself. They slapped against the countertop as I tossed them down, and Julia picked them up, flipping immediately to the pages marked for my signature.

"Of course, you still haven't signed." She spoke slowly in anger, something I'd almost forgotten she could do.

"I was away for three months."

"You've been back for two weeks."

"I've been busy," I said.

"With what? House hunting with your girlfriend?" Julia scoffed. "I'm guessing she doesn't know that I'm the one selling it, much less that only a year ago we were living in that house as a family. Does she know that you still haven't signed our divorce papers?"

"It hasn't come up," I said.

"Goddammit, Art, you are unbelievable. Always with your secrets," she laughed angrily, reaching into her purse for a pen. "Just sign the fucking papers."

"Why? So you can go get married to that walking sweater vest?"

"That walking sweater vest loves me," she said adamantly. "He loves me."

"But I loved you first," I said.

"Well then, be the first to hate me." Julia snapped. She held the papers open at the first blank signature and extended the pen. "This is happening, Arthur, for better or for worse. You need to accept that."

I wanted to scream, to smash the ashtray against the wall, to rip up those fucking papers. I wanted to feel my thumbs crushing her trachea, and simultaneously caress her skin and hold her warm beating chest to my weeping eyes. It felt as though the entire universe was somehow contained just behind my sternum, with all its volatility and dark, unknown spaces. This universe was poised to explode, and in that position, likewise implode upon itself. Perhaps, I considered, it was this condition that caused spontaneous combustion.

I didn't go up in flames, however, and any flames that had existed were utterly and definitively extinguished. Julia collected her signatures. I was still standing there alone when Vivian reappeared from the bedroom fully clothed, her hair damp. Silently, she walked up behind me, and her arms gently wrapped around my middle, her fingers finding each other and interlocking across my chest.

"I need to go," said Vivian. She pressed her lips between my shoulder blades.

"Viv, I—"

"No. Not yet." She collected her things, and gently closed the front door behind her.

I had to stand on my toes to reach the Buddha. I looked over the pale, circular pills, then after shaking one into my hand, I returned him to his place and wiped a spot clean on the counter. Holding the pill between my thumbs and forefingers, I applied only a slight amount of pressure between the centerline of the cross embossed in its circle until it split in half with a dull crack. The tension in my chest began to build as I divided the two halves into fourths. The pieces crushed easily, and the edge of a credit card chopped them into a fine powder before divvying them into four neat and equal lines on the countertop. I stared down at them, studying each one, contemplating their entrance back into my world.

"Lightly, Arthur. Lightly."

"I'm not exactly looking for advice right now, Huxley."

"Yes, I'm aware. What we need is not always what we are looking for."

"I don't need your words of wisdom," I said quietly. "I just want to be left alone."

"Neither is it always what we say we want that we truly do want."

"I mean it, Huxley." I waited for a response, but when I turned to look, he had already gone.

With a rolled up twenty from my wallet, I leaned forward towards the first line, a ball of energy rising within, then inhaled through my left nostril, reviving a sensation that I could have sworn had never felt so gratifying before that instant. Inhale through the right. The chemical burning in my nose felt as warm and familiar as a place by the fire. Shallow puddles formed in my eyes.

There are a million ways to convince yourself that everything will be okay. Some people find their comfort in prayer and religious immersion. Some go to the gym and burn away their worries with their calories. Some get wasted at the bar or go around having random hookups or both. Some just eat themselves to consolation. Others keep their head buried in work to act as blinders to the reality of their situation.

Now, I'm not here to pretend that I'm holier than anyone else, but over the years I feel I've managed to nail down at least a couple solid truths, and one of them is this:

While no single option is the cure-all across the board, there is nothing like a drug.

PART TWO

CHAPTER SEVEN

COVER TO COVER: A REVIEW OF
***Opportunity Cost* BY P.J. GORING**
- Arthur Kimble

Opportunity Cost, by P.J. Goring, is a novel examining the choices made in the life of Lenny Fergus—an accountant diagnosed with terminal cancer—and the subsequent costs and consequences they ultimately incurred. Throughout his life, Lenny was always one step ahead, planning out the next week and next year. He chose to neither marry nor maintain a long-term relationship because of its reputation for being uncertain, and therefore had no children. His friends were always kept at arm's length for the purpose of shielding himself from disappointment and letdowns. Friendship seemed to him more of an inconvenience, and he was never interested in the requirements of its maintenance. But upon receiving the news of his imminent death, he suddenly becomes aware of his empty, suburban home, the friends who refer to his illness as just a part of life, and the missing companion with whom he might have found some solace.

    Suddenly racked with the fear of having led a meaningless and unfruitful existence, and without much of a future to change that, Lenny Fergus decides to use his remaining time to embark on a journey through his life. Moving backwards in time, he visits the people and places that he encountered along the way, in search of a purpose. From speaking with old friends to reconnecting with the former love of his life to visiting his hometown, he becomes increasingly aware of an alternate life he might have lived and is perplexed by those choices which brought him to where he is.

As his sickness takes a tighter hold, Lenny Fergus grows frantic to discover what it was that caused him to navigate life the way he did, and in a compelling revelation of opportunities seized, missed, and disregarded, he begins to see a side to life that never seemed existent before, a side that makes love, friendship, and family worth all of the risks. The question that Lenny must ultimately answer is whether or not it is possible for the decisions in his final hours to give purpose to all the past years of his life.

Opportunity Cost, the eleventh novel by best-selling author P.J. Goring and his first work to be awarded the Pulitzer Prize, paints the portrait of a character that could be anyone and everyone; a character seeking confirmation that there was a purpose to his life; a character realizing the value in being human.

I read over the review a couple of times, making changes and corrections as needed with intermittent sips of my scotch and drags from my cigarette. Once I was satisfied, I emailed it to Samwell and sat back in my chair, checking my phone for the seven-hundredth time. Vivian had not returned my calls or texts all day, and I was feeling exposed somehow. You never realize how much you desire someone until they're not there, and how little you can do to keep them when they are.

After Vivian had gone last night, I'd finished the remaining half bottle of scotch before drunk texting her. I told her how sorry I was. I told her how much I missed her and wanted her to come back. I told her my ex-wife meant nothing to me, and that she misunderstood what had happened. Eventually, Vivian did come back, but not before I'd passed out on the couch. She was gone by the time I woke up, and the only reason I knew she'd been there was because of the Polaroid picture on the coffee table. It was of me only a few hours before, drooling on myself with the empty bottle to my right and my phone still in my hand. Moments like that have a way of being extremely sobering, but I considered how lucky it was that I'd cleaned the drugs off the kitchen counter.

I'd spent the rest of the day napping and reading, avoiding thoughts of the night before. Avoiding thoughts altogether, except the ones that pleased me. Those I don't exactly recall.

There was still this whole matter of the short story that needed to be written. It seemed an impossible task as the cursor blinked at me from the plane of infinite white. I used to love that little black line. There was a time when it would give me a rush greater than any drink or drug ever could. Rather than wonder what had happened, I decided to chew up half a pill and snort the rest. This, of course, ignited my need to drink, and I took a short drive to the liquor store on the corner, telling myself that there was no shame in having a little relapse. It would release the tension of sobriety; give me a reset. I'd be stronger for it.

By that afternoon, I was right as rain having spent the majority of that time keeping myself at a comfortable buzz. The ability to balance and pace my use, maintaining the perfect ratio of pills to booze, hadn't gone away with lack of practice. My tolerance was a bit lower than it used to be, but that would only make my supply last longer. After a hot shower and brushing my teeth, I headed back out to Ryan's and Abi's school to catch the second performance of *West Side Story* that afternoon and to pick them up for my overnight visitation.

The show wasn't brilliant, but it was a good effort for high schoolers, and I congratulated Abi afterward with some flowers. She did have only one part.

There was a restaurant on the downtown strip that, for several years, Ryan and Abi both agreed was their favorite place to eat. As much as it was one of my least favorites, it was worth the unjustifiable cost of second-rate food to see at least an inkling of enjoyment on my son's face. As I watched him eat, I began to wonder if the enjoyment I was paying for was for his sake or mine, but quickly plucked from my side the pin of guilt that was sticking me.

"So, Dad..." began Abi, gulping down a mouthful of cheeseburger.

"So, Sprout..."

"My government teacher is expecting her second baby. It's going to be a girl," she informed me. "She wants to name it Eve, like in the Bible."

"That's a nice name," I said taking a greasy bite of some French fries.

"You think so?"

"Sure. Why not?"

"Are you kidding?" Abi leaned towards me as she realized I didn't outrightly understand her position. "Eve is the reason why women have been overshadowed by male dominance since the beginning of time. Because she couldn't control herself, men have had this ideology that it's necessary to control all women because we can't make it on our own. Eve couldn't handle following a simple rule, then she lied about it and tricked Adam. It's all been downhill from there."

"I see you've put a lot of thought into that," I said, not keen on religious discussion. "But it seems to me that women have it significantly better these days. What about the whole women's suffrage movement? And there are plenty of female politicians. I'm not so sure Eve has much influence anymore. Besides, it's just a name."

"I know it's technically just a name, but that's not the point. I think the sound of Eve is nice, and the name is good, but she's purposefully doing it after *that* Eve. I just don't understand it. Especially since she's teaching government."

"I take it she's religious..."

"Oh, very!" Abi picked through her food, her tone softening. "Which is all right with me. I'm pretty religious too, but it's like the name Jezebel. No one names their daughter Jezebel because she was evil."

"What about Judas? No one names their kid that. Or Adolf."

"That's different."

"Why is it different?"

"Because one betrayed Jesus and the other slaughtered millions of people. And they were men."

"What's in a name?" I started. Abi rolled her eyes at me, but I continued with a smile. "That which we call a rose by any other name—"

"Would smell as sweet. I know, Dad. But a pile of dog crap by any other name would still smell like a pile of dog crap."

"It's not like Eve was evil or anything. She just made a mistake."

"A mistake is something you answer incorrectly, by accident, on a test," Abi argued. "A sin is something you know is wrong but do anyway. And…Eve, evil. I don't think the similarity is a coincidence."

"You might be reaching a bit there," I said. "But doesn't the Bible say something about everyone being a sinner?"

"Dad, you're not getting it." Abi let out a frustrated moan.

"What do you think, Ryan?" I looked over to see him oblivious with his headphones on. "Ryan. Take them off."

My son, who'd been ignoring us throughout the meal, slid them down to his neck and continued chewing after I had to wave my hand at him. "Ryan, what do you think?" He stopped eating and looked at me slowly, his eyes wide as if nothing other than my speaking to him could have been a greater annoyance.

"Think about what?"

"The name Eve."

"I think it's retarded."

"Stop using that word! You say that about everything," said Abi.

"What's stupid, Ryan?"

"The whole thing. It's retarded to think that people are bad because someone ate an apple a million years ago." Once again, I found it interesting that he knew exactly what we were talking about despite the headphones.

"I don't think people are bad just because someone ate an apple, for one thing," she began. "They're bad because she disobeyed God. And secondly, the earth hasn't even been around a million years. It was only created about eight to ten thousand years ago."

"Where's the proof?" asked Ryan.

"The proof is all around. God created everything. It's in the Bible."

"Science suggests otherwise."

"God isn't bound by the laws of science, Ryan. He created science, too."

"See?" Ryan addressed me with a sarcastic smile. "I told you it was retarded."

"No, it's not!" insisted Abi.

"Oh, my God! Yes, it is insanely retarded! There's ample proof the world has been around for millions of years! Tell her, Dad!" They both looked at me expectantly, catching me off guard with a mouthful of food. I took my time chewing, trying to come up with a satisfactory response to them both while also relishing Ryan's request for my input—and his use of the word ample.

"Well," I said finally, "I think that it's important for us to consider ideas other than our own, but even if we think we're right and someone else is wrong, even if we're sure, we still have to respect each other's opinions." Ryan rolled his eyes, recognizing my political play for what it was.

"Ha!" Abi triumphed.

"He didn't agree with you, Abi."

"But he does." Puzzlement suddenly grew upon her young face as she turned to me. "Don't you?"

"Everyone has their own opinion," I repeated. "If they want to believe something different from you, they're entitled to do so. All that matters is what you believe."

"So, you don't believe in the Bible?"

"All that matters is what you believe for yourself, Abi. And don't be surprised if some of your own beliefs evolve over time."

"Evolve?" Her eyes narrowed as if about to impart a secret. "You realize that evolution is only a theory, right?"

"So is creationism! It's just a theory!" Ryan seemed perturbed beyond his control.

"It's faith, Ryan," Abi argued. "There's a difference."

"And that's so much better?! Have you ever even once considered that other people with other religions have just as much faith in what they believe as you do? Having more faith doesn't make you more right. It just makes you more closed-minded." Ryan wiped his mouth angrily and balled up the napkin.

"I know that, Ryan." She spoke with quiet fervency. "But what I have faith in is right. I know it is."

"And they all say that exact same thing," Ryan pressed. "Except your faith is the only one with a history of massacring millions upon millions of people over the past two thousand years because other people disagreed."

"Ryan—" I attempted an intervention, but he continued.

"Your faith controlled everything that people were allowed to know for almost five hundred years. It's called the Dark Ages, and in that time, human progress was at a complete standstill."

"Ryan—"

"Your faith claims that every bad thing that happens to good people is the will of God. Every single thing that goes wrong is all part of His higher plan, but we lowly humans are too stupid to understand it. Well, you can thank your God for all the natural disasters, all the genocides, all the people dying of starvation and disease." I saw through his eyes a moment of swift connection, the spark of thought forming from ideas into words and those words into unretractable sound. "You can thank God for splitting our parents up, too, since that's what He must have wanted."

"That's enough, Ryan." I was as surprised as the two of them by the sudden command in my voice. Ryan had reduced Abi to a trembling little girl, and now was glaring at me, slouched over his plate. I breathed deeply and spoke. "You can feel whatever you want to feel, Ryan, and you can think whatever you want to think. I don't care who you blame for what happened between me and your mother, but you will not drag your sister's faith through the mud just because you're angry about it. Do you understand me?"

Ryan, I'd known, had been pissed off for quite some time. I hadn't held it against him but had, in fact, understood it. To a degree we had all been pissed off, each for his or her own reason, with his or her own justification based on his or her own understanding. There had been collateral damage, and I knew it would take years for that to be repaired. For the past several months, I had prepared myself as best I could for the long road ahead. I knew there would be days of dissention, nights of angst, and the in-between hours of numbness that, in its own right, is pain. I had thought, and wondered, and imagined, and made contingencies, pre-constructed answers, and formed a blueprint of some foundation upon which our lives could be rebuilt. But I had never expected what Ryan said to me next, and I likewise rebuked myself for never considering it as a possibility.

"I'm not stupid enough to blame God," he said, "not when I know it's really all your fault." Ryan uttered his words through gritted teeth.

"What did you just say?"

"It's all your fault." His eyes were a wall of contempt, a wall that I knew had been built to guard the wounds within. I searched for the heart to rebut his accusation, but the only heart I could find would not permit me. "But it's okay, Dad. You don't have to say anything," said Ryan as he stood. "It's not like there's anything left for you to defend anyway."

After turning his back on us and exiting the restaurant, Ryan decided to call Argyle, who subsequently called Julia, who in turn called me. When I answered the phone, she was livid, telling me to bring her children home immediately, reminding me in a most colorful language that, according to the court ordered agreement, she had primary custody. Then she dared me to give her a reason to call the cops, and I considered taking her up on the offer.

Abi had cried at first, yelled at Ryan, but had finally calmed down as I drove them back to Julia's. Tear stains lined her lightly freckled cheeks; the tip of her thumb was creased from where she'd been biting at it. Ryan sulked with his arms crossed, music blasting into his head. He wouldn't look at or speak to me. But his body language said that he was unsure of anything, and in turn, his actions were without forethought, and this scared him a little.

Julia was standing at the door when we pulled up, Argyle behind her like a scrawny bulldog. Ryan wasted no time running to his hideaway, but Abi didn't move as I shifted the car into park.

"I'm not going in." She looked at me, resolute and unafraid. "I don't care what Ryan thinks. I don't care what Mom wants. I'm going with you."

"Listen, Abi—"

"You can't make me go. I looked it up. I'm old enough to decide for myself. I'm going home with you, Dad." Julia waved to her from the front door to get out of the car. "I mean it."

Her eyes were like crystals, filling me with so much wonder and awe that I felt for the first time as though I were looking at a complete individual. A truly independent thinker. She had made a decision, regardless of the wants and wishes of others, and I could only respect it and fight for her side. I nodded, patted her knee, then went to inform Julia. She extended her hands in desire for an explanation, and I reached for a cigarette, lighted it, and exhaled.

"We agreed not to make them choose sides, Julia."

"And I haven't, Arthur."

"I sure as hell got that impression when Ryan was blaming me at dinner for our marriage falling apart."

"Yeah, well maybe he's just insightful."

"Or maybe you're just manipulative."

"I don't give a shit what you think, but I'm not going to stand here while you accuse me of something as fucked up as manipulating my children." Julia glanced over at Abi in the car.

"She doesn't want to come." She looked at me, stunned for a moment, then disbelieving.

"What do you mean she doesn't—"

"She doesn't want to come. She wants to stick it out with me tonight."

"And you're calling me manipulative, Arthur? What the fuck did you say to her?"

"I didn't say anything. She decided this one on her own. And do you mind my asking why the hell Ryan is calling your boyfriend now like they're buddies or something?" Julia stood silent for a moment, then began marching towards the car, ignoring my question.

"Abi, get out of the car. You're coming with me." Abi locked her door just before Julia could open it, her face unchanged by the confrontation. Julia slapped the window, then took on a calm tone after a deep breath. "Sweetie, I know today has been rough. I know you're feeling a whole lot of different emotions right now, but you need to come with me. You'll be okay. You don't have to go with your father if you don't want to."

"But I do want to! I can decide for myself! You can't keep me from my dad!" Abi yelled the words through the glass, and Julia hurtled into a frenzy.

"Get the f— get out of the car now! Arthur, unlock the door!" Her eyes were wide as she tugged uselessly at the handle. "Arthur!"

"No," I shook my head. "She's right. She's old enough to decide for herself."

"She's only fourteen years old! She's doesn't know what she wants!"

"That's funny, because not so long ago you seemed to think she was old enough when the roles were reversed."

"Unlock the damn car, Arthur!"

"Why are you behaving this way in front of our daughter? Just leave her alone and go back in the house."

"Don't tell me how to be with my daughter!" Julia charged at me. "You unlock the car now, or I'm calling the cops!"

"And tell them what? That *our* daughter is mature enough to make her own choice and her father is supportive?"

"You're a son of a bitch, Arthur," she accused from behind her pointed finger.

"Get out of my face, Julia."

"Or what?" Argyle, whom I'd forgotten had been at the door amid the interaction, spoke up as he took his place at Julia's side.

"Stay out of this, Argyle. This doesn't have anything to do with you."

"That's not what Ryan thinks," he replied. "You really want to know why he called me? Because I'm the closest thing to a father he's had for the past three months."

I looked the man in his eyes, the tremble returning to my body in a rage that I knew would be out of my control in a matter of seconds. I took a drag of my cigarette, turning my face into the breeze, somehow finding a peacefulness in its soft hushing; feeling a comfort in the vibrant hues of violet and coral and orange that painted the sky just before nightfall; it was greater than me, open and free. And I was not trapped in that moment. Dropping my cigarette on the driveway, I twisted my heel over it and turned away without a word. Argyle, realizing my intention to leave, rushed past me to settle his weight against the door.

"You better get the hell out of my way."

"Unlock the car."

"Get out of my way!"

"You want to hit me, Arthur?" He leaned in speaking low. "Put one hand on me. See if Abi doesn't find out what a crazy old junkie her father really is."

I stepped involuntarily closer as adrenaline pulsed through me and numbed my nerves for impact, as all the resentment and disdain and hatred began balling up inside my fists. But the breeze returned, and I released it from my fingers like pebbles to the ground.

"That's what I thought," Argyle smirked, then whispered, "It's okay. I'll raise them for you."

I had Argyle pinned against the car, my hands clutching his sweater, and the look of fear in his eyes was enough for me to find pleasure in the action I was about to take. I brought my fist back, poised to strike the man, but my senses were called upon by the voice of one I loved far more than I could ever hate him.

"Don't do it, Daddy! Please!" Abi cried. "I'll get out. I'll go with Mom."

I would have taken the beating as willingly as I would have given it. I would have with my hands tied behind me, with no way of protecting myself. I would have suffered every punch and kick that man could have mustered the strength to serve. I would have faced the blindness of swollen eyes, the cracked and missing teeth, the bruised and fractured ribs. I would have let myself become but a vessel of broken bones, all to keep the dignity of her decisions and the right of her choice intact. But Abi pleaded for me not to, the blue of her eyes the azure of serenity, and the clarity of her will as that of her tears. She exited the car slowly, then approached and wrapped her arms around my middle, her hair brushing the bottom of my chin.

"It'll be okay, Dad."

It'll be okay, she says.

Abi disappeared inside, followed by Julia who was tailed by Argyle stepping away from me slowly. A few moments later I was lighting a cigarette in my car, backing out of the drive and speeding toward the highway, desperate for chemical salvation.

Vivian's phone went to voicemail as I called her for a fourth time. I'd been hopeful that hearing her voice would bring me home and keep me there until the storm passed, but she was apparently still screening my calls. I deserved as much. I'd been pacing my apartment for an hour, contemplating the desire that had been born in Julia's driveway, contemplating the reasons why I should submit to that desire and all the reasons not to. The manner of necessity was different from earlier. I had been helping myself to be well, at least I'd thought. That was gone now. This was not the desire to be well, and the willpower to stand and fight it had abandoned me. I wanted to escape, and that was something I had never planned to do again. But nobody plans for this.

Giving up on reaching Vivian, I collapsed on my bed, bouncing with the impact. I rolled over and stared at the ceiling, noticing the tiny peaks and valleys of its texture, different images forming in its surface like constellations. Invisible lines connected an ancient samurai with his long thin mustache, the fangs of some large cat, a lifeless zombie, and the open fingers of a tiny hand. They had become familiar after lying awake in that spot for countless nights, like decorative furniture that served no real purpose other than to be observed. The lines began to run parallel, and my ability to ignore the beckoning was quickly deteriorating. That's when I considered that not every battle must be won to win a war. Sometimes retreat was necessary to recoup and rest in order to come back stronger next time. But I had already been doing that all day, hadn't I? How much stronger was I for it?

"Strength does not always present itself as such," said Huxley beside me, looking at the ceiling. "Strength is often a combination of different things. For example, when the lines are blurred, it can take a great deal of courage to create your own."

"Courage…I just don't care enough."

"Why do you think that is?"

"Because," I said. "I need reasons to care."

"And you, yourself, are not a good enough reason?"

"It's not as simple as that, Huxley," I told him, the heat rising in my core.

"It never is."

Ricky González was exactly where I'd left him at his desk, his computer displaying a digital ledger and a calculator. Music from a live band was vibrant, and the voices of his patrons sang along merrily with the chorus.

"Art! Good to see you, my friend. I wasn't sure if it would be anytime soon, but—"

"I need a fifty," I interrupted, standing before him without returning his smile.

Ricky removed his glasses slowly and swiveled his chair to face me directly. He breathed in and out easily. "What's going on?"

"If all I wanted to do was talk about it, I wouldn't be here."

"Oh. I see."

It struck me suddenly that, in my frustration, I'd insulted him unintentionally and realized I would have to tell him something. It was an unavoidable means to an end.

"Julia and I…" I said quietly. "I'll just say that it was pretty bad. I just need something to get through it."

"You know as well as I do that it won't get you through shit, Arthur."

"But we both know it'll make the getting through a lot more bearable." He studied me intently. "Come on, Ricky. I'm not looking for a week's worth or anything. Just something for tonight." He was silent for several seconds then sighed.

"I don't have anything that small cut right now. If you want an eight ball, it's a hundred, but...I'll let you have it for eighty."

"Fine."

Ricky stood up and crossed the room to a safe on the floor in the corner. After a moment he returned with a small baggie of blow, the end tied in a knot. He placed it in front of me on the desk, and I stared it down, taking in the bubble of white powder, feeling the anticipation of its absorption into my bloodstream. I opened my wallet and handed him the money. Without counting it, he opened the drawer and dropped in the cash before producing the same plate and razor blade from before.

"Here. Divvy us up a couple lines. I could use a zinger myself." Ricky sat back in his chair. "These accounts are already depressing enough."

The razor chopped and crunched through the lump of cocaine on the plate, the fine powder lined up like hash marks on a prison wall. I took the straw from him and leaned forward towards the first line.

"Arthur." He touched my arm to stop me. "It's one thing to do a little for fun. It's a whole other basket of apples when you go into free fall. You sure you want to do this?"

Ricky locked his eyes with mine, a look of helplessness within them when he realized that I simply had no more fucks to give at the moment. Brushing his hand away, I inhaled the line with a swift, single movement and sat straight with my face to the heavens, the burning in my nostrils as comforting as a child's blanket. I smiled at him through watering eyes.

A few minutes later, I exited Ricky's office, the rest of the eight ball safely tucked into my jacket, and returned to the bar for a drink. Baron's was electric with the whining of a guitar backed by a bass and a set of drums. The people had continued singing, having drunk away the cares of their lives one glass at a time and reached a higher level of existence above the flatlands of reality. I was soaring, however, the chemical having taken hold of my senses at last.

"I know you." Two earthy-looking men stood at the bar beside me, studying my face. "I don't know where from, but I know you."

"That makes one of us," I said.

"Isn't he the pigeon guy?" the other asked. His friend's eyes widened, and he nodded happily.

"Yeah, man, that's what it is. You're the pigeon man."

"You've seen through my disguise," I said before taking a sip of my drink. "I am the pigeon man."

"Hey, Chicken, it's the pigeon man!" One of them called to someone over his shoulder, and a third, taller man appeared, long-haired and scruffy. He grinned broadly and extended his hand.

"No way! This is fucking cool. This guy right here," he said to his friends, "is a genius."

"I am?" I asked.

"Look," said the first of them. "It's Chicken and the pigeon man."

"Can I get your autograph?" asked Chicken, searching for a bar napkin.

"I guess...sure." He stole a pen from the counter and placed it in my hand. "Make it out to Chicken?"

"No, my daughter. Andrea. We've been reading your stories about Huxley since she was six. She's ten now. She's big into the anthropomorphic stuff. Am I saying that right?"

"Yeah, anthropomorphic," I nodded, surprised for a moment that he knew the word, then considered it unsurprising for a man named Chicken. "So, to Andrea?"

"Yup. Andrea." Chicken was beaming as he watched me write on the napkin. "You know, she wants to be a writer someday."

"Writing isn't all it's cracked up to be," I said, handing the autograph to him. "It can be pretty brutal sometimes, actually."

"I believe it. That's why I'm trying to raise her to be the kind of person who welcomes challenges and sees them as opportunities to learn and improve. You know what I mean? I know this sounds cliché as hell, but life truly is what you make it."

"Okay," I said.

"I'm buying you a drink," said Chicken, nudging up next to the crowded bar and standing shoulder to shoulder. "By the way, this is Ollie, and this is Keith, a.k.a. The Hare." They said hello, and I nodded. "My wife Pearl is over there," he pointed.

"What's up with the nicknames?" I asked.

"He's The Hare because he's fast but likes to nap a lot. I'm Chicken because, well, I like to eat chicken." His laugh bellowed.

"And I'm the pigeon man," I said, beginning to think that it wasn't the worst thing to be called.

Chicken, The Hare, and Ollie stood by me, including me in their discussion of summer music festivals which I had no clue about. They were friendly enough, however, and after three more drinks, I followed them to a small apartment a few minutes away. We dived into a bottle of rum as The Hare plugged in an old turntable and set the needle to a vinyl of Pink Floyd. Everyone relaxed on a couple of sheet-covered couches and took turns taking hits from a large, glass bong in the middle of the room. My gaze floated around at the four of them until Chicken put his hand on my shoulder and spoke.

"I dig your vibe, Pigeon Man. But I've got to tell you, your aura is kind of heavy."

"My aura?" I chuckled.

"Yeah," he said, plopping down beside me. "There's a hole somewhere, isn't there? In there." He pointed at my chest.

"No more of a hole than anyone else," I told him, turning my attention to a beer.

"You've got to fill it, man. Let the universe in instead of keeping that empty part of you."

"What are you talking about?" I asked.

"You want to take a trip, man? Make some discoveries?" Chicken's voice had lowered, his eyes narrowing. I cleared my throat and looked past him.

"To where?"

"Wherever you want."

"I think I'm all right just staying here," I said. He smiled then stood and went to the freezer in the kitchen. After moving a few things around, he produced a small plastic bag. Once he'd put the other items back, Chicken returned to the couch.

"Here," he said, holding up a small paper-like square with a technicolored star printed on it. "Free yourself."

The tabs of acid melted on our tongues, though I tasted nothing. I didn't think twice about it, and we continued to drink and snorted a couple lines from the eight ball I'd purchased. Our conversation began zigzagging from one topic to another, the fervency of our opinions increasing with each passing minute.

An unexpected vibration began in my pocket, repeating in quick bursts, and Abi's smiling face beamed up at me. I jumped up and sequestered myself in the bathroom, then answered after a deep breath.

"Abi?" I said, wiping at my nose, trying to sniffle quietly.

"Hey, Dad."

"Are you okay? What are you still doing up?"

"I couldn't sleep. Were you asleep?"

"No. Not exactly," I said, leaning against the sink. "You sure you're okay, honey?"

"Yeah. I was just worried if you were okay."

"I…yeah, yeah. I'm good, baby."

"I know you're just saying that."

"Well," I said, catching my breath, "before you called, I wasn't okay, but now I am. You always make me okay."

"Really?" Abi's voice wavered.

"You always have, Sprout." Our connection was nearly tangible.

"Daddy, I'm sorry. I'm so sorry!" She lost control of her words as they broke with the beginning of sobs. "I didn't mean to cause a problem! I didn't want anyone to get mad!"

"Abi, you didn't—"

"I just didn't want you to get hurt because of me! I don't want to be the reason you have to go away again! I don't want you to leave again! Please, don't leave!"

"Abi, I'm not leaving you. Okay? Never, ever. Last time will never happen again, Sprout. That's a promise. Do you believe me? Do you believe my promise?"

Her breaths repeated in rapid staccatos as she tried to compose herself, the sound of exhalation like static in transmission.

"I believe you," Abi said after a moment.

"And you don't have to be sorry for anything. You did nothing wrong, Sprout. Nothing." There was silence.

"I know you're trying your best."

"You think so?" I finally said, unsure if she genuinely believed it or not.

"That's what Mom said."

"She did?"

"Pretty much." I knew there had been a 'but' to Julia's statement, and I chose for both our sakes not to ask what it was.

"Well, Sprout, your mom is trying her best too." I listened to Abi's breathing settle. "You know, just because we're adults doesn't mean we always know what to do all the time. Sometimes it takes us a while to figure things out, and we tend to make mistakes until we do."

"Is that what you've been doing?"

"Making mistakes?"

"Figuring things out."

"I—I'm trying, baby. I'm trying really hard." Abi didn't speak, but I could almost hear her thinking through the phone.

"You want to pray with me, Dad? Maybe God will tell you what you need to know."

"Well," I began, wishing to decline but realizing that I couldn't. "I guess it couldn't hurt, right?" Moments passed as she waited for me to begin, but in an unspoken intuition, she started the prayer, because, even after all the disingenuous prayers I'd made over the course of my life, I didn't know how to begin the one that might actually matter.

"Dear God, it's me Abigail. And my Dad's here, too, but I guess you already know that. I just wanted—we—just wanted to ask if you could help him figure things out. Whatever it is. And please let him be happy. He deserves to be happy. Thank you in advance. In Jesus' name, amen." She sniffed. "Was that okay, Dad? Do you feel any better?"

"That was perfect, Sprout. I'm feeling much better already." I listened to her smile, envisioning that most beautiful dimpled brilliance. Then the most beautiful synthetic brilliance was rippling out from the bathroom mirror. "You better get some sleep, honey. You don't want your mom catching you on the phone this late," I said quickly.

"Okay. Goodnight, Dad. I love you."

"I love you too, Sprout."

"Dad?"

"Yeah, baby?" My reflection was becoming fluid before my eyes.

"I wish you were here."

I wish you were here, she says.

"Me too." There was the muffled sound of movement, then the vastness of silence as the call ended. Reverie was quickly pulling me away from reality, and suddenly, I didn't want to go.

I didn't want to go.

I didn't want to go.

"Arthur, don't be afraid."

"Huxley!" I cried. "Huxley, I don't want to go!"

"There is no turning back now, my friend. This is the course we are bound to."

"I don't want to! Abi believes. She believes, Huxley!"

"Yes, Arthur, she believes. You should believe, also." His gaze locked with mine.

"I can't!"

"Why not?"

"Because I don't know what she believes."

"Come now," Huxley chuckled. "Of course, you know. How is it that she came to believe it in the first place?"

"It's as vivid as the light," I said. "As vivid as the night."

"Her belief is your star, my friend. Fly to it! Ascend!"

"I'm afraid, Huxley," I said, wiping the tears from my cheeks. "What if I fall? What if I get lost out there? I don't know where I'm supposed to be, but she knows. Why can't she be here? I don't want to be here."

"There is nothing to fear, Arthur, so long as you stop fighting."

"But Huxley—"

"You must stop fighting, Arthur. We will navigate this cosmos together," he smiled. "Together, my friend."

"Together, my friend," I repeated, my heart lifting me.

"Together, we will see this through," said Huxley. "We will see this through."

CHAPTER EIGHT

There are many cure-alls for a hangover, but the one I'd always sworn by was a shot of vodka in a glass of orange juice, followed by two six-ounce cans of vegetable juice, a mug of black coffee, and two cigarettes. Though it was effective in relieving the throbbing behind my eyes, it took half a day to find my feet again after the trip I'd gone on. It didn't quite pull me out of my morning daze either, and I found myself in and out of sleep on the couch, half because I was exhausted, half because I didn't feel like thinking about it.

"Arthur. Arthur, are you okay?" Vivian looked down at me on the couch, her face filled with worry. "I'm so sorry."

"What...What?" I groaned, coming to.

"Are you all right? What happened?"

"Yeah," I said, blinking her into better focus. "What are you doing here?"

"I got your messages from last night. I'm so, so sorry. I just wasn't able to answer, and I couldn't get here sooner. Honey, what happened?" Vivian knelt beside me as she touched my face.

"What time is it?"

"It's almost three in the afternoon." Her eyes locked with mine, and I could see that she'd been crying. "Tell me, please."

"I fucked up," I said after a deep breath. "I fucked up, Viv. I'm sorry."

"What did you do?" she asked.

"I don't remember completely. I ran into these guys...I don't know who they were."

"You were drinking?" I nodded. "Did you take anything?" I nodded again, more reluctantly that time. "What did you take, Arthur?"

"I...dropped acid."

"You did what?!"

"I wasn't thinking clearly," I said.

"I bet you weren't," she frowned. "I take it that's why your car isn't outside."

"It's not?"

"No, it's not. Do you even know how you got home? Did you walk?"

"I..." I closed my eyes in thought. "Yeah. I walked."

"From where?" Vivian waited for me to answer, but I gave her nothing. "You left Baron's and went where?"

"How'd you know I was at Baron's?"

"I called them when I couldn't reach you. They said you'd been there and left with some hippies or something."

"I wouldn't necessarily call them hippies," I said. "Isn't that a derogatory term nowadays?"

"I don't really give a shit if it is," she snapped. "You called me in crisis, and I missed it. Then you went out, got drunk, high from who-knows-what, and then went on an acid trip before walking home in sub-freezing temperatures. Your car's missing, and you're skipping work. I feel badly that I wasn't there when you needed me, Arthur, but this is ridiculous."

"I know."

"I don't mean to lecture you. I'm not your mother. But this is..." Vivian sat on the floor beside the couch. "Did you know that you called me at four this morning?"

"No...What did I say?"

"You said you couldn't do it anymore, that you were too sad and tired to keep trying. You said you didn't want to die, but you didn't want to live either. You said that Ryan and Abi were better off with a dead father, and that Huxley was bullshit. That you hated yourself. That you were such a disappointment…And you wouldn't listen to me or tell me where you were. You scared me, Art. I was so afraid that you were going to turn up dead somewhere. I was frantic, and then Stacy said you hadn't been in. I called the hospital. If you weren't here, I was going to call the police."

"I'm sorry," I said, almost whispering. "I didn't mean to worry you. I don't remember any of that."

"I believe the you right now didn't mean to. But I'm convinced there's a part of you feeling all those things when you're not drunk and high, and you're not telling me. That's not okay. You are not okay. It hasn't been a month since you got out of rehab, and this is what's happened. I'm not saying you have to tell me everything. I'm just saying you need to do something because this isn't working."

Vivian's eyes flooded, the silent tears streaming down to her chin. If I hadn't felt like a complete piece of shit before, I certainly did then. It wasn't her fault. She deserved a real man, someone responsible who had his shit together. Not a man like me. Parts of me that she needed were very much dead or dying. I just didn't have the heart to break it to her.

"I'm seeing a therapist," I said.

"You are?" Vivian sniffled. "Since when?"

"I just had my first session last week. Believe it or not, she said I've already had a breakthrough."

"Who is it?" she asked. I reached around for my wallet and showed her the same card I'd presented to Jack. "Dr. Margaret Hollande."

"Maybe talking with her triggered something. I don't know," I said, avoiding talk of the altercation at Julia's, not because I wanted to hide it, but because I just didn't feel like getting into it. Vivian nodded and forced a smile.

"I'm proud of you for doing this on your own."

"I know I'm not okay," I admitted, avoiding her praise. "I'm trying though."

"I know you're trying. I'm sorry I wasn't here for you. I dropped the ball."

I wondered if somewhere in my subconscious I had manipulated the conversation to my advantage. My impulse said no, but it amazed me that I was the one who'd wrecked himself, and yet she was the one apologizing.

"It's not your responsibility to make sure I'm okay, to keep me sober or to make sure I don't do something stupid," I said. "I'm the one with a problem, I'm the one who has to get myself better."

As she rested her head on my chest, it was blindingly evident to me how little I deserved this woman, and I found it difficult to believe that she didn't see this too. Any decent person would end it right there to relieve her of whatever obligation she must have felt to stick around. I wasn't a decent person though, as my history proved, and pecking at the back of my brain were two realizations: 1) if I truly loved her, I would make an honest effort, and 2) I couldn't wait for her to leave so I could crush a pill and take a shot.

Sure, you can teach an old dog new tricks, but that doesn't mean he stops performing the old ones.

"Good morning, Mr. Kimble. We missed you yesterday," Stacy greeted me outside my office the following day. Her smile faded when she saw me wearing my sunglasses indoors. "Long night?"

"Something like that," I said. "Any calls for me?"

"No, but you do have a visitor." She nodded toward my office. "He's been sitting in there for the past hour and a half."

"Who?"

"Mr. Grant, that productivity analyst who's been hanging around the past few days." Stacy raised an eyebrow. "I don't like him."

"I should have stayed in bed…"

"I told him you were doing an interview with a Finnish bard."

"That's a new one."

"Oh, and I heard a rumor that we're getting a vending machine. Is that true?" she asked.

"Yes," I said dryly.

"Sweet!" cheered Stacy with a fist pump. "Maybe it'll have those baked apple pies you like."

"I doubt it."

"Mr. Kimble." Jerry Grant appeared in my office doorway in that same expensive suit, smiling politely. He approached me with an outstretched hand. "Good to see you again. How was the interview?"

"Very Nordic," I said, shaking his hand.

"Oh, too bad…" He blinked. "I hope you don't mind, but I took a little gander through your collection," he said, holding up a copy of *East of Eden*. "I was always more of a comics person myself. Books like this are too cumbersome."

"Not so much for stronger minds," I said, watching him either miss the inference or ignore it completely. "For everything a time and place, I suppose. Even for comic books."

"No place here, I see," said Mr. Grant, "and no time for clunky old books for me. I guess the two of us balance it all out, don't we?"

"Sure. Would you excuse me for just one moment?"

Without awaiting a reply, I walked past him into my office and shut the door, scanning my books for signs of disturbance. It appeared that only a few had been looked through as most of them were aligned the way I preferred them to be, but my anxiety was still piqued. I took *Brave New World* from the shelf and opened it, relieved to see the two pills I'd hidden. I immediately took a whole one and chewed it up, the satisfying taste of the bitter pill immediately releasing the dopamine I'd been craving for almost twenty hours.

Vivian had never left the day before, staying to make me dinner, get me cleaned up, locate my car a few blocks away in a pharmacy parking lot, and share my bed. I was never able to get my fix, and undergoing withdrawals that entire time, the whole thing was excruciating.

After taking a shot of whiskey from the small bottle in my desk, I put my sunglasses away and opened the door to my office with a fresh breath of energy.

"So, Mr. Grant, how does this work exactly? You're going to follow me around all day?"

"That's the general procedure in small office settings like this," he answered, following me to my desk, "at least for people in positions such as yours. I wouldn't observe your assistant all day, for example. It's easy to gauge her level of productivity within an hour or so. In fact, I made use of the time waiting for you to do just that."

"And what's your verdict?"

"She's a good employee."

"Is that the same as a productive employee?" I asked, taking a seat at my desk. Mr. Grant took the chair across from me. "That is what you're focused on, isn't it? Productivity?"

"No," he smiled, "it is not the same thing. A good employee knows their job, shows up on time, is loyal. They do their best to get the job done."

"Stacy is all those things, I know," I said. He nodded silently, and the mild annoyance I felt towards him turned to disdain. "I hope you don't get bored. I do a lot of reading and writing. That might not interest you much."

"I think I'll manage just fine."

Mr. Grant made himself comfortable, removing his jacket and crossing his legs to support his writing pad. His pen scribbled as I stared into my computer, clicking around randomly as to appear occupied with something important. I shuffled through some old files, copies of previously published short stories. I had only a couple of new emails including the minutes from the meeting I'd missed that morning reminding everyone that the auditor was coming today. An email from P.J. Goring's publicist excited me until I realized it was a generic "we'll get back to you soon" message.

"So," Mr. Grant began, "How long have you worked here at *Verb'd Magazine*?"

"Over twelve years," I said without looking at him.

"That's a good chunk of time. You enjoy your work, I presume."

"Yes."

"What do you do on a daily basis?"

"I do a little bit of everything that's word related. Copy editing, writing, proofreading."

"You write articles?"

"Yes, mostly interviews and reviews. Occasionally I do an opinion piece. Then I have my monthly short story."

"Oh, yeah, I remember hearing something about that. About a bird or something…What's that called again?" he asked.

"'The Adventures of Theodore Huxley'. It's set in 1920s London, about a pigeon named Huxley who solves mysteries with his sidekick nephew, Farnaby."

"You mean solving mysteries for humans?"

"No, it's anthropomorphic." Mr. Grant blinked at me. "It's a version of our world where the humans are animals."

"Interesting. So, basically it's a bird version of Sherlock Holmes."

"No." I frowned. "It's a pigeon named Huxley who solves mysteries."

"Ah. Do you feel like it's been successful?"

"It's gotten good responses, sure. I took some personal time recently and was considering a revamp of the character. Up until now, the feel of it has been smart and slightly humorous. Lighthearted to certain degrees. I'm going to start developing it a bit differently, something darker. Fewer graphics as well."

"Graphics? You mean there are illustrations?"

"Yes, I draw them. I'm not the greatest artist in the world, but I think I do a decent job."

"May I see?" he asked a bit eagerly.

"Sure. The newest issue is there next to you." Mr. Grant looked to the table on his right and found the magazine. He thumbed through, page by page.

"You know, I've never looked at this magazine before."

"Really?"

"I'd heard of it. Literature just wasn't ever my thing."

"It's called a literary magazine, but it covers more than literature. We review and discuss visual arts, music, cinema, sometimes dance…I'd say we're more of an arts magazine."

"That's quite impressive," he commented. "Here, I found your story…The Ivory Cord, Part 4…Hey, these are very good. This is just a pencil drawing?"

"Thanks. Yes, ink as well."

"Do you mind if I read it?" he asked.

"Be my guest, though I would suggest starting at part one. It's over on the shelf."

Mr. Grant walked to where I'd indicated and scanned the date. "Was this your first one?" he asked, waving a wrinkled old issue.

"Yeah," I answered after looking up. He returned to his seat, then searched again for the story. Once he'd found it, he cleared his throat and began reading aloud, much to my annoyance.

THEODORE HUXLEY: THE ELEVENTH HOUR, PART 1

A fog had settled over the streets of London like a lazing river of smoke, and the branches swayed easily in the breeze as the night watch captain peered up at the clock tower. Half past one. They were late. In all his twenty-seven years on the force, he'd never experienced such a generation of tardy creatures. As the old owl muttered to himself, a faint glowing dot appeared, growing quickly.

"Sergeant," he called quietly. "Ready the gate."

"Aye, captain," a younger owl answered from the tree line.

With the crescendo of clicking cobblestones, a badger-drawn cart appeared from the mist, a single lantern at its stern. Two guards were riding atop, facing opposing directions, rifles at the ready.

"You're late," the owl informed them as they approached.

"I didn't know we was in a hurry," one of the guards said, tipping back his helmet.

"What did you think this was, a midnight joyride? Take her in through the south side of the square. Be quick about it."

The captain directed them with his wing and followed behind to the opening gate which allowed them entrance into a large grassy field surrounded by a fortified wall. The cart nearly scraped its wheels against the iron frame of the gate, then with a clang, it closed behind them. A group of guards emerged from a small hut in the east corner to help unload the cargo.

In the center of the square had been erected a massive vault of steel and concrete. Protected within were dozens of rows of gold bricks glowing in the lamp light, the only remaining space reserved for this final delivery from the Bank of England. The captain completed the unlocking procedure to open the vault, and the guards disappeared inside, guiding in the cart of gold.

The door closed behind them, and with a smile, the old captain retrieved a pipe from his jacket and began puffing it to life. The most was thick, yet the moon was still visible above him, and he felt at peace as he thought of his impending retirement.

His thoughts were interrupted, however, by a muffled uproar within the vault. Turning, he beheld a red cloud forming above the square, its body swirling into the sky. It appeared to be escaping from within the vault itself. A metal clanging at the door caused him to drop his pipe and run quickly over, and he soon realized the guards' inability to exit. Dark red smoke began surrounding him as he turned the dial of the lock, his eyes burning, the numbers hardly visible.

The key slipped out of his grasp to the ground, and the captain spit a volley of curses. His lungs tightened and burned. The shouts from within turned to coughing screams until one by one, the voices faded. Recovering the key, he completed the unlocking procedure and waited. The beat of his heart racing, deafening in his ears as each second lasted an eternity. But as loud as the thumping of his pulse was, he could still hear the final cry beyond the door. Then his body stilled, and the world turned to black.

***

"There is something in the air here that makes me well, Doggart. Before the audience ever takes their seats, before the orchestra strikes up the overture and the players have taken their marks, there is a peace in the majesty of this place."

Theodore Huxley looked out from the stage of the Amble Theatre, drinking in the elegance of the auditorium, capable of seating over nine hundred people in its three levels. Four columns were painted a soft crème with golden vines climbing up and branching across the convex curve of the second and third levels. Velvet seats glowed beneath the great chandelier above, lighting the space through a thousand crystals.

"Perhaps it's *not* the best place for a magic show."

Franklin Doggart emitted a husky, deep-chested laugh with a pat on Huxley's shoulder.

"That's not what I meant," he replied. "It belongs here as much as the acrobats, the opera singers, and the Arabian belly dancers."

"It's goin' to be quite a night."

"Indeed, it is," Huxley nodded. "What were you wanting to show me? Something for your performance tonight?"

"Aye, and it's a beauty!" Doggart, a brown burly squirrel, led Huxley backstage where several stagehands were busily making final preparations for the evening. Stationed to the side and standing upright, was a large glass box. He patted the side of it. "This is the water chamber that I'll be shackled in. See that iron ring at the bottom?"

"Will you be escaping the chamber before you drown?"

"That's been done," Doggart scoffed. "No, I'll be submerged in the water, chained to the bottom, and will have to drink the water before I drown. We'll hoist the tank into the air to show it's not simply draining out."

Huxley's eyes widened. "This must be a hundred gallons of water, and you'd have to drink at least a quarter of it. How could you possibly do that?"

"A magician never reveals his secrets," he said.

"Oh, don't use that old excuse," said Huxley. "Besides, I did save your life in Somme."

"You did..." Doggart frowned. "All right, fine. But you best not tell a soul, or I'll have your tailfeathers."

"You have my word," Huxley chuckled.

"Well, the secret is the bottom of the box where there's a small gap leadin' to an empty secondary chamber inside the glass itself. Look carefully. Can you see it? What happens is, there's a special rope disguised as a hoist rope, and as I'm pretendin' to drink the water, it's pulled slowly," he said, pointing. "That rope attaches to the dividers between the main and secondary chambers, and when pulled, it lifts the divider to allow the water out of the main chamber, lowerin' the water level enough for me to breathe."

"Fascinating," Huxley whispered. "Quite ingenious. I can't wait to see it all in action. "

"Beg your pardon, Master Huxley." Dressed in a clean uniform of black and white that complimented the greyish blue of his feathers, Engel, Huxley's valet, approached the two. "The press is waiting."

"Ah, yes. Doggart, would you care to join me?"

"Not for a thousand quid," he laughed again. "You're on your own."

Huxley left his friend, walking down the aisle to the entrance. At his signal, Engel opened the doors, and Huxley was accosted by a small mob of reporters, some writing into notepads, others flashing their cameras before hurriedly changing the bulb to get another shot.

"Mr. Huxley! Will everything be ready for the opening tonight?"

"The question is, will *you* be ready?"

"Mr. Huxley! Are you at all concerned about ticket sales?"

"Only that I won't have enough tickets."

The reporters laughed. "Mr. Huxley, do you have any position on the strike by the trade union coal miners?"

"I'm in support of their right to do so."

"But do you feel that they should continue working out of duty to country?"

"I agree with our king," said Huxley. "Try living on their wages."

"But, Mr. Huxley—"

"Gentlemen, please," Huxley said, holding up his wings to quiet them. "Tonight, the Amble Theatre opens for the first time since 1893, before my father was forced to close these doors. However, it was always his dream to reopen, and my only regret tonight is that he will not be here to see his dream realized. This evening will be an extravaganza, unparalleled by any in our lifetime, and I will be dedicating this night to him."

"Mr. Huxley, some of the public are condemning the

prices of your tickets, limiting your audience to the elites of London. Is this because of the outrageous cost of putting on this show?"

A dark figure appeared behind the reporters, dressed in official black and a brooding countenance.

"No more questions for now," Huxley smiled and gave Engel a nod to see them out. A moment later, he approached the raven standing by the wall. "Inspector Hugo. You're here a bit early. The show doesn't begin until this evening."

"I'm afraid my constabulary duties may interfere with such things," Inspector Hugo replied, giving Huxley a grave expression. "Mr. Huxley, may we have a word in private?"

"Of course, Inspector."
Huxley ushered the inspector to the side of the auditorium and through a single door. A moment later, they were in his office, and Huxley took a seat behind his desk. "Now then, Inspector. I assume you're here regarding the missing gold."

"How did you know?" he asked, quite stunned.

"How could I not have known? The Bank of England's reconstruction required the gold to be relocated. You assured the public it was being held in vaults that were, what did you say, impregnable? You practically threw down the gauntlet to just about every skilled thief in Britain."

"It's a Sceptre vault. It *is* impregnable, designed specifically to house everything at Finsbury Square as securely as the Bank of England," he argued. "But the vault wasn't broken into."

"No?"

"No. The gold, well, disappeared."

"Inspector, we both know that gold doesn't simply disappear, though many a married fellow might beg to differ."

"I knew this morning, but now," Inspector Hugo shook his head, "now, I'm not so sure. The last delivery of the Bank of England had just been completed, and all was accounted for. It's a mystery."

"Well then, in the appreciation of a good mystery, shall we depart to the scene of the crime?"

"I'll take you there, but I can't stay. I've got to go visit the families of the dead," said the inspector quietly.

"The dead? What dead?"

"The constables that were guarding the square. The lot perished inside the vault. Almost twenty of them."

"My god. How?"

"I'm thinking poison gas, maybe chlorine, but we'll need autopsies to confirm that. My first thought was espionage, but this is beyond the capabilities of our foreign enemies. There is one survivor who's still unconscious. Hopefully he'll come 'round soon to shed light on what happened." Inspector Hugo sighed. "As heartless as it sounds though, our biggest problem is the gold. As it stands right now, the British Empire is virtually bankrupt, and I don't have even the slightest explanation to give my superiors, much less King George."

"If there's one thing I know," Huxley said, standing, "it's that there is an explanation for everything, even the impossible. Sadly, it seems that what may be our greatest clue comes at the cost of lives."

"Not bad," Jerry Grant said. "So, what happens?"

"I guess you'll just have to read the rest," I said, thankful that he was done. "But I need to go out for a bit."

"Another interview?" he asked, putting the magazine back.

"No. I need to pick up a package."

"I'll come with you."

"That's really not necessary," I said. "Would that even be productive?"

"We'll find out, won't we?"

Jerry Grant and I rode together toward Columba Regional Airport. While he'd been reading, I'd received an email that the missing remains had arrived and could be picked up at any time. Naturally, I chose to do it immediately with the intent of getting rid of my shadow. The light was clearly not on my side, however.

"Where did you study?" he asked.

"Penn State. You?"

"University of Minnesota."

"What was your major?"

"Business management," he said.

"Is this what you had in mind?" I asked.

"Not exactly."

"What was it you were planning to do?" Jerry Grant looked wistfully at the passing street.

"Gardens," he said finally.

"Gardens?"

"I wanted to start a landscaping company that specialized in gardens. Great big beautiful gardens."

"Why did you study business then?" I asked.

"It seemed like the smart thing to do. My parents owned a greenhouse, so I'd already learned gardens and botany. I didn't understand business though, so I figured that was the smart thing to do. I developed a business model, had a ten-year plan, quarterly projections, the whole works."

"What happened?"

"I couldn't get a startup loan from anyone. Nobody saw the potential in a gardening company," he said. "Then after all that, I still had my student debt. I'm working this job to pay all that off."

"How much debt?"

"Almost seventy thousand. In about fifteen years I should be ready though."

"How old are you now?"

"Twenty-eight." His answer surprised me as Jerry Grant appeared at least in his early thirties. No wonder his hair was thinning. "I'm not giving up though," he said. "This is just temporary. Sometimes, you have to make sacrifices now to get what you want later."

"Sometimes," I said. "Sometimes the wait isn't worth the sacrifice."

"That's just being impatient," he spoke sincerely. "The world has a lot to offer if you just wait for it and play it right."

"It seems to me like waiting and playing are two different things," I said. "One's active, one's passive. They can't both get you where you want to be."

"Not individually. It's a balance."

"Right, but for how long? When did you start this job?" I asked.

"Five years ago," he said. "It's a good company to work for while I wait for the right moment to try again. It's like they say: you have to get back up in that saddle."

"I don't think they meant after twenty years."

"The saying doesn't exactly specify when. It's going to happen though. Honestly, it's probably for the best that it happened this way. I should pay off my student debt first. Once that's done, I can try again."

I concluded that Jerry Grant wasn't so much foolish as he was misguided. It sounded like the classic story of students pursuing an education, then getting crushed with debt, forcing them to become stuck in one job or another for the majority of their lives. I didn't understand the attraction to higher education if it cost you your freedom. Debt is a form of imprisonment, and sure, I wasn't sitting clean myself, but I certainly wasn't drowning.

"I hope so," I said. And I actually kind of did.

At the airport, Jerry Grant waited in the car, perhaps put off by my criticism. I didn't care since it gave me a chance to break away from him for a cigarette. Once I was inside, Gregery smiled at me from his computer, though I couldn't find the power to return it.

"Mr. Kimble," he said, "Let me apologize again for the mix-up. I'm sure this has been a horrible experience."

"It's been terrible," I said flatly.

"I can only imagine." He pursed his lips, conjuring an expression of regret before smiling again. "Please, follow me this way."

Gregery guided me out of his office and through a set of double doors. We continued down a long hallway, our footsteps echoing and mingling with the other sounds of airport workers walking, talking, and periodically banging something. Finally, coming to a small room, he swiped his keycard, and we entered. It was empty except for a long table upon which had been piled several items I could only presume were lost baggage. Gregery walked me to the end and extended his hand.

"There you are, sir. Safe and sound."

I stared down at the cardboard box wrapped in excessive amounts of packing tape.

"You all put it in a box?"

"For safer shipping." Gregery explained. "Now if you can just sign the paperwork, you'll be all set."

The box of ashes went into the trunk as I didn't want any questions about it from Jerry. He didn't seem all that interested, however, hardly saying a word all the way back to the office. It wasn't until we were seated again that he finally asked what had apparently been weighing on his mind.

"Why did you get into this?"

"Get into what?" I asked.

"This job. What made you choose to work for *Verb'd*?"

"Well," I began, thinking of a reason, "I think sometimes that *Verb'd* chose me more than I chose it. It wasn't really on purpose. I just like writing, and I was sick of passing on opportunities to do it for a living. Why did you pick being a productivity analyst?"

"It pays," he shrugged. "Sometimes the firms that hire us give incentives. There's also a 401k and health insurance. It's too expensive for me, but it's there. That's what people do, right? They get jobs that take care of them." Jerry was silent for a while. "When did you first start writing?" he finally asked.

"I was young. Before I was a teenager."

"And it's made you happy?"

"I've been happy sometimes. Sometimes not so much. Like with any career."

Jerry's face was the vision of some inner turmoil at work. Whatever he was thinking, he wasn't sharing it. I wasn't particularly keen to know what it was, though whatever it might be, I felt certain I'd caused it. When he'd first walked into my office, he was confident, sure of his reasons for being there. Now, he hardly seemed to be interested at all in what I was doing—which wasn't all that much of anything.

"Why do you write?"

"Why do I write?"

"Yes."

It was a bold question, but one I felt had no deep and philosophical answer.

"I write because I have to. I'd be miserable otherwise."

"There are other things you could do that would be much more lucrative, much more secure. This is a magazine. Places like this come and go, are bought and sold. This isn't a safe career."

"Safer doesn't always mean better. And this job is fulfilling enough."

"So, this isn't what you *really* want to be doing with your life?"

"That's not completely true," I answered, unsure if this was his own curiosity or his way of getting me to speak candidly about the job I was at risk of losing if he saw fit. "I like what I do. If I had my way, I'd be an independent writer. That's just not in the cards for me right now."

"You're waiting?"

"Waiting…Not really. I like to think I'm setting myself up for success."

"What makes you think that's not what I'm doing for myself?"

"I never said that you aren't. I think you misunderstood me," I said quickly. "What I'm doing is conducive to my ultimate goal. What you're doing isn't, and in reality, it has the potential of getting you stuck."

"What if you're right though? What if I miss my opportunity? What if I already missed it?" His eyes fell.

"What if *I* did?" I asked in return after a long pause. "There aren't any rules to life. Opportunities come only once or they come more than once, but either way, they come on their own time. Not on yours. They don't come when you're ready. It's good to be patient, yes, but expecting the universe to wait on you is just foolish."

"It seems to work for other people," he said.

"What other people?"

"Just other people. Successful people."

"You may need to alter your definition of success, because if there's anyone out there with a life different than other people's, it's not because they were doing the same thing as everyone else. That's for sure. If you want something different than everyone else, then you have to do things differently than everyone else, and you don't apologize for it when they want to know why the hell you're different. If you want change, then make change."

Jerry looked down at his feet for a long time while I absent-mindedly clicked around on my computer. I believed everything I said to him. I had a thousand and one truths to be shared if anyone cared to listen. If you want change, make change. It was motivational as hell, sure, but the moment you start making waves in the cosmos it inevitably has a way of pulling you down in the undertow. It doesn't like to let you breathe. It doesn't allow change for change's sake. If you want change, then you make change. But nobody can control what the outcome ultimately is, and that's where my lack of faith had me by the spine. No amount of truth means a goddamn thing if you can't manage to believe in it.

"You did what?!" A tiny piece of Mexican ravioli fell from Lonnie's mouth back to his plate.

"I know," I said.

"Don't you know it's dangerous to drop acid with strangers?"

"I know."

"They could've been serial killers."

"Well, I wouldn't say all that."

"Rapists," he continued.

"They weren't rapists."

"Did you at least have a good time?" Lonnie asked. "Honestly, I'm kind of jealous. I haven't had a good acid trip in a couple of years."

"I don't remember all that much of it, but according to Vivian it wasn't that great."

"Wait...Vivian dropped acid with you?"

"No, Lonnie," I said. "I called her while I was tripping."

"Oh, shit. How did that go?"

"Obviously not well. But we talked it through yesterday."

"Good. I thought you were going to say she left you," he chuckled.

"She didn't leave me," I said. "But Lonnie, I got fucked up in the way that I didn't want to get fucked up anymore."

"You obviously did want to, or you wouldn't have."

"It's not what I want for myself," I insisted. "Well, I want it, but I don't. Even while she and I were talking about how bad it was for me, I wanted it."

"I understand your remorse," said Lonnie. "It's hard to stop doing what you've essentially made a habit of. Shit goes down, you get fucked up. Sometimes, you get too fucked up. What I think is interesting is that you keep toying with this clean thing, back and forth. You want it, or you don't. You need to make a decision and make it all the way."

"It's not easy when I'm going to be dealing coke and my best friend is literally throwing pills at me."

"Stop being dramatic. You're not going to be dealing. And, dude, this has nothing to do with anyone else. You didn't plan to stay clean, and you know it. I knew it. Better to have those pills there when you needed them instead of going out and risk getting tainted shit…not that it really stopped you, I guess."

"Are you trying to say you were doing me a favor?"

"I was trying," Lonnie shrugged. "Clearly, it wasn't very effective."

"I don't want this for myself."

"You're getting all bent out of shape, Art. What's sobriety without a little relapse?"

"What does that mean?" I asked.

"I'm not saying it's not a big deal if that's truly what you want. It actually ties into a lecture I'm giving next week up in Boston. I'm explaining a concept I like to call 'failing into success'. Do you know what the number one failure of success is?"

"Is that a real question?"

"To understand the question, you need to look at the idea of success in a different light. People often attribute success to certain points. To graduate high school or college is a success. To get that promotion is a success. Making over six figures last year—which I did—is a success. Getting that contract, buying that car, moving into that house;

those are all successes. A lot of people would look at a person and say, 'Oh, look at all that success. They're pretty damn successful.' Those people, however, would be wrong. Do you know why?"

"Just tell me, Lonnie."

"Because they aren't looking at whether or not that success has been maintained. Now, do you know how to maintain success?" He didn't wait for me to answer. "Failure. It's like that idea of one step back, two steps forward. It's imperative to keep a pace like that because each step back solidifies the next two steps forward. It keeps in perspective the place you are coming from in relation to the place you're trying to go. We live in an age of instant gratification. Everything is me, me, me, now, now, now. That's how most people want their success, but success isn't about *achieving* that goal. Success is about *maintaining* that goal. The way you do that, is by failing sometimes, simply because it reminds us of why we were so thirsty for that success in the first place. You say you relapsed. I say you just added fuel to your sobriety."

Lonnie went back to his Mexican ravioli. I watched him, feeling both repulsed by his blatantly flawed reasoning and furious at my inability to pinpoint exactly how. I thought about my conversation with Jerry Grant only hours before, and I knew I was correct. But how was Lonnie wrong?

"Oh!" he said, dropping his fork. "I almost forgot." Lonnie wiped his clean hands on his napkin, ignoring the corners of his mouth that needed it. "So, I'm going out of town next week for those conferences. You remember that?"

"Yes, I'm driving you to the airport, teaching your class, and delivering your drugs."

"Exactly. Which, by the way, I have instructions written down for the pickup and deliveries. Don't let me forget."

"Don't worry."

"Anyway, I'll be gone from the sixteenth to the seventh, almost three weeks."

"That's exactly three weeks."

"While I'm gone," he ignored me, "I need you to watch Becca for me."

"What?" I squinted at him. "You mean, make sure she's not fucking around? I don't think—"

"No, nothing like that. Just watch her."

"What do you mean *watch* her? She's not your dog. She's a grown woman."

"She needs somewhere to stay from the twentieth to the twenty-seventh. Almost a week."

"That's literally a whole week, Lonnie. Your sense of time needs improvement. Also, you're out of your goddamn mind. Becca hates my guts."

"Look, she hates my guts, too, and I'm her boyfriend. Take it for what it's worth. Think of it as a good thing."

"And why doesn't she just stay in your house, exactly?"

"I'm having some remodeling done during that time that requires the electricity being turned off. I specifically scheduled it while I'd be gone, and she would be with her parents."

"So, why won't she be with her parents?"

"She hates them."

"I thought you just said that was a good thing."

"It's her parents. It's totally different." I attempted to protest, but he cut me off. "I know it's a pain in the ass, but please. Help a friend out." I sat contemplating for a moment.

"I get fifty percent of the money from the drops."

"Are you fucking kidding? What kind of deal is that?" he protested. "Thirty-five percent."

"Fifty."

"Forty."

"Fifty."

"Forty-five."

"Sixty."

"Goddammit, okay. Fifty-fifty split. I know women are expensive, but Christ."

"And," I continued, "I get to use your car while you're gone."

"My car?! But you hate my car!"

"Think of it as a good thing."

"Smartass."

"And now I need the instructions," I said.

"What instructions? Oh! Yeah. Here." Lonnie handed over a sealed white envelope. "I included my best methods for cutting it all, too. You should be able to double the product without losing much quality."

"Hold up. You never said anything about cutting it."

"It's standard practice, Art. You want to do this thing or not?"

"Fine," I said after glaring at him.

"Good. You're also going to need this." He reached into his pocket and handed me a small key fob. I studied its metal design, a circle with three X's in a triangular order and a square embossed in the center. "Make sure I get it back."

"I will."

"No, Arthur." I looked up in surprise at his use of my full name. Lonnie's eyes were wide and distressed. "You make sure. I mean it."

"I will, Lonnie."

The room felt incredibly still in my apartment as I took a seat on the couch. I hadn't stopped for the sake of stopping in quite a long time. In contrast to the constant movement and noise and clutter of living, I imagined this must be how it feels to meditate. I closed my eyes, sitting as motionless as possible, settling my breath.

"I believe you're supposed to repeat a mantra or something," said Huxley, facing me from atop the coffee table. "Or hum. Try humming."

"The point is to be quiet," I hinted. "To empty the mind of thoughts." I heard him laugh and opened my eyes. "What?"

"You'd be lucky to even get them organized."

"Maybe I'd be able to if I wasn't interrupted."

"The whole point of meditation is to calm yourself. It's not some magic trick for getting your life together."

"Just be quiet, Huxley. Okay?" He was silent, and I returned to my stillness.

"You're looking much better than the last time I saw you. Quite an experience, I must say."

"Yeah…" I looked down at the floor. "Thanks for sticking with me, for helping me through that."

"It was nothing," Huxley smiled.

"It was something," I said. "Thank you."

"Any time," he said. "And by any time, I mean please don't go on any more acid trips without warning me, for my sanity."

"Quiet, please," I said, closing my eyes once more.

"You should get those ashes out of the box," he said suddenly. "Where are you thinking to put them?"

"Huxley," I growled. "Why do you do this shit to me?"

"Because, deep down, you know you'd miss it if I didn't." Huxley gave me an amused stare that I couldn't return without a juvenile eyeroll.

A few minutes later I'd retrieved the box from the trunk of my car and was seated at the dining table, a pair of scissors in hand to cut the tape. I didn't move, however, staring down at the thing.

"What's the matter?" he asked beside the box.

"I'm not sure where to put it," I said. "Maybe I should just leave it in the box."

"I may be mistaken, but it seems that you've dealt with this for most of your life in a similar fashion. Ignore it, pretend it's not there, keep it boxed away."

"It's worked so far, hasn't it?"

"You think so?" Huxley questioned.

"Why do I need to do anything differently now? What difference will it make at all?"

"It may not make any difference. It may make all the difference in the world." Huxley took a step towards me. "It would be a change, and there would be a ripple."

"That doesn't sound like a good thing," I said.

"It may not be a good thing. But could it really be any worse?" he asked. "Go on, Arthur. Open it."

With a strong exhalation, I ran the blade of the scissors along the tape, the gap between the flaps appearing. I took the wooden container out, and after removing the bubble wrap, placed it on the table, the brass nameplate facing me.

"Who the devil is Ronald Giovanelli?" asked Huxley.

Who the devil, indeed?

CHAPTER NINE

There is something to be said for the history and significance of 'the meal', whether in social or domestic settings. Through the centuries, it has been over dining tables and spreads that countries were founded, plans to destroy them made, ideas born and aborted, relationships blossomed while others wilted. The social consumption of culinary creations has been a keystone in every culture in human history. Yet as grandiose as someone might describe, it was, and always would be, a bunch of people sitting in a room beginning the digestive process which ultimately leads to the shitter. Vivian smiled and shook her head when I pointed this out to her, and informed me that, despite the validity of my argument, I would be meeting her and two of her colleagues for dinner.

The restaurant she chose was called Ghiottone's, serving Italian cuisine just like someone's mama makes in the old country. It was lively with merry voices conversing, the clinking of flatware against porcelain, the chime of wine glasses and a tarantella wrapping softly around it all like magic. Vivian was in a modest cocktail dress, no jewelry save a white gold chain around her wrist from which dangled a breloque with a blue, inlaid sapphire. A man and a woman sat across from her, both failing at the attempt of dressing in standard with Vivian, and my first thought upon looking at them were of Jack Sprat and his wife. The nursery rhyme began bounding through my head in time to the music.

Vivian introduced me to Mr. and Mrs. Sprat who I discovered were writers/journalists/mudslingers for *Slander*, though they tried to denote our positions as equal. They talked fast in between mouthfuls of pasta and gulps of wine, occasionally dabbing at the corners of their mouths with the maroon linens. The only consolation to the sight of them was that they were exactly as I imagined they should look. The two took turns speaking, sometimes simultaneously.

"That Delilah Burnette," Mrs. Sprat continued after taking a bite of bread, "you know, the actress in *Cuffed*...no, you're right...not that great of a movie...But needless to say, Vivian, I heard through the grapevine that she's dating Caesar...You know, that one rapper with the teeth...I know, right? Of all people, I don't see how even he could scrape the bottom of the jar like that...What was that Mr. Kimble? What about a barrel? Anywho...That would be something you should look into, Vivian, since there aren't any pictures yet. But I'm not one to worry about details like that. Besides, you can never count on their publicists to talk. I'm not going to wait for someone else to beat me to the scoop though. I've already got a whole page about it written and ready to go. 'Caesar Cuffed by the *Cuffed* Star'...Yes, I thought so too...Just now! Needless to say, I think he's only doing it because of his recent breakup with January Winters. And you know, she's not waiting around either! Of course, she probably had another man in the bag before dumping Caesar. Not sure who yet, but I've got my suspicions. What, Vivian? I'm not telling who I think it is! A girl's got to have her secrets. But I hope it's Cliff Hanger. God, the glutes on him...I better stop before I have a hot flash. Haha! But needless to say, men are like that—no offense, boys—but it's like men always need somewhere to park their you-know-whats. And Caesar's no different, even though he probably needs a bigger parking space. Heehee! Oh, I'm bad, aren't I? Well, Delilah's probably just his rebound, anyway. She's not the type you want to get tied down to."

"But I thought Cliff Hanger was dating that Russian girl...the model...what's her name? That's right, Ivana Likitov," Mr. Sprat took over. "I thought they were down in Cabo or something just a few weeks ago. Scuba diving, I think it was...At any rate, I could have sworn they were just down there together, and there *are* pictures of that. Why, you took them, didn't you, Vivian?"

"Some of them," said Vivian, tugging at the corner of her linen.

"That's why it's such a scandal, of course!" Mrs. Sprat picked up. "Cliff Hanger just got back into L.A. with her from Cabo, and where was he found? Walking out of The Peninsula the same morning as Alexis Driver, who just so happened to have broken up with that other rapper Proxy last week. Needless to say..."

As the two jabbered on, Vivian kept flashing glances at me over the rim of her glass of water, an amusement taking shape on her lips as she recognized my lack of intrigue and mounting boredom. I watched past the two Sprats at the other patrons talking, laughing, debating, chewing, swallowing, repeating.

A young family, a man and wife with their two children, a boy and girl, entered the restaurant engaged in excited conversation with each other. Perhaps they felt invigorated by the closing in of the holiday season, perhaps it was the air of the downtown strip excited by imminent peace on earth and goodwill toward men. But something in their bodies, the movement and comfortability, the trust, told me it had been there all along. It was something I had experienced and built my world around in a life lost to the treacherous nature of human beings. The man held his little girl's hand, his other arm lightly around the waist of his wife, their son on her other side, his hand in hers as they went to their table. They were all in love, though not with each other, but with the sum of each other, and I continued to wonder if Julia had been right about love, about its inadequacy.

A lack of obnoxious noise being hurled from the Sprats snapped my attention back to the table. Three pairs of expectant eyes stared at me, Vivian's lacking the stupor of the others'.

"No...no," I said, concluding that a negative response was safest.

"I don't understand," said Mrs. Sprat. "You mean to say that you think Fletcher Price is going to live? But what for? What could he possibly have left to do with his life?"

"Ten years doing absolutely nothing but proving he's lost his touch," Jack Sprat added. "Called one of the greatest literary minds in modern history, and it's gone just like that." Mr. Sprat snapped his fingers for effect, however ineffectively. "Someone who can't admit when it's over, that's just a coward, plain and simple. What is that going to do for his legacy? Assuming he's got one worth saving, of course. The man's a fool. I don't care if it was his wife's death that made him crack…what was her name? Sandra? Susan?"

"Miriam," I said.

"Miriam! That's right…Miriam," said Mr. Sprat. Then lowering his voice, "You know, they say she went insane."

"If that were truly the reason," said Mrs. Sprat, "why wouldn't he have just said so? When you have a legitimate reason for failure, why not just embrace it? He can't even admit what the problem really is. He just keeps boozing it up and whoring around. I mean, a man of his age? Come on! It's no wonder he's in a coma."

"And now this supposed new novel he wants to publish…" He shook his head.

"Well, we all know it's going to be awful," Mrs. Sprat giggled. "Really, he's better off dying, for all our sakes."

"Don't you feel even a slight amount of pity for him?" Vivian asked. "Look at everything he's been through since his wife died. Think about how conflicted he must be."

"Of course, I felt a little pity at first," Jack Sprat said. "But after a decade, it's time to get the hell over it! Do what you do, and if you can't, then stop trying."

"What does it even matter," Mrs. Sprat concluded. "It's like I said in my article. Fletcher Price is dead, and nothing and no one is bringing him back to life."

"You wrote that article?" I asked, taking her back slightly at my sudden involvement in the conversation.

"Well…yes. Yes, I did." I flashed an unamused glance at Vivian who adjusted her silverware uneasily. "But I was under the impression that you didn't read our magazine, Mr. Kimble. That it was—beneath you." Mrs. Sprat giggled again like a fucking chimp.

"I don't, and it is." She jerked her head back indignantly at my response.

"Then perhaps it is Fletcher Price," Jack Sprat said. "Are you so deeply interested in him that you'd be willing to stoop so low?"

"Why, look there. It's Elaine Cunningham," Mrs. Sprat interrupted. "There at the door." She craned her neck to see, and curiosity moved their lips in silent question. Vivian only looked forward, avoiding my gaze as she sipped her water.

"I want to go say hello," said Mr. Sprat, wiping his mouth.

"Oh, no! Don't do that," chided Mrs. Sprat. "It's like watching some exotic species in the wild. Best to leave it alone and observe. Who knows what one might learn?" She giggled a third time at her poor excuse for humor. "What do you think she's up to?"

"Business," Jack Sprat snorted. "What else?"

"Couldn't be anything else. Needless to say, she's probably pulling the rug out from under yet another magazine and calling it acquisition." Mrs. Sprat's eyes rolled. "Better hope it's not your *Verb'd Magazine*, Mr. Kimble." Her eyes danced about my face, but I walled up any expression of thought, censoring my next words.

"Who is she?" I asked.

"One of the executives for Slander Media, of course. Nobody knows for sure what she does, but some people call her The Hawk."

Elaine Cunningham's stature was lengthened by her apparent confidence as she moved forward in resolute strides, powered by flexing calves, fueled by the combustion of purpose. Her face, the model of fearless repose, was uplifted to the light as she scanned her surroundings, an ownership of the scene taking hold. In an instant, the Italian ambience of food and family had been elevated with her arrival to an elegance of fine dining where one would have just tipped the valet, bribed the doorman, and felt a certain nudity without a string of pearls. For this woman, however, the valet's tip would have been the brush of her touch as she handed him the keys, the bribe a secretive smile, and she neither wore nor needed pearls.

Even with her signs of graceful aging, she was simultaneously beneath and above beauty, and in that realization was built a hurried and reluctant barrier of distrust within me. When she saw us at the table, she did not smile but acknowledged us with a nod of approval as if we were her subjects presenting the fruitful bounty of the year's harvest. Then she signaled to the hostess to wait, who did so obediently. The Sprats squirmed excitedly at her approach, though Vivian remained unmoving.

"Good evening," Elaine Cunningham greeted, posing in the aura of her status.

"Hello, Ms. Cunningham," Jack Sprat gurgled out from beneath her. "What a pleasant surprise to see you here."

"Is it?" She was not convinced. "Well, when the greater good calls, one must answer." Bright blue eyes fell on Vivian who returned a lackluster expression. "Though, I am surprised to see you, Ms. Ward. I was always under the impression you preferred the finer things." The two blue lights jumped to my face, narrowing in their analysis. "Then again..." A crimson smile made its appearance. "Elaine Cunningham. *Slander Magazine*." She extended a relaxed row of delicate fingers. I shook her hand without much response. "You are?"

"Arthur Kimble. *Verb'd Magazine*." At these words, Elaine's eyes remained unmoved, but their sultry mist cleared and the tendons in her neck ticked.

"So, you're Arthur Kimble. I've heard a thing or two about you. You're an artist, correct?"

"I'm primarily a writer, but yes, I do some artwork as well."

"Right, those short stories, 'The Adventures of Theodore Huxley'."

"That's right."

"Quite a little niche you've made for yourself," she said. "Tell me, how are things going with Jack Dorset? I heard it through the grapevine that he's been in poor health these days."

"You should do a little pruning. He's doing well."

"As well as an old man is expected to do..." A thin eyebrow twitched upward.

"I take it you don't know Mr. Dorset." I leaned back, taking in her analytic stare and returning it two-fold.

"No, but I know his son Stanley. Quite a robust character.

Wouldn't you agree?"

"Robust is—a word." Ms. Cunningham's lips curved again exposing a sliver of her polished teeth. A wave of her hand dismissed my implication.

"Semantics...I'm a businesswoman myself."

"But aren't you in the business of semantics?" I questioned.

"I am in the business of making money, Mr. Kimble. If we all worried over semantics, we'd be a bunch of starving artists." I couldn't tell if she laughed because the concept of being satisfied as a starving artist was absurd to her, or if she truly had that little regard for what she was selling. The Sprats chuckled along with her, though the shifts in their eyes revealed a lack of understanding and a subsequent nervousness. Vivian remained quiet behind the globe of her glass.

"Except for those of us who are not artists," I said.

"Pardon?"

"If you take away a businessman's business," I began, "then he is no longer a businessman, because he cannot of himself produce business. Take away an artist's art, and he will remain an artist because he will simply produce more art. They might both be starving, but only one of them remains the same." Through my peripheral, I caught the hint of a smile in Vivian's lips, but Elaine Cunningham left hers unrestricted.

"Spoken like a true idealist, Mr. Kimble. Your eloquence makes it almost forgivable."

"I guess it's a good thing I'm unrepentant," I replied, suddenly feeling the solidity of the chair I was seated in.

Silence descended uncomfortably for several moments, the Sprats' shifting eyes unsure of what to make of the exchange, and Vivian's never breaking from my face with a strange intensity. My fingers gripped like suctions to my glass, and for a moment, I imagined feeling the convex sides giving slightly under the pressure. Ms. Cunningham nodded as she digested the meaning of my words, her pupils dilating with a fierce, indiscernible concoction of thoughts.

"Are you here all alone?" asked Vivian, altering the course of conversation.

"I don't have the luxury, I'm afraid," she answered. "In fact, I've already kept them waiting far too long, and as we all know, time waits for no man."

"And a woman?" Vivian countered. Elaine raised her eyebrows, casually raining sulfur upon Vivian's head.

"A woman? A *real* woman waits for no man, either." Her eyes glimmered as she drove her words in before facing me again. "A pleasure to have met you, Mr. Kimble."

I nodded before she resumed her course behind the hostess into the adjacent dining area. The Sprats watched Elaine Cunningham move away until she was out of sight. I watched Vivian. Vivian watched the water lapping gently in her glass.

"Isn't she delightful?" marveled Jack Sprat.

To my relief, the dinner did not last much longer, and after a quick exchange of farewells, Vivian and I left the Sprats to their cannoli. But she was unnaturally quiet, her mind having seemed preoccupied with something since Elaine Cunningham had left our table. I questioned what it was, but Vivian shook her head, telling me nothing, and walked ahead into the parking lot. The jaws of frozen air bit our cheeks and snapped at our heels as we crossed the street to her car at the end of the block.

"What's the matter?" I called to her when I realized she was purposefully keeping pace ahead of me.

"I'm fine, Art." She was lying, and I knew it, and she knew I knew it. We'd had our spats before, but it was uncharacteristic of her to be evasive. I was left with no choice but to make my own guess, a guess formulated from words that had not stopped echoing since they'd been spoken.

"What did Elaine Cunningham mean?" I asked. Vivian stopped and turned back to me, her breath billowing.

"Mean about what?"

"When she said that a real woman waits for no man. What did she mean by that?" Vivian looked at the cars passing for a moment, the tip of her nose beginning to turn crimson.

"I don't know," she said with a laugh, looking at all else but me.

"Yes, you do," I said, and she exhaled in a gust of white as she conceded.

"I've been offered a promotion."

"Really? What kind of promotion?" I asked, attempting to mask the wariness in my tone.

"Photographic director…West coast office."

"Really?" I asked with a laugh. "What did they say when you told them no?" Vivian looked at me, a lack of certainty in her eyes. When she said nothing, I stopped smiling. "You didn't say no…Vivian, you're better than *Slander Magazine*. I've told you this a hundred times. It's one thing to be a photojournalist and just do the job, but to actually direct an entire department for that shit…That's completely different. It's like you'd actually be committing to everything they stand for, devaluing yourself the whole time."

"I told them I needed time to consider it."

"How much time did they give you?"

"Close of business tomorrow."

"That's not much time," I scoffed.

"They offered it to me last week."

"Last week?" I stared at her, disbelieving. "Is this why I didn't hear from you for days?"

"You've been dealing with everything on your own plate, Arthur. I didn't want to add unnecessary stress. There's a lot to consider."

"What's to consider?"

"I needed to think about it all clearly. I needed to think about how it affects me and if it supports my goals and what it would mean for us."

"And what would it mean?" I asked.

"Did you not just hear what I said? West coast office, Arthur. That's on the other side of the country. Jesus, we've been looking at houses! But then there's everything that happened the other night…" She finally made eye contact with me. "I didn't know what to do."

"Well, what do you think now?" We faced each other, the heat of our breath filling the space between us.

"This is the opportunity I've been waiting for since I graduated from college," she said stepping forward. "I've been wanting a position like this since I started this career, and I've worked my ass off for this publication."

"You've worked your ass off for *Slander*," I replied, my voice rising. "*Slander*!"

"Why does it matter if it's *Slander*?"

"Because it's *Slander*! They don't even have the decency to sugarcoat what they're about! You're so much better than that, Vivian! You should be working for a respectable magazine where your work will actually be appreciated for what it is!"

"A respectable magazine? You mean a magazine like *Verb'd*?"

"Yes! Like *Verb'd*. What's wrong with that?"

"*Slander* may not be the most upstanding magazine, and you're right. They don't sugarcoat it. They thrive off of unintelligent, simpleminded people. That's no secret. Everyone knows it, and they embrace it. Their bottom line is making money, just like every other goddamn business in the world, only they make it obvious. So, at the end of the day, they're just as honest—if not more honest—than *Verb'd Magazine* has ever been."

"*Verb'd Magazine*'s bottom line isn't money," I said.

"Arthur, wake up! If that was the case, then why are they firing people?" she asked. "Why are they cutting costs? They're no different!"

"They appreciate what I do. They appreciate art and creativity and intelligence."

"You really think that if you weren't profitable to them that you'd still have a job there? You think they would've kept renewing your contract year after year just because of your writing?" Vivian laughed with disbelief. "I go to work every day knowing that *Slander* doesn't appreciate what I do beyond dollars and cents. They don't care what kind of camera I use or what lenses I have or the hours I spend editing. They could find a thousand other people to do my job, but I don't need *Slander Magazine* just as much as *Slander Magazine* doesn't need me. No matter what, I am still a photographer."

"You're a fucking paparazzi." As the words left my mouth, I realized there was no undoing their repercussions. Vivian blinked with her lips parted, the dagger I'd stabbed her with inflicting both pain and shock.

"You think I'm just some paparazzi?" asked Vivian.

"I didn't mean that. I just meant—"

"I know what you meant, Arthur." Vivian stood with her arms limp, her mittened fingers pressed against her thighs. "It's okay though. I don't need you to see me as an artist for me to be one. I just wish that was something you would understand for yourself."

"What the hell does that mean?"

"Until you realize just how amazing of a writer you are and find your own worth, you will always need *Verb'd Magazine* more than they need you."

"That's not true," I snapped. "I'm not the one who wants to stuff my talents into a box for some shit publication! I'm not the one who talks about living up to my capabilities and then turns around to trade them for a bigger paycheck and a nicer office! And I can't believe you would use me and my life and my stress as an excuse to buy yourself time to figure out a way of justifying wanting the promotion!" I shook my head. "You know what, go ahead and be a sell out to *Slander*. Go on out to the west coast. Please! Then maybe you'll finally understand." I finished speaking and noticed the change in her expression as the recognition of a sudden abandonment or betrayal. Her eyes began to glimmer under the streetlights.

"I wasn't going to take that position, Arthur," said Vivian slowly. "I was going to tell them no, because I thought that it would break your heart for me to leave you. It would've broken mine. But it's like you said, it's not my responsibility to make sure you're okay." A crystal descended her cheek. "I thought for sure after everything we've been doing, after I thought we made it so clear to each other how we felt, that you wouldn't want me to go because of how much you love me. Not because of how much you hate *Slander*." She chuckled. "And now you still tell me to go. Arthur Kimble, I would love you as a storytelling garbage man just as much as I would love you as the most famous writer that's ever lived, because I don't love what you are. I love who you are, imperfections and all. But if your only concern with this promotion is how horrible you think *Slander Magazine* is, if you encourage me to do it just to teach me some kind of lesson, and you truly think that it will make me less of a person, then you don't love me like that. All the planning, all the talking, it's not actually something you want...Not with me anyway."

"Viv, that's not—"

"Don't try to convince me you do, because you'll only be trying to convince yourself, and I won't let you do that to either of us a second time."

"Vivian, I'm sorry."

The cavity in my chest felt as though it were collapsing, a feeling I'd experienced before and had promised myself I would never feel again. But it was too late to brace the walls now. Vivian closed the space between us, and the white fingertips of our breathing seemed to reach out and grasp one another in an interlocking collision. She rested her lips upon mine, firmly and sweetly, in a kiss that I had imagined before but had never experienced. A moment later, I felt her warm breath on my ear as she whispered to me, and then without hesitation she withdrew from my arms, quickly taking the remaining steps to her car before driving off.

Vivian didn't look back, and I wished I could thank her for it.

"What did you do after that?" asked Dr. Hollande, the pen in her hand hovering patiently over her writing tablet.

"I went home, went to bed. What else was there to do?"

"I was surprised when you called this morning," she said. "I didn't think you'd be coming back."

"I didn't, either. I still don't necessarily want to."

"Why did you?" she asked. I thought for a moment.

"I don't really know."

"This situation with the house...why didn't you tell her what it really meant to you?"

"I didn't want her to think I'm stuck in the past."

"It seems like she might think that anyway," she said. "Did you believe she wouldn't find out?"

"I don't know," I said. "Yes. I knew." Dr. Hollande took her glasses and wiped them with a handkerchief.

"Have you spoken to your wife since she took the papers?"

"I can't say it didn't cross my mind, but no. I haven't."

"Tell me about your marriage."

"What is there to tell?"

"There must be some reason why you didn't want to sign those papers, something good that you're holding onto. Tell me about the good parts. How did it all begin?"

"I don't see why it matters now."

"If anything, it will put us on the same page when we discuss your wife." Dr. Hollande returned the glasses to her face as she sank back into her chair, ready to listen. I inhaled then let my breath out slowly.

"It was New Year's Eve, 1999. I went to a bar with some friends, the one where we'd usually hang out. It was pretty packed that night. I think there was a band, and I vaguely remember the television being on. Everyone was having a good time. Then the countdown started, and we all hurried outside."

"Why outside?"

"The building that the bar was in had this clocktower on top of it, and everyone went out to watch it hit midnight and start chiming. I remember it was freezing, but everyone just huddled closer together trying to keep warm. That's when I met Julia."

"In the crowd?"

"She was right there next to me, and the people getting closer pushed us together. Everyone was looking up at the clock except for us. We saw each other, and it was…I don't know. We had a moment or whatever. Then the clock chimed, and everyone started cheering and shouting and hugging. Julia and I stood looking at each other though, as if our feet were rooted into that street. That's when she spoke to me."

"What did she say?"

"She said, 'Happy New Year'," I laughed. "And then I kissed her."

"That's quite amazing."

"Yeah, it was all right until she slapped me. Apparently, that whole moment had been a one-sided deal."

"Oh, my. So, she didn't like you?"

"She hated me."

"How did you end up getting married?"

"I didn't see her again for another three months, and then we ran into each other at the grocery store where we instantly recognized each other. I apologized, she apologized, and things just developed from there. By the end of the year, she was pregnant with Ryan, we got married. Julia dropped out of school, and we had Abi, and then…It's funny," I said, looking up at Dr. Hollande. "Sixteen years of marriage, and it all began and ended with a slap in the face."

"That's an interesting way of viewing it."

"I don't really see another way."

"Well, it seems to me that there's more than that moment for you. What was your marriage like?"

"It was good. I loved her. I loved being married to her. It was everything I'd hoped it would be. I guess Julia didn't feel that way, but I just never knew it."

"Is it possible that she did feel that way at some point?"

"I'd like to think so."

"Did she ever tell you she was unhappy?"

"Not until year fourteen. I think, in retrospect though, it was during my first year at *Verb'd* that things started changing."

"How so?"

"Julia used to brag to people about how talented a writer and an artist I was, about how I was going to be known by the world someday. She'd even say it to me when I doubted myself. She believed in me—up until then."

"Why do you think your career decision affected her belief in you?"

"Julia wanted me to take a job offer I'd gotten from a much more profitable and popular magazine. She felt that my choice was selfish and was going to ruin my career which, in turn, would be detrimental to the family."

"So, knowing that she didn't approve, you chose that path anyway."

"Stupid, right?"

"I didn't say that."

"But you're thinking it."

"Not at all. I think you made the decision to go with *Verb'd* because you felt it was a better fit for you and what you wanted for your career. Am I right?"

"*Verb'd* had always been different to me. It stood out because it was unique in what it delivered and what it represented. It appealed to me, and when I was offered a contract and an office, when I sat in that room with Jack Dorset and he told me why it is he gets up every day, I knew I couldn't turn it down, despite the money *Slander* was offering. Any other choice seemed like a commitment to misery."

"After you made your move, what happened between you and Julia?"

"She..." I shook my head, not wanting to revisit a past I'd spent so much time stuffing down into a bottle. "At first she was supportive of me. Then after a year or two, she became distant, uncaring about my writing. She was cold; told me I was letting myself down and, in turn, letting down her and the kids. Then a few years ago, I guess she just couldn't keep it in anymore. She told me I was a failure, that I'd failed her and our children, that I would never be anything but a pawn, that my work was worthless. She also informed me that I was an absentee father, that the work I'd committed to had become more important than them. That was the first time she told me she wanted a separation."

"What did you do?"

"I begged her to stay. I promised I would change. I told her I would be different. All the shit the experts tell you not to do. I convinced her—or convinced myself, I guess—that life would be better, and the man she fell in love with, the man she believed in, would return. Not long after that, she met someone else. Julia kept it secret for a long time, but some things you can't hide forever."

"You caught her in the act?"

"No…" I took a deep breath and exhaled. "You know, before I met Julia, I'd been on my own and was fine with it. Happy even. But once we were together, I started to need her. Then on that day, when I discovered what she was doing…I'd never wanted to cease existing more in my life."

"What did your children make of it all?"

"They were aware we were having problems. They're smart. Kids in general are pretty intuitive about things like that. I just wish we could have talked it over, to at least try to make them understand that we would still be there for them. It's been seeming more and more lately as though Julia wants them to think I don't care, or that I don't want them around. Sometimes I think she even tries to convince *me* of that."

"Why do you think she would want that?"

"I don't know. It just feels that way."

"Is she ever successful?"

"I think with Ryan she might be. I don't know about Abi."

"What about you?" she asked. I looked at the slate green wallpaper, the corner of it starting to peel at the ceiling.

"I realize nobody has this parenting thing down pat, and I don't expect perfection from myself, but when all I can do is try my best, she acts like it's nothing. She treats it like I'm acting out of obligation or guilt. The truth is that I try because, of all the things that could possibly go wrong in this whole goddamn thing, I refuse to let my children ever question or doubt my love for them. I'm not an especially good person, but no matter what I've done, I've always cared. That's why I went back on Saturday to see Abi in the show again."

"Why do you think that?" Dr. Hollande asked.

"Think what?"

"That you're not a good person."

"Because I'm not. I don't do things right."

"Everybody else makes mistakes all the time. Why shouldn't you be allowed to?"

"I'm not everybody else."

"Why should you raise the standards for yourself higher than the rest of the world's?"

"Maybe I didn't raise my standards. Maybe the rest of the world just lowered theirs."

Dr. Hollande wore shoes with only the slight indication of a heel that had tread countless miles. With her legs crossed, her right foot moved up and down lazily and the fading of its black, leather tip was clear evidence of something that my mind couldn't seem to identify.

"Who do you try to emulate, Dr. Hollande?" I finally asked.

"Pardon?"

"Everyone has someone they want to be like, to some degree. Or maybe you did when you were studying to become a doctor, before that maybe, when you were a kid. Who was it for you?"

"I have a rule, Arthur. If any of my clients ask me a question about myself, they must also answer the same question. Fair enough?" I nodded, and she looked off in reminiscence. "I decided I wanted to become a doctor in 1994. I was just in my late teens and had started watching *The X-Files* on television. Of course, my parents didn't want me to watch it because they felt all shows like that were garbage. So, my friend Valerie who was allowed to watch it would record the shows on VHS, and when I came over to her house, we'd watch the tapes. I was always fascinated by Agent Scully. She seemed so…so powerful to me, much more than Agent Mulder, because she was never easily convinced of anything. She was always so skeptical, and her skepticism pushed her to look deeper. I gravitated to that because in my household growing up, we didn't venture outside of things that were comfortable. Thinking beyond what I was told was as exciting as—I don't know—stealing a candy bar from the gas station. When I was young, I wanted to be like Agent Scully. I wanted to be a doctor who looked for answers to questions that people don't, won't, or simply haven't thought to ask."

"A psychiatrist is a far cry from an FBI agent isn't it?"

"I like the thrill of finding answers to the unknown, and the human mind is like the final frontier. The FBI has no jurisdiction there." She smiled as she rested her chin on her fist. "Your turn."

"It doesn't matter," I said quietly.

"We made an agreement, Arthur. A question for a question."

"It doesn't matter anymore."

"Why not anymore?"

"Because he isn't the person I thought he was. It turned out that who I wanted to be like wasn't even real at all. So, it doesn't matter."

"Agent Scully was a fictional television character."

"This isn't a fictional character," I said.

"Then, who is this person?"

"Let's just say it was someone very famous. Someone beyond famous. He was truly great once."

"And now he isn't?"

"No. He's not. Not to me, anyway."

"Why not?"

"I suppose," I began with a sigh, "I don't know. Because he stopped being great one day. I've found it difficult to believe that being great is something that simply ends though."

"You believe that a great person once great must always be?"

"It sounds like a pretty obtuse way to look at the whole thing, but I don't know, honestly. Maybe."

"What is greatness to you, Arthur?"

"What is greatness to me?" Dr. Hollande inclined her head as she removed her glasses. "Greatness is...too many things to narrow down."

"Give me a couple ideas of what it is to you then. Perhaps list a few people you think are great."

"I don't know. Dr. King. Nelson Mandela. Harriet Tubman. Ghandi. You know, the usual."

"All right, and what do these people have in common? Why are they all—equally yoked, let's say—with greatness, in your opinion?"

"Because they all endured incredible hardship. They were oppressed. Misunderstood. Persecuted. Through it all they maintained their dignity, even to death, and the world was better for it. Granted, they didn't live their lives perfectly, but nobody does. And in the face of their struggles, their self-worth remained intact."

"What I'm hearing is that your personal definition of greatness is the endurance of hardship coupled with maintaining one's dignity for the outcome of a positive impact in the world." I shrugged and nodded affirmatively. The arm of her glasses settled on her cheek. "All right. Now, with that being said, do you want to be great like those people?"

"I don't know. I suppose. It's a nice thought. Sure." I leaned forward, folding my hands over my lap. "You've likely heard that quote from Shakespeare: some are born great, some achieve greatness, and others have greatness thrust upon them."

"Yes."

"But he never said anything about the people who give away the greatness they were born with, or who grow bored with the greatness they've achieved, or who fumbled the greatness that was thrust upon them. We all want to be great, Dr. Hollande, but some of us can't be. If we all were, there wouldn't be anything great about it. There have got to be the screw ups. There have got to be the failures and the hypocrites and the cowards and all the rest. Otherwise, none of that greatness would matter at all."

"Do you think we all can't be or that not all of us choose to be?"

"I don't think we all *should* be. I think everyone has their moment to be, but all greatness comes with a price that most aren't willing to pay, and perhaps that's for the better."

"The price being what? Hardship?" she asked. I nodded again. "Do you feel that's a price you're willing to pay?"

"Whether I'm willing or not, it doesn't mean I should."

"Whether you're willing or not, it doesn't mean you shouldn't. Are you trying to paint your lack of willingness as a sacrifice for the greater good?"

I sat silently across from Dr. Hollande, looking at her petite body appearing to be swallowed by the shoulders of her chair. She was perhaps a few years or so younger than I, but even being younger, she must have known something by now about adversity. She was likely from a more conservative family, probably had two old parents shuffling around together in their house still, probably had a boyfriend with a stable job, maybe even a nice savings accumulated over the years. Dr. Hollande was likewise a person who seemed knowledgeable in her field of work, and not purely from college textbooks or professorial lectures.

For her, my words were no mystery. Her mind could tread the trails my thoughts were blazing without getting winded, and she likewise appeared one step ahead of me at all times. Dr. Hollande, I reasoned, was a woman who had experienced life with her eyes open. However, I wondered if she was the type to pay the price or perhaps forego greatness altogether so that she might instead see, and in seeing, understand.

"Sure," I answered finally, exhaling a sigh. "Why not?"

CHAPTER TEN

It's strange to think that all the people who existed over the past several thousands of years were working towards the creation of what we know as the modern world. Of course, most of them weren't thinking about this at all and still don't. People just want to live, and it's for this reason that there has been a history of compromise and cooperation. In general, people will follow the rules of the social contract, the original rules being cut and dried: don't murder and don't steal. Simple enough. Of course, as societies grew, things became a bit more complicated. Don't sleep with the rainmaker's wife. Don't graze your goats on your neighbor's lawn. Initially, these were understood agreements with equally understood consequences. After the invention of writing, these rules became laws often chiseled into some giant rock for all to see.

Over millennia, however, there have remained the existence of unwritten rules. Do not sit at the head of a table that isn't yours. Always say 'please' and 'thank you'. Don't park your car or camel in someone else's parking spot. And never under any circumstances mess with the radio if you're not the driver.

"Unless the driver only has a learner's permit," I argued, pressing the scan button.

"You're making that up, Dad," said Ryan. "I'm driving. I'm the one in charge of the radio."

"I'm older." I watched Ryan roll his eyes in response. "Listen, I control the radio on the way there, and you control it on the way back. Deal?"

"Fine."

"Your focus should be on the road anyway."

"I focus better with music on," Ryan said.

"There is music on."

"When there's good music on," he corrected.

"There's nothing better than the blues and classic rock," I informed him. "Nothing."

"You've been listening to classic rock since before it was classic. Try something new for a change."

"When we're heading back." Ryan sighed and remained quiet. "How many hours of driving time do you need?"

"I don't know," he shrugged.

"Forty-something?"

"I don't know."

"Where's the paperwork?" I asked.

"I don't know."

"Do you even want to have your license?"

"Mom wants me to get it so she can send me on errands instead of doing them herself," said Ryan.

"You don't know that," I said.

"She told me, Dad."

"Okay, but still…Do you want to have a driver's license?" Ryan gave me a sideways glance.

"It doesn't matter what I want," he said.

"Sure, it does."

"Okay, then if it does, and I don't want one, will you take me home instead of making me drive you to the middle of nowhere?"

"It's not the middle of nowhere. It's Annapolis. Besides, you always liked my car before. Don't you like being behind the wheel?"

"No. I don't. Why couldn't we take Uncle Lonnie's car? It drives itself."

"That would defeat the purpose," I told him.

"Can't I just wait until I'm eighteen?"

"No."

"Why not?"

"Because you're right, what you want doesn't matter," I said, "and you're going to drive whether you like it or not."

"Figured."

"But I still want to know whether you want a license or not." Ryan squeezed the steering wheel tightly.

"Yes, but not to be everyone's chauffeur. Why do you even need to go to Annapolis?"

"I'm interviewing someone."

"Couldn't they just fly you there instead of making you drive five hours each way?"

"That would be a waste of money. Besides, they're not making me drive five hours each way. They're making you drive five hours each way." I smiled, finding a childish enjoyment in watching his irritation. "Watch this truck, he's signaling…"

"I can see, Dad."

It was a bright blue day, and were it not for all the bare trees, one might have thought it was summer. Ryan put on his sunglasses, and I considered how much he could pass as an adult. There was as much concern in that thought as there was pride.

"When did you start getting into graffiti?" I asked.

"It's called street art," he corrected.

"Okay, when did you start getting into street art?"

"I don't know," he shrugged. "A couple of years ago."

"You know, I kind of regret having interrupted what you were doing behind the school. I would've liked to see it completed." Ryan glanced at me, trying to hide his surprise.

"But it's illegal."

"You said it washes off, right? It's not hurting anybody," I said. "Have you taken any pictures of the ones you've finished?"

"Yeah, a few."

"I'd like to see them sometime."

"Okay," Ryan nodded slowly. "Sure." His jaw relaxed a bit, and

I noticed his thumb tapping to the beat of the song.

"You like this song?"

"Who is it?"

"The Rolling Stones," I said. "This one is called 'Sympathy for the Devil'. Like it?"

"It's not bad," he admitted.

That felt like a win to me.

The guard rails whipped by like snakes chasing the trees and shrubbery. In the distance, the faint outline of mountains slowly altered along in rambling inclines and declines. I was rarely in the passenger seat, and it seemed a new world was passing us by. The sky was broader and more freeing than one could imagine. There were living things still vibrant and thriving despite the impression of death and hibernation that winter can leave. And Ryan was there.

"Take this exit," I said almost a hundred miles later.

"Need to use the bathroom?" Ryan asked. I said nothing and directed him about half a mile up the road. The large sign for Rex's Wash & Dine peered over the treetops, exactly where it was supposed to be.

"Let's get a car wash," I said with a smile.

"Now? We still have a lot of driving to do. Wouldn't it be better to wait until we're back home?"

"I heard they have great burgers here."

"I'm not hungry."

"You will be," I assured him.

After directing Ryan to back the car into the parking spot three spaces from the far left, we got out and entered through the glass double doors. A young lady with hair extensions and long pink nails was standing at the counter just ahead, her darkly lined eyes looking beyond us toward the parking lot.

"Welcome to Rex's Wash & Dine," she greeted, still looking past. "What you want today?"

"I'll have a double cheeseburger with fries and a Coke," I said.

"Only Pepsi products," she said flatly.

"Oh. Well, I'll just stick with water then. What about you,

Ryan?"

"I told you, I'm not hungry," he said.

"He'll have a cheeseburger and fries," I told her. "Also, I need a car wash."

"Basic, deluxe, or premium?" she asked.

"The la suprema wash, please." The lady finally looked at me with a cold stare.

"Where's your car?"

"Three spaces from the left," I answered. Her eyebrow rose.

"Keys?" She asked. I held my hand out to Ryan, and the keys gave out a muted jingle as they hit my palm.

"Here you go," I smiled. She studied the ring, counting the keys, six in total, then ran her thumb over the single key fob. A friendly smile suddenly came over her face.

"Your order will be right out. Please, seat yourselves."

Ryan and I looked around at the empty diner.

"Hope we can find a seat," he said.

ARTHUR KIMBLE w/ P.J. GORING
ANNAPOLIS, MD - NOV. 20

ARTHUR KIMBLE: This really is a special occasion. You don't do many interviews, do you?

P.J. GORING: Not usually, no.

A.K.: I'm sure you're regularly getting a lot of offers and requests. If you don't mind my asking, why did you take this one?

P.G.: I don't know. It just felt right.

A.K.: You generally live out of the limelight. You even requested no pictures for this interview. It seems that private lifestyle is craved by a lot of high-profile individuals. How do you make that work?

P.G.: Well, it really comes down to making a decision. Do you want to be part of the crowd, or do you not? It doesn't always work for everyone. Some people need that kind of connectivity to others. I'm not one of those people.

A.K.: Do you think that it's your outside-looking-in position that helps you understand and write about people, making your characters so relatable?

P.G.: Maybe. I never thought about it.

A.K.: Where do you go—either physically or mentally—for inspiration?

P.G.: I wouldn't necessarily say that I go anywhere. I find that I'm pretty much always in that mode. It's turning it off for a rest that requires going somewhere else. That's the harder work, I feel, reining in the mind to take it easy.

A.K.: Do you feel it's always been that way, or did you need to work up to that point?

P.G.: It certainly took a lot of work. Don't get me wrong, just because I'm in that mode doesn't mean it's effortless. I wasn't always a good writer. I became one through trial and error. [*laughs*] There are some bafflingly horrible works in my collection.

A.K.: When did you first begin writing?

P.G.: When I was a teenager. Some, not a lot. Certainly not anything expansive. Honestly, I even hated reading. I never would have seen myself as a career author, much less a successful one.

A.K.: What do you consider your biggest success as a writer?

P.G.: Every time I get through the first three quarters of writing a book. [*laughs*] That's the toughest hurdle, to me anyway. So, overcoming that is the key. Sure, on paper, you'll think that book sales are what equates to success. For the industry, you'd be correct. For me, not so much.

A.K.: How difficult was the process of writing your first novel *Almond Joy*?

P.G.: No more or less difficult than writing any of my other novels. There were differences in my writing environment that didn't help, but the environment isn't everything. You just have to learn to tune things out sometimes. I wrote the first half of that book in prison, so, take that as you will.

A.K.: Wait—you were in prison when you started writing that?

P.G.: Yes, I was in Miami-Dade County Jail for six months.

A.K.: Wow. I don't recall your ever mentioning that to anyone before.

P.G.: Nobody has ever asked the right questions.

A.K.: Why were you incarcerated?

P.G.: For dealing heroin. I was an addict as well, so I really don't regret getting caught. It got me clean. If I hadn't been arrested, I doubt that you and I would be talking right now.

A.K.: You graduated magna cum laude from Howard University. You had already written several excellent essays on prominent literature. How did you end up dealing heroin in Florida?

P.G.: That's the thing about a drug. It doesn't care where you went to school, what kind of successes you've had, what family you come from. You could say it's very pro equal opportunity. Life can be tough on top of it. One thing leads to another, and you can find yourself in places you never thought you'd be, doing things you never thought you'd do.

A.K.: How has life been tough for you?

P.G.: In the way it is for most people. We do stupid things. I wasn't what people might consider set up for success. My father committed suicide and left my family with nothing. I had to drop out of school to take care of my mother until she died of cancer in '87. I also fell in love and broke a few bones when I landed. [*laughs*] All the things that make for a bad story.

A.K.: How much of your own life and experiences do you use in your writing?

P.G.: Some of it. It's my lessons learned that I've used more than actual events.

A.K.: Write what you know, correct?

P.G.: Yes, you can write what you know and maybe teach something. But you can also write what you don't know and learn something. I've found the latter to be the more rewarding.

"Want any more lemonade?" asked P.J.

"Sure," I said. "Ryan?"

"Yes, please."

"I think it's pretty neat bringing your son along. Do you two do this often?" The lemonade glugged into the tall glasses on the kitchen table.

"No, actually this is the first time. Ryan needs the road hours to get his driver's license."

"Oh, exciting," said P.J. "Are you looking forward to the freedom of the road?"

"I'm pretty sure I'm just going to end up driving everyone around," said Ryan with a frown.

"Who is everyone? Do you have siblings?"

"Yeah, I have a younger sister. She's a freshman in high school this year."

"What about you? When will you be graduating?"

"This spring," he answered.

"Got any plans for after that?" P.J. asked.

Ryan shrugged. "I guess go to college. I don't really know what I want to do."

"What do you like to do?"

"I don't know…I like making street art. But you can't make a lot of money from that."

"I beg to differ. I've seen some pretty amazing street artists get some high paying commissions."

"But they're really good at it," said Ryan.

"Then be really good at it," he smiled.

Once we'd finished our lemonades, we said goodbye to P.J. Goring and climbed into the car. Ryan's face bore the resemblance of those old paintings of Moses coming down from Mt. Sinai. There was a glow about him, as though the light bulb of an idea had suddenly been turned on.

"What are you thinking?" I asked as we pulled back out towards the highway.

"I don't know," he shrugged. "He was pretty cool."

"Yeah, he was, wasn't he?" I agreed.

The clouds ahead of us were darkened, the sunlight that brightened our journey to Annapolis snuffed away. Ryan finally had his turn manning the radio, and I was surprised to hear a familiar song.

"Is this Alphaville?" I asked.

"Who is Alphaville?" Ryan scrunched up his face. I said nothing until I watched Ryan switch on the wipers as thin drops pricked against the windshield.

"One more," I said.

"One more what?"

"Turn it up to medium," I instructed.

"It's not raining that hard," he said, gesturing to the droplets.

"Still, turn it up to medium."

"*I'm* driving, Dad," Ryan said, the elements of a smile combining on his lips. Seeing that, I couldn't say no.

We discovered that the low setting on my wipers kept time to 'Forever Young' by Jay-Z, and honestly, I couldn't have been happier about it.

Then I remembered the cocaine in the trunk. It's amazing how your mind can ruin anything.

Lou Korkoran lived closer to the heart of the city and higher up than I'd have ever been willing to pay for. He was the database manager for a local corporate law office which he bragged represented several multi-million-dollar companies, all of whose confidential information remained secure because of him. I had always found Lou to have a bit of an ego for his profession, but I supposed, so did the rest of us. It was for this reason that during monthly poker games, we never discussed religion and, especially lately, politics.

"Pair of aces, king high!" Lou boasted after tossing his cards face up on the poker table.

"Jesus, Lou. That's three hands in a row," Samwell observed to my left. "Are you playing an honest game here?"

"I've never cheated in my life," Lou defended with his hands raised.

"You don't have to lie. Your wife's not here," said Sam with a response of laughter.

"What's the deal with monogamy, anyway?" asked Daryl, seated across from me. "Who the fuck invented that shit?"

"A woman," said Lou as he stacked his chips. "No man in his

right mind would come up with that idea. It's your deal, Tony."

"I don't know. I kind of like knowing that when I come home, I have someone to be there," said Tony as he shuffled the deck. "I mean, being on the hunt is fun and all, but don't you guys ever get tired of that?"

"What the hell are you talking about?" asked Daryl. "Marriage was obviously designed by women for women as a way to control men."

"Obviously," said Lou.

"Another perk of being a gay man," said Sam with another chorus of laughter.

"That must be why they call it being gay," laughed Daryl.

"What do you think, Arthur?" asked Phil. "You've been over the fence and back again. Which side has the greener grass?" The table looked closely at me.

"I don't know. I'd say they're both green."

"Yeah, but which is greener?"

"I don't know," I shrugged. "Everyone's got a different yard, so what's greener for me might not be greener for someone else."

"Some people have trees so it might be shady," Phil mocked. "They might not even have grass. They might have that rocks and gravel shit."

"He's got a point, Phil," Sam interjected with a laugh. "Everyone's life is a little different."

"Everyone's wife is a little different," Daryl chuckled.

"You know what my wife told me she wants for Christmas?" Lou asked us. "She asked me if I could get a mosquito net for our bed."

"A mosquito net? What the fuck for?" asked Phil. "This isn't the Amazon."

"She said because it looks romantic." The table suddenly froze for a moment then burst into laughter and protests against the idea. "I know! That's what I said."

"What the hell does it matter once you're inside the net?!" cried Tony as he dealt the next hand. "It'll just look like a net! There's nothing romantic about it!"

"So, are you going to?" Sam asked.

"Going to what?"

"Are you going to get the net?" Daryl clarified.

"Of course, I am. I'll be getting laid every day at least till New Year's." Tony finished dealing, and the room quieted down with our focus on the cards.

"Hey, Daryl. Are you still having your New Year's party?" asked Phil, placing his cards face down.

"I don't know. New Year's is starting to feel old…two cards."

"What do you mean?"

"It's just all the new beginning shit. Everyone makes resolutions, everyone acts like life is going to be different. But we're all going to wake up with a hangover the next morning, just like last year, and everything will seem exactly like it was before. Other than the calendar, what separates the last day of the year from the first day of the year?"

"I don't know. The solar system, maybe," Tony said.

"Fuck the solar system. Who gives a shit that we made it around the sun? Again."

"I just wish it didn't get so damn cold," said Lou. "One card…I was walking down Main Street the other day and this woman jogged by and accidentally bumped into me. Her nipples were so hard I thought she drew blood."

"Shut up, Lou," said Phil with a laugh. "You're so full of shit."

"Did you hear about that guy who got hit by a bus downtown last night?" Sam asked us before knocking on the table.

"Yeah. It was some homeless guy, wasn't it?"

"They don't know who he is. The guy was too mangled up to identify. And he didn't have any teeth apparently."

"Jesus Christ," Lou muttered. "That's a shitty way to go."

"Better than lying around waiting for it," said Tony. "Like that writer who's been in a coma for a couple months or however long."

"Fletcher Price?" Lou asked.

"Yeah. That must really suck," Daryl agreed.

"He's in a coma. How the hell does that suck?" Tony asked. "I heard that it's some of the best rest a person can get."

"But can't you still hear people around you or something? Phil, you're a doctor," said Sam. "Is that true?"

"Phil's a dentist. He doesn't know about comas."

"He's still a doctor! Phil, tell us what you know about comas. Anything?"

"Well," Phil began, "when someone is in a coma that hasn't been medically induced, it means that there has been some type of damage to either the cerebral cortex, which is the whole outer portion of the brain, or the part of the brainstem called the reticular activating system which regulates your waking and sleeping. But the damage could be caused by a number of things, not just injuries from a car crash." He stopped speaking and looked at us all listening intently. "That's all I know."

"I'm confused," Daryl began after a moment. "So, you're not a dentist?"

"Hey, Phil, can you still get a boner when you're in a coma?" asked Tony.

The arrival of Lou's wife an hour later signaled the end of poker night. I'd completely forgotten about it until Sam showed up at my front door ready to go. I'd almost had the courage to decline, but I felt as though if I did, I might be giving away something. What, I had no idea.

"You were pretty quiet tonight," Samwell commented as we arrived back at my apartment. "How are you feeling?"

"I feel all right. Didn't lose much money tonight, so that's a plus."

"I sure as hell didn't win any." He smiled. "Sometimes I wonder about Lou. Honestly, if the whole thing was rigged, I'd still probably go play. He cracks me up."

"Yeah."

After a minute of quiet, Sam watched me intently. "We haven't talked in a while," he said. "How have you been doing? Anything new happening?"

"Not really. I did get that interview finished up today."

"Good. How was it?"

"Did you know he was in prison?"

"Who is Ronald Giovanelli?" Sam asked unexpectedly, staring down at the urn in front of the television. "Is that someone's ashes?"

"Oh, that. It was an incorrect delivery. I'm trying to track down the family. It's been weird. But yeah, they're ashes."

"That's fucking trippy to have some unknown dead person's burnt up remains just chilling in your living room. Borderline creepy."

"It wasn't until you put it that way," I said, taking a seat on the couch. Sam followed suit on the other end.

"So, other than the random dead guy in your apartment, how are you?" He peered at me closely.

"I'm all right," I began. "I feel like the second half of this year has flown by. It's hard to make sense of everything."

"What's got your head twisted?" asked Sam. I lit a cigarette and blew a large cloud of smoke. "Have you been writing?"

"Outside of the interview, no," I confessed after a pause, shaking my head soberly. "No, I can't manage to get myself there. I've got ideas in my head, but they just aren't transmitting to my hands."

"What about Huxley?" he asked. "I don't mean to sit here stressing you out, but you've only got a couple weeks to go. A year ago, that wouldn't have been shit. But now…" Samwell sighed.

"Now isn't a year ago. Nothing is what it was a year ago. Neither one of us is who we were a year ago."

"There's nothing wrong with taking a break."

"I just took one, Sam. After so much time without any kind of resolution, I have a hard time believing that what I need is a break."

"That wasn't really a break though, was it?" asked Samwell. "I know you've been telling everybody that you went on a sabbatical to clear your head and find some new inspiration, but that's clearly not what happened. Something else went on at rehab. You don't have to tell me what it is."

"I hadn't planned to."

"That's fine. I just want you to realize that, whatever it is, you don't have to deal with it alone."

"Isn't that what therapy's for?"

"Therapy," he said, crossing his legs, "is effective to some degree...but you mean to tell me that you've been completely honest with them? Truly?"

"I've told her the truth."

"All or some of it?" he asked, pausing. "Does she know that you're an alcoholic or that you were popping pills? Does she know about your suicide attempt and your rehab?"

"She knows enough," I said. Samwell nodded and turned away. "You're disappointed."

"No," he said with a smile. "I don't need to waste my breath telling you things you already know. All I want is for you to be okay, Art. You're my friend, and any decision you make to get yourself well, I support. No matter what that is."

"I feel like you're hinting at something," I said after taking a drag. "I'd prefer you to be straightforward with me." Samwell leaned in and cupped his hands together in thought.

"Arthur, it's important to know when to walk away from something that's getting the best of you. Some things you can't beat. Some fights you can't win. But that doesn't mean you have to go down swinging."

"Say what you mean, Sam."

"Do what's best for you, whatever that is. That's all I'm saying. Fuck all the rest."

It's difficult in this day and age to find a friend like Samwell. Friendship takes time and patience; it takes understanding but also honesty. You have to be willing to piss off the other person if it means saying what they need to hear. Frankly, friendship sucks sometimes. It can be painful just as much as it can be rewarding.

As Sam was this kind of friend to me, I wondered if I'd ever been that kind of friend to anyone. I couldn't think of a single person whom I was friends with that I was willing to give brutal honesty, or that I was willing to drop everything to be there if they needed me. I considered that perhaps not everyone is capable; that a true friend like Sam must likewise understand that there will always be an imbalance of give and take. To give is freeing, no matter the reward. To take without giving, however, is a crime, and I was guilty.

"I'm tired," I said finally. Samwell looked down at the floor before rising to his feet. He hugged me tightly before leaving. Even his hugs were genuine. What an asshole.

"Is it truly that difficult?" asked Huxley.

"Is what that difficult?"

"Writing. I understand there are times of famine, yet we've never starved before."

"If I could explain it, I would," I told him. "At this point, the thought of sitting down at the computer or with a pen and paper gives me anxiety. I don't know what the hell I'm going to do. Creation is a lot of pressure."

"Is it?" he asked. "As I recall, our first encounter was quite easy. You simply thought of me and poof, there I was."

"That was a long time ago."

"Yes, it was, and you were a boy then. Now, you're a grown man with decades of writing experience and a perfected writing process. Something has changed."

"My head just isn't there, Hux."

"Where the devil is it, then? I'm a character in need, Arthur. I've been sitting, waiting for nearly a year to have some development, some excitement, and you can't explain to me why?"

"What do you know about writing?" I asked. "You don't carry the burden of trying to make something out of nothing. You don't have to choose and wonder and experiment and start all over if it doesn't work."

"When did it become such a burden? Was it when Julia left you? Was it before that, when you started drinking and gobbling up those little pills like candy?"

"I don't need a lecture from my own character."

"You need something from someone. Here I am, and this is what I've got."

"Then go away, because I don't want it!" I yelled. "Go away, Huxley!"

"You will have to face these realities—"

"Leave me alone, goddammit!" I slammed my palm down on the coffee table, seemingly vaporizing Huxley from the room. My cigarette crackled and snapped as I relighted it a few moments later, and somehow, I was already craving the next one.

CHAPTER ELEVEN

The year prior, the family had gathered at my mother's for Thanksgiving, Ryan and Abi and me, my Aunt Beth and Uncle Simon, my three cousins Alan, Christy, and Alexa, and their kids. It had been the first time since Julia and I had separated that I'd seen or spoken to my relatives, but they never brought up the fact that we were there minus one. Everyone was smiling and laughing, including Ryan. We filled ourselves to bursting with my mother's maple bacon turkey, my aunt's garlic mashed potatoes, and after the kids went to bed, we sipped on my uncle's apple pie moonshine. It had been my mother's secret weakness, that moonshine, and before long she was laughing herself to the floor, the brightest smile I'd seen upon her beautiful, wizened face in years. The next morning, we were all surprised when my mother wasn't up before the sun, preparing a breakfast feast. We stayed quiet, however, joking that she'd finally sipped a little too much. But as one hour turned to two, the worry festering in my gut forced me to take a peek into her bedroom. That was when I discovered that my mother had died.

The coroner ruled it a death of natural causes, but at only sixty-seven years old it seemed unnatural to me. My mother's house, a two-story cube built during the Wilson administration, was sold, all her possessions sifted through and either inherited or disposed of. I felt a great deal of guilt at being unable to give each item my full attention as there were so many keepsakes she'd accumulated over the course of her life. "I'm a sentimentalist," she often said, "not a hoarder." But with such a daunting task to undertake while enduring such overwhelming emotion, I was only able to keep a box of photographs chronicling her life. Upon review, I felt satisfied that she'd lived a good one.

The first anniversary of that morning had finally arrived, and I'd determined long before to make a tradition of visiting her grave. Abi and Ryan were with Julia since we'd agreed to alternate holidays, and so I stood alone under the cold blue sky and the drifting leaves of eternal tranquility. But I wouldn't allow the release of my sorrow in its physical form because I didn't want it to weigh on her spirit, even though my rationality told me she couldn't see or feel a thing. Still, she existed, and the existence of who we are has never been anything more than perception in the minds of those who knew us. No one truly dies until all who perceived them in their reality are gone, and perhaps that's all that matters; that our existence remains acknowledged in the world as we perceived it, a world formed by the people we likewise acknowledged.

"She was a fine woman, my friend," said Huxley beside me in the grass.

"Yeah."

"You miss her."

"Yeah."

"I never knew my mother. Did you know that?"

"No, I didn't. Well, I guess I did."

"I was told by some that she was a working bird. They claimed that I was lucky to have been plucked from the nest as such a young fledgling; that I was spared the shame and embarrassment."

"How do you feel about that?"

"I don't know, really. Sometimes..." Huxley exhaled slowly. "Sometimes I feel as though an element is missing from my personality that seems so prevalent in others'. I don't believe myself to be a particularly cold individual, but warmth is something I struggle with."

"You think because you didn't know your mother?" I asked.

"I think it's because you didn't know your father."

"What?" I looked down at him. "What does that have to do with anything?"

"Your mother loved you, but she wasn't necessarily loving. Your father, on the other hand, may have been quite a gentle man. My father was a brute, and my mother a ghost."

"Are you implying that in order to be good at loving, it has to be learned?"

"Perhaps," he shrugged. "Love can manifest itself in many ways. Depending on the person, it can appear as something much alternative to love."

"I think it's just as possible to know what to do by observing what not to do. You're right. My mother wasn't extremely affectionate. I think I've done a pretty good job at being loving with my children though."

"With your daughter. What about with your son?"

"What do you mean?"

"Do you not believe there is a possible difference in how you express your love to Ryan as you do to Abi?" asked Huxley. I gazed down at the headstone in silence.

"It's time to go," I said before stepping off towards the parking lot.

Sam had invited me to spend Thanksgiving with him and his parents who had not succumbed to natural causes yet, but I declined for reasons I couldn't muster the energy to dissect. After leaving the cemetery, I drove Lonnie's car the two hours back home, trying to decide how I was going to avoid Becca who'd been staying with me for an already uncomfortable five days.

For some reason, I'd imagined that she was the kind to leave fingernail clippings in the bathroom sink. I had no idea why, yet I'd not found even the hint of toothpaste left behind or a single strand of long hair curled up and matted to the drain of the shower. In all honesty, she wasn't a bother outside of making me have to sneak cutting all that cocaine. Becca was simply typing on her laptop nonstop in my living room and accumulating a disconcerting amount of empty Red Bull cans. I happened to ask what she was working on one evening, and she looked at me like some wild predator protecting the prey it had just slaughtered.

"Why do you want to know so badly?" Becca had snapped.

"Honestly, I don't," I said. "I was just curious."

"Oh." She looked at me for a few more seconds then went back to typing. It was pretty much always like that, so I was pleasantly surprised when I entered my apartment, and she wasn't there. Her laptop was, however, so I doubted she'd gone far like a doe and her fawn. Or a cannibal and its dinner.

I'd never understood America's obsession with football, at least, not to the extent of memorizing players and their stats, the years they played on whichever teams, and when those teams lost or won depending on what year you're looking at. I could grasp the primal quality of it, however. Just look at history. Everything is wrapped around two opposing forces, dominance and subservience, gods and devils, life and death, prosperity and desolation. And in the middle of those opposing forces, are all of us. I guess you could say we're the football.

My only memory of the game was kickoff. After that, I fell asleep until a rustling around the dining table woke me. Becca stood there carefully moving a few things. I soon realized that it was a meal of rotisserie chicken and side dishes served in Styrofoam.

"What are you doing?" I asked. She froze for a split second, then after a side glance, continued what she was doing.

"Hungry?" she asked.

"What's the food for?"

"Eating. That's why I asked if you're hungry." I nodded in understanding. "So, are you?"

"I guess so. I'm just..." I stood up and walked to the table. "Why did you get all this?"

"It's Thanksgiving." Becca said as if questioning my intelligence. "It's what people in this country do on the last Thursday of November."

"I didn't realize you celebrated Thanksgiving."

"Why? Because I'm a cold, socially awkward bitch?" She frowned at me.

"I mean...Yeah, basically."

"Fair enough."

Becca and I sat across from each other for a few awkward minutes, digging into the Thanksgiving feast with the plastic forks the grocery store had included with the order. I tried not to look at her when I chewed, but the sound of food circulating around in my mouth was getting old.

"So, what are you thankful for?" I asked, coming up short on anything else to say. Becca blinked at me before continuing to chew. Her lashes concealed her eyes as she looked back down at her food.

"I don't know." That was a success. I took another bite of mashed potatoes. "I'm thankful for turkey vultures."

"Turkey vultures?"

"Yes. You know, the big ugly birds that eat dead animals?"

"Yeah, I know what they are. Why are you thankful for them?"

"They eat all the dead shit. Can you imagine what an expensive pain in the ass it would be to have to clean up every piece of roadkill? It would be disgusting. No one could keep up with that. There'd be blood and guts and bits of fur everywhere."

"Yeah, I suppose." The chicken on my plate looked slightly different than a moment before.

"What are you thankful for?"

"Um, I guess…my kids. My…work, my…I don't know. That's about it."

"That's lame."

"What?"

"I said, that's lame."

"I heard what you said. How is it lame?"

"Because that's what you're thankful for by default, which, honestly, isn't any different than being thankful that you don't not have them."

"How is being thankful for them different than being thankful I don't not have them?" I cringed at my utterance of the double negative.

"Because when you're thankful you don't not have something, you're only thankful that some alternative isn't in its place. For example, if someone is thankful for their significant other only because without them they'd be single and lonely, that's being thankful you don't not have that person. It's all about you, not them. When you're actually thankful for someone, it has nothing to do with the alternative of being without them."

"You've been hanging out with Lonnie too much."

"I'm not thankful for Lonnie." I stared at her, not sure what to make of that statement. "I'm thankful I don't not have him. I'm not thankful for my skills in computing. I'm thankful that I don't not have them. I am thankful, however, for turkey vultures, because they pull their weight in the world doing one of the shittiest jobs in nature. I'm not thankful I don't not have them." A triple negative.

"I'm not not thankful for having this meal," I said after a long moment.

"You're not not welcome." It was the first time I'd ever seen her not not smile.

A short while later we cleared the table, and I was heading towards the couch when I felt a cool, familiar moisture graze my arm. "Beer?"

I looked down at the bottle in her hand. "I've been cutting back," I said, feeling that would be rejection enough.

"It's Thanksgiving. I only got a six-pack. Not even enough to get drunk with."

"I wouldn't be surprised if my tolerance has dropped a little."

"Just drink the fucking beer," she said, popping the top and placing it into my unresisting hand. The rush of carbonation being freed made my skin tingle. "Lonnie hates when I drink beer."

"Why?" I asked, taking a spot on the couch across from her.

"I don't know. He thinks it's not feminine enough or something." She popped the top on her own bottle. "Maybe he's afraid I'll get a beer gut. It kind of makes me want one. Cheers." The bottles clinked. The beer went down so sweetly, so smoothly, like a kiss from Aphrodite herself.

"What beer is this?" I looked at the label.

"It's an IPA called Fu-Man-Chew. It's from a microbrewery that just opened outside of town. Like it?"

"Yeah, it's good."

"It's fucking delicious." Becca sat back, an expression of omniscience on her face.

"So, Lonnie won't let you drink beer?"

"Lonnie thinks he won't let me drink beer," she scoffed.

"Is that some kind of reverse psychology?" I asked after another sip.

"Probably. He doesn't like my job either, I think for the same reason he doesn't like me drinking beer."

"He doesn't want you to get a gut?"

"Exactly." Becca gave a half smile.

"I've known Lonnie almost half of my life. We went to college together, and despite his being my friend, he's always been a chauvinistic asshole. I don't understand why anyone would put up with it."

"Eh," she shrugged. "He means well."

"Sure, but he's still a chauvinistic asshole."

"Chauvinists—whether a man or a woman, it doesn't matter—are just insecure. They find it necessary to belittle the other sex because they don't feel confident in whatever role they've been conditioned to believe they should be playing."

"But why put up with it?" I asked.

"Because it's a good dynamic, believe it or not. Unlike Lonnie, I'm incredibly self-aware, and one thing I know about myself is that I will go wild if I'm given the opportunity. Lonnie needs control, but even more importantly, someone to let him have control. That's what I do."

"And in return he keeps you from losing control."

"Something along those lines. At least…most of the time."

"I'm sorry," I said after studying her for several seconds, "I just don't see it. This is the most I've ever even heard you speak, much less be so candid."

"Don't get used to it," she said before putting the bottle to her lips.

"How do you cope with being controlled though? Wouldn't that be against your nature?"

"I suppose in some ways, but that's why I like coding. I can do whatever the fuck I want. I can make or break or build or destroy anything in any way I want to. I don't have to ask permission from anyone, and the only rules that exist are the ones that were designed to have loopholes."

"That must drive Lonnie crazy," I chuckled.

"Like you wouldn't believe." Becca laughed and finished her bottle. "You want another beer?" She asked getting up and heading towards the kitchen. "Yeah, you do."

"Sure," I agreed, looking at the quarter of the beer left in the bottle, then guzzling it down. She returned, popped the bottles and handed me one.

"So, what about you?"

"What about me?"

"You draw?"

"Yeah."

"And you're a writer, right?" Her question hit me hard for some reason, and I found myself swimming in truths I couldn't tread.

"Yeah. I am."

"You don't sound so certain of that."

"I mean," I chuckled again with a shrug, "writers write. Right?"

"Right." She raised her eyebrows. "You don't write?"

"I just haven't in a while."

"Why not?"

"I don't know. I just can't seem to get my thoughts in order to put them down."

"You've got writer's block."

"I guess. Yeah. Or something." I put down a few gulps of my beer.

"Or something what?"

"I don't know."

"You must have some idea."

"Don't you ever go to your computer and find yourself at a loss as to what software or program to create? Or where to take it?"

"Sure."

"And what do you do?" I asked.

"I start making up dumb shit on purpose; useless coding, program things that mean and do absolutely nothing."

"Really? And that works?"

"No, of course not," she laughed. "Sometimes you just have to walk away from something so that when you come back to it, you have a different perspective. You should realize that if you've been a writer for so long."

"What if that doesn't work?"

"Then it sounds like your problem has nothing to do with writing." Becca chugged her second beer then retrieved her third while I sat there, staring at the carpet. "For me," she continued, "creativity is more than just making stuff. It's a living organism of its own. You have to feed it, and whatever you feed it determines the type of shit that comes out on the other end. You know what I mean?"

"I think so," I said, wiping the moisture from my lips after taking a sip from my beer. "You get out of it what you put into it."

"Sort of. That's more of an effort kind of thing. I'm talking about feeding your creativity with what got it going in the first place. You have to go back to the beginning." Becca looked at my expression and sighed. "Look, Arthur, I'm not trying to stress you out."

"You're not."

"You look stressed." She reached down beside her and went into her backpack. "Do you partake?"

"I don't think that's a good idea. The neighbors will probably smell it."

"They're all senior citizens. They don't know what the fuck weed smells like. And if they do, they'll probably ask to join us." We stared at each other, her arm extended to offer me the packed bowl and the lighter.

I took the little pipe and held my thumb over the carb. Flicking the lighter to life, the green nugget smoldered and glowed as I inhaled the smoke before removing my thumb for air. I held it in, surprised at the smoothness of the draw, then suddenly burst into a coughing fit. Becca took the bowl and hit it, all the while smiling at me.

"There you go. That'll help you out." We sat back for a few minutes in silence, occasionally sipping our beers. Then, the old, familiar fingers of warmth began creeping up my spine. I felt relaxed, yet simultaneously active.

"What kind of weed is this?"

"It's a hybrid, mostly sativa, called Jolly Green Giant. A friend in Colorado sent it to me. Good shit, huh?" I nodded in answer. Becca, seeing our beers empty, got up a third time to the kitchen, then returned with a second full pack of beer and the last bottle of the first.

"I thought you said you only got a six pack," I said.

"Yeah, of that kind of beer. This is an amber ale," she said matter-of-factly. She took out two beers and set the others on the coffee table before plopping down on the couch beside me.

"I haven't smoked weed since college. Is this what you meant by going back to the beginning?"

"Does it matter?" she asked in return. We clinked our beers and sipped.

Another two or three minutes passed.

"It was the day we buried my brother, Allan," I finally said. Becca looked at me pensively. "I was twelve, sitting on top of that old silo he and I used to sneak to during the summer. We'd collect rocks and throw them at the birds that were up there. Not to hurt them, just scare them. That's what I was doing. Well, this one rock I threw, it actually hit a bird. I'd never done that before. I'd never tried to. I guess subconsciously I did that time…Anyway, I went over to it, picked it up. It was hurt pretty badly, not moving but breathing so fucking fast. I didn't know what to do with it, so I just laid it next to me and sobbed over it like a baby. I even begged it not to die. And right there, I finally shed all the tears I hadn't been able to before for my brother.

"I stayed up there all night, into the next morning. I'd stopped crying by then. I knew my mother was worried sick about me. She had called up the neighbors, even the sheriff, all the relatives that were there. They were all looking for me. I heard them; I saw them a couple of times. But I didn't say anything. Then I remember seeing my mother down below with that giant, steel flashlight that was kept by the telephone. It was morning by then, so I knew she'd been looking all night. She kept calling me over and over, and I saw...she leaned against the silo and started weeping such defeated tears. I wanted to say something. I wanted to tell her I was there, but I don't know...I just couldn't. And her shoulders were shaking, and she kept gasping every now and then. But then all of a sudden, instantly, for whatever reason, she just stopped. She wiped her face and picked up the flashlight and walked away like it never happened.

"That was the last time I ever saw her cry. About an hour later I went home. She was cooking breakfast when I got there, the table set, acting like nothing had happened. Didn't even ask me where I'd been. Life just kept on going." I looked over at Becca. "That's the beginning."

Becca's thumb wiped something from my cheek. Leaning forward, her eyes met mine for a long quiet moment.

"You want to see what I've been working on?"

The laptop screen glowed on her face, the rectangle of light reflecting off her glasses. I watched as she typed a bunch of mumbo jumbo until a window appeared displaying the pixelated image of a ghost pole dancing on a giant pencil.

"For the past couple months," she began, "I've been working on a program for a software company out of Texas. It's a language translation software, but specifically intended for translating larger bodies of work like novels, textbooks, things like that. The process of correctly translating those things is extremely time consuming since there is more than just word for word translation. For example, some words in other languages don't translate correctly to English, like... *seigneur-terraces* literally means 'terrace lord', but in France, it's what you call someone who sits in a coffee shop all day but only buys one coffee. And there are English words that don't translate into other languages, like *serendipity*."

"Really? Serendipity?"

"Translation software doesn't currently deal with those things. They'll just give a culturally inaccurate translation, and especially for full sentences and paragraphs, the meanings of words are dependent on their context. What I have been developing is a software that identifies and translates not just words, but the context in which they're being used. Especially in plays or novels, writers choose certain words for a reason, for a certain meaning. Direct translation can alter or even lose that meaning altogether. It comes down to context. Until now, it's always taken a human being to do that work, and it takes countless hours to do."

"What do you mean, until now?" I asked.

"This software has an algorithm set to understand contextual differences and inferences based on the language," said Becca. "Essentially, it searches somewhere else in the text to determine what particularly is being said."

"That's pretty amazing."

"That's not the amazing part of it," she corrected me. "What makes this software useful isn't the fact that it can do what a human translator can do. It's the speed in which it gets done. In order to work quickly, it stores patterns of context, evolving its algorithm. When it comes across these patterns repeatedly, analysis takes a thousandth of the original time."

"Wow. Yeah, that is amazing."

"Still not the amazing part. A couple of weeks ago I was running tests on some changes I made to the coding in the algorithm, tweaking the program's ability to remember the context of one phrase in a paragraph and apply it to future phrases within a context sample. What it did was create a method of predicting what the context would be in upcoming words, shortening the time it would take to analyze. To run the test, I uploaded the complete works of Shakespeare to be translated to French. During that upload, however, the internet went out, and what I was left with on my computer was about half of his works, and the first half of "King Lear". I went ahead with the test because it seemed like it would be enough anyway. This is the amazing part: what came out in the French translation was all that plus the second half of "King Lear"."

"Okay…"

"The entire play of King Lear was translated."

"I'm missing the point."

"It not only predicted context, but it also predicted the pattern of the writing. It cataloged context patterns, and from there, plot patterns. Speech patterns. Word usage patterns. Everything."

"And?"

"It finished King Lear on its own. Word for word."

"What do you mean it finished it?"

"It analyzed everything that came before it, and based on that, it translated the first act of King Lear, then went on to predict what would come next."

"Maybe you only think you uploaded half of it."

"I considered that. So, I did a test, using analysis it had stored. I uploaded the first act of 'The Merchant of Venice". It gave me the whole thing back." I looked at her, unblinking, not sure what to make of the information she was telling me. "It finished the play on its own."

"How is that possible?"

"It uses an algorithm to analyze and predict patterns in plot and context. It has such a formulated understanding of the history that it knows what comes next. Precognitive, you could say."

"Christ…"

"I took it one step further though, and this is what really blew me away. Jane Austen was writing a novel called *Sanditon* when she died, and it was never finished. I uploaded all of her completed works, and then *Sanditon*." Becca paused for a breath. "This program finished the book, Arthur."

"How…" I sat back in my chair.

"I did this with *The Mystery of Edwin Drood* by Charles Dickens, *The Garden of Eden* by Ernest Hemingway, and *The Pale King* by David Foster Wallace."

"Those other two were finished."

"Not by the original authors. I did a little hacking around and obtained the original, unfinished manuscripts and uploaded them. It completed all three of them, and as I expected, the Hemingway one and David Foster Wallace one were different than what the contributing authors wrote."

"How do they end?"

"You're going to have to read them for yourself," she said, looking back at the screen. "But this…What I have here is not just a translation program. It's a ghostwriter. One that has no discernable difference between the original author and the program."

"But, that ruins everything."

"What do you mean?" she asked, stunned. "It *changes* everything! Do you know what a program like this is worth? I could easily get seven figures for this!"

"A computer program is creating literature. All the money in the world couldn't make that okay."

"It's taking what is there and making accurate predictions on what comes next. It's not much different than text prediction on a search engine or on your phone."

"You're saying that this program accomplishes in minutes what it takes an author days, months, or even years to do."

"It doesn't just make things up on its own. It uses the past, already created by the author, to piece the future together." Becca leaned forward. "I'm not saying that this is technically right or wrong. I think I realize why you're reacting this way being a writer and all, but it doesn't change how crazy cool this shit is. Seriously. And this stuff is no different than what the author would be writing anyway. This isn't changing what is there."

"What about *The Pale King* or the one by Hemingway? How do you know those aren't different from what they would be?"

"I *don't* know," she said. "But it seems to me that if this software can accurately complete a work that we do know, it's likely that it can complete a work that we don't know. I mean, it understands the author more than the contributors do, in a way."

"But it turns it all into math and patterns and algorithms. That's not creativity."

"How do you think your brain works? It's just a biological computer. It transmits information through electronic signals. It receives information, it processes the information, it assesses, it looks for patterns, it makes predictions, it responds accordingly. We are nothing but the computers of nature."

"Computers of nature? Seriously?"

"Is that so ridiculous?" she asked.

"It's absurd."

"Why? Because if it is then you no longer feel that your consciousness is a higher power anymore? Because if you understand how you work then you won't feel quite as special? People are so egoistic to think they are both a part of nature and likewise above it."

"I never said that."

"You were thinking it."

"How do you know?" I asked.

"I made a prediction based on the assessment of information I have gathered by observing the people around me throughout my life. People operate fundamentally the same way. Simple as that."

"Fundamentally they might, but no two people are the same."

"If that's true, then what the hell are you so afraid of?" Becca challenged.

Fear is something I've always firmly believed is a byproduct of ignorance. Fear will leave people in a rut. It will leave them isolated and lonely. It will make them bitter. Hateful. Weak. I liked to think that I was not someone who feared much of anything, that I was a realist. Being logical took out a lot of the potential for fear because fear is an emotion. I wasn't heartless though. Of course, I was afraid of things. Not a lot of things, but things. I couldn't think about all that though. There wasn't time. There wasn't energy. There wasn't space. If I stopped to think about them, then I might have gotten stuck. That's what the hell I was so afraid of.

"I could ask you the same question," I said. "You observe people, but do you know them? What is the basis for your assessments? How can you understand a society in which you have no part? And why don't you? What the hell are *you* so afraid of?"

"It's people like me that control society to be what it is, like it or not."

"So, you're afraid of losing control?"

Becca stared at me for a long time, absent-mindedly spinning the wheel of her computer mouse with her index finger. "No, I'm not."

"Bullshit."

Calmly, she removed her glasses and placed them on the desk, and with the band that had been around her wrist, she put her shoulder-length hair up in a ponytail. Then, with neither warning nor invitation, she stood, moved to me, and straddled my lap.

"I'm not," she said, before pressing her lips against mine.

Becca smelled like chamomile and orange peels. Foreign and unfamiliar.

Perhaps that's why I didn't stop her.

CHAPTER TWELVE

For the following three days, wintery clouds hovered over Queen City. After threatening a blizzard, however, the sun returned on Monday to melt the thin layer of fluffy snow that had fallen. It seemed the air was somehow fresher and crisper than before. The atmosphere itself weighed pounds fewer, straightening the posture of us all. Sitting in my office, I enjoyed a morning pill, half crushed, half chewed, then lit a cigarette by my window just slightly ajar. I flicked the ashes to the ground forty feet below, following them with my eyes until the specks disappeared. How I wished I could be them.

On my desk, my computer monitor stared back at me, indifferent to the content it displayed. After reading the message three times already, I shouldn't have expected it to change.

Based on your credit, you've been pre-approved for $103,500...

I would need just over one-hundred thousand dollars as a down payment, which was absurd. Even if I cashed in my 401k and scraped the couple thousand out of my savings, that would maybe get me eight or nine grand. Working these drops for Lonnie might bring that up to almost seventy thousand, if I was lucky. There was no foreseeable way I'd get the amount needed in any reasonable time. Unfortunately, impossibilities never stopped anyone from wanting something, no matter how badly one might wish it. In fact, it generally buried the blade of desire even further into the heart.

Jack Dorset had summoned me, and once I'd finished my cigarette, I began the walk through to his office. Helen was as pleasant as usual, complimenting me on my short story which she'd taken a look at in transmission. A moment after taking a seat, Mr. Dorset welcomed me in. He offered a chair and lit us each a cigarette, all the while maintaining a reserved smile.

"Well, Arthur, it seems you've proven yourself quite the storyteller, yet again."

"I appreciate that, Mr. Dorset."

"I want to discuss it with you, actually. This story..." He held up a few printed sheets of paper. "I'm intrigued by your protagonist, this Pamela Miran. First, I was surprised that you wrote about a female since you've only ever had male protagonists. What changed that for you?"

"Well," I began, moving the cigarette to my other hand, "I don't really know. It just felt right. A relationship at odds seemed most congruent with a mother-daughter relationship. Then there's that other element of being without a father."

"Yes, her situation. The abusive daughter of all things. It's not a common tale by any stretch of the imagination. How did you arrive at that?"

"I just had this picture of a woman in my head—Pamela Miran—who was a victim of abuse. But I didn't want the story to be about a domestic relationship between a married couple gone bad. I wanted it to be different, and it just occurred to me. Why couldn't it be her child? I suspect it happens. And in this case, the emotional toll I think is worse for Pamela because it's someone she's *supposed* to love. Someone she can't help but love. It's her child. Whereas with a partner or spouse, it's tolerated because of that sense of obligation, or perhaps a longing for what was, but not because that person is a life created by you. And it really developed into that as I was writing."

"Fascinating, Arthur. As I told you before, I've always viewed you as one of the most gifted writers in my staff, but this just blows all previous evidence of that out of the water. You've really outdone yourself."

"Thank you, Mr. Dorset. I really don't think I could have done it without you though."

"Nonsense."

"No, sir. It's not. You held my place here while I went to clear my head for a while, and now I'm writing again. I feel like I've really tapped into a part of myself that I wasn't even aware of before."

"It's like I told you in our last conversation, Arthur. We're a family. We take care of our own." Jack Dorset took a long drag from his cigarette as he gazed upon the printed words. "You know, this reminds me a lot of Fletcher Price's work, the stuff that really propelled him to fame."

"Oh?" I switched hands again.

"Yes. You know, I was a friend of his long ago. Long, long ago…" Mr. Dorset's words trailed off in pursuit of his thoughts.

"I didn't know that."

"Despite my being several years older than him, we actually attended Princeton together in the late fifties. That was quite a time. But he used to ask me to proofread his work, which I'll be honest never really impressed me. Sure, it was good, but between graduation and his first novel, it was like a similar transformation took place."

"Really?"

"Yes. It was fascinating to read. Of course, once we'd left Princeton we never stayed in touch. Life, you know…but I always followed his work, at first because we'd been friends but later because, well, he was just so goddamn good."

"I don't think I'm anything like Fletcher Price, Mr. Dorset. He's a legend now. I'm just…me."

"As was Fletcher." Jack Dorset stood and walked to the panoramic view of the city. "Arthur, you could be great."

"Thank you, but—"

"But you won't be." His interruption caught me at a loss, his words unexpected and debilitating. "Now, I don't mean that you're going to fail. Failure comes the moment we stop trying. What I mean is, you won't be if you continue to do what you've done today."

For a moment, I felt as though my heart stopped yet simultaneously flooded my head with all the blood in my body. The room became scalding, causing sweat to bead up through my pores until they were visible across my brow. I said nothing, my mind racing with speculation as to the meaning of what he'd just said. But I remained silent, willing my heart to resume beating, demanding dispersion of the pressure beneath my temples.

"I don't understand what you mean…" I said finally.

"No?" Jack Dorset turned towards me, his face shadowed with the light at his back, yet I could see his eyes narrowed with suspicion. "I think you do."

"Mr. Dorset, I'm really not following."

"You wrote this…"

"Yes."

"And you've given it to this magazine to publish."

"Yes, sir. I don't unders—"

"Arthur, this is a good place for short stories, but not like this one. Not here."

"What do you mean?"

"I mean, we aren't going to publish this story."

"Why not?"

"I think you know why," he said in a graveled tone. "Your job is to be creative, but that doesn't mean you can ignore my instructions. A few weeks ago, you came in here with an idea about revamping the whole Huxley series, which—despite my better judgment—I gave you the greenlight to do. Then you bring me this. What exactly am I supposed to do with this?" He tossed the story down on his desk before me. "You will go back to what you have been doing, what you were hired to do."

"Mr. Dorset—"

"You will write about the Huxley that thousands of readers know and love and expect. They want Huxley, and that is what I'm tasking you to give them."

"This is a good story though," I argued.

"Yes, I know it is. But that means absolutely nothing if you continue without some kind of guidance, without regulation." He leaned forward. "Do you understand what I'm saying?"

Did I understand? I wasn't certain. I wasn't even convinced that I knew the man before me, telling me that my work is not acceptable because of the expectations set by faceless numbers, that I must abide by certain rules—rules that I had never known before. Yet, as badly as I wanted this to be an imposter before me, I knew it was not, and though there was a risk that he actually saw through the whole thing, I had to react otherwise.

"Mr. Dorset, when you interviewed me seven years ago, when Sam interviewed me, I didn't feel that I had a chance in the world because I'd always considered this magazine to be of a caliber far greater than what I could offer. Yet here I am, not because I had an epiphany to prove the opposite, but because you and Sam saw enough in me to think otherwise. I only put in my application here because I knew that if I didn't at least try, I would never forgive myself in ten, twenty years. And for the first year here, I only ever wanted to prove my worth to you. To prove that you were right for choosing me. To affirm for you that I deserved to be here. Then I started to truly understand why we were here at all. I began to understand that this magazine was greater than all of us. Even you. This magazine is…it's a monument to art. It's a celebration of artistry in all its facets. It had nothing to do with pop culture and sought the approval of no one. What you're saying to me runs counter to that, sir. So, I ask you, what's changed that I don't know about?"

I studied Mr. Dorset's expression of deep contemplation, a subtle nod indicating that he understood. He stood with the glow of the day silhouetting him against the window. His eyes wandered the room before stopping on the picture of a matador fighting a bull, a painting on black velvet, bordered with a driftwood frame. Jack Dorset stood there for some time before taking a deep breath.

"It's a strange thing, Arthur, that a man will only be as great as he believes himself to be capable, and yet, no truly great man ever believed himself to be great at all, and that is because there is no such creature. Only truly great men know this." He returned to his seat and selected a walnut from its bowl. "I want Huxley, Mr. Kimble. You have a week."

For a moment, I wondered if his statement had been made for the sake of teaching me or humbling me, and with his sudden silence and disregard for my presence, I considered that perhaps I had misunderstood him completely.

"Is that vending machine installed yet?" he asked, staring down at the walnut in his hand.

"No, sir. Not yet."

"Hmm…"

Once I'd exited Mr. Dorset's office, I nodded to Helen as I passed, then turned the corner to return down the hall. Several feet ahead of me, Stanley Dorset emerged from the elevator, speaking jovially with someone who had not yet emerged. The voice was instantly recognizable, however, but even before my brain had the chance to connect its accompanying face, my eyes made the confirmation.

"Mr. Kimble," greeted Elaine Cunningham through a broad smile. "Fancy meeting you again."

"You know him?" Stanley asked with a glint of disgust.

"Well, I wouldn't say I know him. At least, not yet. Would you say that we know each other, Mr. Kimble?"

Drenched in the shock of the moment, I'd stopped walking, stopped moving, and was unable to speak immediately in response to her question. Then a single word entered my mind.

"Semantics…" Elaine Cunningham's eyes billowed with blue rings of fire as her carmine lips curved upward at their ends to reveal two deceiving dimples. Then she laughed radiantly.

"Semantics indeed, Mr. Kimble!"

They passed me together, the arm of her blouse brushing innocently against the arm of my shirt, and I watched them move onward towards Mr. Dorset's office, Stanley ushering her along, yet not swiftly enough to keep her from glancing back in my direction.

"What the fuck is going on?" Sam jumped at the sudden abrasiveness of my words. "What are you not telling me, Sam?"

"What the hell is wrong with you?" He stood to meet my confrontation.

"Elaine Cunningham is meeting with Jack Dorset right now." Sam breathed for a moment, then sat back down. "I said, Elaine Cunningham—"

"I know she is," he said quietly.

"You know? Why wouldn't you tell me?"

"You don't need to know everything, and I don't always have an explanation for things."

"You know what they call her, right? The goddamn Hawk."

"I know."

"Slander Media is known for acquiring other publications. Is Stanley trying to get Jack to sell out?" He rubbed his forehead in agitation. "Is she trying to take over *Verb'd*?"

"Arthur, I don't know what she's planning to do. I don't know what Jack is thinking, or what plan Stanley is trying to hatch. I've wondered myself, but…"

"But what?" Sam turned and walked towards me.

"But I trust Jack. And so should you."

I stood still for a few seconds, contemplating a response to this suggestion. Was I to ignore my instincts or let them have their range?

"I do trust Jack. I just don't trust her. I don't trust Stanley, either," I said, and he nodded. "Can I trust you?" Samwell looked at me in shock.

"What the hell are you talking about? Of course, you can."

"You've been pretty blasé about the whole thing," I said, accusing calmly.

"You don't know how I've been," he said angrily. "You have no idea what's been going through my head about the whole thing. You're not supposed to. I'm your supervisor."

"I thought we were friends."

"Of course, we are, Arthur. But this is work, and at work I can be friendly, but I can't be anyone's friend as any good supervisor knows. Why are you taking this so personally?"

I couldn't give him a reason why. This was striking me to the core though, and despite my initial instinct to strike back, I caught my breath.

"You're right, I'm sorry," I said, taking a seat across from him. "Everything just feels so different."

"He told you he didn't want your short story, didn't he?" Samwell asked. I nodded. "Yeah. I don't quite get that either. But I do understand as far as business goes. It wouldn't be a wise decision to suddenly drop a popular column without a good reason."

"What if there just aren't any more stories about Huxley?" I asked. "Wouldn't that be a good enough reason?"

"To be honest with you, Art, the question I would be asking in such a scenario is, *why* aren't there any more." Samwell studied me. "Are there no more, Arthur?"

"I don't know," I said quietly.

"You think any of this has to do with what you've been dealing with for the past several months? I mean, the stories we've been publishing for the past year were already in the queue. Has it been that long since you've actually written about him?" he asked. I nodded reluctantly. "I know how much Huxley means to you, Art. I understand the connection you have to that character. For it to just stop is, honestly, quite alarming."

"Some things just come to an end," I said. "Some inspirations just disappear, and we have to accept it."

"I don't know if it's that simple."

"Neither do I," I said after a long sigh.

"You'll never find it if you stop looking for it," said Samwell.

"Find what?"

"Inspiration."

"This place always used to inspire me. The simple thought of it used to."

"What changed?" he asked.

"I guess I did."

A pill and a half later, I looked into the magnified eye of a genius lifeless as print on the poster, yet immortal. Turning around to the class, he watched over my shoulder through the slashed curtain.

"'There is nothing to writing. All you do is sit down at a typewriter and bleed.' What do you think Ernest Hemingway meant when he said that?"

"Writing is as easy as bleeding," one young man said.

"As easy as bleeding…Let's explore that idea. If I take a knife and cut my wrists, the blood will pour out on its own until either I'm dead or I've bandaged the wound. Simple enough. Who here has ever written anything, and I mean for the purpose of creativity?" Several hands rose into the air. "How many of you felt that the words just flowed onto the page as easily as blood flowing from your veins?"

"Pretty much never," a woman answered.

"Pretty much never? So, if Ernest Hemingway meant that writing was easy, he was either lying or wrong." I looked at the woman. "Are you saying Ernest Hemingway was wrong?"

"No. I just don't think that's what he meant."

"Oh, okay. What do you think he meant? All you do is sit down at a typewriter and bleed…"

"I think he meant that you're putting yourself—everything inside of you is going onto the page. You're letting what's inside come out."

"So, he was being metaphorical."

"Yeah."

"Is it easy to do what you just said? To put what's inside on a page?"

"Not really. Maybe sometimes. It depends on what it is, I guess."

"Okay. So why did he say there's nothing to writing? That seems to imply that there's no work involved. That it's easy."

"It's not easy."

"It's not easy?" She shook her head. "Who else agrees that writing is not easy? Pretty much all of you. I mean, hell, you're sitting in a class for writing. So, there must be some kind of challenge to it. Right?"

"Maybe he meant that it's easy when you're good at it."

"I can't think of a single successful author of anything who said it was easy. Save for Hemingway," I said. "Yes?" A young woman in the back had held up her hand.

"What if we're focusing on the wrong thing?"

"What do you mean?"

"Well, it doesn't take any effort to bleed. But how easy is it to cause yourself to bleed?"

I smiled. "You're suggesting that perhaps it's what brings you to the actual point of writing that's difficult."

"I mean, isn't the hard part about writing trying to figure out what you're going to write?"

"Write what you know. Mark Twain."

"True knowledge exists in knowing that you know nothing. Socrates."

"I believe that was Plato, actually."

"Quoting Socrates."

The young lady held my gaze, her eyes as firm-set as her jaw, and her determination seemingly more so. But bright blue eyes framed by dark brown hair possess a phenomenon. It's an ocular ruse, of course. Despite what Billy Shakespeare said, the eyes of a person are not windows to the proverbial soul, much less their intellect.

"If you look at it logically, Miss…"

"Lana Dixon," she said.

"Miss Dixon, if you examine that statement logically, you'll realize that it is a paradox," I continued. "If knowing that you know nothing equates to knowing something, then you therefore know something and do not know nothing, meaning that the only true knowledge is not true at all. It's a self-defeating argument."

"So then how do we figure out what to write if we're supposed to write what we know?"

"There's the thing," I smiled. "It's when we start thinking about what we're supposed to write that we go wrong. Supposition is all formed around norms and conventions. It's for this reason that you only ever know of a handful of great artists and writers. They were the few that did not care what they were supposed to write. They wrote what they wanted to. William Faulkner famously claimed that his book *As I*

Lay Dying was written in six weeks from beginning to end without changing a thing. That may or may not be true, but either way, he didn't do it by worrying about what he *should* be writing. It's a testament to freeing yourself. To allowing yourself to bleed. It isn't the bleeding that's difficult. It's having the courage to break the skin and cut down to the arteries. You have to face that fear of the pain you'll feel for opening the vein. The fear that you just might not come out of this alive on the other end." I paused in personal thought. "It's complete misery sometimes."

"So why do it?" one student asked.

"Because misery is beautiful," Lana Dixon answered with a smile.

"So say the children of tomorrow," I said.

I immediately wanted to take credit for that line, but it sounded so good, I was sure someone else had said it first.

After class, I was seated at Lonnie's desk, staring down at the bricks of cocaine in my backpack. I was still in awe at such an amount however small in the grand scheme of the drug business. It was powerful, this chemical. An ounce of it was worth more than an ounce of gold; dangerous, thrilling, levitating in certain quantities. It could kill you, and nothing in the world would change.

In the instructions, Lonnie had written the location of where I'd be making the drops. The first was in a bathroom on the other side of the campus. Third stall. There would be money in the tank. The brick would go in the tank of the second stall. Simple as that.

The cocaine seemed almost heavy as iron as I walked across the campus quad where students were still milling around in abundance. I kept my eyes to myself, hoping to avoid being spoken to or noticed by anyone.

"Professor Kimble," someone called, and I turned to face them.

"I'm not a professor," I said.

"You should be, then." Lana Dixon walked up to me, spinning a ring of keys around her finger. "That was an interesting class. Mr. Lemmon doesn't teach like that."

"No?" I questioned. "How does he teach?"

"Let's just say that you can't teach what you don't know."

"True, but you'd be surprised how much you can learn by examining questions without answers," I said. "My mother used to tell me, knowing is ten percent thinking. The other ninety percent is just admitting you have no idea."

"Smart woman," said Lana.

"I'm glad you enjoyed the class, but I need to keep moving. I have some work I need to get done."

"Work? It's getting late. It's time to relax."

"Time doesn't slow down, and neither should I."

"Come on. Let me buy you a drink."

"At a bar?" I asked.

"No, at the water fountain," she smirked. "Of course, at a bar."

"That would be inappropriate, Ms. Dixon."

"Why? You're not a professor, remember?" Lana Dixon's smile curled up. "See you next week, Professor."

Without another word, she left me standing there in the middle of the quad with six kilos of cocaine hanging from my shoulder.

I found the bathroom without a problem. In the third stall, there was the money all neat and bound in a plastic bag just like good drug money should be. I was quick about taking it and moved to the next stall. The tank opened easily, the two bricks sank safely in their plastic wrap to the bottom, and I was out.

In my car, I'd finally stopped sweating, and it occurred to me just how easy that whole non-transaction was. I pulled the money out of my bag and looked it over. At least twenty grand was in there, just as Lonnie had said, though the sight of it was surprisingly underwhelming.

The second drop was equally as simple. Just off the highway at a gravel rest area, a semi was parked for the night. I wasn't all that into big rigs, but it was quite a sight with chrome wheels, cherry red paint and a hood ornament of a topless woman leaning forward as though preparing to take off. The key was inconspicuously left in the door, and I quickly got in and shut it behind me. The money was exactly where it was supposed to be, and after the quick exchange, I returned to Lonnie's car and headed onto the highway.

The final stop was in a neighborhood just on the outskirts of downtown Queen City. On the corner of East Hardy and Lennox, there was an old newspaper box against a wall, just in the shadows. I parked at the other end of the block, just in sight of the box, and watched the street for a few minutes. My heart was beating quickly, the realization that I was much less alone than at the college or in the rest area, making me question if I was insane or simply stupid. I considered that it couldn't be so bad if Lonnie did this regularly, but after a few more seconds of thought, that knowledge didn't make me feel any better.

With three deep breaths, I opened the door to my car and began walking quickly towards the corner. The lights of a passing car glided over me, causing my gut to knot itself up. Then I was alone again, in the quiet, in the dark. At the box, there too was a key, an open door and...

"No money?" My brain took off with so many thoughts I couldn't keep them organized. Was this the wrong box? Was it the right box, and I'm being set up? If this is a setup, is it by the police or the dealer? I cursed under my breath, closing the box then opening it again like an idiot expecting a magic trick. The idea of just leaving jolted me around, and as I was about to step away, a man rounded the building, not five feet away, scaring the hell out of both of us. We could see each other clearly, our eyes taking in every detail with adrenalized accuracy.

"Are you..." he began.

"No," I said, though it occurred to me that, unless I was the person, there was no way to answer that one way or another.

"Sorry." The man walked quickly away.

I sat in the car for several minutes, watching, trying not to believe that I had somehow fucked up the drop, fearing the fact that I was still in possession of two kilos of cocaine ten minutes longer than I should be.

"Since when did you develop such impulsive behavior?" asked Huxley in a fit. "What's to become of me if something happens to you, eh? Did you ever consider that? Am I to be the victim of some pubescent's horrible fan fiction? The subject of some cheap animated film?"

"Don't be so dramatic," I said, looking around. "I don't like this situation any more than you do, but your freaking out isn't helping anything."

"This situation calls for some sensibility. Don't try to convince me that you thought this through."

"Obviously not. If I did, we wouldn't be here."

"Oh, that's just bloody fantastic, Arthur. Just splendid!"

At any moment I expected a SWAT team to descend on me from all sides, and a knock on my window almost made me shit myself. A tall, bald man leaned casually against the car, a cigarette burning between his fingers. I stared for several moments until he knocked again.

"You the man?" his muffled voice asked.

"What?"

"I said, are you the man?"

"I don't know what that means," I said. He motioned for me to crack the window, and I obeyed.

"Listen," he said quietly, "it's hard to find good help sometimes. You get a guy that's wet behind the ears, and this is what happens."

"Okay. I'm sorry."

"I'm not talking about you. You did everything perfectly." He took a drag and exhaled the smoke through his nose. "Put the passenger window down."

"What?"

"Put the passenger window down." The mechanics whirred as the window lowered. Within ten seconds, someone bundled from head to toe came whizzing by on a bicycle. The money plopped into the seat, and I instinctively pushed it to the floor. "Go ahead and leave it in the box."

"The box over there?" I pointed.

"Yeah. What other box is there?"

"Okay. And then what?"

"Then you go the fuck home," he said.

"Okay."

"You have a Merry Christmas."

"Merry Christmas," I said.

The man flicked his cigarette then headed down the street in the opposite direction of the cyclist, rubbing his hands together vigorously.

As quickly as I could, the cold wind biting my chapping lips, I returned to the newspaper box and dropped in the bricks. On the way back to my apartment, I considered how stupid of a career the drug business would be. Although, looking at over sixty thousand dollars in cash beside me, I realized how easily that could be overlooked—and how horribly I needed a drink.

Lonnie's house appeared inhabited with all the windows lit up, though I knew he wouldn't be back for another week and a half. I walked with my backpack up the small flight of stairs to the front door and knocked, my palms beginning to sweat despite the cold. Becca appeared in the crack of the door then allowed me in without a word. I followed her robed figure into the living room where she took a seat on the couch.

"So?" Becca stared at me expectantly. I reached into my backpack and extended to her a stack of hundreds.

"Five grand." Looking at it, she seemed almost hesitant to react, then calmly accepted the money. "I need a drink, if it's all right."

"Sure."

Restraining my urge to run to it, I walked to the refrigerator and took out one of several beers lined in two neat rows. The bottle opener was on the counter, and within seconds, my thirst—though unquenched—was not so desperate.

"What did they think?" Becca asked from the living room.

"What did who think?"

"Your job," she said, appearing in the doorway with her beer. "What did they think about the short story?"

"They didn't hate it," I said before taking another long drink.

"But?"

"But they didn't like it. They don't want to use it."

"Damn. Five thousand dollars spent for nothing." She turned and went back to the couch. "Too bad."

"You know, any business would see a reason to refund my money."

"I'm not running a business. I did you a favor."

"A favor isn't something you pay for," I argued.

"I never promised you a masterpiece. You offered to pay me this money in exchange for using Ghostwriter. I let you use it. Now I'm keeping the money."

The sound of her typing filled the room as I stood there feeling stupid with my beer. I wondered how a person I'd always considered to be so attractive could suddenly appear so vile. The thought made me feel disgusting.

"Don't you know better than to fall for your best friend's girl?" Becca asked.

"I haven't."

"Then why are you staring at me?"

"You don't want to know," I said.

"If you're feeling dirty, don't worry. It goes away after a while." She didn't look away from her laptop.

"You're trying to tell me your conscience is clear?"

"No," she chuckled. "I just tied that son of a bitch up and locked him in the basement."

"That sounds like an acquired skill," I said, and she didn't respond.

I finished the beer and was about to leave when Becca said, "Lonnie isn't as good of a man as you."

"If you say so."

"You're a man who knows what is right and tries to do it—more or less."

"That doesn't make me an especially good man."

"That's because you fail. That inner turmoil gets you. What do they call that, the anti-hero?"

"We all have inner turmoil," I said. "Even you."

"You think I feel guilty for the other night?" she asked.

"I know you do. And you love it."

Becca smiled weakly, never looking at me. "I make it a point not to feel guilty for anything."

"They call that being the villain," I said matter-of-factly.

"Perhaps. But you don't feel guilty, either." She eyed me, a glint of amusement in her smile.

"How do you know?"

"Because you wouldn't be talking to me. That's your inner turmoil right now, isn't it? That you think you should feel guilty, but you don't." She took a sip from her beer. "You'd like to fuck me again, wouldn't you?"

"No," I said after some thought. "Nothing personal, but no." Becca smiled and raised the bottle to drink.

"Now, that's what they call being the hero." I made no response before stepping outside. As the door shut behind me, I could see Becca chugging the rest of her beer.

CHAPTER THIRTEEN

My eyes followed the movement of the pallbearers as my brain caught itself up with everything that had happened over the previous four days: the monthly conference on Tuesday where Jack Dorset had not been in attendance; the iron bars of tension and uncertainty twisting together as Stanley Dorset took his father's place; the shrieking of the metal bending under pressure almost audible in the silence. Sam had been out of the office all that morning but present in his chair at the table, his face locking away his preoccupied mind as he flipped a pen end over end atop a folder of papers. Stanley informed us that his father had suffered a heart attack the night before and was indisposed for the time being. He told us there was nothing to worry about, however, that his father would return in just a few days, and that we should go about our work as normal. In the interim, Stanley would be acting on his father's behalf.

After the meeting, several of us chipped in some money on a card and flowers for Mr. Dorset, but when Stacy went to deliver them to his office, she found the door locked and Helen's station unattended. Stacy left the gift on Helen's desk. Sam had nothing to say about the matter except that Jack Dorset was getting up there, and these things should be expected. The day went on and ended. We all returned on

Thursday, the heaviness of an ominous rain cloud hovering with its burden. Then, we received the news, expected as it was, and the rain fell in torrents. A silent uncertainty still loomed over our heads, and nobody chatted. Nobody smiled in sincerity. And it was all wrong.

Jack Dorset looked pretty good for a dead guy; perhaps even better than the last time I'd seen him breathing. I'd never imagined what he might look like with makeup on, but if I ever had wondered, I knew then. His hair was uncharacteristically slicked to the side, clothes pressed and perfect. It's a strange thing looking at a person in a coffin because you half expect them to suddenly pop their eyes open, sit up, and reveal it was just an elaborate prank. I found myself standing transfixed, staring at his chest, watching for any indication that maybe—just maybe—it might rise. For that simple sign of life. That thump-thump. But no. Jack Dorset was as dead as a golden toad.

"It's like a giant sardine in a can," Sam muttered beside me.

"You mean him or us?" I asked. We looked down at the casket. "What's up with that?"

"With what?"

"They put a fucking rose in his hand. What was he, a gardener or something?"

"I don't know."

"Nothing ever makes sense at these things. What's natural at all about a bunch of people getting dressed up, standing in line to look at a corpse, then after saying a few words going to eat a catered meal?"

"People have to eat."

"And that fucking rose."

"We need to keep moving."

"They don't serve alcohol at these things, do they?"

"You don't need that, Art. Come on." We stepped away from the casket towards Stanley Dorset who was standing beside a large wreath that resembled a flotation device on a sinking ship. A black and white photo of Jack Dorset as a younger man was centered in the circle.

"Thanks for coming," Stanley greeted with a smile.

"Of course," Samwell returned, shaking his hand. "He was like a father to me. I can only imagine what a loss you must be suffering right now."

"Suffering…" he repeated revealing his teeth in what could have passed as a well-mannered growl. "I hope I can count on you—both of you," he continued, looking at me, "to assist me with carrying on his work, ensuring its evolution."

"Evolution?" I asked. "Into what?"

"Into what he wanted," Stanley answered. "What else is evolution for but improvement?"

"I don't know. A couple words come to mind: adaptation, survival."

"We're both looking forward to seeing where the future of *Verb'd* might lead," Sam interjected before taking the high road and walking away.

Sam and I settled ourselves in the end of a pew towards the middle of the sanctuary, and I began inwardly chastising myself for not having prepared my nerves with a shot of whiskey before showing up. I scanned the room in search of some holy wine or whatever Catholics drink. Of course, there wasn't any. I supposed funerals aren't lively enough to serve alcohol. Dozens more people entered the chapel over the next several minutes, all going to view the body, shaking hands with Stanley, then chatting amongst themselves. Eventually, the presiding priest took his place at the podium to lead us in prayer with a somberly resonating, "Let us pray."

"What the fuck is she doing here?" Sam whispered to me, head bowed, eyes closed.

"Who?"

"Elaine Cunningham." I shot my eyes open and looked behind us. After surveying the mourners for only a moment, I spotted her, eyes unblinking as they seemed to be penetrating the casket, unconcerned with the prayer. The blue orbs shot suddenly over to lock their gaze on me, and despite my desire to look away, I couldn't. Or I wouldn't. Perhaps I didn't want to. She inclined her head towards me with the upward curve of her lips, then bowed her head. Once the prayer was over, Samwell was invited to the podium.

"There is a lot that can be said about the life of Jack Dorset. It spanned all of eighty-six years, traveled six of seven continents, crossed three oceans, and produced over forty thousand pieces of writing. Jack Dorset's life was unusual, namely because it was the life that most people don't experience. Not because they can't, but because for one reason or another, they just don't. He wasn't afforded an easy beginning. The son of a New York steel worker, Jack grew up one of five children in a household that could scarcely afford to feed two, and it was for this reason that Jack began his career in print early as a newsboy. At the time, he was an illiterate six-year-old without much interest in education. But he knew his way around Manhattan and memorized where all the wealthy executives and business owners could be found and when. He made a point to not only know them by name but ensure they knew him by name. It was a clever business tactic that proved lucrative for him.

"It didn't take Jack long to realize the impact of what he did for the people around him, the importance of what was printed within the pages of those newspapers. However, being unable to read made it impossible to appreciate. He knew—he felt—there must be something within those pages that was valuable. Empowering. And he needed to know. So, Jack taught himself to read. Every day, he'd stash one paper aside for himself, take it home after long hours of hawking newspapers, and go through each letter and each word. Eventually he was able to get through the pages. Pretty soon he found himself saving up for heavier reading and purchased his first piece of literature The Old Man and the Sea. This changed more than just his life. It altered his reality, the world around him, and the way he perceived the people he interacted with. This was the discovery he made as a child, and the discovery he wished to share with the world ever after: that the purpose of words—of anything created by human beings—the purpose of art—is to enhance the perception and experience of one's own existence.

"It was for this reason that Jack Dorset taught his younger siblings to read and write. It was the reason he managed to get a position as a freelance journalist for *The New York Post*, how he earned his way into Princeton, graduating at the top of his class. After covering the Vietnam War, he eventually put together his first globally lauded journalistic work of comparative humanity, and all the while writing the four novels which proved he was as adept at writing fiction as he was at delivering the truth; perhaps, even proving that some of the greatest truths are found in fiction. Finally, thirty-three years ago, Jack Dorset established *Verb'd Magazine*, a publication that I've been privileged to be involved with for almost twenty of those years.

"In times like these, we ask ourselves, what is life? What am I doing with it? What am I missing? I've been forced to ask myself those questions. Of all the things Jack Dorset taught me, however, one lesson stands out above all others. He told me once that, whatever you do or don't do, wherever you go or don't go, however high life lifts you or however low it beats you down, it's only life. Jack Dorset lived an extraordinary one simply by not worrying about it."

Samwell closed the black leather folder containing Jack Dorset's eulogy and stepped down with a solemn expression that resembled a man struggling to pry a heavy weight from earth's gravitational clutches. Or maybe, it was releasing it to the earth. Perhaps both. He took his place beside me as the priest returned to lead us in another prayer, and I couldn't help but wonder if it was truly any damn use.

"I'm going to resign."

That day was uncharacteristically warm for December. Vanilla skies bathed the cemetery through marbled clouds, the color of the grass vaguely desaturated. There's something to be said for cemeteries with their ornate sculptures and works of art, their green landscapes carefully designed and manicured, flowing willow branches and long swaying arms of oaks and birches worshipping the heavens in a restful breeze, wildlife free and coexisting peacefully. It's funny that the same place could invoke such fear in the midnight hour, suddenly having become a refuge of vengeful ghosts and lurking mad men, skeletal hands bursting from the not-so-restful resting places of the deceased, and the shadows containing in them a most certain death if the spirits should be provoked. In the light, there is peace and beauty, and in the darkness, there is misery and discontent. Such a vastness of differing countenance in a cemetery is almost perplexing with such a simple change between the night and the day.

"I said, I'm going to resign," Sam repeated.

"Yeah, I heard you."

"Are you?"

"I don't know," I said. "I'm in a contract."

"You know why she's here, right?" I shot a glance back at the group yet to disperse from the tent. Elaine Cunningham stood chatting with Stanley and a few other people I didn't recognize.

"It doesn't matter," I sighed. "They're going to do what they want."

"And what are you going to do?"

"I said, I don't know."

"How are you so relaxed about this whole thing right now? Just last week you were chomping at the bit with anxiety."

"Where are you going to go?" I asked, deflecting. "Any job offers?"

"I'm still debating." We continued walking further from the group. "Art, I really think you should consider your options."

"What options exactly?"

"Options about what's next for you. Why don't you go with me?"

"Go where, Sam?" I asked, releasing my agitation. "You don't even know where you're going. Unlike you, I have responsibilities. I have kids. I can't just up and quit on a whim."

"It's not a whim. I've been mulling it over for a while."

"A while? Really? How long is a while? A few days? A few weeks? Months?"

"A couple months."

"Oh, like when they started firing people. Before they required expense reports. Before you told me that everything was fine and there's nothing to worry about."

"I was doing my job."

"You were full of shit, Sam!" I whirled around towards him. "And you still are! You told me to trust you, and despite my gut feeling, I decided to. I trusted your bullshit like a fucking idiot! You knew there was something going on the whole time!"

"I didn't know any more than you did."

"But you knew enough to consider resigning."

"If you're looking for a bad guy to blame, I'm not it."

"Then who is? Stanley?"

"I don't know."

"Elaine Cunningham?"

"I said, I don't know."

"How about Jack Dorset?"

"Come on, Art—"

"None of them ever told me to trust them while simultaneously pulling the wool over my eyes, Sam."

"Goddamn it, Art, just say what you need to say."

"You're no fucking different, Sam! You're no fucking different. After all the years and the trust we built, come to find out you're just the same as all the other people I can't fucking rely on!"

"Rely on to do what, Arthur? You don't want people who tell you the truth! You don't want honesty!"

"What the hell does that even mean?"

"You've been feeding everyone your bullshit for so long you can't even tell it apart from what's real anymore. You demand truth and honesty from everyone, but you can't even be honest with yourself!"

"I am honest with myself!"

"Yeah? So, have you admitted to yourself that you're still struggling with addiction? Have you admitted to yourself that rehab didn't cure you and never could?"

"I'm not struggling."

"Arthur, you still get high! You might be able to convince the people who don't know you, but I do. I know you're not clean. I can tell when you're high, I can tell when you're not. Like right now."

"I'm not high right now!"

"No, but you've been wishing you could be this whole time."

"Fuck you. Fuck you and the high horse you rode in on."

"I'm not on any high fucking horse. See, this is exactly how you react to honesty. You can't handle it one little bit. You start freaking the fuck out."

"This isn't honesty, Sam! This is bullshit! Everyone I know is full of shit! You, Jack, Vivian, friends, strangers, my goddamn ex-wife!"

"Why the hell do you think she's your ex-wife in the first fucking place?!"

I swung on Sam before I realized it myself. I didn't regret it like I expected to, however. As he rubbed his jaw where he'd fallen, I was certain he'd had it coming.

"So, this is what it's come to, huh?" Samwell asked quietly.

"This is what it's fucking come to."

I left him lying in between the graves, the loathing that had been simmering within me suddenly boiled over. And I no longer cared who got burned, even myself.

"There was a time when friendships lasted a lifetime," sighed Huxley. "How those days have flown."

"People are shit," I said, getting into my car. "No one is who they claim to be. No one can be trusted to stand behind you without pulling a knife. Sometimes I feel like it would be easier to not know anyone at all."

"Wouldn't that be a lonely existence."

"It already is, Hux."

Not twenty-four hours later, the acquisition of *Verb'd Magazine* was announced through a three-sentence email blurb. As of that moment, we were all employees of Slander Media, an irony I couldn't help but chuckle at disdainfully. I finished crushing the pill on my desk and inhaled it. I should have realized this was coming. Sam had seen it. Then again, maybe I had too and simply shut my eyes. Thinking back over the past few weeks spelled it all out like *Sesame Street*.

"I'm resigning," I said calmly, my heart racing as I stood at Jack's desk.

"Resigning…" repeated Stanley Dorset, smugly sitting back in his father's seat. The walnuts, I could see, had been tossed in the waste bin in the corner. "I'm afraid that's just not possible. We have a signed contract with you that doesn't expire for another four months."

"You know you don't want me here," I said. "Just let me walk away. I'll take half of what I'm owed."

"If you walk away, we don't owe you a damn thing. We pay you to do a job. If you don't do it, you don't get paid."

"Unless there are creative differences," I said. "Which there are."

"I don't see any," he said.

"Well, I do."

Stanley smiled and rose to his feet. He approached the window, much in the same way his father had, and looked out into the city.

"We've never liked each other," he said. "For one reason or another, we've always seemed to be at odds, and always revolving around something with my father, may he rest in peace. You two saw eye to eye on most things. You understood each other in a way that I never could. I tried, but I failed, and he had no interest in understanding me. So, what was I to do?" Stanley turned back to me. "I'm not a vengeful person, I don't think. I know I have a tendency to fly off the handle, to make impulsive decisions sometimes. However, the decision to hold you to your contract is one I've been considering for a few weeks now. We all knew that my father would be dying soon. Why do you think we took so much effort into shaping up this ship of his?"

"I'm resigning," I said again after a long pause.

"Don't you care to hear the truth about what happened?" he asked.

"I know the truth," I said. "I knew Jack Dorset well enough that I don't need you to try to warp what happened. I won't be working for you; I won't be working for *Slander*."

"The name isn't changing, you know," he said.

"We both know the name doesn't mean anything."

"You think you're noble by making a stupid decision?"

"It's not a matter of nobility. It's a matter of principle. I stand by *Verb'd* and what it represented."

"And what is that exactly?"

"*Verb'd* stands for the creation of art, in all its forms, the turning of ideas into actions. And just as importantly it stands for the protection of creation." Stanley appeared to think for a moment, then closed his mouth, looking at me lazily.

"That's quite poetic, but there's something you don't realize that I will share with you." Stanley sat on the edge of his desk. "This whole acquisition was my father's idea. His orchestration. He didn't want me taking over this company as much as I didn't want it. Rather than see it run into the ground, he decided to sell." His eyes met mine as I searched them for the lie.

"I don't believe it," I said with half-hearted conviction. "He would have never sold out, especially to Slander Media."

"Slander Media was the only bidder willing to keep on existing employees, actually. Sure, they're taking *Verb'd* back to the drawing board, but at least people aren't losing their jobs."

"Don't act like you care."

"I'm not acting, Mr. Kimble. In fact, I was furious that my father had decided to let the productivity analyst come through. You know, Mr. Grant suggested we let you go."

"Did he?"

"My father wouldn't hear of it. At the moment, it annoyed me, but now I'm glad he didn't. I don't want to see people fired. Look at your assistant, Susan."

"Stacy."

"That's what I meant. Look at her situation. She's getting ready to have a baby. I don't want her to lose her job. Besides, she's a lesbian." Stanley leaned.

"Wow." I shook my head disgustedly.

"Despite what you think, I'm not the bad guy. I never was. I'm sorry that you believed so sincerely in my father, but you have to understand that no matter what someone's intentions are, they're still just as vulnerable to being human as the rest of us."

Years projected into my thoughts, years in Jack Dorset's employment reaping all he could impart to me. Everything I understood about this job, this cause, I'd learned from Jack, and as much as any disciple, I believed in it. It was as true to me as the impermanence of life. And he had become my truest mentor, the mentor who taught me to never sway from my principles and codes, because without that, there was no identity worth having. To think that he had become so removed from his ideals brought to question everything he'd led me to believe, and it instigated within myself the familiar clashing of the armies of logic and emotion.

On the side of logic, there was the fact that art is not creation with the intent of duplication or similarity. Art is creation uninhibited and unprecedented. There was the fact that art is not unique to certain people and is not understood only by those with special skills, talents, or of a particular upbringing. Art is the single natural language of all humanity that ever has, does, or will exist, and each individual within humanity speaks a dialect whether it be writing, music, film, theatre, dance, visual arts, and even culinary arts. There was the fact that art is not strictly apropos. Art is eternal.

On the side of emotion, there was distrust for anyone and anything who suggested that there was no purpose greater than the escalation of our own greatness. There was loyalty, built upon the foundations of our sacrificial toils, fueled by an all but spoken belief in the existence of a purpose greater than ourselves. There was loathing, a loathing for those naysayers of dreams; those hunters who, in covetous destruction of that which they could not of themselves conceive, mounted on their walls the aspirations of others; those who disregarded their dreams and evaded their aspirations, and those whose vanity corrupted them both.

And there was love, a love for those who dared to dream of greater things than there are in heaven and earth, for those with aspirations far too wild to be tamed, and those who humbly bore their naked souls for the sake of relief and liberation.

But emotions are suppressed by logic, and likewise, logic is suppressed by emotion. It is from this inner struggle to balance the two that conflict is born, and it is this conflict from which evolves our hope and doubt, our fear and our courage, our love and our loathing. And it is from this which art is born, the art of hope and the art of doubt, the art of fear and the art of courage, the art of love and the art of loathing. It should be understood that it is not essential for these arts to exist together, but it should also be understood that the art of hope could not have been conceived without knowing the emotion of doubt, nor courage without knowing the emotion of fear. The art of love could not be conceived without knowing the emotion of loathing. But in those instances when, in the deepest and most tumultuous of inner conflicts, the artist captures both within a singular frame, he has created the purest art of all: the art of love and loathing.

It had never entered my mind that I could even begin to loathe Jack Dorset. Yet, there I was, and it exhausted me. The disappointment and bitterness were seeping over onto everything that existed around this, around me. I had to think of something else. I needed to wipe it all away, or bury it, or blot it out. Just stop giving a shit, because, in the end, nobody else does. Not even Jack Dorset.

"So, Mr. Kimble, will I see you tomorrow?" Stanley asked.

The trees were naked at Queen City Community College. It may have simply been the events of the day weighing on me, but it appeared that a hue of gray had been glazed over the grounds. Before getting out of my car, I chewed up a whole pill and chugged two beers from the six-pack I'd purchased en route to the campus. Within ten minutes, I was convinced that I could have a good class, and almost felt motivated to say something profound. Or at least pretend to.

Not many students were walking around when I arrived, yet it still felt a bit disconcerting to be carrying a couple bricks of cocaine around campus. If I'd had my choice, I would have dropped them off immediately. Lonnie had instructed me to wait until after classes, however, and so they went straight into his office, locked away from discovery.

It was the second week of teaching, and I'd become completely confident that no one had learned a fucking thing in this class. Honestly, I didn't really care. While I wasn't going to be popping out A's like a Pez dispenser, I wasn't planning to deviate from Lonnie's generous grading scale either. I'd made last week's assignment simple: write a creative piece of any kind with a minimum of five hundred words. I couldn't imagine that even high schoolers were getting off this easy. I considered this a fail-proof assignment, and even gave them the first half of the class period to finish up any last-minute adjustments before getting into the lecture.

"I want to talk today about what makes a story good, about what makes it interesting. What do you all think? Let me get some opinions."

"A good plot," said one student.

"The characters," said another from the back.

"A good plot, characters, yes. These are both essential parts of a story, but what about them makes them good? What makes a plot worth reading through? What makes a character worth getting to know?"

"Relatability," said Lana Dixon.

"That's a good reason. What else?"

"The development."

"Okay," I nodded. "What does it mean to develop a plot or a character?" The classroom remained quiet. "Development is more than just taking them from point A to point B. Development means that, by the time the character gets to point B, they're different from how they were at point A. There's been a noticeable change or an evolution in their personality or the way they think. Perhaps what they believed is altered or even opposite from what it was. And the most effective way to do this, at least in my experience, is to put your character in difficult—sometimes impossible—situations. If your character is afraid of bees, you move them next door to a honey farm. If you have two characters who hate each other, you make them an assignment requiring teamwork."

"You take them out of their comfort zone," said one.

"Exactly. Take them out of their comfort zone. Give them a rude awakening. Your characters might hate you for it sometimes, but they'll thank you later." The class chuckled.

"What if it's not always as simple as that?" asked Lana. "What if your character is a superhero or something?"

"Every hero has a weakness. Super or not."

"Not all of them."

"Well, not all weaknesses are physical," I said. "Some weaknesses come in other forms that I like to call pressure points. This is when your character's challenge is metaphysical, a matter of belief or purpose. If your character fights crime, then you put them in a situation that forces them to make a judgment call that speaks to their ethical standards and not just the law. If it's a religion, make them have to choose either faith or evidence. If it's love, give them a choice of whether or not to sacrifice. Chances are, the character will tell you what they will or won't decide to do. And this leads to plot development."

"But how do you know that their making the choice you want them to make?" asked the young man to my right.

"By asking the most important question of all: why? Why are they choosing this instead of that? Why are they saying one thing instead of another? Why anything? And figuring out the answer to this will help you determine whether it's the right decision for your character. Always ask why. About everything. This is how you go from writing about a character or a place or event to understanding them. This is what differentiates the great writers from the good writers. This will make what you write stand out from the rest."

"But what if you can't figure out the answer?" asked Lana. "What if you just don't know why?"

"Then I'd say you've discovered the purpose to writing your story," I said. "To find out."

Hollywood frequently likes to depict bars as these casual places where the hot chick is always one empty bar stool away, dripping with pick-me-up vibes. Or perhaps she's in a bind and needs a bailout, and Mr. Studly just so happens to be right there to innocently save the helpless little damsel resulting in the most well-intentioned fuck of his and her life. Shenanigans ensue and by the end of said story, they wind up falling in love, despite the forces of life against them. They defy the odds in the name of their love and hold up that great big middle finger as they drive off into the sunset. It's a beautiful story, but little did Mr. Studly know that little Ms. Vixen is a right-wing conservative and he's a hardcore liberal, and by the time they reach the interstate, not even an act of Congress will keep them together. Of course, the director has already called a wrap before anyone sees that part. Roll the credits.

For this reason, it's best to embrace the reality that bars are generally noisy with shitty rock'n'roll in the background, and there are at least three people between you and the hot chick (if there is one), and the thing about her is that either she's best buddies with the bartender and under his or her protection, she's already with someone, or she suffers from acute resting bitch face. No matter, desperate times call for desperate measures, and when the world is flattening out around you, the risks don't seem quite as high. There is a plethora of tactics to get the object of your carnal attraction to open up even when they don't necessarily want to, but they all boil down to one thing: finding common ground. What people fail to realize is that this is more than having the same songs on your road trip playlist or binging the same television shows. Sure, that all fills what would be an awkward silence, but those things don't matter. That's not why anyone is there.

From birth to earth, we all live a linear existence. Yet, each one is unique, no matter how closely they may run parallel to one another. We look up at the same blue sky with different eyes, wonder at the same moon with different thoughts, and still you are always there, and I am always here. So, what are the two of us doing in this bar, right at this moment? Why the intersection? The answer could be made as convoluted and insane as anyone might desire, but it all comes down to one simple thing: sex.

"Sex?"

"Sex."

"Fuck off, creep."

The indirect approach wasn't as effective as it used to be. There was a time when stringing together words was like stringing together a hundred pearls. Hardly anyone wears pearls anymore.

"You had me on the edge of my seat with that little dissertation." Lana Dixon's voice interrupted my thoughts, and I turned from staring into the bottom of my glass. "I'm not going to lie, Professor. I'm a little disappointed with the conclusion."

"I'm not a professor. And who said that was the conclusion?" I asked, flicking the ashes of my cigarette and turning my body to face her.

"It had the characteristics of a conclusion."

"That was just the introduction. I've yet to prove my argument."

"You mean to tell me it's *not* all about sex?"

"Not hardly."

"How disappointing," she said before sipping her drink.

"Did you follow me here or something?" I asked.

"Don't get full of yourself, Professor," she laughed. "This is a college town, even if it is only community college. Is it so unlikely to believe that we just ended up at the same bar?"

"You asked me to have a drink with you last week, and then we run into each other this week. I was never any good at math, but I feel pretty certain that the odds are low."

"Well, then, maybe that makes this encounter all the more fortuitous."

"Or it means you're dangerous," I said. Lana shrugged, walked to my other side, and sat down where the woman I'd repulsed away had been.

"There are worse things to be, but what's wrong with a little danger?"

"It's been known to have adverse effects on a person's health," I said before ordering a round for each of us and lighting a cigarette.

"That's been known to have adverse effects too, Professor." She nodded towards my cigarette before producing her own.

"I already told you. I'm not a professor. Not even a substitute professor."

"That explains a lot."

"How so?"

"You actually know about writing, or, better yet, you love the idea of ideas. That's no small feat."

"To believe is to love. To know is disappointment."

"Who said that?"

"Me. Just now."

"How uplifting."

"What can I say? It's a curse." We received our drinks, and she lifted her glass, the ice clinking as mine met hers.

"Here's to being cursed." Lana Dixon's clavicles bore a resemblance to the curved chrome of motorcycle handles. I took another long sip.

"You never did tell me what your argument actually is," she said.

"Honesty. It all comes down to honesty, and then avoiding it at all costs."

"Honesty," she smiled, the twin orbs of light reappearing in the darkness. "But honesty can be a lot of fun."

"Is that so?"

"Haven't you ever played truth or dare?"

"Once or twice, perhaps. The fundamental flaw with truth or dare is that there's no way of knowing whether the other person is actually telling the truth. I've come to the conclusion that everyone playing is either a liar or a loser. In many cases, both."

"That's why the dare is so much fun."

"The dare is dangerous."

"Says who?"

"Says anyone who's ever played the game," I said. "It's better suited for horny teenagers at a house party."

"You obviously never played it as an adult. It's so much more interesting."

"Is it?"

"Go ahead. Give me the choice," said Lana, straightening up. I smiled and shook my head.

"Okay. Truth or dare?"

"Truth."

"What is...Where were you born?"

"Right here in Queen City," she said.

"See? Everyone is a liar," I said before taking a drink.

"What makes you think I'm lying?"

"Let's just say I've met a lot of people from Queen City," I said.

"That's a horrible thing to say," she laughed. "But, alas, it is true."

"Nobody's perfect."

"So they say. Okay, now it's your turn. Truth or dare?"

"Dare."

"I dare you to finish your drink."

"It's full," I protested.

"Exactly." Lana watched with fiendish amusement as I drank up my double scotch. "I'll buy your next one just for being a good sport."

"Thanks," I said, grimacing. "All right, truth or dare?"

"Dare."

"Chug your drink," I said. She laughed and shrugged in surrender. It took her less than thirty seconds to suck up her rum and coke through the straw, all the while looking me dead in the eyes until the staccato croaking of an empty glass could be heard.

"There." Lana smiled, setting it down on the bar. "Truth or dare?"

"Truth," I answered, despite my better judgment.

"Truth…How long have you been a supplier?"

"A supplier?" I asked, hoping that I hadn't paused too long. "A supplier of what?"

"Oh, come on. Don't ruin the game," Lana said.

"I don't know what you're talking about." My mind was flashing around for the recollection of any hint as to how she might have known. Perhaps she was just guessing, but such a coincidence was unlikely, even if I was a newbie at drug trafficking.

"I'm talking about the exchange of goods for money. You know."

"No, I don't." I thought back to the night she'd asked me out for a drink, that I had done the drop immediately after we'd spoken. Had she followed me? If so, then why? I'd heard about undercover cops infiltrating college campuses to bust drug rings. I hated to think she was one of them.

"Yes, you do," she insisted. "I'm not a cop, if that's what you're thinking."

"Why would I be worried about your being a cop?"

"Because there are only two ways that I could possibly know

that you've got twenty-two thousand dollars stashed in your car. It's a very nice one by the way. A Tesla, right?"

"It's a rental, and that's quite an assertion," I said, beginning to sweat. "Let's say hypothetically that I did have a ridiculous amount of cash in my car. You could only know that if you were a cop, or…"

"Or…" Lana smiled.

"You're the one who gave it to me."

"You are as smart as you look," she winked. "I told you I'm not a cop. To lie about that would be against the law."

"It doesn't seem you have much regard for the law."

"No more than it has regard for me. I'm just a dealer. You're the bigger fish if they were looking to fry someone."

"Why are you telling me this?" I asked.

"Because I like you," she said, casually. "You have a nice face, much nicer than Professor Lemmon's. You're a better professor in general. I guess I just can't help but wonder why you're moving bricks."

"It doesn't concern you," I said.

"You're the one who said to always ask 'why'," said Lana, grinning.

"When you're writing," I said, getting agitated. "Ask 'why' when you're writing."

"Isn't the best way to understand something to ask questions?"

"You're clearly a smart girl. Why are *you* dealing?" I countered.

"Because there are things I want that I can't get with a regular job. The economy is shit, and there's a demand out here."

"What could you possibly want that's worth breaking the law for?"

"You tell me," Lana said. Her eyes became intrusive yet calming. I could say nothing back to her, and she broke from my gaze to signal the bartender for refills. "There's nothing wrong with wanting. If you wonder why I care, I don't necessarily. I just think you're interesting. You have a lot of good things to say."

"You've hardly heard me say anything," I said, lighting a fresh cigarette.

"Why don't we change that?" asked Lana.

"Because as of today I'm not coming around here anymore. I was just the understudy, and now my part is over."

"It doesn't have to be," she said. "There's still a demand around here that isn't being met. You could make this a regular thing, you know."

"I've seen enough movies to know that once you start, you don't stop until you're in federal prison."

"That's actually pretty rare," she said.

"Is it?"

"I've been dealing for three years, and I've never had a close call with the cops."

"Because you're white."

"Because I'm smart. Most people doing this shit are idiots and half-assers. It would be a nice change working with someone who's got some sense."

"You mean me," I specified.

"Why not?"

"I told you. It's over. I'm not getting tangled up in this shit."

"You have an opportunity," she said, "whether you want it or not. You can get whatever it is you're after."

"I never said I'm after anything."

"Everyone is after something. Even if they don't know what it is." She leaned towards me. "What is it you want, Professor?"

"Why do you keep calling me that?" I asked.

"Because it suits you." Lana picked up my pack of cigarettes and took one, putting it between her lips for me to light.

"You're asking me to continue doing something that I shouldn't be doing in the first place, and to do it specifically with you," I said after placing the lighter down. "Am I understanding this correctly?"

"I'm telling you that you can have whatever you want. Doesn't that make it all the more worth doing?" she asked. "You can't tell me you don't find some excitement in all of this."

"All of this," I said, "is over as of tonight."

"Why?"

"I told you why."

"But it doesn't have to be."

"It needs to be."

"Only because you don't see the advantage in continuing?"

"Only because it's wrong," I said. "People like me don't do this kind of thing. I'm a father. I have a career. I have good reasons to not do it."

"I'm guessing it's those reasons that got you here in the first place," said Lana. "There's something that you want. What is it?"

"That's not your business," I said, and she chuckled.

"Maybe you're misunderstanding me. I don't want to be involved in your personal life. I never meant for you to actually tell me. Things can be twice as enjoyable with limited points of contact, you know. In many ways."

"So, you've been asking me for my own sake?"

"When was the last time you asked yourself?" Lana peered closely at me. "I mean, really?"

She'd hit me with a fair question, and despite my best efforts, I couldn't actually remember ever asking myself before. As a parent, need entangles itself with want until they are one and the same, and I'd been one for almost seventeen years. I was a writer for a reputable magazine that gave me the freedom I wanted to create. More or less.

Dr. Hollande had asked what I expected out of life, and while I still couldn't answer that, I wondered how much more could be expected than what I'd already gotten. In most cases, that would be considered good fortune. A happy existence. And yet, it didn't answer the question that this college student was posing.

What did I truly want? Only one thing came to mind, and I only needed fifty thousand more dollars to get it.

CHAPTER FOURTEEN

There are several moments throughout a person's life in which they encounter the self. It's not usually a great experience, dripping with self-disdain and judgment, sizing up all they have done and even more so what they have not. It's a time of reflection, literally, in the mirror, sizing up one's self for everything they believe they are in contrast with everything they are told they should be.

Yes, told.

Expectation is something acquired over time and molded by whatever tribe or society you are lucky (or cursed) enough to be a part of. No one has ever, in the history of this god-forsaken planet, tried to live up to a standard completely their own. As much as people might like to believe otherwise, that's just not how this works. In that reflection in the mirror, no matter how beautiful or worn down, smiling or not, sucking it in or letting it go, a person does not simply see their self. They see all of the people that they wish they could be, how close they are to being there, and likewise the people they despise, however much of them exists in their reflection, whatever damage they've inflicted.

Despite knowing this, I thought I saw myself in the reflection and only myself. I was all I ever thought I would be, and there was no more wishing. I was the one who'd inflicted the damage onto myself, and there were the scars to prove it. I had passed what could reasonably be the middle of my life. I was on the decline. My hair was receding. My skin was losing its elasticity. My zest for life had become bland. This, I assumed, was getting older. I used to believe that the world was my oyster, and while this wasn't necessarily incorrect, not every oyster holds a pearl.

In my peripheral vision, I could still see my reflection with the straw, inhaling the lines of powder on the dresser top. Behind me, Lana Dixon breathed in and out easily, still with her youth tightly in her grasp. Her hair was in a clean mess over the pillow, chest rising and falling in slow and steady rhythm. I finished the warm beer remaining on the nightstand before pulling on my pants. As I put on my shirt, Lana's eyes fluttered open, and she turned to look at me. Despite her smile, I couldn't manage to produce one of my own.

"Come back to bed," she said, reaching out. Her fingers glided over my back as I sat putting on my sneakers.

"I can't."

"Oh, come on. There must be some way I can tempt you."

"I agree," I said. "But that doesn't change my answer," I said, rising to put on my jacket. She watched silently as I approached the door.

"Not even a kiss goodbye?" asked Lana.

"I'm not much into goodbyes."

"But isn't parting such sweet sorrow?"

I looked back at her, marveling at all the wild things in her eyes.

"Take a lesson from someone who knows. Never quote Shakespeare before drinking your morning coffee," I said. Lana's smile faded, her eyes dropping to the blanket that kept her from exposure. "You asked me what I really want. You can't be angry if that isn't you. You should be glad that you're getting what you want."

Lana nodded thoughtfully. "Yes. I'm getting what I want."

A certain, unexplainable relief came over me when Lonnie informed me he'd arrived back a day early. At the same token, I felt hesitant to go see him. Lonnie opened the door to his house, clearly having just gotten out of bed. He smiled and waved me in.

"Art. What's up, man? Becca was just about to make some lunch. You hungry?"

"No," I said, unshouldering my backpack. "Thanks anyway."

"What's in the bag?" Lonnie cheesed. "Money, money, money. Right? Let's go to my office." He led me down the hallway with a smile, and we entered a room with a small desk and a single window. "This is where all the magic happens."

"Very magical," I said, before sitting down. He lit a cigarette, and I followed suit.

"Well?" he smiled.

"Sixty thousand dollars." I set the pack on his desk and unzipped it.

"Excellent!" Lonnie happily inspected the three stacks of twenties as I set them down. "You have any problems at all?"

"No," I said.

"Great. Hey, before I forget, my manager got me a gig in Tallahassee last minute. It's for this weekend, but I also have an appointment for my car to get an oil change on Saturday morning. Think you could take it for me?"

"Sure," I said. "No problem."

"Thanks." Lonnie went back to counting.

"I need to talk to you about something."

"What's up? You need a refill?"

"Well, yeah, but that's not what I wanted to talk about. You know Lana Dixon from your class?" Lonnie nodded. "She's the one buying the cocaine. She's the dealer."

"Are you sure?" He stared at me. "How'd you find that out?"

"She told me."

"But why would she do that?" he asked, pointing his cigarette at me. "Did she know you were the one making the drop?"

"Apparently so," I said, exhaling a stream of smoke. "She knew about you, too."

"What?" Lonnie's eyes squinted in astonishment. "There's no fucking way. I make sure there's no one around." He flicked his ashes. "So, is this a problem now?"

THE ART of LOVE (& LOATHING)

"Not exactly," I said. "She says she wants to team up."

"Team up? What does that mean?"

"Join forces. I don't know. Work together. Her idea is that, if we pool our resources, we can at least double our take."

"No thanks. I don't want to be a dealer. I know you sure as shit don't." Lonnie watched me as I sat silently. "You're thinking about it?"

"I'm over half-way to goal with just two drops," I reasoned. "Another two, and I'd be there, maybe even past it."

"That's not the way you want to get there, Art. Trust me. The money isn't worth it."

"But the house is worth it. Ryan and Abi are worth it."

"Even more reason not to get into dealing. It's going to come back to bite you. I'm telling you. I've seen it happen. Why do you think I'm so excited about getting this hosting gig and getting away from the college? It gives me an excuse to stop." Lonnie sighed. "If you want to take over what I've been doing, then that's your business, but you don't want to become a dealer. You'll never get out."

"So, you won't be doing this at all? You're giving up all the money?"

"It's too much for me to figure out how to keep laundering it. If I just spend it fresh, the IRS will be up my ass. That's another thing you need to consider. How are you going to explain having a hundred grand in cash? You can't."

"I don't see how you were all gung-ho about this business just a few weeks ago, and now you're trying to talk me out of it. Why should I give up my chance to have what I want?"

"This isn't what you want, Art. You might think it is, but it isn't."

"So, what am I supposed to do? Quit after getting this far?"

"Why not? Find a different house. Stay where you're at. You don't need all that space anyway."

"What about excess, Lonnie? I thought that was just wealth with a purpose."

Lonnie shrugged and looked out the window at a tree branch.

"I'll give you the money," he said finally.

"No."

"Come on, man. This is easier than all that shit. No crimes committed. No possible prison time. A nice, clean gift from one friend to the other. A gift for your kids. That's what this is all about, isn't it?"

While my conscience had a tendency to be disconnected and at times downright lazy, this was not one of those times. All I could think about was my betrayal. There was no excuse for what Becca and I had done, despite being drunk. Becca herself had been intoxicating. Perhaps, I considered, I had been the same to her. Guilt suddenly swept over me as Lonnie was offering me everything I wanted while I had secretly violated his trust only weeks before. However, the greatest guilt of all engulfed the other as I realized that I felt no remorse for the act itself. I didn't deserve his gift, that much was certain. You can't always get what you want, but sometimes, you shouldn't even if you can.

"Thanks, Lonnie. I just can't."

"Okay," he said, looking strangely defeated. "But if you change your mind, let me know." Lonnie shook my pills from a bottle into a small plastic bag as I placed a fifty on his desk. Beside it, I silently set down the key fob he'd given me. Lonnie stared at it for a moment, motionless, then continued putting my refill together.

"I didn't lose it," I smiled.

"Keep it," he said without looking at me. "You're going to need it."

Within thirty minutes, I was back in my apartment building, rounding the slight corner towards my door, key in hand. Before I could reach the lock, the door of the apartment across the hall opened just slightly for an older woman to peek through at me. When she saw who I was, she opened the door further and stepped out in a gray dress that covered her from ankle to jaw and the shadows of a sunhat deepening the gauntness of her cheeks. As it had been the only outfit I had ever seen her wear, I imagined a collection of identical dresses neatly hanging up in a closet that smelled like moth balls.

"Mr. Kimble."

"Hello, Ms. Foster." I had no intention of engaging in a conversation with her and continued to slide my key into the lock. My neighbor stood silently watching me, however, and I looked over my shoulder at her. "Did you need something?"

"Mr. Skiddles," said Ms. Foster hoarsely.

"I'm sorry?"

"My cat. Mr. Skiddles. Have you seen him?" She kneaded the palms of her hands with her fingers, her eyes two shimmering circles of concern.

"To be honest, I didn't even realize you had a cat."

"So, you haven't seen him?"

"No. Sorry." I turned the key and prepared to enter when she spoke again.

"This is what he looks like." Ms. Foster held up a can with the picture on the label towards me. The printed face of a cat, orange with highlights of white and brown, looked at me with green eyes as it prepared to take a bite of some type of meat from a crystal bowl.

"I haven't seen your cat, Ms. Foster."

"Well, if you do, he responds to the name Mr. Skiddles. That's his name."

"Mr. Skiddles…"

"Yes. Take this so you don't forget what he looks like." She held out the can.

"No, thanks. I think I—"

"Please, take it."

"Ms. Foster, I—"

"So you don't forget. You can't forget."

The old woman's pleading wouldn't stop until it had cut my heart strings.

"If I see Mr. Skiddles," I said, taking the can, "I'll make sure to let you know."

"Oh, thank you!" Ms. Foster released a smile of relief that revealed two rows of thin, stained teeth. "Thank you so much, Mr. Kimble."

"Sure thing."

I hurried into my apartment with a nod and closed the door,

glad to be away from the old lady. In my kitchen, I stood by the trashcan, preparing to drop the cat food in, when the printing on the metal top caught my eye: 'BEST BY JUN 86'.

The rest of the week shot by like an echo, bouncing in and back out of existence faster than could be realized. Outside of editing the final draft of my interview with P.J. Goring, I did practically nothing in my office but maintain an even buzz. I gave Stacy a paid week off, not really caring whether that was within my professional capacity or not, and she was as happy as Cratchit on Christmas morning; I, the redeemed Ebenezer. A few times, in some heightened sense of pleasure, I even managed to write a few lines. Reading them back to myself proved dissatisfying, however, and I deleted them as quickly as they were typed.

"What was so bad about those lines?" asked Huxley, apparently peeved. "I thought it was a rather good start."

"It wasn't going anywhere," I told him before taking another drag of my cigarette. "More random, unfocused nonsense. It's about all I'm good at anymore." Huxley watched me pour some more whiskey into my glass.

"I wouldn't say all that," he frowned. "Perhaps the problem is your clarity."

"I feel clear. Relaxed and clear."

"Then why does there seem to be a fog?"

"I don't know," I said, looking back at my laptop screen. "I don't have the energy to think about it right now."

"What do you want to think about?"

"Honestly, Hux? Not a goddamn thing," I said before leaning back and shutting my eyes.

That evening, Ryan, Abi, and I entered the crowded shopping mall that had been seemingly decorated overnight with all the trappings of holiday cheer. Bing Crosby's softly crooning voice echoed from the walls, reminding children that they better watch out, and they better not cry. Abi walked a few feet ahead of me and Ryan, subconsciously avoiding the edges where each giant tile in the floor ended and met another.

I'd brought them shopping to find a Christmas present for their mother, though they were at a disagreement as to what the gift should be. It wasn't a case of the two of them having separate ideas, however. Ryan was simply so disinterested in Christmas that he wouldn't agree to anything Abi saw or suggested.

She'd first found a silver necklace with an infinity symbol hanging from its chain, but he said it was too common. Abi discovered at the same jewelry store a pair of rose gold earrings with pink, teardrop crystals. It would clash with her complexion. At another store, Abi picked a pair of lambskin gloves lined with cashmere. Ryan argued that Julia wouldn't want to cover up her painted nails. A scarf was too itchy. Shoes were never a good gift for anyone.

"Well, what then?" Abi asked, releasing her frustration. "What do you want to get her?"

"I don't know," Ryan shrugged. "Something useful. Let's get her a toaster or something."

Abi raised her eyebrows in shock. "A toaster?"

"Yeah, with the big slots for bagels." Ryan spoke innocently enough, though his indifference suggested to me that he was enjoying the disbelief on Abi's face.

"Nobody eats bagels except for you, Ryan. That's a selfish gift, and Christmas is about giving and being unselfish."

"But what good is jewelry or shoes if she already has a bunch of them? It's just going to get put away somewhere." Ryan's point seemed to hit home with Abi, and she looked around slowly in thought.

"Your mom loves coffee," I said.

"Yeah, but she already has a coffee maker," Abi answered.

"She doesn't use it though, because she always wants espresso." Ryan allowed the fragment of a smile to appear as he arrived at a conclusion. "We should get her an espresso maker."

"Then she won't have to go buy her espresso every day!" Abi agreed with a glow.

"Practical, useful, and thoughtful. I'd say we should find an espresso machine." I smiled at them both, satisfied in us all as we'd come up with a solution together. The only downside was that I knew they could never afford it with their allowance money, so I was going to have to spot the difference.

We made our way across the mall and up the escalators to the massive store with about every imaginable gadget for the home one might ever contrive. Towards the center of the store, we found a small collection of espresso and cappuccino makers with their shining, stainless-steel bodies and levers. For several minutes, we looked them over like a trio of monkeys, randomly pushing and pulling buttons and knobs, peering into the cavities and remaining clueless as to how they worked. Finally, a young saleswoman walked by without regarding us, and I hailed her down for assistance.

"Can you tell us what the differences are with these things? We're pretty lost," I said earnestly.

She looked silently over my shoulder at the machines then breathed.

"They're espresso machines."

"Yes, I know. But what are the differences?"

"Well, that one," she said pointing, "is $69.99, that next one up is $99.99, and that big one is $149.99." It took a moment of silence for me to realize that was her answer in all its finality.

"Why?" I asked, receiving a confused stare from the young lady.

"Why what?"

"Why are they priced differently? Why is one more expensive than the others?" She thought about it for several seconds, looking at the machines again without a step closer.

"That one's bigger than that one," she answered, pointing again, "and that one's bigger than both of them."

"So, it's eighty dollars more for a bigger batch of espresso?" I began to realize what I was up against. "If you don't know anything about these things, then it would save us both time if you say so. I can find someone else."

"Okay, then," she said flatly before turning to resume walking towards her original destination. I looked after her in subtle astonishment before glancing back at Ryan and Abi who looked as confused as I felt.

"Maybe this was a bad idea," said Abi.

"No," I shook my head. "We'll each do a search on our phones for these three espresso makers and compare what they say. Sound good?"

We huddled together next to the display and began typing for the information we needed. It only took us a few minutes to realize that we were in way over our heads. None of us knew what the differences in water pressure per square inch implied, what a tamper was, or the supposed better quality of the manual machine process. When I discovered that a good grinder could cost an additional hundred to two hundred dollars, I surrendered to determining the quality of the purchase based on price. Seeing as the cheapest one didn't include a grinder, it was the hundred-dollar espresso maker that we left the store with—no gift wrapping, thanks.

Outside the store we collapsed onto a bench, the strain of thought and comparative analysis having wiped us out in addition to depleting any holiday cheer I had summoned for myself.

"Hot cocoa?"

A sweet, aged voice spoke from behind us, and we turned to see the local Mrs. Claus pushing a small cart of steaming pots and cardboard cups. Beside her, a couple kids dressed as elves stood blank-faced, awaiting orders. It seemed to be the best pursuable option as it wasn't possible or wise to take Ryan and Abi for a shot of bourbon.

"Sure," I said. "You want some?" The two of them nodded and Mrs. Claus sent her elves to work while she made in-character conversation. Surprisingly, it wasn't so hard to play along.

"It's wonderful to see families out together, really getting into the Christmas spirit. Mr. Claus has been holed up all year in his workshop, so he's super-duper excited to be here today!"

"He's here in the mall?" Abi interrupted excitedly.

"Yes, indeedy! Right around the corner there," she answered, gesturing a finger to our left.

The elves marched around with our hot chocolate. We sipped them carefully, the flavor and warmth lifting our spirits.

"That'll be thirty dollars," she said, never losing her smile.

"The price for yuletide cheer rises every year," I said.

"Inflation."

"You'd think the North Pole would be immune to that sort of thing."

"Well, at least your receipt for the hot cocoa gets you ten percent off for a picture with Mr. Claus," she said. "You should stop by and say hello. He loves having visitors!"

"Aren't we a little too old for that?" Ryan asked, to which Mrs. Claus stood defiantly erect.

"Certainly not, young man. Christmas is for everyone, no matter how old, no matter how young."

"So, you're saying that if my dad wanted to sit on Santa's lap for a picture there wouldn't be anything weird about that?" Ryan argued.

Mrs. Claus began looking slightly uncomfortable at the retaliation of words.

"You should, Dad! Let's go get our picture with Santa! It'll be fun!"

"I don't think that he'd like it if I sat on his lap. I don't think anyone would like it."

"We'll all do it together! Please, Dad?"

"I'm not sitting on Santa's lap," Ryan protested with the whipped cream topping of his drink evident upon his lip.

"Dad," Abi said quietly, poking her eyebrows up pleadingly. "It'll be just like old times. Why not?"

Her smile disarmed me from my inhibitions more quickly and effectively than a glass of the smoothest whiskey. Mrs. Claus had already begun walking away when I felt no choice but to agree.

"Okay, Sprout. We'll go get our picture with Santa."

Ryan scoffed and continued ensuring us of his rebellion as we walked in the direction of Santa's meet and greet. It was easy enough for Ryan to conclude that I'd given in to Abi's begging because I had a bit too soft of a spot for her, which may or may not have been true, but as our steps continued, the sound of sleigh bells ring-ting-tingling and the freedom in embracing childish impossibility for the sake of enjoyment carried me. My feet felt lighter, my body relaxed, and my smile unlocked.

Ryan fell behind us but kept following, catching up as we took our place at the end of the line. I actively sealed up the cracks and crevices in my mind, refusing to allow in the other realities of my life. I struggled to maintain this defense until the reinforcement of being next in line finally arrived. Then it was easy. We walked through as a staff member opened the rope for our entrance. Our shoes clicked and tapped down the little plastic cobbles until we reached the old man on his throne of red and gold. He ho-hoed to us, fixing his spectacles as he saw me.

"Merry Christmas! Who wants to take a picture with me?" He asked jovially.

"All of us," said Abi happily.

"All of you?" Santa croaked a bit, glancing up at me as he struggled to stay in character. "Well, all right, but your dad is going to have to stand. My old knees are only good for children these days." His smile returned as he ho-hoed again. He tapped his knee for Abi to sit, then his other for Ryan who did so reluctantly, keeping to the edge of Santa's lap as if about to make a break for it. I stood beside them watching. "So, what are your names?"

"I'm Abi, this is my brother Ryan, that's our dad. His name is Arthur."

"Nice to meet you, Abi and Ryan. Have you two been good this year?"

"You don't have to do all that," said Ryan.

"Why, what do you mean?" asked Santa.

"We know you're just some dude in a costume."

"Ryan!" Abi cried. "Don't ruin it."

"Now, now, Abi," Santa consoled her. "You're both so big, I wouldn't expect you to believe, and that's okay. It's not about whether you believe in me, anyway. Or the gifts or the tree."

"Oh, yeah?" Ryan asked dubiously. "Then what is it all about? Jesus?"

"Well, Jesus is a whole other barrel of sugarplums. A lot of people have different reasons for Christmas, different beliefs about why we celebrate. But at the core of it all, it's just about love."

"Right," said Ryan, clearly not having any of it.

"Now, Ryan, hear me out," Santa continued. "When I say that it's about love I don't mean the feel-good love that makes us all want to hug each other and hold each other and spend our time together. I mean the love that still exists when we don't. Families are so busy nowadays, it's easy to make mistakes and it's easy to forget. But there's still love. Christmas is just that day we put aside to remind each other. Christmas is about the love we don't feel all the time. That's the greatest love of all, because it survives on meager rations. It can take the hits, the disappointments. The let downs. And Christmas, well, that's when we can look each other in the eyes and say, it's all right. Now, you may not believe in *me*, but you can believe in *that*, can't you?"

The three of us remained silent, Ryan looking at the floor, Abi smiling with flushed cheeks, and I wondered if this guy might actually be the real Santa. I'd seen many over the years, some more alcoholic than others, some with fake beards, some with real, some with pot bellies and some with stuffing. None of them had ever been challenged as to the validity of their claim, and I doubted that they would have responded with such compassionate earnestness if they had. Maybe it had been all of us who were wrong. Maybe Santa was real after all.

The photographer motioned for us to take the picture, and we closed in around jolly old St. Nick. A few minutes later, I looked down at the photograph of me, Abi, Ryan, and Santa Claus and marveled at the happiness I thought had been evaporated long ago. Perhaps, I thought, even happiness was something we just had to believe in.

As we walked along the mall heading back towards the entrance, Abi announced that she needed to use the restroom. Altering our direction for her, we arrived at the restrooms, and Ryan and I stood quietly as she went in. I watched my son nodding slightly with the beat in his headphones and taking a few aimless steps until he stopped. His eyes looked ahead towards a toy store, though after a few moments, I realized it wasn't the toy store he was watching. At the entrance, a Marine stood tall in his uniform with his blue pants and black coat, his rank glowing gold over red on his arms. The white belt around his middle was perfectly fitted, accentuating his lean form. Decorating his chest were a few rows of colorful bars and two small medals dangled freely below. Beside him, a large cardboard box stood just as erectly containing several toys. My eyes went from the Marine greeting passing shoppers back to Ryan's face, and I recognized an unusual tightness in his jaw, a narrowing of his eyes in concentrated admiration.

"Is that a Marine?" Ryan asked me suddenly, pulling the headphones down.

"Yeah. Why?"

Ryan said nothing else, but rather stepped off with a clear intention of talking to him. I wanted to follow, unsure of what to make of his sudden decision, but my feet wouldn't move. Ryan stood before the Marine who smiled and held out his hand.

"How you doin', son?" he asked with a brisk hoarseness.

Ryan took his hand and shook. "I'm good. Just doing some Christmas shopping."

"That's good, that's good. You getting any toys today?"

"No. I'm kind of old for toys."

"Is that so? How old are you?"

"Sixteen." The Marine paused for a moment then took a deep breath.

"So, you're getting ready to graduate this year or next year?"

"This year," Ryan nodded. "I skipped a grade."

"I'm Staff Sergeant Kopek," he said. "What's your name?"

"Ryan."

"Ryan, have you thought at all about what you're going to do after you graduate?" By that point, I'd overruled my feet and took my place behind Ryan.

"We're still exploring options," I interjected. Staff Sergeant Kopek looked at me and smiled.

"You must be this young man's father." He shook my hand with a vice grip.

"I don't really know what I want to do," Ryan said.

"You ever thought about the military?"

"We're trying to go the academic route, actually," I answered.

"That's good. You can never learn too much." He smiled at

Ryan. "The Marine Corps provides a lot of good opportunities for assistance with secondary education."

"Do you like being in the Marines?" Ryan asked. Staff Sergeant Kopek leaned towards him with a smile.

"Some days I do. Some days I don't. But I'll tell you, there isn't a night when I don't get down on my knees and thank God for the United States Marine Corps."

"Staff Sergeant Kopek!" Abi's voice rang out from behind us, and the Marine looked over and smiled in recognition.

"Well, hello, Ms. Abigail."

"Are you doing Toys for Tots here, too?" she asked, though continued without waiting for an answer. "Staff Sergeant Kopek has been at our school a couple times this week promoting Toys for Tots. It's a program that takes donations of toys and gives them to kids whose parents can't afford them. It's a really great cause!"

"It sounds like it," I agreed with little enthusiasm.

"Did you donate a toy?" Abi's question struck unexpectedly, and I fumbled with my words. "Come on, Dad. We need to do it. It's not like Ryan and I need toys, and we can afford it." The Marine, Ryan, and Sprout all looked at me silently, and it became clear that I had no choice in the matter.

Abi led the way into the toy store and took her time deciding what toy we would donate, considering the possible children that it might go to, imagining their likes and dislikes, where they might be, and what would be appropriate. After twenty minutes or so, she'd selected something, I swiped my card, and we returned to the staff sergeant outside the store. She gently rested the toy atop the others.

"I hope that helps," said Sprout sincerely, her eyes aglow with the joy of humility.

"Thank you, Ms. Abigail," smiled the Marine. "That's gonna make one very happy kid on Christmas."

"Well, it's time we get going," I said trying to usher my children along.

"Stay warm out there," he said. "And Ryan, here's my card if you have any other questions about the Marines. I'd be happy to answer them any time." I considered intercepting the card but restrained myself, watching Ryan take the information. "Have a Merry Christmas."

"Merry Christmas, Staff Sergeant Kopek," said Sprout.

"I wish you could keep this car," Abi commented, burrowing herself into the heated seat. Ryan seconded her opinion.

"Yeah, it's not so bad, I guess." I still hadn't gotten used to the giant screen, but it had become less of a bother. "Uncle Lonnie's going to want it back though. We've still got it for two more days."

"*You* do," said Ryan. "We have to go back home and ride around in mom's station wagon." I got a touch of pleasure out of him preferring something with me than with his mother, even if it wasn't technically mine.

"Thanks for taking us shopping," Abi smiled. "Mom's going to love her gift."

"Yeah, thanks," Ryan seconded.

"No problem, guys. I had a good time."

I took that moment to think, to capture. This is what I'd been chasing so desperately, at least it felt like it. Abi and Ryan smiling, with me, together. The earth was warm and bright despite the winter evening. There was nothing more important, nothing less simple. As much as it pained me to admit that Lonnie had been insightful to the degree of accuracy, he was right. This was all about them, and they shouldn't have to pay for my sins.

"There's actually one more place I want to take you," I said as I steered the car into a U-turn.

"Are we getting ice cream?" Abi asked.

"It's too cold for ice cream," said Ryan.

"Better than that," I said, the excitement mounting in my chest.

They continued to guess as we drove toward the edge of Queen City, past the piercing lights and traffic. They began to recognize the houses. The streets and the park.

"Why are we going to our old house?" Ryan asked. I remained silent and pulled into the driveway. "Dad, why are we here?"

"Because," I said, "it's not your old house anymore."

"What are you talking about? Mom is selling it."

"That's right," I said. "And I'm buying it."

"You're buying it?" Abi repeated.

"You can afford it?" Ryan asked, and I frowned.

"I know I'm not made of money, but yes. In a few weeks, all the paperwork will be completed, and we can start moving in." I turned to them with a smile. "I might even put that tire swing back up."

"Really?" Abi's eyes sparkled.

"Why are you buying it?" asked Ryan.

"What do you mean, why? So that we can live here," I answered.

"Why here though?" Ryan was apparently not sharing Abi's excitement. "We just moved out a week ago. We lived here for a long time. Why do you want to go back?"

"I thought you guys would be happy. This is our family home."

"I'm happy," Abi chimed in, smiling.

"I mean, it's not that I'm not happy. I just…"

"Just what, Ryan?" I looked at him, his face the picture of a concentrated search.

"I'm just surprised. That's all."

While I didn't think he was lying, I didn't believe him completely, either. There was more going around in his brain that he deliberately kept hidden, and he didn't appear afraid that I knew it. However, what I wondered, more than the details of what he'd repressed, was why he'd decided to stay silent. Ryan was not often self-censoring, even at the expense of another person. So why now?

"I think this is the best Christmas gift ever, Dad," said Abi, breaking my thoughts. Ryan looked out the window as I smiled at her.

"I'm glad, Sprout. I'm really glad."

A couple minutes later we were on our way back to my soon-to-be-former apartment, and the conversation quickly turned toward the subject that had been itching in the back of my mind.

"Are you going to join?" Abi asked Ryan whose expression of deep contemplation quickly faded.

"Join what?" he asked.

"The Marines, obviously."

"I don't know. I might. I might not," he answered with a shrug.

"You've got to finish high school first," I said, looking at him in the rearview.

"I know."

"Yeah, you can't drop out this close to graduating," chimed in Abi.

"I said, I know."

"Have you been thinking at all about any colleges?" I asked. He looked out the window, shifting as we drove over a pothole.

"I mean…I've looked at a couple. I think I might start with community college though. It's a lot cheaper."

"And then move on to a university?"

"Sure. Yeah." His lack of commitment didn't satisfy me, and I was about to tell him so when a set of flashing blue lights popped on behind me.

"What's going on?" Abi asked. "Are they pulling us over?"

"I guess so."

"What did you do? Were you speeding?"

"No. What makes you think I did anything?" I asked.

"They wouldn't be stopping you if you didn't," said Ryan.

"I didn't do anything, guys," I said as I pulled to the side of the road. "It's fine. There's seriously nothing to worry about." Despite my words, I could feel Sprout's anxiety, and I took her hand. "It's going to be fine."

Two officers approached the car, one on each side discreetly touching the trunk. I'd already rolled the window down and smiled when he appeared.

"Evening, folks. How are you all doing tonight?"

"We're okay. Just going home from Christmas shopping," I said.

"Do you know why I stopped you?" he asked.

"Honestly, no," I said. "I know I wasn't speeding."

"No, you weren't," he agreed. "I stopped you because your passenger taillight is out. Were you aware of that?"

"Really? No, I didn't know. This isn't actually my car."

"Whose car is it?"

"It belongs to a friend of mine. I'm not all that used to driving it. The thing is practically a spaceship," I joked.

"Okay," he said unamused. "I'll just need to see your license, registration, and proof of insurance."

"Sure," I said. "It's just in my back pocket." I shifted to retrieve my license and handed it to him.

"Registration and insurance."

"Oh, yeah. I'm not sure where..." I looked around for a split second before deciding on the glove compartment in front of Abi, and I reached for a handle that was not apparently there.

"Is there a problem?"

"There's no handle," I said. "I'm not sure how..." I turned my attention to the screen, pressing a few of the menu buttons, perspiration beginning to form under my arms. Finally, a button marked 'glovebox' appeared. "Got it."

When the light blinked on inside, my heart moved up to my throat as two large medicine bottles full of pills appeared before me, resting happily beside the documents. I lifted my elbow in a way that might avoid any chance of the officers seeing as Abi told the one on her side that the car was awesome, and how she wished we could keep it a little longer. Ryan muttered that the officer doesn't care. I was still cotton-mouthed and sweating as I grabbed what I needed and shut the compartment.

"Like a spaceship," the officer repeated. He studied the two documents, then informed me he'd be right back.

When you're in anxious situations that you don't know what the hell is going to come of something, time feels a lot longer than it actually is. That time is exponentially longer when waiting for two cops to pull your information while you have a couple giant bottles full of unprescribed amphetamines poorly hidden in your car.

"Can we listen to music?" asked Abi, reaching to the digital console.

"Sure," I said, considering that it might calm my nerves. Christmas music began playing, and I realized this would not be the case. The

THE ART of LOVE (& LOATHING)

last refrain of "Jingle Bell Rock" was finishing up when they finally returned, and they smiled in that solemn police officer way. The one at my door handed me back the papers, informing me to fix the headlight, and he'd let me go ahead with a warning.

It's suspense akin to this that people love about a good heist movie. The bad guys (who, incidentally, you find yourself rooting for because their crimes are somehow justified, or they're just too darn charming to hate) are for sure getting away with their millions. They get stopped unexpectedly but play it cool, and the officer or whoever it is that stops them has no idea that under a tarp or behind a curtain or hidden in some compartment is the loot. They get away scot-free, and you get your complimentary refill of popcorn before leaving the theater.

I was being paranoid, I decided, and for no good reason. It was unlikely they'd be found, and even if they were, there were plenty of worse drugs out there, and these could be excused away. I had calmed my heartrate until, to be helpful, Abi pressed the glovebox open and reached for the insurance and registration in my hand. In what seemed like one swift action, she took the slip, placed it in the glove compartment, and closed the door.

I witnessed this in slow motion, frozen, only releasing my breath when the compartment closed. Of course, Abi didn't push the door all the way, and it fell back open with a jolt, dislodging the contents of the compartment. The bottles rattled to the floor between Abi's feet along a stick of lip balm and a small makeup case. The officer shined his light directly on the pills.

"What you got there, sir?" he asked.

"Just my blood pressure meds," I lied. "I need to make sure I have them at all times."

"Two big bottles of them?" the other officer asked.

"I commute a lot."

"Young lady, would you hand me those, please?" Abi obeyed, confusion clouding her face.

"You already told us you don't drive this car. It's not even yours."

Frank Sinatra's voice came sweetly through the sound system, slow and clear, the slight drawl of his singing contributing to the melancholy in his tone and the song itself.

...Have yourself a merry little Christmas...

"These sure as hell aren't heart meds," the second officer said, holding up a single pink pill. "There must be at least a couple hundred here."

"All right, sir. I'm going to need you to step out of the car."

"But I haven't done anything—"

"Out of the car, sir."

...Let your heart be light...

"Keep your hands where I can see them."

"Please, is this necessary?" I asked, opening my door. "I've got my kids with me."

"Yeah. I know," the officer said, shaking his head.

...From now on, our troubles will be out of sight...

As I held out my arms, I wished I could have believed Ol' Blue Eyes just then. But as they were handcuffing me, three quietly frantic minutes later, I could see in Abi's young blue eyes that there was no erasing this. There was no forgetting or overlooking, no matter whose fault this was or wasn't, no matter what I said or did from this point forward. And Ryan's eyes...well, I couldn't see them at all.

...And have yourself a merry little Christmas now...

CHAPTER FIFTEEN

Potential is a key in an ignition. Potential is a pile of wood doused with kerosene. Potential is a bin of LEGO. A crayon held in the hand of a child. Potential is the outcome of war and peace. The money in a poor man's pocket. A baby in the womb. Potential is the difference between what's on the inside of a person and what's on the outside. Potential only exists in the middle, the invisible link between what is and what could be. It isn't the end game. It's not even the game itself. In fact, it only exists virtually by the absence of the possibility it presents. In order to exist, potential relies on the existence of something that does not yet—nor may ever—exist. So, what of a person who does not "meet their potential" as they say? Was it ever truly there to begin with?

My father once told me that every man has a duty to his life to live up to his greatest potential. I was just a kid at the time and had no idea what he meant. A few months later, he left, and I concluded that either I was never part of his potential, or he couldn't follow his own advice. After sitting in a jail cell for sixteen hours—or at least what felt like sixteen hours—I began to wonder if maybe it had been him who was never part of my potential. It's funny the shit you think about when you have nothing else to do.

"This is quite the cage," Huxley commented, looking around the cell. "I've seen worse."

"I can't believe I'm here," I said. "I can't believe this is happening to me."

"You can't?" he asked, mildly amused. "What exactly do you think happens when you start dealing drugs?"

"I wasn't dealing drugs, Huxley. I was spending time with my kids."

"In the vehicle of a drug dealer."

"Who keeps large of amounts of drugs stashed in their car?"

"Drug dealers," he said. "It's rather elementary."

"Would you mind not being a fucking smartass right now?" I snapped. "Do you think this is funny or something?"

"On the contrary. I'm feeling quite disappointed."

"Are you, now?"

"I am. There is an alternate universe in which you are a free man, Arthur. You have chosen to exist in this one, however."

"There's no such thing as an alternate universe," I said. "Don't be stupid."

"I'll do my best."

"Did you come here just to tell me how shitty of a human being I am?"

"I said no such thing, Arthur," Huxley replied defensively. "I may be your character, but you will not put words into my mouth that don't belong there."

"Leave me alone, Huxley! I want you to leave me alone!"

"If that were true, I wouldn't be here right now."

"You always have something clever to say," I seethed. "Why can't you just shut the fuck up sometimes?!"

Static hissed at us from the loudspeaker in the ceiling.

"When you hear the buzzer, open the door and walk to the C.O. office on your right." There was a crackle, and a buzz sounded followed by the muted clang of the steel door being remotely unlocked. I stepped out, the cold tile floors trespassing through my socks. Several correctional officers sat on a raised platform behind computers, shuffling paperwork, typing, and bullshitting.

"Step up over here." One officer wearing a Santa hat pointed to the line taped to the floor in front of her half window. "Full name?"

"Arthur Ryan Kimble."

"All right, Mr. Kimble," she continued, "you're being released on bond. I've printed out your forms for release as well as the terms of your bond. Here's a copy of your arrest record and your summons to appear in court with the date and time. Here are all the items on your person that we confiscated, if you'd like to take these now…" A large Ziploc bag with a sticker seal was slid my way, and I retrieved my wallet, keys, shoes, cellphone, and jacket.

"I'm missing my cigarettes and my lighter."

"If everything is there, please check this box," she indicated with a pen, "and sign here. If you are missing anything, you must declare it now. Are you missing anything?"

"Yeah, I'm missing my cigarettes and my lighter."

"Are you missing anything?" she asked again, this time her eyes sending a cautionary stare.

"No." I checked the box and signed. The correctional officer shuffled a new paper to the front.

"If you feel that you have otherwise been mistreated or had your rights violated while in custody, you may file a complaint with the Queen City Corrections administrative office. Any complaints will initiate an investigation request that may or may not be fulfilled, and if fulfilled, could take anywhere from 90 days to one year for completion from the time an approval of such an investigation is declared. Do you understand your right to file a complaint?"

"Yes." I signed. Next form.

"Sign here stating that you will comply with the terms of your bond." Scribble. "Sign here stating that you understand when you are to appear in court. Signing this is not an admission of guilt. Failure to appear will be seen as not only noncompliance of your bond but also contempt of court, and a bench warrant for your arrest will be initiated." Scribble. "On this last paper, please indicate how you would rate your experience."

"Rate my experience?"

"The scale is one to ten, ten being the best experience, and one being the worst experience. The three categories of rating are cleanliness of the facility, friendliness and efficiency of the staff, and quality of the food. You may leave additional comments in the section below." She slid the paper forward to me, my mind a giant question mark. "The scale is one to ten, ten being the best—"

"I understand, thanks," I said. I took the pen and put fives for all.

"Sign here." Scribble. "All right, that's about it. Your feedback is important to us, so please feel free to leave a review of your stay here at Queen City Corrections on our Facebook page. While you're there, don't forget to like us, and be sure to follow us on Instagram and Twitter." I blinked at her. "You're free to go. You can follow the arrows there to the exit. Do you have any questions?"

"Yeah, do you guys have a blog?"

"I suggest you get the fuck out before you assault a correctional officer," she said.

The sky above was gray, overcast simply because it was winter. The grass was also gray. The trees, gray. The birds and the buildings and the people gray. Yet, Elaine Cunningham's lips were still a deep and brilliant red within the monochrome, her eyes remained blue fire. The sight of her surprised me, and despite my best efforts to hide it, I had a feeling that she could tell.

"Merry Christmas, Mr. Kimble."

"What are you doing here?"

"Giving you the gift of freedom, of course," she smiled, spreading her hands.

"You posted my bail?"

"You're welcome."

"How did you even know I was here?" I asked.

"It's my job to know where people are and what they're doing. I must say, I was surprised to find out about the amphetamines in your system. Well, almost surprised. Hardly anybody lives without some kind of vice, and honestly, who truly knows anyone anymore?"

"Why did you take the trouble of coming out here?"

"I told you, Mr. Kimble, I'm giving you the gift of freedom. Isn't that enough of a reason?"

"Not when your gift comes with a price tag, as I'm sure it does."

"I wouldn't call it a price tag, necessarily. Maybe more like a gift-back."

"Then it's not a gift," I said. She drew in her breath to speak. "I know. Semantics, right?"

"I can't take back the bail I posted," she said after a chuckle. "It was never an exchange of goods or services. I can only hope that it might influence an outcome."

"That outcome being…"

"I want you to say 'yes'." Elaine Cunningham smiled, flaring her eyes.

"Yes, to what?" I asked, rubbing my hands together against the freezing temperatures.

"Why don't we adjourn to my car. I'll give you a lift back to your home."

Elaine Cunningham drove a silver Porsche, and well. Her command of a room seemed to extend to her command of the road, and her calf muscles flexed with each depression of the pedals. The silence between us stretched on for a minute or two, though for some reason it didn't feel awkward at all.

"Mr. Kimble," she finally said, "I'd like you to assist me in developing the new *Verb'd Magazine*."

"There is no *Verb'd Magazine*," I said with a hint of disdain. "You wrecked it. Remember?"

"I would say that's simply a matter of perspective. Mr. Dorset was running the publication into the ground. I kept that from happening."

"It's not worth having if it's changed into something else."

"But that's the thing, Mr. Kimble. The only element of *Verb'd Magazine* that I want to change is its lack of success. Contrary to what you may think, I do appreciate art. I was never any good at making it, and truth be told, I'm a bit envious of people who can. But I've always enjoyed it." The tires screeched for a second as we rounded a corner, though she didn't seem to notice. "Like it or not, I want the same things you want."

"You don't know what I want," I said.

"You're a man of principles, yes? A man ruled by his convictions?"

"Hardly."

"You've been jaded."

"It's a good color on me." Elaine pulled the car over, her eyes blazing as she faced me.

"You want normalcy. You want something you can rely on, that you can trust. You want evidence for the faith you've put into your work, into your art. You want something to make sense. You want structure. You want all these things, and the further you go down this road, the further away from those things you become. Does any of this sound familiar to you?"

"It's intriguing."

"Yet," she continued, "you can't manage to stop from continuing on, and the questions you've been asking all this time about the world, you've begun asking about yourself. That's scared you. You need something to pull you out now. You need something to keep you from losing yourself completely. You need something to believe in that's real." She looked me dead in the eyes for a long quiet moment, and it seemed that I could feel her in the most intangible way.

"I suppose that's where you fit in."

"That's where I fit in." Putting the car into gear, we rolled back out onto the road.

"So, what is it you want me to do?"

"I want you to work with me in making *Verb'd* everything it could be, everything it should be. A publication that paves its own way, bigger and more unapologetic than ever. A publication that boasts its principles and ideals of what art is. Of what creation is. I want you to help me bring all the potential it had under Jack Dorset to a reality. I want you to see its future the way that it was meant to be seen. I want you to raise *Verb'd Magazine* from the dead. But first…" She pulled into my apartment parking spot, then turned to me again. "First, I need you to believe that it can be done, because that is the only way any of these things can happen. Can you believe, Mr. Kimble? And if you can, will you believe?"

Elaine Cunningham waited on bated breath as I sat contemplating what she wanted from me, how she'd gone to such lengths to coax me into saying yes. It occurred to me then that I was the one in demand. She needed me more than I needed her, and I felt the power.

"I want a new contract."

"Done."

"And my old one bought out."

"I'll give you five thousand dollars."

"Fifty."

"Ten."

"Fifty."

"Fifteen."

"Fifty-five."

"This isn't how negotiations work," she frowned.

"Fifty-five thousand, and you can have all the belief I have left."

"All of it?"

Perhaps it had been stripped of me. Perhaps I'd never actually had it in the first place, but my resolve to follow a certain path, to embrace particular ideals and shun the rest, to never trade my dignity for gain, that was all gone. It was all right though, I reasoned, because it was a sacrifice for family.

"All of it," I said.

I watched her smile return, and it pleased me for some reason. "Welcome to Slander Media, Mr. Kimble."

The Christmas tree lights were shimmering, casting shadows through the branches of the faux tree. I stared at it, past it, for longer than I can recall, and I thought of nothing. In a sudden burst of energy, I walked into the kitchen. I reached for Buddha. A bottle and a glass. A card and a pill. An escape and a prison. An anguish and a solace. It was all irrelevant and yet paramount. The universe was so small it was crushing me, yet so vast that I felt lost. But being lost was lovely. Being crushed was relieving. As I stood there, feeling the drug lift me up and the drink set me down, I knew nothing, and through that, everything.

I was four drinks in when Lonnie showed up at my front door, knocking loudly while calling my name. Slowly, I walked down the hall and opened the door halfway before turning back toward the kitchen.

"Well, merry fucking Christmas to me," Lonnie said, following behind. "Thanks for calling to tell me my car was impounded. You know it's now considered evidence, right? A hundred-thousand-dollar car stuck in there as fucking evidence. Thanks, by the way, for asking to use it in the first place."

"You wanted me to get the oil changed!"

"A Tesla only gets an oil change every hundred thousand miles at a special service center, moron! It's an electric car! But either way, I didn't tell you to take the kids for a joy ride while you were at it!"

"Then what exactly did the mechanic do when—" I blinked at him in a moment of sudden realization. "That's where the pills come from? From the fucking auto shop?"

Lonnie let out an exasperated sigh. "What did you think? They just rain down from the sky, and I collect them in buckets?"

"You could have at least given me a heads up," I said. "It was great watching them fall right at my daughter's feet."

"They wouldn't have if your daughter hadn't been riding in the car. You know, I don't understand why the hell you were pulled over to begin with."

"Because one of the taillights was out." Lonnie looked puzzled. "Yeah, that brand-new, super-powered, six-figure car you brag so much about had a taillight out."

"I don't see how that's possible," he said slowly. I lifted my hands in ignorance before gulping the rest of my drink. "That car isn't even six months old, Arthur."

"Why don't you just ask your mechanic?" I remarked. "That's not even the important issue right now. Is there anything else in that car that I should be concerned about, because I'm already being charged with possession with intent to sell and two counts of child endangerment." Lonnie said nothing. "Lonnie, I need to know. Is there?"

"Hello?" My stomach dropped as I heard Samwell's voice calling from the front door. "Arthur, it's Sam," he said, coming down the hall, and I concluded that Lonnie must have left the door open. There weren't enough seconds to cover the remaining lines from the pill I'd crushed. No time to hide the bottle or the glass. Sam appeared, looking first at me, then the pills, to the bottle, to me, then to Lonnie where his eyes stopped roving. "You son of a bitch!"

Samwell moved swiftly around the counter towards Lonnie who backed away, his hands raised in defensive preparation. I yelled for Sam to stop, moving to intervene, but he was on Lonnie before I could get there, and the two tumbled over onto the floor. Lonnie shrieked beneath him at first until a fist slammed into his cheek, then his eye, then between the two. Samwell was cursing vehemently, his body a mass of fury that I had to throw my whole self at to pry him off. A few moments later, we were all three on the floor, separated, breathing heavily and sweating.

"Sam, what the hell, man?" I finally said.

"What the hell yourself, Arthur. You literally get out of jail for possession and the first thing you do is come home and get fucked up with this piece of shit?"

"Fuck you, man," Lonnie spat through a bleeding mouth. You don't fucking know me."

"Arthur, what the fuck are you doing?"

"What the fuck am *I* doing?" I repeated angrily.

"You don't want this for yourself. I know you don't."

"Who are you to speak for me? You don't know what I want, Sam."

"Well, apparently neither do you! I've seen you at your best, at your clearest, and I might not know exactly what you wanted then, but I know that you never wanted this! You've dug yourself into a hole you say you can't get out of, but in reality, I don't think you actually want to get out of it."

"It's his goddamn hole to dig. It's his hole to stay in if he wants," Lonnie interjected.

"You shut your fucking mouth, you fucking snake," he said,

pointing his finger at Lonnie. "You say you're his friend and yet you feed him drugs knowing that he's just out of rehab? How the hell do you sleep at night?"

"What are you talking about?" Lonnie asked. "What do you mean just out of rehab?"

"He just got out of rehab not even two months ago! A real friend would know that!"

"Arthur's been out of rehab since August, asshole! He was only there for two weeks before he left!"

Listening to this all unfold one word at a time, I sat there knowing what was about to be revealed. For some reason I didn't feel any way or other about it. It was a strange feeling, like lying in a boat out on the water. The sky becomes infinite, and you are released to the slow and steady movement beneath you. Carried away. And closing the eyes. It is another existence altogether. The sound of my name came to me from the land though, once, then again.

"Yes, Sam," I said, opening my eyes. "It's true."

Samwell leaned back against the wall, looking at me, though without any hint of anger or hurt or disappointment. It was the moment when that thing happens, revealing a fragment of the world as being contrary to what you previously believed. The heaviest of fragments that induce no tears. They inflict no pain. The revelations of their existences become instantly accepted, as if they were known all along. And you just keep on going. I recognized it from somewhere, but Sam got to his feet before I could place it. He stepped over me towards the door, paused with his hand on the knob, then walked away.

"What a fucking lunatic," Lonnie said. "Can you believe that prick?"

"Get out, Lonnie."

"What?" He sat stupidly looking at me.

"I said, get out." My voice was relaxed, my eyes glued to the wall where Samwell had been.

"What the fuck is your problem?" he asked, standing. "Come on, let's get another drink. You're not thinking—"

"I fucked Becca," I said, looking up at him. "I fucked Becca right over there on the couch, there in the kitchen, and in my bed. It meant nothing to me. It meant even less to her."

Lonnie blinked several times, his mouth hanging open. After a few moments, he slowly made his way out, never bothering to close the door behind him.

"Hello, Arthur," said Huxley from the kitchen counter.

"Hello, Huxley."

"How are you?"

"I'm tired."

"It's been a long day."

"It's been a long life."

"Not as long as you may feel, I wonder."

"Feeling is all we have, Huxley."

"Is that so?" He glanced around. "Where have all your friends gone?"

"I got rid of them."

"Why?"

"Because."

"I suppose that's a good a reason as any."

"Why do you have to be a sarcastic little shit about everything?"

"I am what you make me. Nothing more."

"I didn't make you so you could be an asshole."

"No, you made me simply so that you wouldn't have to feel the guilt of having killed me."

"What?"

"It's true. You created me to avoid your guilt, and I understand. I'm not bitter."

"I created you because I wanted to."

"Wanted to what?"

"I just wanted to."

"Come now, Arthur. We both know that isn't true."

"You don't know anything."

"I know that you're hurting, Arthur. I know that you've formed a self-destructive pattern over the course of your life because for one reason or another, you just can't seem to love yourself, much less like yourself. And you feel that since there is nothing to love about yourself, you'll hurt yourself, pushing others away in self-punishment to avoid the added baggage of dragging them down to witness it all."

"Why would I do that?"

"Guilt, Arthur. That's all. Plain old, ordinary guilt."

"Guilt for what?"

"Now that, I must admit, not even I know. I'm not sure you do, either. You haven't spent much time trying to figure it out because it's easier to pretend that it's not there. But, Arthur, one little flea might be tolerable, but soon enough he's going to invite his friends."

"Stop with the shit, Huxley. What the fuck do you want?"

"What is it *you* want, Arthur? I am here because you want me here."

"I want you to leave me the fuck alone!"

"If that were true, I'd—"

"If that were true, you'd be gone. I know, I know."

"I don't make things the way they are. I am your character. I came into existence because you wrote me into it."

"Is that what happened?" I laughed. "Well then, let me grab a pen and paper." I shot up and went into my bedroom, rustling through the clutter on my desk before finding them. I sat down there, bent over the paper. "I should've done this a long time ago."

"I am your character, Arthur," Huxley said, still in the kitchen. "I am privileged to have been a part of your story."

> *Huxley made his way down Lexington Avenue, the Midnight Marauder dodging in and out of the crowd ahead. At times hopping, flapping his wings, and running, Huxley did not let his man out of sight.*
>
> *"Uncle! Wait!"*
>
> *"Cut him off at the intersect, Farnaby!"*
>
> *"But Uncle—"*
>
> *"Just do it! He's not getting away from me this time!" The busy streets narrowed, and Huxley caught a glimpse of the Midnight Marauder ducking into a small alley. He entered moments behind him, the sound of commerce and community cut away. The alley was dark, and he stepped forward cautiously. "Come out, you coward. There's nowhere to run this time. The jigs up!"*

"Indeed, Mr. Huxley," a voice ascended from beneath Huxley's feet. Huxley looked down to see the Midnight Marauder rise swiftly out of the puddle. As suddenly as he'd appeared, Huxley heard the thick popping of a blade piercing skin, felt the fire of steel burning in his chest. "At this moment, my sword is deep in your abdomen and just a hair short of severing your spine. I will end your suffering momentarily, but first I must tell you this: there is no glory in your ending. There is no pride to be had from this death here in the mud of an alley. You wasted your life. Your life's work means nothing, nor will it ever. You were never more than just a curious little bird."

The sword withdrew from Huxley's body, and the Marauder forced his head down into the murky puddle. The putrid water filled Huxley's beak, his will incapable of keeping his breath. The water filled his lungs, and in panic, his wings flapped wildly, but with little strength for the blood pouring from his wound. His body writhed beneath the Marauder's heavy paw. Then, after an eternity of seconds, Huxley lay still. The Midnight Marauder waited a few moments longer before releasing. He stood and spit on the lifeless form at his feet before disappearing into the city.

Between the tall buildings, a single drop of rain found its way to land on the dead body of Theodore Huxley.

I stopped writing, my hands shaking.

"Huxley?" Silence. "Huxley?" I stood slowly and walked to the doorway. A puddle had formed in the place where Huxley had been. Or perhaps it had been there all along. I dropped the pencil and went to the kitchen where the crushed lines had been waiting for me. One in the right. One in the left. A gulp of whiskey. I looked around the room and felt what I equated to be absolutely nothing. Nothing but me and Ronald Giovanelli.

PART THREE

CHAPTER SIXTEEN

On the evening of January 20th, Nadine M., 22, from Sacramento, California, took the six-hour drive to Los Angeles. Armed with one wreath of flowers, a box of ten white candles and their accompanying cardboard discs, two lighters, and one framed black and white photo of Fletcher Price, she was unable to find parking and walked the remaining mile to reach Cedars-Sinai Medical Center. She knew that somewhere inside, lying in one of the twenty-four rooms dedicated to such neurological injuries, was one of the greatest authors and playwrights of our time.

"I think I was one of the first hundred people to join the Faith For Fletcher movement. I think there are, like, almost thirty-five thousand people now. That's how we ended up organizing these vigils, just to show our support. This is the sixth Sunday in a row I've been up here, even on Christmas Eve and New Year's, and it's amazing to see how the crowds keep growing every weekend. We want him to know we love him and are hoping and praying for his recovery. Fletcher Price has made such a huge impact on all of our lives, and even though the past ten years haven't been very good for him, we want him to know that we miss him, and he's still important to us."

Flickering candlelight illuminated her face and the faces of hundreds more gathered along the sidewalk in the dusk of evening. Their glowing visages speckled the path that ran through the heart of Cedars-Sinai, their voices serenading the replica of Michelangelo's *Moses*, the tablets of the Ten Commandments tucked under his muscular, marble arm.

The Riveras, a man and woman with two teenage daughters and one teenage son, had come from Reseda with very much the same items in a backpack. They'd also brought an old copy of *The Untimely Death of Friedrich Puddle*, the fourth play by Fletcher Price, and were reading from the yellowing pages, each with their own part. Mr. Rivera played the painter Friedrich Puddle, his wife the painter's assistant Hans, their two daughters Princesses Georgia and Gigi, and their son the Court Minister Lazaro.

PRINCESS GEORGIA
Where dost thine eye behold such as an abstraction but with such creation as abstraction might be obtained? What jostled planks and forlorn skies might bear grander beauty than that which must be conceived to enter earthly shade? Nay, even beauty hath no borders yet this conceived art is not art nor is conceived, and I am beleaguered by such folly and of the persuasion that you, Friedrich Puddle, have succumbed to thine own contrived and perverse manner of blindness. Yet I see no scales over thine eyes, and therefore no scales can be removed.

PRINCESS GIGI
Good sister, it is not his eyes but his head that is ill, and a sick head can all but be removed as a remedy, for health itself requires a head. By thine own nature art thou a healer, and by mine own am I with wits. Yet, neither healing nor wits can alter the workings of the mind. Shall pestilence befall us now as our own subjects assemble at the gates? Is it our fate or the fate of our lineage that we inherit such thrones only to be drowned in our own blood? They cry for blood, so blood must be spilt.

HANS
I pray thee, Princesses, speak of bloodletting and blindness as

thy whims may please, and seek the approval of thy subjects for the sake of thy lineage, but my master's hands are tied. Even now, the ropes twist and burn to the bones! If it is the work of his hands that displease, take his hands! If it be his is eyes that defile reason, pluck them from their sockets! If his tongue doth offend, rip it from his jaws! But prove thy mercy and exalt thy compassion by sparing his life, for not a breath on its own can offend, nor can the simple beating of a heart defile!

PRINCESS GIGI

Speak no more, slave, or I shall rip out thine own tongue as it doth offend me!

PRINCESS GEORGIA

Sister, he speaks for our benefit and the benefit of his master. Shall even a faithful servant be reprimanded for loyalty, or his master for earning it so? It is the art that offends, yet the art hath no tongue. The art defiles yet has no eyes. The art displeases and has no hands. It must be burned, I say. What could I not behold upon this offending canvas that I might not view from an open window?

MINISTER LAZARO

What might an open window offend if it is as the canvas? Should your majesty burn the window as well or set fire to the fields? Are not one and the other but a reflection? I say, Majesties, if a man's horse goes lame, does he not take the horse out and slay him? If a woman's child is born with hindering deformity, does she not throw it into the river?

PRINCESS GIGI

Speak plainly, Minister.

MINISTER LAZARO

Do not spill blood for the sake of the mob, for then thou art not rulers. Do not spill blood for the sake of vengeance, for then thou art not merciful. Let Friedrich Puddle's blood be spilt for Friedreich Puddle's sake, for he is sick in the mind and dull in the wits. He is beyond healing and such a disease may be infectious, that in a month's time, a year, or a century, it may prove fatal to logic! Let his life be sacrificed for his own sake and the sake of our people! In this way, thou art

just and noble rulers. In this way, thou art merciful.
PRINCESS GEORGIA
Indeed, I believe you speak truth.
PRINCESS GIGI
And I.
PRINCESS GEORGIA
But what of the prisoner? What say you, Friedrich Puddle?
FRIEDRICH PUDDLE
What say I? Should I speak in favor of myself and in the same speak my own condemnation? Or should I speak to the pen, that history might make a martyr of me?
PRINCESS GEORGIA
Thou dost speak true, for thy fate is truly beyond thy grasp.
FRIEDRICH PUDDLE
My fate, Princess, but not my life. For it is not life that I breathe, but air, and it is not life which pumps through my veins but blood. Life is action. Life is thought and forethought and recollection. Life is not yours to take, nor is it mine to keep. It is but a passing wave, as the world through the eye of a vagrant. What one perceives once will never be again, even as it might be seen a hundred times over. All is new, as it ages and as it dwindles. Thou speakest of creation and abstraction as if one begets the other, yet the world you see is abstract by your own perceptions. What is red to thee is crimson to me, and what is freedom to me is bondage to thee. Nay, I will not defend nor offend, for abstraction requires no defense. It is reality. It is I in these bonds, it is the mob at thy gates, it is thy minister and his slithering tongue. It is the two of thee upon thy thrones. It is my servant and his loyal heart. In all these things there is reality, and in all these things there is abstraction, for one is not without the other.

Gregory L. of Philadelphia, Pennsylvania, had traveled the furthest, though his initial purpose for flying into LAX was a business meeting with a multi-million-dollar vitamin water company.

"I got here about a week ago, meetings all week and whatnot, and I just had to come. I grew up reading Fletcher Price. I can't overstate his impact on my life. I've always had something he's written on hand. In the good times and bad. Fletcher Price is the one person who understood me. So, I guess I owe him. We all do."

It was a heartfelt spectacle. The hands which all had turned countless pages of Fletcher Price's books, plays, and poems were joined together, or clasped in prayer, or grasping the ends of dripping, glowing wax. Some were still turning those pages, revisiting the worlds and wonders which he'd penned, places and people that had been conjured from his own mind. It was a mind that was still now, not asleep, but for all intents and purposes, inactive.

The gathering, as holy as it was, did not move my soul. Once I'd found a spot to sit on the grass of a small hill, I took a pill I'd stashed in my wallet and began chewing it slowly, bit by bit. I wanted to care. I wanted to feel as these people did, sorrowfully hopeful, doubtfully expectant. Where had they been ten years ago? None of them seemed to care about the past forty years of Fletcher Price's work since *Happy* was published. But at the prospect of his dying, the prospect of a great mind becoming no more than a mass of decomposing tissue, they had burst forth like rats from a flooding sewer.

It seemed apparent that they had appeared for the possession of the experience, to take what was not theirs. It happened often, in all tragedies, in all places. For some reason there was this overwhelming dissatisfaction that people had for their own lives, however regal or bourgeois they may be, and in reaction they interjected themselves into affairs that had nothing to do with them. It was a need for emotion, for tragedy. For a story to tell. For a purpose. That was why they were there now. That was why I despised them.

"You look like a man who could use a little green." A scratchy voice with a slathering of Eastern Europe spoke from my left. Wearing a wrinkled button up and poorly knotted tie, a balding man nearing his sixties had walked up beside me without my noticing. A handful of stubby fingers brushed over his tanned baldness as he smiled innocently through smart, round glasses.

"I don't carry cash," I said.

The man plopped down in the space to my left and began packing some pre-ground weed into a bowl.

"I love they legalized this shit. Smoking right out in the open makes me feel—how you say—liberated. But that's half the fun, no?" He flicked his lighter and took a long, deep draw, holding his breath for several seconds before coughing out the smoke in spurts. "Ah, that's good. You sure you don't want any?" he asked, extending the bowl towards me.

"No, thanks." I resumed looking out over the crowd, a momentary silence ensuing.

"My name is Dominic. Dominic Markovski." The fingers were now pressed in line and pointing at me. I looked at them briefly and shook hands. After saying nothing he asked, "What's your name?"

"Arthur Kimble." The glowing end of his pipe crackled and brightened.

"Arthur Kimble," he repeated squinting his eyes. "Not *Verb'd Magazine* Arthur Kimble…are you?"

"Once upon a time," I answered with a deep breath.

Dominic's eyes widened with a satisfied smile that he'd learned something about me. "I knew you looked familiar."

"If you say so."

"I must confess something to you," he said quietly. "I am Bulgarian."

"What's wrong with that?"

"Nothing. I wasn't finished," he said. "When I moved to America a few years ago, I read your magazine to help me learn to read English. I read all your stories about Huxley and his adventures."

"So, that's how you knew who I was," I said.

"I recognized you from your picture. You are head writer, no?"

"That's the title they gave me," I shrugged indifferently.

"I am big fan of your work, Mr. Kimble. As I said, I read all your stories."

"Thanks."

"*All* of them," said Dominic leaning in. "This last one was a surprise."

"You didn't like it?" I asked, looking back to my view of the people lining the street.

"Oh! No, I thought it was great! I loved it!" Dominic rocked his body, wrapping his arms around his knees. "Honestly, I haven't read anything like it in a long time. It shows a different side to your work."

Though being confronted by a fan was a new and welcome experience for me, his adoration of my work stirred in me a feeling of uneasiness. I studied him again, taking more time to focus on the hazel-wreathed pupils behind the glasses. I could not detect sarcasm in his voice, perhaps because of his accent, but his eyes confirmed his sincerity. "What did you say your name was?"

"Dominic Markovski. But, please, call me Dom."

"You're not a journalist, are you? Covering the vigil?"

"Who? Me?" He laughed with wild amusement. "Listen to my English. Do you think I have a knack for words?"

"You don't have to be proficient in English to be a journalist nowadays."

"Sadly, you may be right," he nodded.

We remained quiet for some time, but then he slapped his knee. "How about a drink? This place is depressing as hell." The surge of need had long been pounding through my arteries, and the pill I'd chewed up hadn't exactly made the situation easier. "First round's on me."

Reasoning that to decline would be rude and with the 'free' element added to alcohol, I accepted his offer. We'd soon hiked our way down the street and into a large corner bar, crowded and noisy. Dominic signaled to the bartender and ordered us each two beers.

"So, you never told me what it is you do."

"You could say I do odd jobs…" Dom shrugged.

"Odd jobs?"

"For celebrities. Rich people."

"Are you a gardener or something?"

"Perhaps, you could say, I am a fixer."

"Like a plumber?"

"Eh, maybe. Well, not like a plumber. Some of my clients call me the specialist. Others call me the custodian. My favorite is the illusionist."

"That's quite the variety of monikers, Dom, but they don't really tell me anything. To be honest, with titles like that, I'm inclined to walk away."

"Please, forgive me if I'm wrong," he smiled, "but I took you for a man who might appreciate a little mystery."

"Perhaps when it's printed on paper, but when some random guy comes up to me, knows who I am, then starts telling me he's some kind of magician that cleans up particular messes for celebrities..." My words stopped as Dominic smiled with a nod, and it suddenly became clear what he was telling me. "You make problems go away. That's what you mean. Like damage control."

"Yes. Like damage control."

"What about problems that shouldn't go away?"

"My clients don't pay me to be ethical, Mr. Kimble. Only to protect their reputations."

"So, you're a kind of covert publicist," I said, feeling that there were too many publicists in the world already without one of them running around behind the scenes playing spy. He laughed heartily again.

"No, no! Nothing like that. Publicists are like metal detectors that control what goes out to the press. What I do is control what they detect in the first place." I laughed with him, the coolness of the beer on my palette relaxing me.

"You're the inside man," I said. He stopped laughing, suddenly staring without amusement into my eyes.

"I told you. Illusionist." After a long moment, his smile reappeared with the laughter of his intended joke, revealing straightened teeth, teeth which almost appeared as bars imprisoning a trove of secrets. "I started my own business here once I learned enough of the language. I worked alone out of my car at first, but now I've got an office with a beautiful view, and best of all, I have a secretary with—no joke—the nicest pair of tits you could buy in this town."

"That's quite the rags to riches story. What's your secret to success?"

"My secret to success?" he repeated, seemingly surprised at the question before continuing earnestly. "Do whatever you have to do,"

Dominic said quietly, "whenever you have to do it, and don't…look…back."

"So, ruthlessness, essentially."

"You call it being ruthless. I call it being ambitious," he said before sitting back on his barstool and turning to the crowded room. "And fuck as much as you can."

"Ah." I looked over his angular profile, increasingly distrusting the happenstance of our meeting. "Did you sit down beside me at the hospital so that you could make friends with me? Or was there another reason you introduced yourself?" My poignant questioning took him by mild surprise. "See, I'm not here because I want to be. I'm here because I have to be. Booze or no booze, I'm not enjoying myself, and now I've got someone talking to me out of the blue who earns a living by making people's beds for them, which, frankly, is a job I find difficulty in mustering very much respect for."

"You're entitled to your opinion," he nodded. "But I like my job. Why don't you?"

"I never said I don't like it."

"No, you definitely did. Just now. You find it impossible that someone might actually recognize you and want to talk to you because they enjoy your work. You don't believe there's any way I could want to pass the time with you because you dislike what you do so much. It's pretty obvious."

"You're right. You're not a journalist."

"Is that your way of telling me I'm wrong?"

"That's my way of telling you to fuck off."

Dominic Markovski nodded, puckering his lips as he looked down at his patent leather shoes. He didn't stand though, as I thought he would, nor did he make an insulting return. He just sat there, looking at his shoes. His presence began to increasingly bother me, not because he was still there, but because he was completely reserved and without retaliation. By his silence, he was compelling me to feel something I did not wish to feel yet could not stop.

"I'm sorry for being rude," I said. "I…appreciate your compliments about my work."

THE ART of LOVE (& LOATHING)

"I accept your apology," said Dominic looking up cheerfully.

"So, Illusionist, do you have any interesting stories?" I asked.

"Do I!"

I continued listening to him talking about some of his clients, though in keeping with strict anonymity. Of course, there had been the affairs, the domestic altercations, the orgies, the drug addictions, some occurring hand in hand.

He told me the story of a professional athlete who'd begun experimenting with sexual encounters of a bestial nature and had been blackmailed by his ex-girlfriend. Dominic had taken care of it.

Another was of an action star who'd accidentally shot a stuntman in the face while filming, though whether it was an accident or not was debatable as the star had caught the stuntman balls deep in his wife the week before. Dominic had taken care of it.

A famous musician had a group of young fans join her after a show in her dressing room for an orgy, and when he said young, he meant in their early teens. Dominic had taken care of it.

"So, you see what I mean by damage control," he laughed over his glass of whiskey. "It's a dirty job, but most celebrities will pay anything to keep their good name."

"You know their secrets though. That's your leverage?"

"Los Angeles is a city of low hanging fruit, my friend. And you'd be surprised how low they can hang."

Dominic Markovski was, in my mind, an anomaly. The immigrant entrepreneur who presented himself as no more than an unkempt sleaze. He didn't flaunt whatever money he must have with such a business as he described, and I wondered if perhaps he was lying. Truthfully, I had considered it often in the past hour, but between Dominic's insistence and my personal lack of giving a shit—save for the free drinks he was throwing at me—I didn't struggle with letting him say his piece.

"But enough about what I do. Even crazy stories like mine can get boring," he said before ordering us each a shot. "So, Mr. Kimble, what brings you to the City of Angels?"

"It's personal," I answered.

"You said you were here because you had to be. That doesn't sound personal."

"It's a long story," I sighed.

"Good thing I've got time," he smiled.

I looked around, slightly annoyed, and simultaneously relieved that I might actually tell someone; that I wouldn't have to carry the weight alone.

"I'm returning someone's ashes. Well, exchanging them," I corrected myself.

"You mean, like a *person's* ashes? As in cremation?"

"Yeah."

"Exchanging a dead guy's remains…That honestly sounds a lot crazier than any of my stories. Are you sure you're just a writer?"

"At most," I smiled. "It's not that crazy. It was just a mix up at the airport switching one with another."

"That's a little crazy."

"It was just an accident," I said.

"Not everything that appears to be accident is accident. The universe has its own way."

"If you say so."

"This family, they live out here?"

"Yup. I'm supposed to meet them tomorrow afternoon." Dominic took his shot and belched.

"Well, if you need a lift, let me know. Getting a cab is impossible midday, and they're all a bunch of crooks."

"I'll think about it," I said, pretty certain that I would pass up the offer. I took my own shot and shivered with pleasure.

"Tell me about your work. What's it like being a famous writer for *Verb'd Magazine*? Your family must be proud of you."

"I'm not really famous, and I don't have much of a family to speak of anymore."

"Ah," Dom nodded in understanding. "You and the wife parted ways."

"That's a very mild way of putting it, but yes."

"You are sad?" he asked after a pause.

"No. I just want my kids back. I even closed on a house a couple of weeks ago, but my ex-wife filed a protective order against me as if I might actually hurt my kids."

"Why would she do that?" he asked in shock.

"It's a long story. Either way, the courts will decide in a few days whether or not they're safe to be around me," I chuckled disdainfully.

"You said you bought a house for them?" he asked after some silence.

"Yeah. It was our home from before, when we were all still together."

"Well," he said after a pregnant pause, "I don't know all that has happened, but I hope the courts are good for you. Even I can see that you love your children." He sighed. "It's too bad that life isn't any easier when you're famous."

"Like I said, I wouldn't consider myself famous."

"But you're a successful writer," he said. "And you love what you do."

"Love is a very strong word," I said. "I guess I used to love it."

"Oh?" Dom raised his eyebrows in genuine concern. "What happened?"

"Corporate America," I chuckled irritably. "They were acquired by another company a couple months ago."

"But they are still *Verb'd Magazine*. They just published an issue last week."

"Just because it has the same name doesn't mean it's not different."

"A rose by any other name will still smell sweet, yes?"

"A pile of shit by any other name will still smell like shit," I frowned. As Dom nodded solemnly, I looked away, trying to remove myself from that room and see Sprout, see Ryan, to recall their faces in detail.

"Change is not always easy, but it is always necessary."

"It's a place that, at one point in time, felt like home. I felt like I was where I belonged. Where I was supposed to be. But now…Maybe it stopped being home a long time ago. Maybe it never was home to begin with."

"Let me tell you a story. Before I came to America, I lived in a Bulgarian village named Kabile. It is very old but still very beautiful to me. My ancestors lived there for hundreds of years, and I was happy to be there. Life was simple. However, I was born when the Bulgarian Communist Party was still strong. Opportunities were scarce, and I always wanted more. Finally, we became democracy like United States. Still, I was unsatisfied because all my life I'd heard stories about living in the West. I was told that a man could be whoever he wanted to be, wherever he wanted to be, and no one could stop him. That, to me, was freedom. Sure, we had democracy, but what good is that with no opportunity. That was why I finally came here.

"I made this place my home. But it did not take a long time for me to realize that opportunity is not free. I work harder now, longer now. I am not an honest man by trade. I have sacrificed my principles to have what I want. To do whatever I wish. And I believe, what I have learned, is that home is not a place that a man must go. Home is a place that he must make. It is about finding the place where you fit instead of hoping to fit into something else. It is about being free to—to pursue happiness. Like in our Constitution. Home is an idea. Not a place. But that's just the opinion of an immigrant." Dominic took a gulp of his whiskey and glanced around the room.

I churned over his words, that home was only an idea, a place that exists in our minds as opposed to our physical world. It occurred to me that, if Dominic's assertion was true, even the homeless might still find a happy domicile. Yet there I was, a man with a career and a place to live, an individual with desires that, in their own right, were obtainable. I was a father. Despite all this, I still felt as no more than an aimless wanderer, always passing through, but never actually going anywhere.

"Which one do you want?" Dominic asked, gesturing towards a pair of women sitting across the bar. Their lips were plumped, their eyes outlined and fluttering with accentuated lashes, and their figures were thin and fragile. They wore beauty and were beauty from the deepest layers of their skin to its tanned surface. Their eyes were hungry and that was their confidence.

"Which one do I want?" I repeated for clarity.

"I prefer brunettes, but since I am such a fan of your work, I'll let you have first pick."

"They're not merchandise to select at a store. They're women."

"My friend, not all women are merchandise, and not all merchandise are women. These two, however, are both."

Even though it ran counter to my personal beliefs on the matter, it turned out that Dominic was right. Five minutes later, they had joined us, sipping delicately on Long Islands. Apparently, they already knew Dominic and alluded to his work which silenced any doubts I'd previously held of his honesty. The brunette, Lara, leaned against him, and the blonde, Kara, against me, ensuring that every movement she made required the brushing of her body against mine. They acted thrilled when he introduced me as a writer, and I pretended not to realize that neither of them read *Verb'd Magazine*, much less had heard of it. They were quite familiarized with *Slander Magazine*, however.

The girls laughed, drank, flattered, flirted, bit their lips, whispered, hinted, lusted, touched, and took. It was a swift succession of actions carried out with professional seduction. Dom took us to his beach house overlooking the Pacific. Lara produced a glass vile of powder from her bra, pouring out a small pile onto a square mirror conveniently placed already on the coffee table. The lines were drawn and quartered expertly, then they were gone just as quickly, the sweet chemical burn in the nostrils, familiar, like a lover in the throws of euphoria. It was glorious, smiling and laughing with them. Smoking, snorting, drinking, snorting some more. It was a release that ensnared, and as I realized that it was happiness at its most synthetic, I also realized that I didn't give a damn.

CHAPTER SEVENTEEN

I woke with a start, uncertain of the time and even more so of the place. Sheer curtains drawn across a wide, balcony door glowed vaguely, dimming the indirect sunlight. The silence of the bedroom was accompanied harmoniously by the waves crashing against a nearby shore. Kara was still asleep beside me, breathing heavily, her beauty still intact upon her face. Her hair was thick with product, stringy and unkempt now, and her small, naked breasts seemed flat as the earth pulled them towards its core through her torso.

Vivian appeared in my thoughts for some reason, the natural beauty of her sleeping countenance. How I'd often wake and look at her, not with awe or love, but in a peaceful admiration for the woman herself. I blinked her away quickly and forced the lump in my throat back down with a gulp of vodka that had been abandoned on the nightstand. The burn of warm liquor brought me back to Los Angeles, into the bedroom, and into the present.

Carefully, so as not to wake the woman beside me, I slid my body off the edge of the bed, standing and swaying before regaining my equilibrium. I leaned against the wall as I put one leg after the other into my jeans, pulled my t-shirt over my head and donned my shoes to walk out into the hallway. It was a bare house with few furnishings, but the colors were contrasts of vibrance and pastel. The morning was bright in the living room, and I made a beeline for the bar, pouring myself a whiskey and water before walking it to the great pane of glass that separated me from the beach. The Pacific Ocean stretched out endlessly, each row of waves becoming miniscule lines and then fading out into a sheet of green sapphire.

"It's beautiful, isn't it?" The words took me by such surprise that my glass slipped through my fingers onto the tile floor. It landed straight up, unbroken, yet cracked from the bottom to the side. "I'm sorry, I didn't mean to startle you."

Fletcher Price was snowy-haired and somehow athletically framed even in his old age. A neatly groomed mustache perched above his lip in distinction, as did the glass of liquor flat on the palm of his hand. He watched me through dark eyes that revealed a glimmer of pleasure at the shock he'd evidently intended to invoke. Legs crossed and jaw tightened, his majestic posture appeared as though inhabiting a throne, asserting some position of power, the activity of his thoughts hidden save for the rubbing of his thumb along his fingertips.

"Aren't you supposed to be in a coma?"

"Life calls for a bit of rebellion every now and then, don't you agree?"

"I suppose." I swallowed through the dryness in my throat.

"To be honest, it was a bit thrilling to read *Verb'd Magazine's* featured short story last month. It's been so long since anyone's wanted to even touch my work, let alone print it. Of course, Dominic was quite disappointed, since he truly is such a fan of yours."

"Dominic works for you?"

"Dom works for himself."

"This whole thing was a setup?" I bit my lip in agitation at my lack of insight.

"Yes, but, please, don't be angry at Dom. He really was quite torn about the deception, and that—"

"Wait." I pointed at him. "Wait, wait, wait. Your work?"

"My work."

"You said your work...talking about the short story."

"Is this the functionality of your brain with a hangover? Serves me right for not setting a curfew for you."

"What do you mean *your* work?"

"I think it's pretty evident, Mr. Kimble. You know what you did. I know what you did. In fact, the only people in the house who don't know are Kara and Lara. But that's not their fault. They work hard."

"I don't know what it is you're talking about."

"Is this really how it's going to be?" Fletcher Price stared at me expectantly for a moment then sighed with the shake of his head. "You've got some nerve, and I mean that as a compliment."

"Again, I don't know what you're talking about. You've gone to a hell of a lot of trouble just to get me here, so you obviously believe you have a reason. I just legitimately have no idea what that is."

He rubbed his thumb again, staring forcefully at me as though attempting to read the bottom line of an eye chart.

"The short story published under your name last week, where did you get it?"

"I didn't get it anywhere. I wrote it."

"Dom!" Fletcher Price called. Dominic appeared from the opposite hallway, cleaned up in a tailored suit. "I need you to help jog Mr. Kimble's memory."

A blur of stories I'd heard the night before whirled through my mind, and I realized how badly I did not need my memory jogged. Dominic approached me, his expression annoyed, his body language unforgiving. "Mr. Kimble, where did you get that short story?"

"I told you. I wrote it." Dom closed his eyes regretfully, then kneed me directly between the legs. A shot of pain coursed like a bullet through me.

"Mother fucking son of a bitch!" I yelled, crumpling to the floor.

"Apologies, Mr. Kimble," he said earnestly. "You okay? You want a bag of frozen—"

My fist found its retaliatory mark, and we both were coughing on the floor.

"Fucking asshole," I seethed.

"I said I was sorry, you motherfuck!" Fletcher Price looked on, unamused.

"Well?" he said finally.

"Why the hell do you think I didn't write it?"

"Because I wrote it, Mr. Kimble. I wrote it, and what's more, no one has ever seen that story save two other people. So, I need you to tell me exactly how it ended up in your hands."

"That's not your story," I repeated. Dom had recovered faster than I and was prepared to give me another punch as I was rising.

"I have the original written version of it here in my hands," he said, waving a few pages in the air. "Tell me."

"I don't—" I broke off from completing the sentence again when Dom reared back to lay another on my jaw. "Okay, okay! Jesus Christ…" He relaxed as I stood then assisted me with dusting myself off. Fletcher Price cocked his head sideways in expectation. "May I have a cigarette?" Dom took a silver case from his jacket pocket and presented the cigarettes lined up neatly. I selected one then lowered myself into a chair. "Thanks," I said after he lighted it.

"Any time. Would you like another drink?"

"Scotch and water, please." I exhaled a stream of smoke and squinted at Fletcher Price.

"Please, Mr. Kimble, continue."

"I got it from a software developer. A coder, working on this translation program for some company out of Texas or wherever. The program was supposed to translate large works like textbooks and novels. The way it was designed, the algorithm—I don't know the lingo—but basically it learned how to predict what was written…Thank you." I took my drink from Dom and another drag of my cigarette.

"Predict?" repeated Fletcher Price.

"The example I was shown was the complete works of Shakespeare. After so many examples to learn from, it was able to take the first half of a play and finish the second half."

"What do you mean finish?"

"I mean finish. Word for word. As if the program was Shakespeare himself."

"Sounds like something out of a bad novel."

"It's true. She showed it to me, and I couldn't believe it myself," I said, sipping my drink. "But seeing is believing. The same thing happened with Hemingway and David Foster Wallace, their unfinished works."

He stared out the window slowly sipping from his drink. "This software, what did you say it was called?"

"I didn't. But honestly, I don't know. The developer had started calling it Ghostwriter."

"Ghostwriter?"

"Yeah." Fletcher Price's eyes were captured in his thoughts. "So why exactly aren't you in the hospital? I can't imagine people who were in a coma just 24 hours ago would be out drinking, smoking, and kidnapping people."

"No one was kidnapped," Dominic said. "You came here of your own free will."

"Okay, lured then," I said. Dominic shrugged.

"You mean to tell me that this computer was able to not only translate these incredibly large volumes of literature from one language to another, but could also create in minutes what the original authors spent potentially thousands of hours doing?"

"That's what I'm saying," I nodded. "And here we thought it was the factory jobs at risk of being replaced by robots and computers. I guess it's all a matter of time."

"If what you're saying is true, then there is more at risk with a software like this than our petty writing careers, Mr. Kimble." He shifted in his seat to face me more directly. "Do you understand the implication of literature, of the written word no longer being a free form of expression and becoming an art form controlled by parameters?"

"He who commands the language commands the world. I've read *1984.*"

"Or she. He or she," said Dom.

Fletcher Price rolled his eyes. "As long as creation remains a product of the people, that power is dispersed. If human creation is something that can be simulated, mass produced, then he who controls the software controls the world."

"Or she," I said. "Honestly, I wouldn't worry too much about it. I mean, what about human perseverance? Ingenuity?"

"Ingenuity? How do you think this Ghostwriter software came into existence in the first place?"

"Fair enough," I conceded.

"It seems to me," Dom said from the bar, "that while you both make good points, you are forgetting about one important element in art. Perhaps the most important element."

"And what is that, Dom?" asked Fletcher Price.

"The human experience." We sat silently for a long moment. From the bedroom, either Kara or Lara emerged, still naked.

"What's going on?" she asked through a fog. Dom quickly ushered her back amid her protest, and I saw him reaching for his wallet when they disappeared.

Fletcher Price took out his own cigarette case, selected one, then slid a small compartment door to the side. He pressed the tip of the cigarette in, rotating it powder white, then held it out to me. I accepted without hesitation, and he repeated the process for himself. I lit mine and couldn't help but smile. Sweet, sweet deliverance.

"As intriguing a discussion as it is, I fear we've strayed from the path," Fletcher Price said after settling back in his seat. "You still didn't answer my question. How did you get that short story?"

"It was just there. It was included with the software as test documents." His eyes searched the ceiling.

"What if I don't believe you?"

"Then you don't believe me."

"That short story has existed for almost twenty years without an ending."

"That's a long time to sit on an unfinished story."

"The muses are fickle creatures," he replied, turning his head down to study his cigarette. "Fickle and unforgiving. I couldn't for the longest time, no matter how much I wanted to, no matter how much the characters begged. But you did. Perfectly. Or, at least, it seemed that way before you told me about this computer program."

"That's why I'm here, because you thought I actually finished it." He said nothing.

The waves breaking on the shore hushed our silence, and I looked out at the beach once more before going to the sliding door and stepping out, the freedom within the Pacific breeze washing over me. Fletcher Price walked up beside me. He was nearly a head taller than I, a height deceptively concealed in the chair.

"So…" I said.

"So?"

"You could've just called me, you know. Long distance is free nowadays."

"To be truthful with you," he said, his eyes squinting, "that short story was only part of it. I was going to ask your help in finishing some other works for me, but…"

"But what?"

"It's clear that what I need is the software." After a moment of silence, I laughed at him, both amused and disgusted. He remained solemn. "If you give it to me, I will keep your literary indiscretion a secret, Mr. Kimble."

"All that concern you just expressed over its very existence, and now you want to blackmail me for it?"

"I realize the hypocrisy, but I can assure you I have honest intentions." He sighed deeply. "We are very much alike, you and I."

Smiling, I shook my head. "I'm not concerned with whatever reasons you want to claim. You spent the last two months holed up in a hospital, or god knows where, getting people to feel sorry for you. They had their vigils, their dedications, their fundraisers, all that, but you knew that it was only a matter of time before they'd get bored of you. Cue the software that will just magically spit out a novel for you, and you see your ticket back into the limelight."

"Mr. Kimble—"

"I have no reason to trust you, I have no reason to believe you, because at the end of the bitter day you're just a scared old man willing to do and say anything for his personal gain. Fucking pathetic to think I used to idolize you. I thought you actually gave a shit about the purpose of art, the sanctity in its creation, that not only were you a master of the language, but you weren't a goddamn sellout. Fletcher Price isn't dead. Fletcher Price is nothing but a fraud." He stood there looking into his drink.

"You are correct, Mr. Kimble. I suppose that I have become quite the connoisseur of deception. Yet, to be truthful, I find the present scenario quite removed from my personal comfort in that it would be useless to conceal my cards from you. My reasons for my lifestyle are my own, and I feel no need to explain myself or my actions. However, it seems that deception is a tool we have both become adept at wielding, and despite the specifics, it is a tool we both find necessary for our survival, or at least, for our existence in the worlds we wish to inhabit. Deception—however we may use it—is precisely what makes you and me alike.

"Though, what does make us different isn't whether we deceive others, but whether we deceive ourselves. I may be a man who has acquired a taste for violating his own standards and embraces deception when there is something to be gained, but I would never attempt to convince myself that I am not. Lying to oneself reaps no reward."

"You think I'm lying to myself? About what?"

"Beyond persuading yourself that you are not a liar or a fraud as you put it, only you would know, Mr. Kimble. We are merely equals in the art of deception, despite our differing styles."

"Deception isn't an art, Mr. Price. It creates nothing, and destroys everything, and there is no beauty in destruction. There is no hope."

"Oh, Mr. Kimble!" Fletcher Price exclaimed with a laugh. "How wrong you are! The forms they take may differ, the construct and the meanings may vary, but the colors…the colors of creation and destruction are all beautiful! And as for hope, there is hope in all things. Hope is what drives us to press on after destruction. Hope fosters belief, and belief is the lifeline of deception. So, you see? It is a balancing coexistence, like life and death. Like love and hate."

Far above was the single remaining star in the morning sky, and

I considered the possibility that there was nothing between it and me, that if one were to have a string of infinite length, it could connect us from its point in space to mine upon the earth. The despairing paradox in that was, even with no obstacle to hinder me, I could still never reach it for the distance.

"I need an answer." Fletcher Price looked at me expectantly. "Give me the software, save your career. From what I understand, that's about all you have left."

"I've either lost everything I ever cared about, or I've destroyed it," I said finally. "You went to a lot of trouble in hopes that you could coerce me into doing something for you, something by every right you should be able to do yourself, because, for one reason or another, you can't. After all this time, you can't do it anymore. And now the only thing you have to show for your life is a legacy that's in jeopardy. Mr. Price, from where I'm standing, you're the only one with something to lose."

"How much do you want?" he asked, his voice leaking desperation.

"Even if you could pay me enough, I don't have the software. The developer does."

"Then give me the name. All I need is the name." Fletcher Price's eyes were pleading, and despite my reservations, I couldn't help but feel sorry for him. "Please, Mr. Kimble. I'll give you anything."

Where the hell was that asteroid?

"What was that house number?" asked Dom.

"One, four, seven," I said.

Dom and I had left his beach house an hour before, just in time to hit traffic on the Pacific Coast Highway. After picking up my things from my motel, we weaved in and out between countless cars until Dom finally got us into the neighborhood of the late Ronald Giovanelli. I hadn't wanted him to drive me, but after calculating the cost of a cab to and from, I realized I'd be a fool to pass up his offer. We didn't speak the whole way there, either by mine or our mutual choosing. Every once in a while, I'd glance over at him, one hand gripping the leather steering wheel of his 1968 Charger. Even knowing what he did for a living, in no way did he appear to be anything but a nice guy, and I considered how difficult it must be to harbor your feelings in a job like his. It had been his choice though, hadn't it? There was a need, and Dom filled it.

The car stopped in front of a small house with desert landscaping that included a cactus and a large circular rock that I had to assume was some kind of bench. An orange tree cast shade over the spot, and in its own way, I felt the calling to sit. Rest a while.

"What are you doing?" I asked as Dom got out of the car.

"Going with you."

"Why?"

"Because it's interesting."

"Just wait out here," I said.

As I walked up the stone path, I could see the front door open to permit fresh air to enter through the screen door. I gave it my most pleasant knock and waited. Several seconds later I repeated the knock, and after another long wait, I knocked a third time.

"Maybe she's not home," said Dom from the car.

"Mrs. Giovanelli?" I called through the screen. Beyond the door, I could see a sliver of the living room, the back of a large chair, the top of a silvery head. "Mrs. Giovanelli. It's me, Arthur Kimble. I'm here with your husband's ashes."

I opened the screen and stepped inside, repeating her name as I approached the chair. As I moved through to the living room, I saw the familiar urn on the side table. A pair of pale hands were folded on a tiny lap, a black dress reaching down to the floor. In the following moments, I discovered that my suspicions, which seemed a bit far-fetched to begin with, were thankfully incorrect. Mrs. Giovanelli was not dead.

"You must be Mr. Kimble," she smiled through thin lips. Her old eyes sparkled with life, cheeks and face wrinkled but bright and colorful. "I'm sorry for not getting the door. My knees are hurting quite badly."

"No worries."

"Please, sit down." She gestured to the old, plastic-protected couch across from her. "There is tea there. Please help yourself to some of the sandwiches as well."

"Thank you," I said, taking a seat.

I wasn't sure why, but I'd been hoping and expecting for this transaction to go quickly. However, it's never easy saying 'no' to a sweet, little old lady who, despite her ailments, had gone to the trouble of preparing a spread.

"Not at all. Ronnie always liked to have a home that was inviting. He had so many friends, you know. Wonderful people. Of course, he was a wonderful man. But when you get old, people pass one by one until it's either you or them left. I guess I'm the lucky one," she smiled. "It's all a matter of perspective. Thank you for coming all this way, Mr. Kimble. I'm sorry I wasn't able to make it a bit easier on you. My doctor warned against flying."

"Really, it's no problem," I said. "Thank you for covering some of the cost. To be honest, I was worried that it might get lost again."

"Wouldn't that have been dreadful." Mrs. Giovanelli laughed heartily, and I tried to laugh, too. I only managed a nervous sounding pair of 'hahas'.

"Here you go," I said, trying not to sound in too much of a hurry. Her eyes teared up as she took a happy breath.

"Oh, Ronnie. Back from your one last adventure, I see." She took the urn and placed it in her lap, running a thin finger along the nameplate. "He was always going off on adventures as he called them, chasing this and climbing that. We used to go together long ago, but over the past few years, he had to go alone. Diabetes hasn't been kind to me. That's how he died, you know."

"Diabetes?"

"Oh, no. He was healthy as a mule. Ronnie died on one of his adventures. Fell from a cliff."

"Oh, I'm sorry."

"Don't be. He certainly isn't, I'm sure." She swallowed. "I miss him though. Even when he was gone, it wasn't so bad knowing he was out there somewhere. Now he's here. But not…Anyway, here you go." She motioned to the urn beside her.

"Thank you," I said, taking it and reading the name. The room fell silent, comfortably. Then she cleared her throat.

"How about that tea?"

"No thanks," I said, still staring at the box in my hands.

"Grief is always a difficult process. Believe me, I understand. And I see from your expression that you haven't moved on from the anger yet."

"What?" I asked, looking at the old woman.

"Anger. You have a lot of it. I can see it all around you." I said nothing. "Perhaps it isn't only grief?"

This woman, this stranger, looked into my face from her chair, and I felt the unrestrainable bursting of my heart. I needed something to rescue me, but there was nothing. Only the truth.

"I can't tell what the hell I'm doing anymore," I said. "I thought I was surviving, just doing what you do when you lose everything. But I feel like I'm losing more now than I ever did before, and no matter what I do, nothing changes. I feel like the brakes to this thing have been cut. I can't stop moving or slow down, and there's no steering away from the cliff I'm headed towards. It's only a matter of time before I go over the edge. Then there's nothing else to lose. There's nothing left to hold onto or hope for. All that comes next is the freefall and waiting to hit the ground.

"I miss my children. I miss my wife. I miss home. I just want to go home. I'm so alone, and it's all my fault! It's all my goddamn fault!"

I wept at this old widow's feet, and she placed her frail hand on my head in consolation. Her touch was warm somehow, and that warmth travelled through my skin and down my neck, finding a home deep within me. She said nothing as I buried my tear-soaked face in the skirts of her dress. Then, several minutes later, I stopped crying as quickly as I'd started.

"Thank you for meeting with me," I said, standing with the urn in my hands. Mrs. Giovanelli nodded with a smile.

"You're welcome."

Stepping outside, Dom was smoking a cigarette in the shade of the orange tree.

"You okay?" he asked as I put my sunglasses on.
"Just get me the fuck out of here."

CHAPTER EIGHTEEN

For some reason, I'd never been able to perceive the month of February as a winter month. Despite coming and going faster than any other, I always felt as though it should belong to spring. Wishful thinking doesn't save lives, however. Neither does it build bridges or create wealth, and it certainly doesn't raise the temperature. I watched the frost on my windshield refusing to melt beneath the sun's unhindered rays. Even nature has its way of giving the glorious middle finger.

"...Good morning, Linda from Cincinnati!"

"Good morning! I can't believe I got through! I'm so excited!"

"We're excited, too! I understand you have a matter-of-perspective story for us."

"Yes, but I'm not sure about this one. I feel like it's a doozey."

"Trust me, it can't be any worse than some other stories I've heard."

"If you say so...Well, I was married to my husband for over fifteen years. We had such a wonderful marriage. He was always a gentleman, listened to me, met my needs, and he was successful in his own independent way. Our favorite pastime was hitting a round of eighteen holes together. We'd go at least twice a week if it was possible. We did this religiously for well over a decade."

"Why do I get the feeling there's a deep, dark bombshell hovering somewhere?"

"Well, long story short, my husband was murdered last year in a home invasion."

"Jesus! I didn't see that coming. I'm so sorry."

"Thank you. It's been difficult, but I've managed. I've spent a lot of time on the golf course feeling connected to him."

"You said this was a matter-of-perspective story. Are you calling about his death?"

"Well, not so much his death as the way he was killed...the intruder beat him to death with my five iron."

"Wow, that's just horrible."

"They caught the man that night; shot him dead."

"Linda, your story is intriguing, but we're on limited time. Where is all this going?"

"Okay, well, that five iron was my favorite club, of all my clubs. And I knew that it would be confiscated as evidence. So, before the police arrived, I washed off my husband's blood and put his five iron there with his blood."

"Wait...you did what?"

"I couldn't let them take my five iron. I'd had that club for years! I knew I wasn't ever going to find another one like it."

"Have you actually been using it?"

"Yes, and I swear, it drives better than ever."

"I'm sure it does."

"But, every once in a while, I start feeling so guilty for using the weapon that murdered my husband to win on the golf course, and I can't even bring myself to practice my putt in the office. Can you help me?"

"Linda, I can absolutely help you. What you're exhibiting is something I call 'destructive growth'."

"Destructive growth?"

"That's right. So many things happen in our lives that will try to tear us apart, to unravel who we are as people. For some, that can be getting fired from a job, having to file bankruptcy, being diagnosed with a life-threatening illness, or, in your case, losing a loved one. It's easy to let these things get the better of us, and honestly, who can blame someone for getting discouraged about things like that. There's a process for everything, but eventually, the healthiest thing we can do is confront what it is that's brought us down. Every time you use that five iron, what goes through your head?"

"I hope I get it on the green."

"Besides that."

"My husband was murdered with this club."

"Precisely, and it has an effect on your psyche, tearing it down little bit by little bit. But let me encourage you, Linda, because this is simultaneously building you up, and making you stronger. Tragedy is difficult to experience and process, but repeatedly reminding yourself of and holding onto tragedy will only open the doors to strengthen the parts of you it bends and breaks, very much in the way a tree grows stronger with every storm. What you're doing is a very brave thing, Linda, and I commend you for it."

"Really?"

"Absolutely. So, the next time you reach for that five iron, remember that, while you might feel guilty about it, you're becoming a stronger woman. And isn't that what your husband would want?"

"Yes. Yes, he would! Thank you so much! I feel better already. I think I might cut out of work to hit the course right now."

"You do that, Linda, and thanks for calling in!...Don't touch that dial. We'll be right back with another Slice of the Lem—"

I clicked the radio off, hoping to avert the imminent aching of a thirty-pound weight in my gut.

"Let's talk about Abi," said Dr. Hollande. "How old is she again?"

"Fourteen."

"Was she present for the protective order ruling a week ago? It's been a week hasn't it?"

"Yeah. And no, she wasn't. Neither was Ryan, fortunately."

"Why fortunately?"

"Because they might have actually convinced them that I was the bad man everyone says I am. Julia's lawyer brought up everything, you know. He used my drinking and drug use and my suicide attempt against me, as if I would ever hurt my kids. I'm not a danger to them. If anything, I'm a danger to myself."

"Are the two completely unrelated? If you hurt yourself, aren't you hurting them, too?"

"I suppose…"

"Was Abi aware of your drinking problem before?"

"Yes."

"Tell me about that." Dr. Hollande folded her hands on her lap.

"It was last summer," I began with an exhale. "I had Ryan and Abi over for their visit. I was a little buzzed from day drinking as usual. Back then I could hardly go an hour without a drink. I thought I was better that way, that I was friendlier and more relaxed. And I thought I was hiding it well. This particular night, I was a little tipsier around them than usual, and once they had gone to bed, I completed the circuit. I got sloppy drunk. But everything was fine until Abi got up to go the bathroom and tripped. I still don't know on what, but she hit her head on the doorknob and got a deep gash in her hairline. It was bleeding horribly, and obviously she started freaking out. Ryan and I rushed to the bathroom to see what was going on, but I was so drunk I could hardly speak without slurring my words and my vision was blurred. I couldn't even assess her injury thoroughly. I did grab a handful of napkins though. That was a proud moment." I shook my head.

"Was she all right?"

"Ryan looked her over and thought she would need stitches. He was worried about a concussion, too, but instead of calling an ambulance, I thought I could drive her to the hospital. Ryan knew what was wrong with me. He could probably smell it. But I didn't give him a choice. We argued about it for a minute…I don't remember what I said to him, but he backed down. Anyway, we got in the car. We made it about halfway to the hospital before I fell asleep at a red light…"

"What happened then?" she asked after a long silence.

"I woke up the next morning in the back seat of my car. Ryan had managed to drive us the rest of the way, took care of everything, got us home…He's a brave kid."

"What did Julia do?"

"She swore to me that I'd never see my kids again. And I believed her." I inhaled through my nose and sighed. "The next day, I climbed into the bathtub and slit my wrist, but Vivian found me before I could get to the other one."

"How do you think what happened with your kids that night impacted your relationship with your daughter?"

"I don't know...I think that's when she realized I wasn't okay. You can only hide it for so long. There's not much worse than when your child catches on to the fact that you're fucked up."

"What are you afraid of happening with your daughter?" asked Dr. Hollande. I circled one of the metal studs in the arm of the couch with my fingertip.

"She's such a beautiful person, and I'm afraid that I'm going to ruin her."

Through the haze on my window, the woman's gaze broke from luminescent eyes above high accented cheekbones. Alabaster skin glowed behind the vapors of her breath. Two symmetrical, shadowed valleys led smoothly to her lips, blue and glittering, only the tips of her teeth visible, and wedged between them in a sensuous bite was a breath mint causing her lips to protrude. I supposed there were worse advertisements to have as your office view. Those eyes though. Why was it always the eyes?

"Mr. Kimble?" My attention was retracted back into the room.

"Yes."

"Yes?"

"I mean..." I coughed. "Sorry, what were you saying?"

"I was saying thank you for allowing me the opportunity to interview." The young man before me slouched in his chair, a smile stapled to his chin.

"Right. Um...Yeah." I shuffled through some papers. "Dylan, right?"

"Yes, sir."

"Okay. So, you graduated from Georgia State, did the whole journalism degree. How was your time there?"

"Oh, it was great."

"Okay," I said. After waiting a moment, "Can you elaborate?"

"It was a great experience. I liked it a lot. I learned so much," he nodded. "It was really cool."

"Cool…" I looked back down at the resume. "Why do you want to work for *Verb'd Magazine*?"

"I grew up reading *Verb'd*, like, religiously. So many years."

"Okay," I paused again. "So, you enjoy the magazine?"

"Oh, yeah. For sure."

"What do you anticipate doing with a career in journalism for the long term?"

"Well, I see *Verb'd* as a steppingstone so to speak. I feel it could really get me the experience I want in order to get in with some of the better, more prominent publications."

"More prominent…"

"You know, *GQ* or *Maxim*. I'd really like *Maxim*."

"*Maxim*, huh?" I breathed for a few seconds, feeling my foot shaking with agitation. "Okay, Dylan. I appreciate your coming in." We both stood and shook hands. Mid-stride to the door, he turned back.

"So, when do you think I might get a return phone call? Because I'm, you know, weighing my options with a couple other places."

That fucker pushed his glasses up with an index finger and waited for an answer from me with his mouth open. I didn't mind the wrinkled shirt, the khakis, or even the cheap shitty tie with some hypermarket brand Matisse print all over it.

"Are those Nikes?"

"Yeah," he smiled, lifting one of his sneakers. "They're Jordans."

"So, they're not yours?" I asked.

"Huh?"

"Never mind. I'm more of an Adidas guy." Dylan stood like a cow in a pasture. "I'm sure you can find your way out."

The kid finally nodded, exiting my office as he fumbled with thoughts that halfway made it to vocalization. Slumping back in my chair I looked out at the billboard again, the tips of the woman's hair silver and frozen.

"Here are the resumes for the rest of your interviews today," said Stacy, appearing minutes later in my office to rescue me from my chasm of thoughts.

"How many more do I have to suffer through?"

"Four. But a couple look like they might be promising."

"You think so?" I asked hopefully.

"I don't know. I was just trying to be encouraging." Stacy gave me an apologetic smile. "Did you see the vending machine?"

"No, I didn't. Any baked apple pies?"

"No. It's still empty." She sighed. "Oh, well. Here you go."

"Thanks. You know, I've been meaning to ask. When's the baby due?" I looked at her beach ball of a baby bump.

"March fifteenth," she smiled.

"On the ides," I nodded. "I'm not sure if that's supposed to be lucky or unlucky."

"I don't think it's either," she said. "We're having our baby shower in two weeks if you want to come. We'll be unveiling the gender."

"*At* the shower? Wouldn't you want people to know before they buy clothes and toys?" I asked. "What if it's a girl and somebody buys a football or something."

"Nobody gives a football at a baby shower," she frowned. "And even if they did, women play football, too."

"I'm just saying."

"Times are different, Mr. Kimble."

"But aren't you worried?"

"Worried about what?"

"Worried about your kid being picked on or isolated," I said, "for being too different from everyone else. The world is a pretty rough neighborhood, you know."

Stacy bowed her head with a smile, then approached my desk and looked me in the eyes.

"Of course, I'm worried, Mr. Kimble. I don't want my child to have a difficult time because they're not like everyone else. I don't want them to be judged because they dress or think or act differently. But what I don't want more than that, is for them to try to act counter to who they are, or adjust their appearance based on what other people want to see, or voice popular opinions instead of honest ones, and despite it all, to still be judged. If I can succeed in that, then I never have to worry about my baby doubting their value or trading their dignity."

For what may have been the first time, I looked closely at Stacy's face. She was young, yet always pleasant and hopeful. She wasn't jaded like everyone else, or at least, if she was, she hid it well. Best of all, however, she believed in the possibility that the future isn't all doom and desolation. The world was bright for Stacy, not because the world is bright, but because she made it that way.

"Tell me about your son. He's almost seventeen?"
"That's right."
"A senior in high school."
"Yeah, he tested out of kindergarten and went straight into first grade. He's always picked things up quickly in school."
"You must be proud of him."
"Yes."
"What are his plans after high school?"
"I don't know. Sometimes I think he'd want to go to arts school, but other times I think he'd rather just start working towards being a street artist. Of course, back in December, he was talking with a Marine recruiter in the mall. So, honestly I'm not sure where his head is."
"Does that frustrate you at all?" she asked. "That he doesn't know what he wants?"
"Not really. He's a kid. I just don't want him to do nothing."
Dr. Hollande blinked at the floor, then shifted in her seat. "How is your relationship with Ryan? Can you describe that for me?"
"Now? Non-existent. He hasn't spoken to me since I was arrested."
"Has Abi?"
"Yeah, a few times over the phone."
"Why do you think he didn't?"
"I'm still not sure why Abi did," I said. "I guess he's pissed off at me, and for good reason."
"Pissed off or hurt?"

"Why not both? He doesn't want anything to do with me."

"Did you try to reach out before the protective order was put in place?" She eyed me for several seconds, waiting for an answer.

"No. I didn't. But what would I have said to him?"

"That you love him and miss him. That you're sorry."

"He wouldn't have believed me."

"Perhaps. But what is he to think now that the window of opportunity to communicate with him has closed without a single conversation?" she asked, though I had no answer for her. "There's nothing you can change about the past. You can't undo what's been done. But how do you think you can change the future? What can be done to show him that you really do love him?"

"It's not that simple," I said. "I told you what happened that night I was drunk. Would you want anything to do with your father after some shit like that? He's given me more chances than he probably wanted to. I don't deserve him. Maybe that's the real reason why I didn't call, because I don't feel like I deserve him even if he did forgive me."

"Suppose you're right," Dr. Hollande said. "Suppose you don't deserve him. Does that mean he doesn't deserve you?"

"He deserves better than me. A better version that I just can't be anymore."

"Why can't you be?"

"Because it's just too fucking late. The only thing I would do—the only thing I've ever done is drag him down. He's so much like me...so much like me, only so much better. I want him to stay that way, even if it means cutting myself out. I don't want him to end up feeling the way I feel. I don't want to be the reason why he does what I do."

"What is it you do?" asked Dr. Hollande.

I looked down at the carpeted floor, noticing for the first time that there was no padding beneath it.

Helen had been let go, and in her place outside Jack Dorset's old office sat Max, a fair-skinned flamboyant man who surprised me by decorating his desk with pictures of his wife and three young children.

"Mr. Kimble! How are you this bright winter's morn?"

"Hello, Max."

"Would you like anything to drink? I've got this fantastic espresso machine my wife gave me for our anniversary present. It'll perk those creaky bones right up!"

Elaine appeared from within Jack's office before I could decline. "Good morning, Mr. Kimble," she greeted with a smile. "Max, why don't you make us some espresso with that new machine of yours."

"Already on it, ma'am," Max replied almost singing. I could've sworn his cheeks were lightly rouged.

It had been a while since I'd entered that room, though it resembled a whole new world altogether. The blinds were gone, replaced by cream colored drapes which were tied open with thick maroon cords. The sun shone brightly through like a sanctuary, except the air wasn't dusty or stale but rather crisp and sweet. On the walls, some modern pieces of art hung, their color schemes having been clearly matched to the rest of the room; except for one painting that was still positioned where it had been before. The matador remained frozen within the fluid motion of evading the bull's deadly horns. And the desk. It was still there, too.

"Please, sit." She gestured to one of two chairs facing her before taking her own behind the desk. I remained standing. "How are interviews going?"

"Well, I started by calling all the people that quit and offered them their jobs with a pay increase and a sign on bonus."

"Any takers?" she asked.

"No, but I've had two interviews today and have four more this afternoon."

"Let me know how those go." She shuffled some papers to the side. "There's something important I needed to discuss with you." Elaine rested her hands on her desk, fingers folded neatly, manicured nails staggered between her smooth knuckles. Her chest rose with a slow inhalation of anticipation, but Max entered with the two espressos.

"Here you go," he said happily, carrying a matching pair of tiny mugs. "I added some flavoring I know you'll both love." He placed them before us. "Caramel with a dash of cinnamon, and my own special ingredient." Max winked at me, and I felt a flush of nervousness. "Can I get you two anything else?"

"No, thank you, Max."

"Oh, and Ms. Cunningham, your two-thirty is here."

"Is he?" She looked at her small wristwatch. "Perfect timing. Show him in." Max nodded and turned away as I took the mug and blew gently over the foamy surface, the steam curling away. One small sip, and Max's secret ingredient became clear as I tasted the comforting warmth of Irish whiskey.

"Mr. Markovski, Ms. Cunningham will see you now."

I nearly spewed the espresso out over Elaine's desk upon utterance of the name. Ideations about the impending conversation brought sweat to my temples, and I began formulating a defense against anything and everything I might be accused of. I remained facing forward, however, and it wasn't until he was standing beside me that I turned to look at Dominic's smiling face as he reached to shake Elaine's hand.

"Thank you so much for meeting with me. I hope it wasn't much trouble penciling me into your busy schedule."

"No trouble at all. Mr. Markovski, let me introduce you to Arthur Kimble, the writing director here at *Verb'd Magazine*." Dominic showed no indication of having met me before as he offered his hand.

"Pleasure to meet you. I have long been an admirer of your writing. I feel as though I already know you," he laughed.

"Do you?" I asked, forcing a smile as we shook hands.

"Max," she said into her intercom, "get Mr. Markovski an espresso."

"Please, call me Dom."

"All right, Dom," she smiled. "I was actually just about to bring Mr. Kimble up to speed on our discussion from the other day. Since you're both here together, perhaps you'd like to present it to him."

"Of course." Dom shifted his weight to look at me. "Mr. Kimble, I represent Mr. Fletcher Price, the author. I assume you are familiar with his work?"

"Somewhat," I said, certain at any moment the destruction of my career would begin.

"It is no secret that Mr. Price, despite his unparalleled success over the course of his life, has suffered over the past several years after the loss of his wife. He has not produced anything for the public of much success, and his reputation has been tarnished by poor judgment and rash actions which ultimately put him in the hospital with a coma for quite some time. Last week, as I'm sure you know, he recovered and was released to go home."

"We were very pleased to find out," said Elaine. I supposed even she could kiss an ass.

"Thank you. He was pleased with so many warm well wishes. It was certainly unexpected." I tried not to roll my eyes. "I must tell you, however, that when he woke, Mr. Price was a changed man. I do not know if it is from reflection, or perhaps, he spoke to God. I don't believe in such things personally, but there is no doubt that something is different. The evidence is that, upon returning home, Mr. Price began to write and write and write some more and is now editing a new novel." Dom looked at Elaine with a chuckle. "I know I may be biased, but as his representative, I have read the work. It is, in my humble opinion, Mr. Price's magnum opus. It was truly life-changing."

"Didn't he announce a new book just a few months ago?"

"That's been scrapped," Dom said.

"Okay, then. What's the title of this magnum opus?" I asked skeptically.

"It is called *The Art of Love*."

"That's very original," I scoffed. "Who came up with that name?"

"I did," Dom smiled.

"I had a feeling." Dom stopped smiling. "What is it you're leading up to?"

"Ah, yes. I'll cut to the chase, as they say." He returned to a relaxed position. "Mr. Price understands how detrimental his actions over the past several years have been on his image. Many have forgotten, lost hope, even slandered him." I glanced at Elaine whose eyes remained steady without the hint of a flicker. "This is why he wants to have an exclusive interview, detailing the long journey he has been on, before and after the loss of his wife. Mr. Price wants to set the record straight before releasing a new novel."

"What's the record exactly?"

"I may be his representative, but if you wish to know, he must tell you himself. For this reason, I made a call to Ms. Cunningham, and for this reason I am here today. Mr. Price specifically would like you to be the one to interview him and write this exclusive."

We stared at each other for several moments.

"This would be a huge boon for us," Elaine said finally. "It could easily be the story of the year. Despite the bad publicity, people love hearing someone's confessions."

"They should join the clergy then if they want to hear confessions."

"Mr. Kimble, I don't understand why—"

"I think you understand perfectly, Dom. I'm not interested in being part of this."

"Why not?"

"Because I'm just not."

"This isn't a request," Elaine cut in. "You're being assigned this article."

The espresso was still hot, and I sipped slowly on it, perhaps in hopes of making it easier to swallow this bitter pill.

"Fine." I gave in. "I'll get with Stacy about coordinating a day in the next few weeks to do this."

"Mr. Kimble," Dom began, "I'm afraid you're misunderstanding. Mr. Price wishes to chronicle the details of his life, open the eyes of his audience to who he really is. In order to do this thoroughly, you must go to the places he has been. You must see the world through his eyes."

"You're going to follow him for a couple of weeks," said Elaine.

"A couple of weeks?" I repeated. "You mean travel and live with him for an extended period of time?"

"Two weeks," explained Dom. "Until you have what you need to make this article complete."

"Ms. Cunningham," I said, "I was under the impression that you needed me to focus on staffing my department. Who is going to train the new hires?"

"You're not the only one who is capable of doing that. This takes priority. I'll be having Jan and Vincent take over the interviews. I've also got some of my staff from other locations coming to run this little machine of ours until everyone is up to snuff."

"I have kids. I can't just up and leave out of the blue."

"I'm sure they will understand once you've explained the situation." Dom's knowing eyes narrowed as he spoke. A light tap on the door, and Max entered with Dom's espresso. Dom thanked him and blew gently on the dark steaming liquid, his gaze never leaving my face. "Mr. Price was right," he said.

"About what?"

"He said you wouldn't want to do it."

"Then why is he asking me to?"

"I asked him the same question, and to be honest, I found his answer a bit puzzling."

"What was his answer?"

"He said, and I quote, 'because he is the one who will see.'" Dom shrugged. "I can't imagine what that might mean. Do you?"

Elaine Cunningham picked up her mug held it just below her chin, the heat rising in waves over her silent smile.

"Mr. Kimble, it's a pleasure to meet you." The young man smiled at me through circular lenses, his handshake satisfyingly assertive.

"Stewart Andersen?" I asked.

"That's me."

"Thanks for coming in," I said, leading him to the chair in front of my desk. "You had about an hour drive here, correct?"

"That's right. It's a beautiful day for it though. I certainly didn't mind." He sat, the folder of papers in his hands rested flat on his lap.

"Well, Mr. Andersen—"

"You can call me Stewart," he said.

"Stewart, let's get right down to it," I said, taking my seat across from him. "Why don't you tell me a little bit about yourself."

"Of course," he said cheerfully. "I've been writing since I was a kid, reading just as much. I've always been a big fantasy fan, but I enjoy reading literary fiction as well. I feel that my style of writing is a fair mix of both. I'm certainly no Tolkien," he laughed, "but I do all right."

"Any family?"

"Yes, I've been married for four years, and we have two girls, Drea and Kisha."

"That's wonderful," I smiled.

"They truly are," he said. "I don't know what I'd do without them."

"Tell me about school," I said, quickly changing topics.

"I attended Boston University, studied journalism as my major. I also earned a minor in sociology. I edited two years for my campus paper, *The Daily Free Press*. I believe I included an article I wrote for that in my resume."

"Yes, about your theory on human development, the human equation," I said. "It was interesting, reading an article that sticks it to all the bigwigs of psychology. It certainly made me think. I only wish there had been room to develop it further, but I understand how much space is limited in a campus paper. Excellent work though."

"Thank you. I enjoyed it quite a lot."

"It says here you were a journalist for another paper... *The Latest*? I've never heard of them."

"Yes," he nodded. "It was a venture that I and two friends from college put together. The focus was investigative journalism, but we shut down after a few months. Nobody wants to talk to someone they've never heard of. I've been a copyeditor for a regional sports magazine ever since."

"That's a shame. Small press is the backbone of our national integrity, if you ask me."

"I couldn't agree more. To be honest, that's the reason I applied here specifically, because this isn't some incorporated publication like everywhere else. I've always had a deep respect for it."

"Sorry to burst your bubble," I said, "but in case you didn't hear, *Verb'd Magazine* is under knew management. Our founder Jack Dorset passed away in December. Slander Media acquired us."

"Is that so?"

"I'm afraid it is."

"But you still operate under the same name."

"Yes. That's about the only thing that isn't changing." I watched his face turn down in disappointed thought, reminding me of a person I'd forgotten about. "You know, Stewart, on paper you're exactly what I'm looking for. Meeting with you, it's easy to see you're personable and sharp and talented."

"Thank you."

"I'm going to offer you the position you applied for, head writer of *Verb'd Magazine*," I said.

"Really? Thank you," Stewart beamed.

"But I want you to say no."

He blinked in silence, digested my words unsuccessfully. "I'm sorry? You want—"

"I'm offering you this job because you would do well at it. Hell, you'd probably be more successful at it than I was. But in good conscience, I can't advise you to accept my offer."

"That makes no sense. I've wanted to work here for a long time."

"You wanted to work for *Verb'd Magazine*, the one that operated on certain principles that, well, they're just not implemented anymore."

The applicant studied me closely for several ponderous moments before he spoke. "Why are you still here, then?"

"Pardon?"

"If what you just said is true, then why are you still here?" he repeated. "It's obvious that you don't like the idea of Slander Media taking over, and honestly, I don't blame you. Comparing what the two produce is like night and day. One, as you said, had clear principles, and the other has none. But you not only stayed, you accepted a promotion."

"I sold out, Stewart," I said. "They gave me that proverbial offer

I couldn't refuse. I used to believe like you, that there are still a few shreds of goodness in this business, but it turns out that we're wrong. This is it."

Stewart thought for a few seconds, then chuckled. "Mr. Kimble, I've been reading your work in this magazine for several years. Maybe I'm being too bold right now, but I think you're full of shit."

"Do you, now?"

"*Verb'd Magazine* meant something to you—more than that, the integrity of art meant something to you. It was all in your writing, in your reporting, in your ideas. It always has been. I don't believe that you're the sellout you think you are. I believe that you're hopeful, somehow still, that there is something left to be salvaged and restored. Now, you can tell me all you want to decline this offer, but if you're extending it to me, I'm going to accept it. Because we both know that it's the people that made *Verb'd Magazine*, not the name, and as long as you haven't given up on people, then *Verb'd Magazine* can be saved. If I'm wrong, then send me on my way, but if I'm right, let me on board."

It was clear the kind of person I was faced with. Stewart Andersen had ideas, incredible ones, gliding to and fro through the firmament, searching for a place to land. They had their sights set on this place, ready to make a home. To grow. To thrive. Stewart Andersen was an idealist and unrepentant. And in this realization, I knew there was only one thing I could do.

"Mr. Andersen, I'm sorry, but it seems that you're overqualified for this position. Thank you for applying, and please feel free to use me as a reference if you ever need."

Stewart Andersen paused, then nodded, the disappointment turning bitter. "Thank you for your time," he said, then stood and left the room.

As I watched him go, I felt as though something had broken, but determined that a shot of whiskey would repair it.

"What was your father like?" asked Dr. Hollande.

"My father," I repeated. A fire engine grew louder as it roared down the road, then was gone.

"Did you know him well?"

"No. I didn't really know him at all except for his name and what he looked like. Benjamin Elroy Kimble. A tall man with a mustache. He left when I was eight, not that he'd been there much before that."

"What was his profession?"

"He was a musician. Played guitar in a band called Bad Tom. They went on the road pretty often, then one day he never came back." Another fire engine raced by. "My mother didn't keep his pictures up for very long. I have maybe a handful of memories of him."

"What kind of effect do you think that had on you as a child?"

"I was more or less indifferent, I think. I was only sad because my mother was, and then when she wasn't, because my brother was."

"Was your brother older or younger?"

"Allan was older by two years, kind of close to our father, but in a strange way. I guess he worked harder for his attention. Allan thought that he left because of him."

"Why did *you* think your father left?" A pair of police sirens sped down the street.

"I didn't know why he left. I don't really remember what I thought. I was just sad. Everything was sad. And then it was angry."

"Angry?"

"Everything was angry and heavy, like life was suddenly a burden we all were forced to carry. I can understand this for my mother. She had to become the sole provider out of nowhere. If it wasn't for my aunt and uncle, we'd have been homeless. But after so long, the tears stop. You don't ask why anymore. That anger though…that never went away. Our father never reached out to us. He didn't even come to Allan's funeral four years later."

"Do you feel that his absence has influenced you as a father?"

"If so, I hope in a good way," I said. An ambulance came and went. "I'm not so sure that absence is the worst thing there could be though."

"How so?"

"Better an absent parent than an abusive one. Better an absent parent than a self-destructive one. Better a dissolved marriage than a volatile one."

"So, you're saying that it's better to not have something than to have the bad version of it," said Dr. Hollande, resting her temple on an index finger.

"Essentially. The only bad part about that is the wondering. I wonder if it would have been so bad. I wonder what having that relationship is like. You sit and wonder and imagine your whole life, and the most upsetting part of it is that you'll never know. There's never a clear answer for how things could have been. Only what you imagine."

"What do you imagine, Arthur?"

"I don't know." I tapped my fingers on my knee. "I don't know. I can't really speculate at this point."

"Why not?"

"Because I can't. It's just…too difficult. Besides, what's the point?"

"Well, perhaps you could compare and contrast what you imagined might have been your relationship with your father to your relationship with your children," she said. "To see how much of a difference there is or isn't."

"There are only two outcomes to doing that," I said. "Either I imagine a father better than me, and I feel like a failure, or I imagine a father worse than me, and I feel like a failure."

"I don't understand. Why would you feel that way in both scenarios?" she asked.

"Because those scenarios have nothing to do with reality, and in reality, I feel like a failure."

The siren of an ambulance blared outside the window as it returned the way it had come.

CHAPTER NINETEEN

The plane touched down in Oklahoma where the cornfields used to sway. Long ago, the ground was fertile, perfect for raising acres of wheat and grazing cattle. Not far was a river. Cavities of water lay in wait underground for the children of settlers to drill down and release it. At first, only a handful of families lived in this valley, then a few more settled until there was the population of a small town. The church was built, a schoolhouse, a grocery store. War broke out in 1917, and they planted beans. The federal government paid a farmer for a few acres of land to pave a landing strip to export them. After the landing strip came a couple of gas stations and restaurants, then hotels, department stores, and by 1938, there were just as many blocks of suburbia as acres of cultivated land. This is where and when Fletcher Price was born.

The yellow cab made its way from the single-strip airport and out to where hundreds of cookie cutter houses were neatly arranged into grids that radiated out in geographic rays from the heart of Canary, Oklahoma. There was nothing spectacular about where we stopped. The home looked like an oversized Monopoly piece with a small brick landing for a porch, pure white with sea-grey shutters. I walked up the steps to the old screen door and knocked against the metal frame. A woman appearing to be in her sixties opened the door and smiled politely.

"Are you that reporter fella?"

"Guilty as charged. I take it this is the right place. My name is Arthur Kimble, I'm supposed to be meeting Dominic Markovski and—"

"Fletcher Price. Yes, they're right here inside." She held the screen open in invitation. The house smelled old, with a hint of what resembled peanuts and Werther's Originals. "I'm just so thrilled to have this visit. I been livin' here since I was a little girl and I never ever knew that this was the childhood home of Fletcher Price. It's amazin' the things you don't know until you know an' then it's like, wow! I never knew that!" She laughed merrily to herself.

"Do you remember ever finding skeletons in the closet?"

"Do what now?" Her smile vanished.

"Such a sense of humor," Fletcher Price smiled holding a bottle of water. He approached with an outstretched hand. "Good to see you again, Mr. Kimble. I was worried you may not come. Dom never doubted you a second."

"The thought did cross my mind."

"Well, I'm glad you're here," he said, smiling with an odd sincerity.

"You're looking well, Mr. Kimble," said Dom.

"You of all people should know that appearances can be deceiving," I said. We stood there silently for a few seconds.

"I believe the photographer is ready." Dom cleared his throat. "Shall we?"

The back screen door was as squeaky as the front, leading to a deck with two descending stairs. The yard was small and green, and to the right was a clothesline suspended from two rusty poles. A pair of wicker lawn chairs had been placed on either side of a small table, and adjusting the lens on her tripod-mounted camera was Vivian.

She looked up at me, for some reason unsurprised, then smiled at Fletcher Price. "I think we're all set. How are you feeling?"

"I'm feeling excellent, dear," he said. "Thank you. Just make sure you only get my good side. Of course, with all the technology you kids have today, you can make every side a good side, can't you?"

The two laughed as I stood watching, my shock turning to something akin to envy. Not of Fletcher Price, but of the moment in which she laughed.

"Mr. Kimble," she greeted flatly. "Please, take a seat."

I nodded silently and took a chance at looking her in the eyes. She didn't look back at me, however, and it appeared that the precedent was set. There was to be no recognition, no warmth, and I'd never wanted to hold her more than in that moment.

"Shouldn't you have a pen and paper or something?" he asked, looking down at my empty hands.

"Us kids and our technology," I said snidely, taking a small voice recorder from my pocket.

Vivian's camera flashed.

ARTHUR KIMBLE w/ FLETCHER PRICE
CANARY, OK - FEB. 6

ARTHUR KIMBLE: I am sitting in the backyard at the birth home of Fletcher Price, the prominent writer of such acclaimed novels as *Revelry* and *A Long Day's Night*, and plays including *The Untimely Death of Friedrich Puddle* and *Goners*. His newest book and the first in nearly a decade, *The Art of Love*, will be released this spring. This is also the first interview in over ten years that he has afforded the public, and what an honor it is to be speaking with him. Mr. Price, it is so good to see you healthy, especially after recovering from the coma you were in. But my own observations aside, how are you feeling?

FLETCHER PRICE: I'm feeling better than ever, and please, Art, call me Fletcher.

A.K.: All right, Fletcher. That's great to hear. So, we're going to be visiting a few places from your past over the next couple of weeks, and this of course would be the first one, the home in which you were born.

F.P.: Yes, and that's no exaggeration. I was quite literally born in this house. My mother didn't even have time to make it to the hospital. I guess you could say I've always been fast and easy. [*laughs*] Jokes! Jokes!

A.K.: [*laughing*] It says a lot about a man who can joke about himself.

F.P.: Well, all kidding aside, to laugh is one of the healthiest things a person can do. My mother used to tell me that, and she would laugh every day. And sing. She knew some great songs from the old country.

A.K.: The old country, as in Italy?

F.P.: That's right. She made the crossing in 1929, at the age of twelve. Couldn't speak a lick of English, but she knew so many great little songs.

A.K.: Do you remember any?

F.P.: Oh, heavens! I don't know, that was such a long time ago. Even if I could remember, you wouldn't want to hear me sing. She did it so much better than I ever could. A voice like an angel. Right over there actually, she'd sing while hanging the laundry out to dry, alternating in and out of humming when she had the clothespins in her mouth. There's an old picture somewhere of me as a baby in the laundry basket while she's doing all that.

A.K.: What about your father? What did he do?

F.P.: Well, he was born here in Canary in 1907, and worked the farm until he was old enough to learn a thing or two about airplanes when they put in the landing strip. He wasn't interested in flying, just the mechanics. As the town grew, he found his calling as an auto mechanic, electrician, airplane mechanic, you name it. I couldn't tell you much more about him.

A.K.: He was killed in action in World War II, correct?

F.P.: Yes. At Normandy.

A.K.: How old were you?

F.P.: It was early 1943, so I was five years old when he was drafted and attached to the 4th Infantry Division, if I remember correctly. Killed June 6th the following year.

A.K.: That must have been a difficult time for you and your mother.

F.P.: It was. I have only little snippets of memories from that time since I was so young, but I remember the chaplain coming up the stairs and the Army officer with him. I was looking out the window, and I called to my mother who was in the kitchen. She came around, looked outside, and I've never experienced or observed that kind of pain and instant sorrow wash over somebody's face since. Like a—like a waterfall. It was loud, too, like standing next to Niagara. You couldn't hear anything…couldn't hear the sounds of her crying. She was moving, and heaving her body, and the tears, and her mouth open like she wanted to scream, but you couldn't hear anything over those falls. [*shrugs*] That was a long time ago.

A.K.: What did your mother do after that?

F.P.: She had a big family back in New York, and after a few years of trying to do it on her own, they took us in. Explains this accent. [*laughs*] That was in 1948, so I was about ten. We stayed with my Uncle Tony and Aunt Marie, and they had a couple kids my age, Judy and Alexander.

A.K.: So, your mother tried to stay here in Canary and survive as a single mother, but that apparently didn't work out. That must have been difficult for her.

F.P.: I suspect so, but as her son, she wouldn't have told me if she was unhappy. Remember, she laughed every day, even after my father died. Now, I think that she did it more for me than for herself.

A.K.: And how did you handle that change, moving to a big city like New York from, in comparison, the deep country?

F.P.: I took it like any other kid. On the chin. [*laughs*] No, I was targeted for a short while being new, got into a few scraps with the other kids. That's kind of how it goes, and I can't deny I was a little angry. I didn't understand. My father had died, and I had to say goodbye to everybody I knew. I even got around to blaming my mother. But it's part of being a kid. I had to grow up to realize.

A.K.: To realize what?

F.P.: You know…to realize that being angry didn't help me, didn't help my mother. I never felt alone though. The family, they were everything. If I didn't have all of them, I probably would have gotten into a lot more trouble. They took care of us.

A.K.: I'd like to talk about someone you credit with really jumpstarting your appreciation for words, for reading and writing.

F.P.: Oh, you mean my Great Uncle Luca.

A.K.: Exactly. Can you tell me a bit about him?

F.P.: Good old Uncle Luca. [*laughs*] He had a beer belly the size of a basketball, was always puffing away on these fat cigars the size of sausages. He loved to tell dirty jokes, too. You want to hear one?

A.K.: Absolutely.

F.P.: What's the difference between a pick-pocket and a peeping tom?

A.K.: What's the difference between a pick-pocket and a peeping tom?

F.P.: One snatches your watch, and the other watches your snatch. [*laughs*]

A.K.: [*laughs*] That's a good one.

F.P.: [*sighs*] Great Uncle Luca...Yes, I do credit him with piquing my interest in language, but probably not in the way you'd expect.

A.K.: Oh? How so?

F.P.: You see, my Great Uncle Luca could hardly read or write, but nobody knew this. I figured it out when I would ride with him in his delivery truck in the summer. He was a milkman, and he was always telling me to read him this or that. It started with street signs, then order paperwork, the occasional newspaper. Well, one morning I climb into his truck, bleary-eyed and tired, it's still dark outside, and he put a book in my hands. It was a second edition of John Steinbeck's *Of Mice and Men*. He asked me to read it to him, so, I read it. I'd never seen a grown man shed a tear before. It was just one tear, and he caught it right as it was about to roll down his cheek. Reading that book changed the course of my life forever, not just because it's a wonderful book, but because, well, it became clear to me just how important language—the written word—truly is.

A.K.: That's incredible. Do you still have the book?

F.P.: I do, in my library at home. Every so often, I'll open it back up and read it. It's good to remember, to remind myself.

A.K.: Remind yourself of what?

F.P.: Everything. [*smiles*]

MR. PRICE IS courteous enough to give a tour of his first home, and from there we take a ride back into the city. As we pass the houses and buildings from his early youth, he watches through the open window, a soft tranquility in his face. We come to a little diner called Hackam's Deli, an aged brick building still with its original sign in the window. This was where Fletcher Price first earned nickels for delivering sandwiches to customers shortly after his father died. He is all smiles walking back in over seventy years later, and we order our own sandwiches which are mountains of deli meat, cheese from a local dairy farm, and fresh veggies all crammed between two thick pieces of freshly baked bread. The toothpick does little to hold it all together, and we end up using their plastic cutlery to eat.

F.P.: These sandwiches haven't changed a bit! [*laughs*] We used to ride bicycles up and down this street, me and the other boys. We'd have races to see who could deliver the sandwiches the quickest, sometimes even betting the nickels we were about to earn.

A.K.: Did you win often?

F.P.: Well, let's just say I never lost.

THE CANARY, OKLAHOMA, cemetery is only a few blocks from the deli, and we stroll along the sidewalk to reach the high iron gates allowing passage through the stone wall surrounding the graves. This is where Fletcher Price's father, Kent Price, is buried. After walking a bit further, we stand over the headstone, and Fletcher Price requests a moment alone. Watching from the distance, nothing is audible, but his lips are moving. One can only imagine what such a prolific wordsmith might be saying to his late father.

The steam stacks of a distant factory sent thick columns into the sky to dissipate into the atmosphere. Canary had, at one time, been bustling with life and promises of a brighter tomorrow, but all that remained from those days were the empty exoskeletons of innovation and the ghosts of generations past wandering through. I felt as one of them, my reflection on the window pale and gaunt. The red, burning cherry of a cigarette burst into a glow as I took a drag. The subtle circles under my eyes were deepened in shadow. I appeared older than I remembered, recalling that I hadn't really taken a look at myself in a mirror for quite some time. I turned up the cheap whiskey, guzzling the second of six tiny bottles from the mini bar. I glanced over at the door when the knock came, and I breathed deeply in anticipation of who would be standing there when I opened it.

"Ms. Ward," I said.

"Arthur…you're drinking?" she asked, noting the bottle in my hand. "You know that's not free right?"

"*Slander* can cover it," I shrugged. "I already got approval from Elaine to get as smashed as I want. I'll be responsible though. I'm cutting myself off at drunk."

"I find that hard to believe."

"That she approves?"

"That you're cutting yourself off."

"Sticks and stones. You know, cavemen turned those into tools and took over the world."

Vivian stood silently, looking at me in a way I couldn't decipher, and I wondered why I had addressed her with such immediate abrasiveness.

"Are you okay?" she asked finally.

"Yeah," I said. "Are you?"

"Yeah."

"How's the new position going?"

"So far, so good. I heard you're now the new writing director. I take it Sam left."

"Yup. He jumped ship after Jack Dorset died," I said. I took a breath, "I'm glad to see that it's going well."

"Thanks," said Vivian, smiling weakly. We stood there stupidly for several more seconds before she cleared her throat. "I thought you knew."

"Knew what?"

"That I'd be here. I could tell earlier that you didn't."

"That's what happens when you don't read emails," I said before putting the cigarette to my lips.

"The way things ended with us…I'm not sure how you feel about everything, but I just want you to know that I intend to remain professional, despite any feelings I have. We're here for this assignment, and I won't interfere with that. I'm hoping we can agree on that."

I couldn't understand why she had to be such an honest woman. It almost angered me how she was always so thoughtful and rational. Why couldn't she have been even a little bit upset? Why couldn't she let her emotions slip for just a moment? Then I considered that she was better off not being like me, almost as much as not being with me.

"I do," I said. Vivian smiled, and I immediately wanted to take it back.

"Get some rest, Mr. Kimble," she said, turning down the hallway.

"Vivian," I started. She stopped and looked over her shoulder at me.

"Yes?" she asked.

Despite knowing what it was I wanted to say, I couldn't find the words to say it.

"See you tomorrow."

I closed the door and drank the remaining bottles.

Loud knocking erupted, and lying on the bed, I covered my ears. "Arthur!" Vivian's voice punched through from the hall. Huffing, I stood, marched to the door and opened it.

"What do you want?"

"Why aren't you dressed?"

"It's the middle of the night! What are you talking about?"

"No, Arthur," Vivian shook her head disgustedly. "It's 10am, and we've got half an hour before our bus is here. Now, get your shit together and be down in the lobby in ten minutes, or I swear to God, you'll be hitchhiking your way to New York." She stormed off.

"Fuck." I closed the door, then in sobering comprehension swung it back open and called after her, "We're taking a bus?!"

"You look like shit." Fletcher Price looked down at me where I'd kept myself wedged into the seat with my face covered for the first few hours of the trip. "Water?" I looked up at him through squinted eyes, then took the bottle he extended. He dropped into the seat beside me. "Here, have a couple aspirin." He produced three pills, which I also accepted, then watched me interestedly. "I want to ask you a question."

"What?" I asked.

He stretched his legs out into the aisle and crossed his feet. "How do you and Ms. Ward know each other?"

"Who said we know each other?"

"Please, Mr. Kimble, I'm not a psychic, but I wasn't born yesterday." He waited for an answer.

"We both work for the same company," I said reluctantly.

"I mean besides that."

"It's a long story that I don't care to get into right now." Fletcher opened his hands, extending them to reference our current location. "Besides, I thought I was here to interview you."

"Why not take some time to get to know each other while we're at it?" he asked.

My annoyance finally gave out as I sat up. "Look, can we stop the charade like everything is all hunky-dory between us? I still haven't forgotten about the time you had me kidnapped."

"I never had you kidnapped, Mr. Kimble."

"Call it what you want. We're not friends," I said. "If I ever gave you the impression otherwise, then that was my mistake."

Vivian's eyes looked over the seats at us from the front of the bus, and I softened my expression. Almost a minute of silence passed before he sighed.

"These roads don't look much different after all these decades," Price said. "Pastures and fields almost to the horizon. You know, there was a time when I wanted to just walk away from it all and live on a farm somewhere. Peace and quiet…more precious than gold."

"Why didn't you?" I asked, not even avoiding the bate.

"Responsibility," he said with a singular nod.

"Responsibility to what?"

"To the readers. The audience. To my wife, most of all. Although, sometimes I think she wanted to get away from our life as much as I did. Perhaps, even more. There's a truth to the saying that a man's strength is his greatest weakness."

"I've never heard that before."

"Maybe it's not a saying. I don't know. Anyway, it would've been nice for just a while to live without all this."

Somewhere in his vision was a life he'd only ever imagined, a life disconnected from the inalterable reality of what has been.

"It must be tough being popular."

"People will tell you all the time," he continued, ignoring me, "that responsibility is more important than desire." He glanced at me with a knowing smile. "They're very misguided people."

"Mr. Price." His nurse, a middle-aged woman who never took off her knitted sweater, stood beside him with a stethoscope. "It's time for your medication and to check your blood pressure."

Fletcher Price silently pulled his arm from his sweatshirt and presented it to her.

"What about your responsibility to the ones you love?" I asked him, continuing our conversation.

"Your responsibility to the ones you love equates, first and foremost, to ensuring that *you* are okay, that *you* are well and happy. Thriving if possible. The better you are for you, the better you will be for them." He popped a paper cup's worth of pills into his mouth.

"Is that why you spent the last ten years wasting away?" I asked. He paused before sipping his water.

"Yes," he said finally. "When you've lost your reason to be good to yourself, and you can't find a reason within, why continue?"

"What about the readers and the audience?"

"It's like Miriam always used to tell me. We don't owe them a goddamn thing. Of course, she and I frequently forgot this, and we paid dearly." Price looked out the window again. "She probably far more than I."

The nurse pumped up the cuff around his arm, quieting him as she listened for his heartbeat.

The tires of the bus rolled out a baritone hiss, an occasional bumping over potholes, like a piece of music. The engine hummed ahead, tying the parts together, and even the trees whooshing by in almost rhythmic fashion added their own inaudible yet unmistakable pattern to the harmony. Clouds parted and rejoined in lovers' union across the blanket of a satin sky. Behind a pane of frozen glass, I beheld it all, yet would never remember it, because it was all overshadowed by that one ever stalking storm.

ARTHUR KIMBLE w/ FLETCHER PRICE
NEW YORK CITY, NY - FEB. 8

NEW YORK CITY, the most populated town in the United States, and no more recognizable a place in it than that of Times Square. Fletcher Price and I are sitting at one of the metal café tables, sipping coffee from one of the many Starbucks in the vicinity. Surrounding us, billions of dollars in advertisements illuminate in broad daylight, beckoning us to catch a Broadway show, see the latest blockbuster out of Hollywood, or purchase the finery and clothing from any of the dozens of shops and retail stores. Then there are the people, a million little dots of life crammed into a few blocks, and somehow, they seem to make it work.

FLETCHER PRICE: I haven't visited this place in nearly fifteen—twenty years. It's nothing like it used to be except for how busy it is; it's warmer than I remember. But it's still beautiful. It'll always be beautiful.

ARTHUR KIMBLE: What are some of your first memories of this place?

F.P.: Well, the first thing I did was hate the hell out of it. I didn't want to like being here, but you can't live here and not get drawn in. My first job, aside from the part time deal with my Great Uncle Luca, was cleaning up the family convenience store. His was one of the only places that had candy at the time, since sugar was still rationed for a while even after the war. I was making about ten or twenty cents putting in a couple hours of work a day. At least once a week I'd catch a movie at the cinema down the block from here. I remember walking up to the ticket booth and feeling like such a big man to be paying with my own hard-earned money.

A.K.: Did you have any favorite films or actors at the time?

F.P.: Well, all the greats. Who didn't love Cary Grant, Jimmy Stewart, Marlon Brando, Grace Kelly. She was breathtaking. I remember especially becoming a fan of James Dean in that one picture, um, *Reckless Without a Cause*, I think it was called.

A.K.: *Rebel Without a Cause?*

F.P.: [*snaps fingers*] That's right, *Rebel Without a Cause*. I wanted to be that rebel so badly when I was a teenager. That was before I saw him star as Harry in *East of Eden*, which as you know was an adapted Steinbeck novel. Now, I had grown to love all things Steinbeck at that point, and after watching that film as a late teen, how all the amazing qualities I loved about the novel had been fleshed out, I didn't like James Dean anymore. I realize now it wasn't his fault, but...Then, when he died, I felt almost responsible, as if my dislike for him had driven him into that fence. I felt horrible. Of course, that was just me being a silly kid.

A.K.: You mentioned wanting to be a rebel. Did you ever get involved in gang activity or any crime in your youth?

F.P.: We were all getting into our own version of trouble, but rarely ever getting *in* trouble. My mother's side, they had their ways. Their get out of jail free cards. But the first time I ever got in trouble was for stealing a comic book. They kicked my ass for it, and by 'they' I mean...

A.K.: Your family?

F.P.: It's like I've always said. If anyone's going to kick your ass, let it be family, because they'll take care of you afterwards while you lick your wounds.

A.K.: Did your mother have to be stricter on you?

F.P.: I really don't think she ever found out about that. [*laughs*] I really don't. It was taken care of, so I don't think anyone felt the need to tell her. I never got into much trouble again after that anyway. My Uncle Tony told me once that a son who worries his mother doesn't deserve her. And I believed him.

A.K.: Wise words.

F.P.: Yeah, those old bastards had a saying for everything. Don't cross a street you can't pave yourself; if you can't afford to lose it, don't buy it; leave the gun, take the cannoli…

A.K.: Wait, really? They said that?

F.P.: [*stares silently then bursts into laughter*] No, no, no, I'm just pulling your leg.

A.K.: [*laughs*] You got me. So, tell me about your mother. How did she deal with everything?

F.P.: My mother, bless the dead, she never stopped working hard for me, even though she didn't have to. We were taken care of with the family. She never married again. I don't know if she ever really dated anyone. As an adult, I can only assume, but she never brought anyone around me. She never let me know. I always appreciated that.

A.K.: What kind of work did she do?

F.P.: Seamstress. [*standing*] Why don't we stretch our legs? My ass is getting cramped.

WE WALK ALONG toward the Rockefeller Center Station, Fletcher Price remaining quietly thoughtful. The F Train takes us beneath the East River and into Brooklyn, the most populated borough of the five that comprise New York. We get off at the Carroll Street Station, then turn right onto 2nd Place.

F.P.: It's just a couple blocks. This is the street I lived on with my mother and my uncle's family. It's a lot prettier than it used to be. That's the thing about old stuff. Everyone puts a higher value on things that age. Except for aging people. Just steady depreciation. [*stops walking*]

A.K.: Is this the place?

F.P.: 30 2nd Place. This is it. [*staring*] It's smaller than I remember.

A THREE-STORY red brick townhouse is snuggled in between the rest, a painted metal fence outlining the yard. A small shrine to the Virgin Mary faces the street from the lawn, an American flag with a thin blue line waving above it.

A.K.: Would you like to knock on the door?

F.P.: No. I'd rather just keep walking.

FLETCHER PRICE PROVES that even at the age of seventy-nine, he has the energy and sprightliness of a man of thirty or forty. He leads the way down several blocks, reminiscing of playing ball in the street and riding bicycles around from one park to the other. Eventually, we cross Hamilton Avenue.

F.P.: This is Red Hook.

A.K.: Red Hook?

F.P.: I know, if you're not from New York City, all the boroughs and districts can be confusing. This is like a small village in the larger city of Brooklyn.

A.K.: You mean if New York City was a state?

F.P.: Sure…

A.K.: Where are we headed?

F.P.: Here.

A.K.: It's a pizzeria.

F.P.: You don't like pizza?

EACH SLICE OF pizza we order could be the size of three. Topped with pepperoni and layers of melted cheese, it's exactly what someone would expect of New York-style pizza. We sit at one of the two tables inside the little eatery.

A.K.: You don't mean to tell me that you ate pizza here as a kid, do you?

F.P.: It's good, right?

A.K.: Very, but I don't see—

F.P.: This right here, at this table—well, not this exact table—but in this spot, this is where I first spoke to Miriam. It was the summer of '61, just after I'd finished my studies at Princeton.

A.K.: You met your wife at a pizzeria?

F.P.: It was an old Irish pub back then. See, this was the Irish side of Hamilton Avenue. The south side where the Hookies lived.

A.K.: Hookies?

F.P.: The nickname for people who lived in Red Hook. It was predominantly Irish at the time. We, the Italians, were called the Creekies because we lived on the north side of Hamilton Avenue. Back then there was a lot of hate between the sides. We were always fighting and causing trouble. So, for me to be in this bar was a risk.

A.K.: But you did it anyway.

F.P.: You didn't see her then. She was the most beautiful creature I'd ever laid eyes on. I was twenty-three at the time, she was nineteen.

A.K.: How did you end up in here to begin with to even see her?

F.P.: No, no, I first *spoke* to her here. The first place I saw her was in Times Square. Right where you and I were sitting earlier. I saw her, red hair playing in the breeze as she crossed the street. Miriam had these freckles across her nose and cheeks. Eyes that radiated like emeralds. We rode the same train, and I followed her here on a path not too different from the one we just took. It was a risk to come in here. They'd have kicked my Italian ass if anyone realized.

A.K.: What did you say to her?

F.P.: Well, I looked up at her as she walked over to me, met those eyes, drew in a breath and said, 'Can I have a pint, please?' [*laughs*] And the rest is history.

A.K.: What about the Irish and Italian thing?

F.P.: We worked through it. You know…

A.K.: Her family accepted you?

"Turn the recorder off." Fletcher Price looked out the window onto the road. "Please." The rollers of the digital cassette tape on my phone stood still.

"Okay."

"Back then, it was more than just a dislike between the Irish and Italians. There were gangs, mobs at the time on both sides. You hear about the Italian mob a lot because, well, they just did it better. Irish gangs weren't so infiltrating into the backyard of democracy. But at the bare-knuckle truth, it wouldn't have been unheard of for either side to kill a man just for being in the wrong place at the wrong time. I was an Italian in an Irish pub. In the lion's den.

"Miriam…She was different, and I knew this before ever speaking to her, because when I'd first seen her, she wasn't just crossing the street. She was painting in Times Square, with her easel and her palette. She wore this big smock, and she wasn't painting the Times building or any of the magnificent structures around. She was painting the people, all together walking, blacks, whites, yellow, red, brown, all together. Poor and rich. Native and immigrant. You have to understand, in that era in a city as large as New York we always felt crowded, fighting for our space, protecting what was ours because there just wasn't enough room to share.

"But all those different people she was painting, they all seemed to fit just fine in that one canvas. To be honest, it wasn't her eyes that attracted me, or even her hair, not her beauty. It was her mind and her art, how she saw the world in a way I never had—never could. That's what stole my heart. And when I asked her for a beer, I could see on her face that she knew what I was. Miriam just smiled and brought me a beer. I did this almost every day for three months."

His eyes squinted, wandered back outside and up towards the clear sky painted with streaks of airplane trails.

"When I'd get home," Price continued. "I'd sit in my room and write in this little notebook, verse after verse of poems about Miriam, about how much I loved her. I realized that I'd have to do something to get her attention. I couldn't just keep ordering beer and saying nothing, but in Red Hook I couldn't get up and start talking to her either. So, I wrote one of my poems down on a little napkin, and the next time I visited, I slipped it into her hand when she gave me my beer. I was ecstatic. That night, I was sleepless with anxiety. All the fears and insecurities and what-ifs came spinning up into my head.

"Well, I came in the next day, and when she handed me my beer, she slipped a napkin into my hand. Smiled at me. I was over the moon. It was all even better than I'd dreamt. I put it in my pocket and left before I'd even finished my beer. I was so anxious to know what she'd said. Once I'd crossed back on the other side of Hamilton, I stood under a streetlight and took the napkin from my pocket, opened it and discovered that it was actually the same napkin I'd given to her with my poem on it. The difference was that she'd corrected—this makes me laugh—she corrected my grammar, and at the bottom she wrote in all caps, 'YOU CAN DO BETTER'. That's when I truly, deeply fell in love with Miriam. I knew I had to have her as my wife. Nothing and nobody else would do."

"You didn't really know anything about her though," I said.

"You kids these days…you overthink everything, you fear vulnerability, and you believe reason to be the higher power. Arthur, all this that I've told you, that was everything anyone would need to know. The rest of it—the Irish and Italian thing, who her family was, any money they might or might not have had—that wasn't her. She didn't see me as some poorly written wop. She believed I was more than that, and she wanted me to see that, too. Love doesn't need a reason. Love is above reason. People who say or believe differently are simply afraid. They've been hurt. It's so easy to forget that, despite the changes we face in our lives and in ourselves, love has never changed."

"That's easy for you to say. You two spent your whole lives together."

"It wasn't always easy."

"But you stayed together," I said. "You didn't give it up. You still loved each other. So, it is easy for you to say, because you've never experienced what it's like to have the most wonderful thing end in the blink of an eye without any warning, not because that person died but because they just decided, without explanation, despite anything you did or didn't do. They took any and all choice away. They left you powerless."

I pressed record.

A.K.: You said you wrote her a poem. You wouldn't happen to remember how it goes would you?
FROM HIS INNER jacket pocket, Fletcher Price produces a small booklet and reveals within the cover a dark, yellowing square of paper upon which are many scribbled lines. He puts on a pair of square reading glasses and looks down over the old napkin.
F.P.: Let's see, the title I wrote is "The Parallel". Very creative stuff. All right, here goes:
> *In a house along the street*
> *Is a girl I'd like to meet.*
> *Her hair is red, her voice is sweet,*

But we are parallel.
We both are living on the shore,
But she is rich, and I am poor.
She is the harvest, and I the moor,
And we are parallel.
But what are spaces in between?
Potential places for our dreams
To fill and grow and sew and glean
Within the parallel.
So, I will venture to that place
That I might look upon her face
And I might feel her warm embrace
Across the parallel.

CHAPTER TWENTY

There is a reason why the word 'recreation' is used when describing casual drug use. Whether you want to admit it or not, there's an undeniable amount of fun to the whole thing. Certain feelings and stimulations and associations can heighten the experience of a drug, and one cannot argue the effects of increased dopamine in the brain, regardless of the stigma. It's no different a physical response than when eating a warm piece of homemade apple pie, winning a friendly game of flag football, or masturbating—except magnified by a thousand times. It all feels so damn good, and, for this reason, addiction exists.

The truth is, everyone's addicted to something whether it's work, food, exercise, relationships, sports, the list goes on. Of course, it's all a matter of choice. The only difference with drugs is that, if you want to stop, you're battling more than the desire for dopamine and a weak resolve. You're battling the physical need for that other chemical. This is why people who cut out sugars from their diet aren't curled up in bed, sweating bullets and shivering in pain. Withdrawal from a drug is terrifying. It hurts down in your bones and seems to last for an eternity.

"You look like shit," Dom said, standing over me in the bus aisle.

"You're not the first person to say that," I mumbled.

"Why are you shaking?" I rolled my eyes and leaned my head

against the window to watch the evening set in. "What's the matter, Mr. Kimble?"

"Go away." Dom took the seat beside me.

"Do you know why I'm here on this trip?"

"You're Price's henchman. Why wouldn't you be?"

"I'm here to make sure you don't make this whole thing crash and burn. I'm not a henchman. I'm not a butler. I'm a fixer. You pose a potential problem that Mr. Price cannot afford. At the same time, I'm not a babysitter. So, when I ask you what's the matter, it's because I have the feeling that you're on the verge of fucking something up." I said nothing to him, wishing I could just silence the world and go to sleep. Wishing that I'd had more willpower to ration my pills. "You're withdrawing, yes?"

"I'm fine."

"I've seen this many times," Dom sighed. "It is debilitating."

"I said, I'm fine."

"How do you expect to do your job like this? I've watched you get worse sitting here on the bus yesterday and now today. You can't will or think this away. Your physical body is in shock."

"What the fuck do you want me to do?" I finally snapped. "I'm out. My supplier is hundreds of miles away."

"Yes, I know." Dom reached into his inner jacket pocket and produced a small plastic bag, a handful of happy pink pills inside. "I am good at what I do because I anticipate and prepare." I reached for the bag, but he pulled away. "However, I'm not your dealer. I'm not going to dish them out to you because you can't control yourself. There are six here. You may have six more in four days. Do you understand?"

"Yes," I nodded, never taking my eyes off the pills.

"No." Dom leaned in and spoke slowly. "Do you understand?"

I summoned the courage to look him in the eyes and saw fire.

"I understand."

Dom tossed the bag at me. "Get yourself cleaned up. We are stopping in one hour."

"One hour? We're not even halfway through Florida," I said.

"And if you weren't so preoccupied, you'd know why," said

Dom before leaving me.

Two glowing circles rose up over the Florida State Fair like two giant eyes, spinning in neon. There was a miniature horizon to the fairgrounds, bright towers pricking the black sky with their needles, and over everything was a hue of gold and multicolored roses.

"I haven't been to this place in almost thirty years," said Fletcher Price, the light of a child in his eyes. "Still smells like popcorn and cream soda...How many tickets for a hundred?"

The ticket booth attendant stared down at the bill. "Um...at twenty-five for thirty...that's...one hundred twenty? Yeah, a hundred and twenty," she nodded, pleased with herself.

"Excellent. One hundred and twenty tickets, please." Price smiled, slapping his hand on the counter. Gazing about him, he looked momentarily entranced. "My, the lights are brighter than I remember."

"Thank you for bringing us," said Vivian in between shutter clicks.

"Oh, yes!" he suddenly cried. "Everyone, get in for a picture!" Turning to the attendant, "Excuse me, would you take a picture of the six of us?"

Vivian begrudgingly handed her camera to the woman at the counter before showing her the simplicity of what was needed. Ike, the bus driver, and Dana, Price's nurse, stood beside him with his arms around them before beckoning the rest of us to join.

"Smile!" the attendant instructed us, smiling herself.

I stood on the edge of the shot, feeling relieved from my suffering only a couple of hours earlier. The camera flashed, and Fletcher Price clapped his hands.

"All right, gang. Let's get this party started."

Row after row of vendors and carnival games lay out before us, all manned by workers droning their sales pitch through megaphones, their voices nasally and strangely satisfying. He stopped at a game of wooden rings and glass bottles, telling us all that back in his prime, he could win easily.

"I'm glad you're feeling better," said Vivian, stepping to my side as we watched him toss the rings.

"Thanks," I said. "I guess it was just road sickness."

"Who's next?" asked Price after losing. "Ike? Dom? Ms. Ward?"

"I'll accept that challenge," she said with a smile that, upon seeing it so closely after so long, flooded my senses with an overwhelming warmth.

We watched her, everyone cheering as I stood silently. She furrowed her brow in concentration, the same as when she used to edit photographs or read a good book. I'd never noticed before, however, and I wondered how I could have missed it.

"Your turn, Dom," said Vivian.

"No, thank you," he laughed. Vivian turned to Ike and Dana, receiving the same responses. Finally, she turned to me, extending the rings. How brilliantly her eyes lit the darkness.

"I don't know. I don't think so," I said.

Fletcher Price began chanting my name, and the other four joined him until I submitted, taking the rings from her and stepping to the line. I stood still, targeting one of the many bottlenecks in the small formation. Then, tossing the ring in what I considered a decent arc, I watched as it pinged the glass and bounced at least five feet away.

"Two more tries!" the barker cried.

After adjusting my footing and settling my shoulders, I repeated the process again, tossed, and missed once more.

"You can do it," said Dom, and Vivian moved up beside me.

"Go for the one on the edge."

"Yeah?" I asked, following her finger. "That seems like a longshot to me."

"Exactly," she said, smiling once more.

"You owe me a funnel cake if I miss."

"You owe me a funnel cake if you make it."

"How do you know I won't miss on purpose?" I asked.

"I guess I don't."

Vivian backed away, leaving me with the single remaining ring. Turning slightly, I faced the edge of the bottles lined up in a large triangular formation. With no more than a second's aim, I released the ring, watching it spin through the air until the hole caught the edge of the bottle lip, tinging, ringing against the glass, then settling around it like a necklace. They let out a whooping cheer as the man running the game very unenthusiastically handed me a giant stuffed panda, completely pink and yellow.

"You mean I have to lug this thing around?" I asked, looking at Vivian stupidly. She burst into a laugh, and I couldn't help but smile, and for a split moment, I felt a choking ache in my throat.

"Serves you right for trying," she said. "Come on. Let's go get my funnel cake. Anybody else want one?"

"Not just yet," said Fletcher Price. "I want to give that spinning ride a try." His nurse's eyes bulged.

"Mr. Price, your heart is—"

"Oh, Dana. For the next three hours, you're fired," he laughed, leading her in the direction of the ride. "Unless, of course, I have a heart attack. In which case, you're immediately re-hired."

"Let's just meet back here in an hour," said Ike as he and Dom headed in the opposite direction. "Don't get lost!"

"We won't," said Vivian, and we walked together towards a food vendor.

A few minutes later, we sat at a table, her enormous funnel cake nearly toppling off the flimsy paper plate. She tore a piece and started blowing on it frantically.

"Hot?" I laughed. She chuckled.

"Have some, Art," Vivian said before eating the bite. "Oh my god."

"What?" I asked, taking a piece for myself.

"This is the best funnel cake I've ever had. I'm not even kidding."

After cooling off my own piece, I heartily agreed as I chewed, the powered sugar melting in with the fried cake.

"Wow," I said. "Just...wow."

I caught Vivian watching me, a peculiar look of happiness on her face. "I haven't seen you smile like that in such a long time," she said quietly.

It hadn't occurred to me that I was smiling, and the acknowledgment of it almost made it disappear. "How have you been?" I asked.

"I've been well. California is a nice place to live for the weather. Not so much the traffic." She took another bite. "What about you?"

"You know," I shrugged. "I'm all right. Queen City is the same as always...I bought that house."

"Ah." Vivian nodded before taking another bite. "Are Ryan and Abi happy about that?"

"I..." There wasn't a single part of me that wanted to tell her, to utter the truth that I'd not spoken since its development. Why she made me feel the need to, however, I'll never know. "I haven't seen them in a while. Go figure, right?"

"Why not?"

"It's a long story," I said, looking away towards the Ferris wheel, rotating in the distance.

"It's okay," said Vivian, touching my arm, her understanding smile pouring into my soul. "We don't have to talk about it."

After only a couple of minutes, we'd devoured the funnel cake, and Vivian laughed at our moment of gluttonous weakness. I laughed, too, and we headed back into the crowd. As she talked of her new west coast apartment, the strange neighbors, a snake on the loose in her building, and her antique office desk that has a locked drawer with no key, it occurred to me how much I enjoyed the sound of her voice. It didn't even necessarily matter what she was saying. It was like music on the breeze, a revival of the heart.

One hundred and fifty-five feet up in the Sky Eye Ferris wheel, we looked out from the gondola, the fair spread out before us like a child's toy town, little toy people on little toy rides, except all that was imagined as a child was becoming real in every wishful way. The tinkling of a carousel's song reached us in waves. Up there, the rest of the world was not so far away, and the sky was not so close. And Vivian was there.

If only I'd found a way to tell her that I loved her.

ARTHUR KIMBLE w/ FLETCHER PRICE
KEY WEST, FL - FEB. 10

FLETCHER PRICE: It's amazing what a little sunshine can do. Changes your whole perspective.

ON A BALCONY overlooking the Atlantic Ocean, Fletcher Price sips a glass of iced tea in cool, white linen loungewear. Blades of a wooden koa fan turn lazily above us as he flips through a large leather notebook, the pages aged and thinned as the skin on the back of his hands. His eyes scanned over the writings with fond familiarity.

F.P.: There are so many of these.

A.K.: How many works do you think are there?

F.P.: In just this one? Oh, I'm sure two to three hundred. That includes doodles and thoughts. So many unfinished works. That's the thing about creative minds. They don't rest easily.

A.K.: How many of those are there?

F.P.: These notebooks? I couldn't say for sure. Dozens, at least. We're talking about five decades. None of that includes published works, however. These are all more personal. This, right here in my hand, this is the process. If you really want to know the mind of a writer, read what they keep to themselves.

A.K.: Would you be willing to read a few things for us?

F.P.: Sure, sure...let me take a look here. Here's one: "Which is more intimidating, something obviously greater or something potentially equal?"...Let's see..."Who we are is not what we are. What we are will die with us. Who we are could die or live forever depending on how we lived."

A.K.: Do you remember the context of what you were writing?

F.P.: Oh, no, this is from so long ago. There's no telling why I wrote some of these things. Well...I do remember this one. It says, "if you cannot silence a voice, drown it out..." I was exploring the villain in my novel *The Lyre*. That was back in the early seventies. It's amazing what sticks and what just...[*waves hand*]

THE SINGLE-STORY house was Fletcher and Miriam

Price's first home together, and where they lived for over half of their marriage which spanned from 1962, until her death in 2006. Fletcher Price recalls their lives in the southernmost part of the country, their cocker spaniel named Chippy, late nights on the pier, and the paintings that Miriam created which are displayed throughout the house.

F.P.: I remember sitting over at my writing desk when she came up behind me and wrapped her arms around my neck; she smelled like jasmine…and she told me we were having a baby. I'd never been happier. Pure joy. And the radiance that glowed from her very core was indescribable. A few weeks later…

"Listen, do you have to keep that thing on? I feel like I'm talking to an answering machine."

"It's part of the process, Fletcher. You wanted to be interviewed."

"Not by a damn computer." Sighing, I turned off the recorder. "Thank you."

"You were saying, a few weeks later?"

"A few weeks later, she was out in the yard, playing fetch with Chippy. I was working in the study. Suddenly, Chippy starts whining from outside, and at first, I don't think anything of it until it gets louder and louder and more panicked. So, I take a look outside and there she is face down. I ran faster than I think I ever had. Miriam had passed out. I knelt beside her, was shaking her, yelling her name. It felt like an eternity trying to revive her, but it only lasted a few moments before she woke back up. We went to the doctor, and he said she was just dehydrated and needed to rest. That night she lost the baby."

Fletcher's eyes dropped to his limp hands.

"I'm sorry."

"What are you going to do? These things happen. There was a period of grieving, but we moved on. Creativity was our release of all that, and we were better for it." He nodded and looked the room over. "Let me show you around the neighborhood."

Fletcher and I, Vivian, and Dom padded along the sidewalk,

relieved to be in the pleasant warmth of the island. He led us through several blocks of houses until we reached Duval Street where, in the winter months, dozens of vacationers were enjoying themselves, popping in and out of bars and shops.

"Miriam and I walked this way so many times, especially midday like this when the sun was at its highest. Of course, in the summer, we'd wait until the evening when it was cooler, but even then, the music could be heard all down the way, and there was always something beautiful to see and to feel. There's always been so much life here, different from New York City. I think that's why we loved it here so much. Miriam, especially. She used to say all the time that she would be happy anywhere in the world with me. But if she had to choose a place to be without me, it would be here.

"You know, as long as I've lived here, I've never been in the Hemingway house. I always felt it incredibly irreverent, the way they sell tickets to walk through his home like a goddamn carnival show." He shook his head. "Heaven forbid they do that to me."

"Why did you choose Key West," I asked, "other than the weather?"

"It was on a postcard that Miriam found in a book she purchased at a nickel and dime store. Someone had used it as a bookmark, I guess. I still have it in the house." Fletcher squinted at the street. "Our families weren't very happy, but they got over it."

"This was about the same time that you published your first novel, wasn't it?"

"Close. I published that one in New Yok, just before moving."

"Which book was that?" asked Vivian, snapping a photo from a few feet behind us.

"*The Number Three*," he said, smiling in reminiscence. "It's about a newlywed couple in a place much like this one, and the wife finds an old journal—about two hundred years old—in the attic of their house. She, of course, begins reading it, and discovers that the journal was written by the wife of a rich man who was overseeing the original settlement of their town. The journal details strange occurrences and behaviors the writer experienced. As the wife reads the journal over the course of several days, however, the same occurrences seem to be happening to her; experiencing the things she is reading about. She ends up responding in much the same way that the author did. Ultimately, the journal is a confession of the eventual murder of her husband."

"So, the woman reading kills her husband?" she asked.

"I didn't say that," Fletcher smiled.

"What does it have to do with the number three?"

"I guess you'll just have to read it and find out. I have a first edition you're welcome to have."

"Why is it," I began, "that so many of your protagonists are women?"

"Why not?" Fletcher shrugged.

"It's just more characteristic for male writers to focus primarily on male protagonists and female writers on female protagonists."

The blue skies were deceiving as they suddenly began to deliver a shower of rain. The four of us began walking back around the block to the house and, in a couple of minutes, were watching the downpour from his old green porch. Vivian went inside to dry off her camera and change her clothes as Dom took a phone call in the living room.

"This was Miriam's favorite thing," said Fletcher, slowly moving back and forth in his wicker rocking chair.

"You know, we still haven't talked about this new book of yours," I said, leaning against the railing, lighting a cigarette.

"We'll get to it eventually," he said.

"Okay," I nodded, looking out at the rain in thought. "Isn't Key West kind of far for two newlyweds from New York City to move?"

"I don't think so."

"What about your families?"

"What about them?"

"You both just up and left," I said. "Postcards are nice, but you had no connections down here. You severed the ties all because your wife saw a postcard. That doesn't seem a bit odd to you?"

"No." Fletcher spoke flatly, circling the end of the arm rest with his fingertips.

"Seems to me like you two might have been running from

something." This statement caused his jaw to tighten and set his stare beyond the porch. "What were you running from?"

"I told you our families didn't like each other."

"But you said they got over it. Cultural hate doesn't just die away like that. There was something else."

He closed his eyes and sighed. "In your preliminary research for this interview, did you happen to look at my wife's history?"

Not wanting to admit that I hadn't done any research, I responded, "Why do you ask?"

"Her family name was Dorset," he said quietly. "As in Jack Dorset."

"Wait…you mean…" He nodded in silence, and my thoughts jumbled together in a pile.

"Jack Dorset was Miriam's brother. He felt like I was taking advantage of her, was afraid I would only use her to my personal benefit."

"That doesn't make any sense," I said after some thought. "Jack told me that the two of you were friends. What would cause him to think that?"

"He claimed that I had stolen my first book from Miriam," said Fletcher. "He claimed she had been telling him about the idea for over a year, had been working on it, and then I stole it for myself. That was the end of our friendship."

For a long moment, I considered the man sitting before me, the lifetime of inspiration he'd bestowed upon me through his writing, and of the immense disappointment with the last ten years that killed my infatuation for his work. I also considered Jack Dorset, the man who'd taught me everything I understood about art, about creating it and the principles by which it should be created. I'd come to doubt the man even more quickly than Fletcher Price though, and oddly enough for the same reasons.

"Why would he say that if it weren't true? Why wouldn't your wife simply set the record straight?" I asked. Fletcher remained silent. "She didn't because it was true…"

"I never stole anything from Miriam, ever," he said resolutely.

"But you never wrote that book, did you? Jack was right all

along." He sat motionless, without a word, and I took a stunned drag of my cigarette. "You're a real son of bitch, you know that?"

"Arthur, I can explain."

"No explanation required," I said. "You're a con, and you've been one from the very beginning, plain and simple."

"But it isn't simple," he said, his desperation growing.

"Then explain it to me."

"We loved each other, truly and deeply. But love comes with a cost, Arthur, just as much as with a reward. It comes with pain and sacrifice, with disappointments and fears. It's unfair sometimes, and it can be coarse and unpleasant. But," he said, raising a finger, "the reward of completion, of companionship, it outweighs all of that."

"What the fuck does that have to do with this?" I asked. "Are you trying to justify what you did?"

"I don't need to justify a goddamn thing," he said, finally getting angry. "We lived our lives as a team. We were always on the same side."

"A team? Taking the work of a mentally ill woman to launch your career isn't what I'd call being a team."

"What the hell do you know about it?" he spat out. "Miriam and I loved each other in a way you could never understand. How could you possibly ever let someone be on your side when *you're* not even on your side? Always boozing it up or getting high so that you don't have to face yourself…You're an ungrateful, irreverent son of a bitch, pitying yourself when everything a man could desire exists at your very fingertips."

"You don't know anything about me."

"Oh, I know. I know all too well about the blinders, the ego, the expectation, the selfishness. The excuses, all the excuses! The self-loathing and sabotage…we both might have allowed ourselves to become this way, but the difference between us is that you still think you can carry on hating yourself and your life without eviscerating the joy from the people around you. We're thieves, Arthur. We take everything and give nothing in return, but I'm not the one expecting an apology."

As his words chewed and clawed into me, his face shook and contorted in the last-ditch efforts of holding back a tear. And in that moment, within those accusations, it suddenly became clear what was before me. The truth had been there all the time, but only now did I recognize it, and it astonished me.

"You didn't write a word of it...any of it. It was all her the whole time. That's why you needed Ghostwriter."

Fletcher Price's shoulders surrendered to the gravity of a thousand years.

"You are the one who sees." He spoke softly, all the vitality having left him. "Could you please call Dana? I'm not feeling so well."

Fifteen minutes later, Dom, Vivian, and I watched as he was whisked away in the back of an ambulance.

"What happened?" Vivian asked as we stood there.

My gut ached; my ribs and my throat. My arms were too heavy to take the cigarette from my mouth. My feet were directionless. My mind was a vortex. How could I say anything when I was standing naked in the middle of the goddamn world?

Without a word, I walked away from her that time.

A few hours later, the sunset long past, the fire drew dazzling spheres of light encircling the woman's glistening body, her arms and her legs flexing every muscular fiber within as she danced. The light blurred behind the booze. The world swayed, but in a sweet lulling way, as if Mother Earth wished to calm the restless human race. Shhh. Sleep. That's what we needed. But I didn't wish to sleep. I didn't wish to rest, because resting is leaving the mind to its own devices, and I didn't trust those devices, not even when I was awake. Especially when awake. Consciousness is better though. There's always one way or another to escape reality.

It was nearly 10pm when Vivian found me, my eyes transfixed on the fire dancer.

"Are you okay?" she asked quietly.

"Yeah," I said, pulling my focus back to the boardwalk. "How is he?"

"He's suffered a minor heart attack, but the doctor says he's stable."

"Okay."

"Art," she said, sitting on the bench beside me. "What did you two say to each other?"

There's a ray of hope that leaks out of unknown places, and eventually it hits you right in the solar plexus. There's no breathing then, but it's not panicked gasps you suffer through. No one gets knocked to their knees. But there's no breathing, no movement. Even the moment itself, time, is still and sweet. It runs its hour and second hands in sweet caresses down your cheeks and tells you that there is loveliness and honesty and faithfulness in a world that forever has been tucking you into bed with nightmares and terrors. The lack of breath is relieving. It is transcendent. Then, the body does what it must, the diaphragm relaxes, the lungs expand, and all the dead, bitter air sucks its way back in.

"What's going to happen with the interview?" I asked.

"We'll be here until tomorrow when he can travel back to LA. I checked with the home office, but they still want us to stick around until he's well enough to finish the interview."

"What if he never is?"

"The only thing that would change would be the headline," she said. "An exclusive is an exclusive."

"I wish I was surprised to hear you say that."

"Come back to the hotel with me. You'll feel better after a decent night's sleep."

Even after an hour of sitting in silence, she remained beside me, and everything was all right.

CHAPTER TWENTY-ONE

THE STORY, FOR BETTER OR FOR WORSE

Julia and I sat on the couch in the late evening, semi-competitively questioning Alex Trebek's answers. Her body was nestled into mine, wrapped in my arm, her hands on the baby bump that was our mystery future.

"Oh, my god," she whispered.

"What's wrong?" I asked, sitting up.

"Oh..." Julia suddenly smiled and let out a single giggle of excitement. She took my hand and placed it on her stomach, moving it around slightly. "He was kicking just now."

"Really?" I looked past her in blind concentration of what my hand was feeling for.

"Yeah," she said. "Where'd it go?" Julia guided my hand around for several seconds then frowned. "I guess he stopped. It's like he knows when you're trying to feel him."

"Yeah," I said, disappointed. "I think you might be right." We relaxed again.

"What do you think he'll be like?"

"I don't know," I said after a moment's thought. "Pretty fucking awesome most likely, if he's anything like his mother."

"If he's anything like his father, you mean," Julia smiled, and we kissed. Her eyes looked into mine, the dimple still in her cheek. "What if…"

"What if what, honey?"

"What if I'm not a good mother?" She'd asked me this before, and before, I'd told her that I knew she wouldn't have to worry about that. I searched her face for the answer she needed.

"What if I'm not a good father? I don't know anything about raising a kid," I said. "But maybe the point isn't to be good at it. Maybe the point is that we just be the best mother and father we can be. Maybe that's all it takes to be good." Julia tucked her head on my shoulder. "If that's the case—and I believe it is—then I know you're going to be a wonderful mother."

"So are you," she smiled. After a pause, "A good father, I mean. Not a mother." We laughed and kissed again.

~

"Ryan, we'd like you to meet Abigail Leigh Kimble," Julia said, her smile glowing. Ryan stood up on his toes, curious about the new member of the family. Julia seated herself for him to more easily look at his sleeping sister.

"Agibail?" He pointed, looking up at us.

"Abigail," I corrected gently.

"Wow," he crooned, looking upon her face as though it were the universe in a bottle. "She a girl?"

"Yes, that's right," Julia answered. "She's your baby sister."

"Me baby sisi?" he asked, pointing to himself, his eyebrows raised.

"Yes, your baby sister," I said. "Yours and no one else's."

"Me sisi Agi." Ryan beamed at the newborn. He raised his little finger and ever so softly placed it on Abigail's tiny fist. "She so sof'," he whispered, witnessing magic.

~

Abigail's eyes were closed when I woke, her breathing finally calm as she lay in her crib. Julia had been up all night with her, rocking and soothing her aching gums. She'd insisted I sleep so I'd be rested for my interview in the morning. On the back of the chair in our room, my clothes were neatly laid out. Julia had picked a dark red tie with black pinhead dots. When I was dressed, I was greeted with a tired smile and loving eyes.

"I made you breakfast," Julia said. "We can't have your stomach growling during your interview."

~

Abi giggled with her toes poking just over the edge of the cushions as I crept around the couch on hands and knees. Ryan was curled up in a ball beside her, laughing through his pearly little teeth. I rose up suddenly, roaring like a monster as they screamed in delighted terror. The tickle monster attacked their necks, their ribs, and their little feet. Ryan's foot shot out on impulse and kicked me in the mouth, cutting my lip on my tooth.

Blood poured out. Ryan was horrified and Abi started crying. Julia drove me to the ER, Ryan in the backseat repeating how sorry he was. By the time it was all done, our son and daughter were sedated with sugar-free popsicles, I was four stitches heavier and guaranteed a scar, and Julia was laughing at my temporary speech paralysis from the anesthetic.

~

"I'm pregnant." I looked at Julia who was smiling, her hand in mine as we drove.

"You're pregnant?" I repeated. She nodded happily, squeezing my fingers. Why I couldn't have just smiled and been happy...

"What's the matter?" Julia asked hesitantly. "Aren't you excited?"

"Of course, honey," I tried to convince myself. "I'm just wondering if it's affordable right now."

Yes, I actually said that.

"Affordable?" Julia stuttered. "We're not buying a fucking car. We're having a baby...You don't want it," she neither asked nor stated.

"I never said that! It's just that initial surprise...I can't help but have that as my first thought, how I'll pay for things, the financial side. It's not that I'm not happy or that I don't want it. I do. I'm just immediately in strategy mode..."

Just as good as an apology.

"It's you and me in this together, Art," she said.

Just as good as acceptance.

~

Julia and I parked outside the doctor's office and went inside. Abi and Ryan were at school, and I had taken the day off from work. After waiting forty-five minutes past the actual appointment time, the sonographer led us into the examination room. Julia always flinched from the cold jelly, but this time she didn't move. A few minutes later, the sonographer stepped out to get assistance. The doctor couldn't find the heartbeat either.

I was in tug-of-war between relief and heartbreak, and so I expressed something in the middle, neither tears nor joy.

"I guess it works out," Julia said that night. "You were right. We couldn't have afforded it anyway." She bled for three days, and I couldn't wait to get back to the office.

~

"I want to try again," said Julia, pushing a cart down the frozen aisle of the grocery store.

"Try what again?" I asked.

"Having a baby." I looked over a selection of precooked meals as if trying to choose. "You don't?"

"I didn't say that."

"Then what is it? I know we can afford it now that you've gotten this promotion to head writer. We can plan ahead." Julia was so earnest and hopeful. Her eyes searched me for something. I don't know what.

"I watched what happened to you last time," I said. "I don't want you to have to go through that again."

"I can take better care of myself. I know it can be different this time." Julia put her hands on my waste. "I promise it will be."

Two weeks later, Samwell drove me from work to my own doctor at the hospital and wished me luck. The room was clean and crisp, the surgical table cold and metallic. The nurse applied iodine, and Dr. Cho smiled at me as he gave me shot after shot of anesthetic. "Are you sure?"

"I'm sure." I said, staring at the ceiling. The cauterization smelled like burnt hair.

"At least you won't have to wrap it up anymore," Samwell chuckled later as I sat at my desk, a bag of frozen peas on my crotch.

~

Julia emerged from the bathroom with the pregnancy test in her hand. She tossed it into the wastebasket as she had eight or nine other times in recent months.

"I don't understand," she said, sitting on the bed beside me, her face stricken with disappointment. "I've been tracking my cycle."

"I'm sorry, honey," I said, rubbing her back as I had eight or nine other times in recent months.

"What would you think if I tried fertility treatments?" Julia asked. "I already talked to my doctor about it, and she was saying its effectiveness is higher than ever."

"You mean the shots?"

"Well, that's only part of it. First, they start just by insemination. That shouldn't be too bad for you," Julia teased.

"You mean turkey basting it?" I asked.

"Ew, gross," Julia laughed. "Seriously, what do you think?" She was bright, the dimple having returned, the splendor of what she was longing for riding on one word from me.

"Honey, what if the fact that you haven't been able to get pregnant is a sign?" The light went out. "What if having more than two kids just isn't in the cards for us?"

Julia never brought the matter up again.

~

"I might as well use my education for something," she said after telling me she was going back to work.

"Honey, that's wonderful! You're going to do great," I smiled and hugged her tight, feeling the bubbling tingle of happiness.

Julia became a paralegal at Hinkle, Lam, and Bowman, PLC. I encouraged her, praised her, and picked up some of the slack around the house from her new career. They were long hours, but she was motivated in a way I hadn't seen in years. After a while, an early night was being home by 9pm. A late night had become 2 or 3am, and sometimes there was no night at all. Julia would still be around for the kids, for me—when she was in the mood—but otherwise would be engrossed in one case or another.

"I'm pregnant." Julia studied my face, a clear uncertainty in its meaning. She forced a smile. "Finally, it happened."

"I guess you'll have to take some time off from work," I said.

"I actually put in my two weeks' notice today." I watched her go back to putting plates up in the cupboard. "They weren't very happy, but they said that if I ever want to come back, they'd have a place for me."

"Nice," I said. I went to the store for paper towels and came back drunk a few hours later. Julia was already in bed.

My time became devoted to my work. I didn't attend any of her appointments, and Julia never asked me to. I rarely came home straight from work, and Julia never complained. I sipped whiskey at dinner, and Julia paid it no mind.

Julia had a stillbirth just over five months in. I was at the office when she called me from the hospital. I worked late that day and never asked her how she got home. A few weeks after, she went back to work at the law firm.

~

It was a doozy of a fight, one of so many that I have no recollection of its cause. I was drunk though, so maybe that's why. Despite the chasm that had opened between us, I could still see to the other side where Julia no longer laughed, no longer sang, and never truly smiled. There was never a conversation, only an argument. It was a Valentine's Day.

"I had a vasectomy." Julia spun around to face me.

"What?! How could you do that and just not tell me?" she yelled. "What the fuck, Arthur!" She stood from the couch and breathed, her hand on her hip. "When did you get it done?"

"Almost two years ago." I watched the blood drain from her face, her lip beginning to shake. "I couldn't get you pregnant if I wanted to."

"So, all that time we were trying—"

"You were trying…Yes. That was why you never got pregnant. It wasn't you; it was me." I reached into the refrigerator to replace the beer I finished. "Which begs the question: who was it?"

"Who was what?" she whispered.

"Who knocked up my wife?" A tear ran down her cheek. "You want to fucking cry, now? Fuck you. You don't get to cry." Julia moved to leave the kitchen. "Oh no. You're not going anywhere until you hear what I have to say. For half an entire pregnancy I sat around knowing full well that someone else's bastard baby was growing inside of you, and I had to think about how exactly that came to be. Pun intended. I don't know why the fuck I did. I cried until I couldn't cry anymore, and then some more after that. I thought I'd never stop crying, that is until I found out that you gave birth to a corpse. I cried then too, but only because I couldn't stop laughing.

"I hope it hurt your body. I hope you had to look at it, had to see its undeveloped face, its shriveled and decaying body. I hope you watched them pull that dead baby out of your diseased and blown out cunt, and that you still do whenever you close your fucking eyes."

Julia crumpled to the floor, weeping at my feet. I hurt her on purpose. I thought I would feel better when I did. But that's just not how it works when it's someone you love.

~

Three years later to the day, I sat alone in that same living room, in that empty house, the lights off, surrounded by unpacked boxes. The new urn replaced the old in front of my television. With Buddha seated on the coffee table staring back at me, I took a sip from the bottle in my hand. The beer was warm because, though I'd put it in the refrigerator, I'd forgotten to plug the damn thing in.

A knock at the door hardly earned my attention. After a minute and two more knocks, I went to answer it.

"Good evening, Mr. Kimble." Dom was standing in the cold, his collar turned up.

"The fuck do you want?"

"I need to talk to you. About Mr. Price. It's important."

"Everything's important..."

"I have something for you from him. Please..." I glanced up at the sky shrouded by the city light.

"Fine."

"How are you?" he asked, standing a few feet away as I returned to my seat.

"Living the dream. Obviously."

"Obviously...I noticed your new car in the driveway. I've been looking at getting a Tesla myself."

"Want a beer?" I asked, ignoring his comment.

"Sure."

"It's warm. I haven't plugged in my refrigerator." He opened the bottle and tilted the neck in my direction before taking a sip.

"Not so bad," he said, nodding at it.

"Did you come on your own, or did he send you?" I asked after lighting a cigarette.

"Does it matter?"

"Whatever he wants, the answer is no. I already made that mistake twice."

"I think you should hear me out before you make such a hasty decision."

"I think I've already heard enough."

"What is it about him you hate so much?"

"I don't hate him."

"You've got some kind of chip on your shoulder, at the very least."

"Why do you like him so much? Knowing everything you do?"

"He's a good man. He's an honest man."

"Are you shitting me? He's been lying to the entire world for decades."

"Tell me of a single person who hasn't," he said. "Who is more honest, the man who swears he is honest or the one who admits to his dishonesty?"

"Neither. They're both dishonest. The only difference is that one is lying to himself and the other is lying to the people around him."

"And which do you think is worse?" Dom watched me take a pill from the jar. "Why do you do that?"

"It helps."

"Are you trying to convince me of that or yourself?" I looked up at him as I crushed the broken pieces beneath a credit card.

"It helps."

"Okay," he shrugged. "If you say so."

"Are you trying to get me to admit to you that I'm lying to myself?"

"If it is yourself that you are lying to, why should I care if you admit anything to me?" I continued crushing the pill into powder. "I have noticed in society, throughout history, all over the world, that a man is expected to be tough, to be strong. Many a father and mother have believed—and still believe—that what they call 'tough love' makes a weak boy into a strong man. My father beat his tough love into me more times than I could ever count, and I only learned to hate, and hate only makes you weaker. I've often asked myself, what gives a man strength? Perhaps it is his god, a higher power that will swing low and carry him forward. Or maybe, it is his ambition. A man sees something he wants, and either he feels empowered enough to go get it or he does not. Either way, it all depends on what he is willing to do. Perhaps a man finds strength in his partner, in his lover, in someone who—no matter what—will always be there by his side.

"The problem with these things is that a man's god is simply just that: a possession of man, and therefore is no god at all. Ambition is limited by what a man believes himself to be capable of, and in his weakest moments, a man will talk himself into believing that he is powerless. And a lover…The only lover worth having is the one that remains conditionally. So, what is a man to do? How might a man stay strong? How do you think, Mr. Kimble?"

We sat in thoughtful silence as he waited for me to conjure some sort of an answer. I failed.

"To me," he continued, "strength is a decision just like love and hate and hopelessness and all the other places we go within ourselves.

Strength is not simply a measure of how much a person can lift or can carry. Strength is the ability of a person to understand when to put things down so that he might continue forward, no matter how hard it is to let go. And when he chooses to do this, all the goodness that has been stuffed down and imprisoned within can be freed. You have goodness within you, Arthur Kimble, if only you would choose to let go." Dominic nodded and stood up. "Well, I have a plane to catch. Do yourself a favor and plug that refrigerator in." He crossed the room towards the front door then halted. "Oh, I almost forgot. This is for you, from Mr. Price. He asked that if you should decide to read it, please read it soon." Dom laid a thick rectangular package and a sealed envelope on the small table between us.

"What is it?" I asked.

"I don't know," he said. "Good luck, Mr. Kimble."

Dom opened the door and left me and my pills behind. I stared at the lines I'd made, then picked up the envelope and opened it. Inside were three sheets of folded paper. The handwriting was shaky, and almost illegible in places, but I deciphered through it line by line:

Dear Mr. Kimble,

Miriam never wanted to be a writer.

She never asked for it, never sought to develop it. She felt it was more of a curse than any kind of blessing, really. It hurt her, in so many ways. We frail and fragile humans are so easily addicted to things that elevate us and that likewise bring us down. This was similar, but to such a heightened degree. Perhaps you can imagine a drug—not even that, a molecular substance, an energy that you physically need to stay alive, yet this substance is at the same time incredibly toxic. You're helpless to it. Nothing ever makes sense without it, and yet you never feel more confused than when it's coursing through your body. Confusion becomes synonymous with understanding. Chaos with order. Up is down, right is left, love is hate. Misery is happiness. That was her life. Why, I don't know. I tried to understand, but I never could.

Night after night, I would sit and watch as she wept bitterly over her typewriter, the tears falling onto her fingers as it took all the strength in her body just to press the keys. As she poured out her soul on each page, she underwent such self-inflicted wounds that it might as well have been torture. I wanted to stop it. I wanted to fix it. I wanted to relieve her from that burden. I'd tell her so, sobbing like a child for her and her pain. At the same time, I loved her words. They healed pieces of me that were aching, and because of that I felt like a traitor, guilty for being healed by the product of her suffering. I confessed this to her once, but Miriam only took my face in her hands and said to me, "My love, if it is for you that I suffer, it is for suffering that I can smile."

It was her idea to publish her works under my name. It was never about fame for either of us. It was just the right thing to do. She believed that art—any art—kept in a drawer somewhere is not art at all. Hidden away, it has no meaning or purpose. Miriam believed that art requires more than simply an artist. It requires an artúre. She created this word herself to describe someone who is more than simply a spectator, or a critic of art. An artúre is one who connects to the art, and through the art, to the artist. The artúre and artist become personally bound by way of the art.

She saw this not only as a double-edged passion but a duty. A purpose. That was her 'why'. For all things. It was her reason to keep fighting, because that's truly what she was doing. Miriam was fighting a war that raged on and on with only brief intermittent periods of calm; a war that she would keep locked within herself, until she couldn't anymore, and then it would manifest beyond tears. She would become violently angry and erratic. In the early days, it would seem to happen without warning, but as the years went on, she began to recognize its onset and would shut herself away for days. Sometimes weeks. I wouldn't see her at all, but I knew, behind that closed door, she was battling something. But not alone. Never alone. The characters she created, the people in her stories, they were as real to her as you and I. They were always right there beside her in the trenches.

Over the course of her life, the struggle she endured with every work grew exponentially. There was less and less reprieve. Then one day, she lost. Not the battle but the war. Perhaps it was fatigue. I don't think it was hopelessness, or that she destroyed herself. Who can say?

In my weaker moments I've considered myself to be the one who let her down. I was her husband. Her partner. I'd made her a promise. Maybe I just hadn't done enough, hadn't yoked myself equally. Of course, I realize now that's not true. As difficult as it is for me at times to remind myself, it's not true. I didn't know what she had been working on at the time. It seemed the process was enduring much longer than it had in the past, but she told me it was because—of all her writings, of all her art—this was her greatest. You could say, her magnum opus. So, I stepped back, further than I ever had.

I wasn't there for her at the end. I wasn't there to pull her back in. She'd become someone else, and I just didn't realize. Was there anything I could've done to change the course of things? I don't know. As much happens in our lives, we get so many opportunities. We get lost in the possibilities until our heads start swimming, and we have no awareness of the moments that are escaping us second after second, and we miss them, blind, as if they had never existed at all.

What is it we're chasing, Arthur? What is it we're trying to find? Whatever it is, it's something constantly changing. It's terrifying. It's like being in the dark, following a string and never really knowing where it's headed, never knowing when the floor's just going to drop out from underneath you. Never knowing if all the time you're just walking around in circles. You try to believe. Try to have faith. But all the faith in the world, all the belief—it's never enough to be certain. So, why even do it? What is it all for? Not long before her death I asked Miriam that very question, and she told me something I've been struggling to understand ever since. She said, "What better reason does one need, than to simply ask that question?"

Miriam never finished the greatest work of her life. She was close, but to this day, it lacks an ending that even the most advanced technology failed to create. Her protagonist, her anti-hero, is waiting on the precipice. I couldn't finish it for her, because I didn't understand. Maybe, just maybe, Arthur, if she'd been able to complete her final masterpiece, then I would. But that didn't happen, and I still don't. I was foolish to think some computer program might understand. Dominic was right: without the human experience, it is meaningless.

And now here we are, a place where we will never be again. I'm not asking you to do this for me, because we both know I am undeserving. I'm not asking you to do this for Miriam, because, though she was deserving, she would never have allowed herself to be the reason. I'm not asking you to do this for yourself, because this will not save you. I am asking you to do it simply because it should be done.

I'm placing her work, unfinished, in your hands. This is the only copy, every word, every line. This is all the truth an old phony like me can offer. Perhaps, when this is all over, I'll understand what it was that I missed, but even if I never do, at least someone will.

Humbly yours,
Fletcher M. Price

CHAPTER TWENTY-TWO

Once upon a time, a very famous artist painted a picture of a shiny green apple. This apple was alone in the center of the canvas, surrounded by a white plane. Out of its flesh had been taken a single bite, and the juices had run down the peel and dripped off. At the unveiling of her work, the artist announced that the name of the painting was "The Bite", and everyone immediately began trying to guess what this piece of art was supposed to mean.

In attendance at the unveiling was a priest, an atheist, and a philosopher, each as respected as the artist for being experts in their particular fields. After the unveiling, as everyone was eating their hors d'oeuvres and sipping their champagne, the priest was asked what he thought the meaning of the painting was.

"The meaning of the painting is very simple," said the priest. "The apple represents temptation and the bite is man's failure to conquer it."

The atheist quickly disagreed. "Of course, you would find a spiritual meaning," she said. "What this painting is *actually* about isn't the apple at all. It's about the beauty in the white emptiness that surrounds it, empowering the apple to have any context it wishes—or no context at all."

The philosopher disagreed with both the priest and the atheist.

"This painting isn't about the bite taken, but the bites not taken," he said. "It represents infinite possibility."

The debate continued for some time until finally, they decided to approach the artist and ask her themselves. After telling her their individual hypotheses, the three waited with bated breaths for the answer.

With a laugh and shake of her head, the artist said, "Stop worrying about it, and enjoy the fucking bite."

STEWART ANDERSEN w/ ARTHUR KIMBLE
QUEEN CITY, CT - MAR. 21

STEWART ANDERSEN: For over thirteen years, Arthur Kimble has occupied an office here at *Verb'd Magazine*. Beginning as a staff editor, he quickly advanced to the position of head writer and is now the writing director. Throughout all that time, he conducted over one hundred and twenty interviews, reviewed over seventy-three books, and for ten years, gave us "The Adventures of Theodore Huxley". It's my pleasure to be interviewing a man whose commitment to the craft is as undeniable as his proficiency. Mr. Kimble, thank you so much for sitting down with me.

ARTHUR KIMBLE: I'm pretty sure this was mandatory, [*laughs*] but you're welcome just the same.

S.A.: I'm pretty sure it's mandatory for me to say that. [*laughs*] All right, Mr. Kimble, for the past month it's been nonstop for you about pretty much one topic, and that is your experience with Fletcher Price before his passing three weeks ago. First, I'll ask, how did you come to be the last person to interview him?

A.K.: Well, as you know, I was assigned to write an article about him, and I spent a week travelling around with him to different places from his life.

S.A.: You were assigned, or Mr. Price requested you?

A.K.: He requested me personally, and then I was assigned.

S.A.: Do you know why he did that?

A.K.: No. I don't.

S.A.: You didn't ask him?

A.K.: No. I had more important things on my mind.

S.A.: Fletcher Price was more or less plagued with scandal for the last few years of his life. Some people even think he faked his coma several months ago. Can you describe that final time with him? What was he like?

A.K.: Nobody fakes a coma, at least not for a whole four months. [*laughs*] Conspiracy theories aside, Fletcher Price was an ordinary man who lost his wife of forty-three years. People will quickly pass judgment on public figures, but the way I understood him, he had a lot of goodwill and spoke of the past ten years with considerable regret.

S.A.: Do you think that might have simply been a show he put on for the article?

A.K.: No. I don't.

S.A.: The article you wrote for Fletcher Price has yet to be seen by anyone. As writing director here, do you think that you'll ever have the article published?

A.K.: Perhaps. It all depends on if and when people are ready to read it.

S.A.: Speaking of reading, that brings us to the subject of Fletcher Price's purported novel, *The Art of Love*, a novel that no one claims to have seen except for you. I'm going to take your word that it exists because I respect you as a journalist, and because you're my boss. [*laughs*] The biggest questions that rise are, why hasn't the novel been published yet, and why hide it?

A.K.: I wouldn't say that it's being hidden any more than another author's unpublished work. My guess is that it's just not ready to be published yet.

S.A.: Was that not the premise of the article in the first place, to serve as publicity for the book?

A.K.: I can't say what his reasons were, because he never told me. I can tell you though, that Fletcher Price only wanted what everyone else wants.

S.A.: What's that?

A.K.: A fresh start.

"Mr. Kimble," Stacy said, peeking into the office. "You have a call on line one."

"Can you take a message?" I asked.

"It's Anita Pine." There was a long silence.

"I can come back," said Stewart. "I know where you work."

"Okay, fair enough," I said, trying to chuckle. Once he'd left the room, I picked up the phone. "Ms. Pine."

"Hello, Mr. Kimble. How are you this morning?"

"I'll let you know in a minute."

"I just spoke with the D.A.," she said. "They want to offer you a deal, and to be honest, it might be in your best interest to take it."

"But I'm innocent. The burden of proof lies with them, and they don't have any."

"The drugs in your system that night combined with the over two hundred pills in the glove compartment, the key fob with the symbol associated with the drug cartel they're after, and the traces of cocaine found in the trunk may or may not be seen as circumstantial, and they don't like to lose. They're going to throw it at you any way they can to make it stick, and if they do, you could be in prison for up to five years. How is that going to help your case getting your kids back?"

I stared out the window, a freshly lit cigarette in hand. "What's the deal?"

"Give them something. In return, they'll drop the charge to a class one misdemeanor for first time possession."

"What do you mean, give them something?" I asked after a pause.

"Information. Where did the cocaine come from? Who supplied the pills?"

"I already told them whose car it was, and they're doing nothing."

"Mr. Lemmon was out of town. There's no evidence that suggests he knew anything about it, and he denies ever giving you permission to use the car. So, unless you have something to tell them that will definitively clear you, it's not looking good.

"Listen, Mr. Kimble," she exhaled, "I understand that you want your children. It's easiest to do that without a conviction of anything, but the odds of that are not in your favor. A drug felony conviction will make it nearly impossible for you to present a good case for yourself to get them back, especially with the prison sentence likely to follow. They're convinced you know something, and as along as they think that you're holding out, they're going to try to nail you to the cross. Take this deal, accept the misdemeanor. As a first-time offender, you'll likely get a year of probation, and that will give you a stronger case for your parental rights. Ryan and Abigail need their father. Taking this deal is what's best for them."

As a mid-lifer, I'd become well-acquainted with getting screwed. But no matter how many times, no matter what the position or how softly those sweet nothings are whispered into your ear, it doesn't get any easier.

"How long do I have to think about it?" I asked.

"You have until your trial tomorrow at 10am," she said.

"Okay," I sighed. "I'll let you know. Thank you."

Twenty minutes later, I stepped out into the midday warmth. The comforting sun had returned and although the summer was still months away, something in the sky was hopeful.

A few minutes of walking brought me to the Starbucks on the downtown strip. Overcoming any hesitation, I entered, taking a glance around the incorporated café before approaching the table by the window.

"Thanks for meeting me," I said.

"No problem." Samwell smiled before drinking his coffee.

"How have you been?" I asked, taking the seat across from him.

"You know. The same as always. Aren't you going to order something?"

"No," I said. "I'm not really in the mood for it."

Sam's face was relaxed, not altogether expressionless, but unrevealing.

"You look well, Art. I'm glad."

Why did he have to smile like that?

"Thanks."

"What did you want to see me about?" Samwell finally asked after sitting silently for several seconds.

"Because...I owe you an apology. And not any run-of-the-mill apology," I said, "but a real one."

"Okay." He placed his coffee to the side, folded his hands on the table, and waited.

"I want you to know," I began, feeling my weakness with apologies, "that I regret the way I treated you. I regret how I took our friendship for granted, for taking you for granted as a person. I guess after all this time of hating myself, I just—"

"Nope. Try again."

"What?"

"You're about to make an excuse for your actions," he said. "That has no place in an apology. Try again."

After thirteen years, I knew what anger looked like on Samwell's face, and there was none.

"Okay..." I cleared my throat. "Sam, I betrayed your trust, took advantage of it. I didn't mean to, it's just that—"

"Try again, Art."

With a deep breath, I realized there was no explaining myself to him. He wasn't interested.

"I'm sorry for hurting you. You're the best friend I've ever had, and I wasn't the same for you. I'm sorry for lying. I'm sorry for blaming you. I'm sorry for taking advantage of our friendship."

Samwell studied me diligently, looking into my eyes with the curiosity of a child staring into an anthill.

"You're forgetting something," he said.

"I'm sorry for hitting you."

"And..."

"I'm sorry for...I don't know. Everything, I guess."

"Everything," Samwell repeated.

"I want to show you..." I said a few moments later. From my pocket I produced a coin and placed it before him like an offering. "Thirty days."

Sam picked it up and ran his thumb across the triangle embossed on its face.

"To thine own self be true," he read aloud, then looked at me.

"Who are you, Arthur?"

The question astounded me. It was something I had never asked myself, never even considered, and I wondered why not. It wasn't a complicated question, and the answer required nothing outside of myself. Yet, a concrete answer evaded me.

"I'm an alcoholic. A substance abuser." My hands empty, I wished I'd gotten that coffee.

"That's *what* you are," he said. "I'm asking *who* you are."

"Who am I?"

"Yes." He waited, watching me struggle in thought.

"I'm Arthur Kimble."

"That's what other people call you." Samwell smiled. "*Who* are you?"

I didn't want to admit it. To do so felt like a defeat, but he already knew the answer.

"I don't know who I am," I said, my throat tightening.

"Good," he said, reaching for his coffee.

"Good?" I asked. "What does that mean? How is that good?"

"Because, if you haven't decided who you are, then you can still be anyone you want. You can become whoever you want to become." Samwell smiled. "It's only when you're sure you know who you are that it's too late."

"Too late for what?"

"Too late for whatever it is you really want." He sipped his coffee and looked out the window. "I accept your apology, Arthur. At the same time, I don't know if I can trust you."

"You can," I said. "Sam, I'm different now. You can trust me."

"Thirty days of sobriety doesn't magically change people. It might appear that way on the outside, but on the inside, you're still the same."

"That's not true," I argued. "I'm not the same that I used to be."

"You are," he said. "But that's not altogether bad. It just means that I'll need time to trust you the way that I used to. You'll have to earn it."

"That's pretty self-righteous of you."

"Why should I let you in at the risk of being taken advantage of again?" he asked.

"But I'm not going to do that again."

"Says you." He crossed his arms. "Between the lies about rehab and using and drinking, how much more was there? How do I know there aren't other things you've lied to me about?"

"Because I didn't," I said angrily. "I apologized. What more do you want from me?"

"What do *I* want from you?" he asked laughing in shock. "I don't want shit from you except effort, some real fucking effort, to be good to yourself."

"I am doing good for myself," I replied.

"Great. Keep it up," he said. "It's not you as a person I don't trust, Art. You realize that, right? It's the addiction I don't trust. It's those goddamn demons you buddied up to for all this time that I don't trust. I love you now just the same as I did before, and I've always got your back, but I owe it to myself to be the best me I can be. That means not letting other people hurt me whenever they want. That means protecting the parts of me that are susceptible to damage. That means not allowing myself to be a tool for your self-destruction because I can't live with that on my conscience."

Samwell Epstein was the best person I knew. From head to toe, there wasn't a bad bone in his body. In some ways, it's difficult to not resent people like that. With every one of their good deeds, they hammer in the fact that there's nothing on earth you can do to deserve having them in your life. That's a nail no one likes in their coffin.

"I'm sorry, Sam," I said. "You're right."

"Art..." Samwell looked down at his hands, then up at me. "I'm so happy to see you."

I'm happy to see you, he says.

"Yeah," I smiled. "I'm happy to see you, too."

S.A.: What were some of the destinations you visited with Mr. Price?

A.K.: We started out at his hometown, Canary, Oklahoma, then to his home in New York City.

S.A.: That's where he met his wife, correct?

A.K.: Yes, Miriam Dorset, the sister of Jack Dorset who founded *Verb'd Magazine*.

S.A.: Really? I had no idea.

A.K.: I'm not so sure many people did. They were pretty successful at keeping their private lives private.

S.A.: Where did you travel after that?

A.K.: Well, we took a bus down the coast to Florida. We were headed all the way to the Keys, but Fletcher Price altered the route just a bit, and we stopped in at the Florida State Fair. Apparently, it was one of his and his wife's favorite things to do every year.

S.A.: That must have been fun.

A.K.: The man liked his funnel cake. [*laughs*]

S.A.: I can't say I blamed him. But do you know why he took you there specifically?

A.K.: Why does anyone willingly go anywhere from their past? Memories.

"Miriam and I had so many good times here," said Fletcher Price as he leaned against the bus, his eyes absorbing the sight of the fairgrounds.

"What do you remember the most from the fair?" I asked, lighting a cigarette.

"Her look of complete captivation as we circled high on the Ferris wheel; the way she laughed, completely free from everything."

"Everything?"

"You know how life gets," he said. "For some, it's more difficult to escape than for others."

"I see."

"I don't want you to get the impression that our marriage was always wonderful all the time," said Fletcher. "It was here at the fair that we had one of our worst fights."

"Really? At the state fair?"

"Miriam swore that she was going to leave me." I watched him bow his head. "She meant it, too."

"May I ask why?"

"Things had been tense for some time," he said after a deep sigh. "It had already been over twenty years since my first book, and I'd published about fifteen or sixteen more by then along with several plays. I was involved in the screen adaptations for three of my books over the course of two years. Then there were hundreds of book signings and lectures and guest appearances. To put it simply, Arthur, I was fucking tired."

"I can imagine. Was it wearing on her as well?" I asked, blowing out a puff of smoke.

"Not as much as it had on me," he said. "It was 1983, if I recall correctly, and we were here. I felt so alive as we walked through the avenues of carnival rides and games, and the look of elation in Miriam's eyes, it filled my heart to overflowing with the kind of love and joy that comes only from witnessing the birth of your child, hearing the music that explains your soul, or the discovery of your counterpart. Miriam and I never had a child, and before then, I'd only heard the music. It was here that I truly discovered Miriam and understood the people we were in relation to each other.

"I was ready to forsake all for her. I was ready to turn my back on the world so that I could spend every remaining moment of my life in her presence, and I told her so. I told her I was done with the career. We had enough money to live comfortably for the rest or our lives. We didn't need it. All I wanted was her."

"I thought you said you had one of your worst fights," I said. "Why would she threaten to leave you for that?"

"She was angry at me," he answered. "Not because of how sincerely I meant what I told her, but because of my willingness to stop doing what came naturally to me, what she called my 'why'. Miriam told me that she didn't want to be married to a man who trades his purpose for something as simple as love. That she doesn't want me if I'm not whole, and how could I ever be if I left that behind. She walked away, leaving me to stand like a fool with a pair of funnel cakes." Fletcher chuckled. "I ate both of them."

"Wow," I said, flicking the butt of my cigarette into the parking lot, the sparks bursting in their last throws of existence. "So, the writing continued."

"The writing continued."

"For her."

"For me," he smiled.

A breeze swept over us, and silently, we drank it into our nostrils, filling our lungs.

"That explains the past ten years," I said.

Fletcher nodded and turned his eyes to the sky.

"No armies can conquer as that of a broken heart, Mr. Kimble." He stood up straight and, with a sigh of relief, placed a hand upon my shoulder. "But the heart is a resilient little thing."

Fletcher Price retired to the bus as I lit another cigarette.

"Mr. Kimble!"

The afternoon was finally drawing to a close. Stewart's interview with me had long ended, and I sat lost in my thoughts. Stacy's panicked voice found me though, and I was slightly relieved.

"Mr. Kimble!"

Jumping up from my chair, I rushed to the door of my office. "Stacy, what's wrong?"

"Mr. Kimble, my water just broke," she said, her eyes wide and wild.

"Shit…"

Stacy was in the passenger's seat having contractions as I tried to navigate through rush hour traffic towards the interstate. St. Anthony Medical Center was seven miles away, yet at that time of day, seven miles seemingly stretched to seventy. With a woman giving birth in the vehicle, that made it closer to seven hundred.

"In through the mouth, out through the nose," I said.

"In through the nose, out through the mouth," said Stacy, following her own instructions.

"Are you sure you're in labor?" I asked. "Like, you're certain?"

"Yes, I'm certain."

"No offense, but if I have to catch your baby, I don't think we could work together anymore," I said.

"That's definitely not going to happen," she said, rolling her eyes. "Don't get yourself worked up."

"My wife did this twice. Why would I get worked up?"

"You know, you really need to stop doing that," she said.

"Doing what?"

"Calling her your wife. She's not your wife anymore. She's your ex-wife. Do yourself a favor and accept it."

"Why are you choosing right now to bring this up?" I asked.

"Because you can't get mad at a woman in labor." Stacy continued her breathing as I merged onto the interstate and bore down on the gas pedal.

In ten minutes, we arrived at the emergency room entrance, and I walked her to the registration desk. Immediately, the nurses put her in a wheelchair and began assessing her. A few minutes later, they were ready to take her to the delivery unit. Hanging back, I watched them begin to wheel her away when she grabbed the nurse's arm, and they turned around.

"Please, don't leave me," said Stacy.

"What?"

"Stay with me until Bailey gets here."

"When is that?" I asked, wishing like hell I'd just called an ambulance.

"I don't know. Can you please just come?" she begged. "I'm scared, Mr. Kimble. I need you."

I need you, she says.

As mature and responsible a woman she was, sometimes I forgot that Stacy was only twenty-three. Over the four years she'd been my assistant, I couldn't count how many times she'd kept my life in order, taken care of me and my hangovers, even lied on occasion to cover my ass. The truth was, I'd become so accustomed to needing her, that it hadn't occurred to me that she might need me, too.

"All right," I said, and we took off toward the elevators.

Having a baby is a bunch of hurry-up-and-wait with a sprinkling of urgency and trips to the bathroom. Rarely is it ever the way it's portrayed in the movies where babies practically fall out into the waiting hands of a doctor. In most cases, women aren't cursing and kicking people either, although I can understand why Hollywood might like to make that a staple of the cinematic delivery.

After calling her wife, I sat in a chair beside Stacy, holding her hand through each contraction, my fingers turning purple, then tingling as the blood returned, then back to purple. I remained by her side as the midwife checked the progress of the delivery and shared Stacy's excitement when it was announced that the baby was in position. It was time. For the next two minutes, the room was organized chaos as an entire team of trained professionals prepared to bring this new human being into the world.

"Mr. Kimble," Stacy said, struggling to keep her voice even. "What if..."

"What if what?"

"What if I'm not a good mother?" she asked. "What if I'm not good at this?"

I'd never noticed before that Stacy's eyes were green.

"You know, I remember asking myself the same thing when Ryan was born. I questioned whether or not I would be good at this. I wondered what the hell a person like me was doing even having a baby, because what did I know? I was doing the best I could to make sense of the world for myself. How would I ever be able to guide this whole other person?

"Then, the doctor told us that Ryan was breech and the umbilical cord was wrapped around his neck. If we didn't have a c-section immediately, he could suffer brain damage or even die. And do you know what happened?"

"What?"

"I forgot all about my fears of being a bad parent, because all I cared about in that moment was Ryan. He became the one thing in the world that mattered to me." I smiled at her. "And that's never changed."

"All right, Mrs. Whittaker," said the midwife. "Are you ready to do this?"

"I'm ready," said Stacy with a confidence I wasn't sure I'd ever had myself about anything.

"Stacy!" Bailey rushed out of breath into the room.

"Bailey! You're here!" Stacy shone like the stars, and Bailey marveled at her light, and the two held each other as counterparts do.

I returned to work having forgotten my laptop and homework on my desk in all the excitement. The offices were empty, the light dim through the windows as the sun bid our side of the world farewell once again. While packing up my things, my stomach growled, and it suddenly occurred to me how hungry being at the hospital had made me. As I began considering where I could stop to eat on the way home, a fluorescence in the hallway caught my eye.

The vending machine that Jack Dorset had promised us was stationed there clean and bright and filled with snacks. Excited for some reason at the prospect of being the first to use it, I reached for my wallet, took a pair of ones, and fed them to the machine. I scanned my possible choices, then saw the bright, tidy row of baked apple pies, selection A2. I could hardly believe it had actually happened and failed to suppress an astonished chuckle. My salivary glands began to activate as the buttons depressed smoothly. The machine whirred as it processed my cash, and the springs turned, pushing the pie forward. Just as it was about to fall, the mechanics stilled, leaving the pie dangling over the edge in cruel suspension.

For a long while, I stood there, looking at it, considering my options. Finally, I positioned myself next to the vending machine, hands flat against the metal and plastic, bracing myself to push. Then, I stopped. I couldn't understand why, but I stopped. And after another long look at the apple pie, I picked up my briefcase and walked away.

The house was still marginally warm when I arrived home, though dark, and it was deflating. After microwaving a bowl of chicken noodles, I turned the television on to fill the emptiness as much as to be distracted from it. The urn still sat in front of the screen collecting dust, and as I chewed, I stared at it, and as I stared, I thought.

A minute later, I placed my bowl down on the coffee table and picked up the urn, feeling the weight in my hands. As most thoughts will, the one I was currently having in that moment led me to another, and I carried the box into my bedroom. After clearing a space on my dresser, I set it down, adjusted it, then blew the gray haze off its lid into the air. Standing there for some time, I read the nameplate over and again: Benjamin Elroy Kimble.

"Don't get any ideas," I said. "This doesn't mean I've forgiven you."

Again, as most thoughts will, the newer thought led me to yet another, and I went to the closet where unemptied boxes had found a home. In a matter of minutes, they were in the middle of my room, lids open, and I rummaging through them until I found what I was looking for. Returning to the couch, I opened the folder for the first time and began to read.

Miriam Price's final novel was printed on several different kinds of paper, and some parts even written by hand. Edits and corrections scarred and pocked the pages as I slowly turned one after the other, reading them, sometimes twice, and moving on. It was a story I'd never expected, unlike anything she'd ever written, unlike anything I'd ever read, and at times I cried tears. At other times, I laughed out loud. But the night stretched on, and at last, just before two in the morning, I turned the final page over and sat in silence. It was in need of an ending, and without even a moment of forethought, I reached for my laptop.

The rising light had long found its way into the house through bare windows by the time I lifted my hands from the keys. I took a drag from the eighth cigarette that had begun to smolder out in the ashtray and milked the last drop of coffee from my fifth cup. The cursor blinked a happy hello and goodbye on the screen making me wonder how I'd ever found the thing so intimidating.

A familiar fluttering at the window snipped the string of attention away from my laptop and, looking up, I smiled.

"Hello, Huxley."

"Hello, my old friend."

"The story isn't over," I told him after a long silence.

"No, and I don't suspect it will be for quite some time," he said from the windowsill. "That's all right though. Isn't it?"

"Yes," I nodded. "It's all right."

"In the meantime, you have a decision to make. Until 10am, wasn't it?"

"Yeah," I said, looking down at the time. "I've already made it."

Huxley nodded in approval as peace finally descended on the two of us.

"I'm glad you're here, Hux," I said.

"So am I, Arthur. So am I."

THE END

ABOUT THE AUTHOR

The Art of Love (& Loathing) is Stephen Daniel Ruiz's debut as an American novelist. His other professional work includes dozens of short stories and poems and one stage play. These writings span subjects from addiction, relationships, parenthood, and mental illness to questions of philosophy, moral dilemmas, and ethicality.

Growing up, Stephen Daniel Ruiz began writing prose and poetry, though he spent an equal portion of his youth focused on songwriting. As an adult, his overseas service in the U.S. Marine Corps did not diminish his love of writing and music. After his return to civilian life and the birth of his fourth child, he refocused his lifelong passions and dedicated his energy to perfecting his skills as a writer of both stories and songs.

To get to know him better and to read more of his work, visit www.sdruiz.com. If you've enjoyed this book, be sure to pass it along and leave a review online.

And of course, thank you for reading.

CPSIA information can be obtained
at www.ICGtesting.com
Printed in the USA
BVHW011915130721
611837BV00015BA/955/J